THE
REGULATORS

SHADOW
OF MALICE

WWW.BENBRUCE.CO.UK

First published in Great Britain on Amazon Kindle Direct in 2019 by Ben Bruce

Cover design by Sean Strong

Edited by Bee-Edited

Thanks to Mark and Becka for the feedback.

ISBN 9781999846930

For my parents.

1

It was raining heavily, soaking him to the skin. The few clothes, if you could truly call them clothes, offered no resistance to the element's torturous assault on his body.

Not that he noticed.

He didn't feel the rain's icy touch on his skin or the wind slicing through him, cutting into his fragile frame as it sought out the wounds that crisscrossed all over him, making them ache more and more. The longer he went on, the more the heavy rags he wore slapped against the cuts and sores on his body, stinging every time the material found an open wound.

Not that he noticed.

His bare feet scuffed against the wet tarmac. The rough texture of the road had already cut his feet, opening up old wounds, creating new fissures from which blood seeped out, spreading like dark red clouds in puddles, marking his route. He stumbled, knowing that his legs weren't working how they were supposed to, but not really understanding why. He didn't have time to understand why. He only had one thing in mind.

The streetlights seemed to be looking for him, their pools of light spreading out, reaching towards him, hoping to snare him, illuminate him, expose him. He knew that he had to stay away from them, but the nearer he got to his destination, the harder it was to stay in the shadows.

He continued forward, hoping that he was heading in the right direction. How could he know though? This wasn't a place he knew. It wasn't a place he had ever lived. He didn't know where he was, he couldn't even be sure he was still in his own

4

country. Everything seemed strange, everything scared him. He just wanted to find his destination. To be safe.

Would he be safe?

He had been told they wouldn't believe him. That they would simply take him and return him back where he came from, but he knew he couldn't believe that anymore. He had believed it for too long. He had to believe something else now.

Maybe it was the first springs of adolescence, or a deeply hidden genetic trait that had come from his forefathers, but he had started to ask questions. Quietly, he had tested the limits to see if he could find a chink in their logic. He knew he had let that message keep him captive as much as the chains, locks, ropes, and cells they had used. Now, he ignored that message. Something from his life before, something his carer had always told him had finally won out. "Always trust the police, son," his carer had said. "They're here to help."

He had to believe it was true. If it wasn't, then he would be caught again, and he would be punished. If that happened, he hoped they would kill him. That was better than the life he had lived for the last... how long was it? He didn't know. He didn't even know how old he was anymore. He must have missed so many birthdays. Too many to even count. It felt like a lifetime. It had been a lifetime for him. A lifetime he didn't want to be part of anymore. However old he was, he had lived long enough like that, and if the alternative was death, then that was better than staying there.

Even he knew, despite his young age, that such a realisation was a drastic one to reach. He had been five – he could count to five when he had gone into the house – and now he knew he was older. Much older. He had been able to tell that by looking at the other children that had arrived after him. They seemed to get smaller and smaller. Maybe they were bringing younger children, that was probably happening as well, but he knew he was becoming one of the older ones, and that meant that, sooner or later, his time would be up.

He stumbled on, wobbling from side to side, panting as he went, wondering if he would ever find what he was looking for. Perhaps this town didn't have one? That was possible. It didn't look the biggest place in the world. The roads were quiet. All the shops and pubs looked shut. There were no lights on in any of the houses. Perhaps this was just a village. He knew about villages; he had been to some on trips to the petting farm with the foster home before all this happened. Villages had farms, they had post offices, but they didn't always have police stations.

As he ran on, he became certain this wasn't a village. The buildings seemed to go on and on, and he found himself heading deeper and deeper into the warren of streets. The buildings got bigger, closer together. This had to be the right place.

Still the rain poured, the wind howled, his eyes stung. Was it from tears? Was he crying? He didn't know. He hadn't cried for a long time. He had shut that side of himself down a long time ago, a weakness that he never wanted to show anymore. Emotion got you into trouble in the house. It got you hurt, got you killed. He had learned about the hurt and heard about the killed. Some people left and never came back. He had been lucky; he hadn't been one. Until now. But this was different.

Finally, he saw what he was looking for. The blue light from the sign glowing like a beacon of hope, and now he knew he was crying. He gulped as he ran, getting closer and closer, his feet slapping on the wet slabs below, his head bobbling on his weakening body.

When was the last time he ate?

He scrambled up the stairs on his hands and knees and pushed the glass door to the reception room open, spilling inside and falling to the floor.

"Help," he croaked.

The officer behind the desk looked on with shock. "What the hell?" he exclaimed, standing up from his desk.

The boy looked up and saw the officer standing there for a moment. It felt like forever, but finally, the man moved, opening the door as he scurried towards him, bending down.

"You alright, lad? Can you hear me?" the officer asked, scooping him up in his arms, but there was no response. The boy, exhausted from his efforts, was on the verge of passing out. He felt the relief, and the exhaustion hit him in unison as the warmth of the officer's grasp made him realise how cold he had been out there.

"I need some help here!" the officer hollered to his colleagues deeper in the station before grabbing his radio and calling for an ambulance. The child's eyes flickered open, and he looked at the police officer. He closed them again. He was safe; the officer would help him. The police always help people. That's what he had been told.

2

Yorkshire hadn't quite been as Thea Watts had expected. For a woman who had spent her whole life in London and the South, she had grown up on the idea of it being a bit "grim up north," but from the moment she had arrived, she had known that was wrong.

York might have been a city, but it was different than London in many ways. It didn't have the same sprawling reach of the capital. It didn't take long at all to be outside of the urban area and into the often-spectacular countryside that surrounded it. The Yorkshire Dales lay to the west, whilst the Yorkshire Moors were to the northeast. Thea had visited both and fell in love with the seclusion.

There was Leeds as well if she needed to get more of a metropolitan feel, but even that, compared to the vastness of London, felt small and intimate. Everything was a different pace. It suited her right now. She had all the freedom in the world to think and reflect on what had happened before.

It had been eight months since she left the NCA. She had asked for the transfer, but she knew she would have been pushed. Her name had been noted, her card marked. Sooner or later, they would have found a way to get her out of the firing line, and by asking for a transfer, at the very least, she still had a career.

The move away from London followed, and now Thea Watts found herself in the CID offices of the Fulford Road Police Station in York. It was a dated building but still of a decent size. Inside, the place looked like it might crumble at the touch, it was so desperately in need of renovation. Everything was old and falling apart, at complete odds with the modern NCA offices in London. No one seemed to mind, however. No one seemed to care.

She had been seconded to the Sexual Assaults unit. It was somewhere no one wanted to be. Only a very hardened person could hear some of the stories that came through her unit and not be touched by them.

That was becoming a problem. At least, it was becoming a problem according to her Sergeant, Oliver Wilkes. He was a well-meaning man, someone who Thea liked. He wasn't like Frank who had been decidedly old school. Wilkes was one of the new breed of middle-management types. Positive reinforcement, hands-on with his people, always making sure to look after their mental wellbeing. Not a bad idea considering the sort of cases they dealt with in his team.

He sat there, opposite her now in his office. He wore a smart grey suit, white shirt, and dark blue tie, his light brown hair neatly cut, short, and well styled on top, fading down to a trace of stubble that followed his strong jawline. Even sitting, you could still see that he was taller than most, six-five, but slender. No extra muscle, no hint of fat. Healthy looking, like a long-distance runner perhaps.

"Thea." He had his head cocked slightly as he spoke. Empathy. "I do worry, you know." His accent wasn't Yorkshire, that was clear. Perhaps the north Midlands, Lincolnshire, something like that. Thea had never asked. As much as Wilkes was a nice guy, they were never going to be friends.

"About what, sir?" she asked. She hadn't wanted to sound surly, but she knew she had.

"You've been here a while now. You know what this job is like, it takes a toll. You need people around you to talk to, and from what I hear, you're not really doing that. Is there someone at home you're talking to?"

"No, boss, there's no one. But I'm good. Honest."

"I know you are now." Thea shifted uncomfortably in her seat. She knew where this was going. "Thing is, this sort of stuff creeps up on you later on. It hits you in the middle of the night, when you're staring at the ceiling struggling to sleep, and then it doesn't want to go away. I've been there."

Thea nodded. She knew Wilkes was waiting for her to say something, but there was nothing to say. He was right. It would get to her. It had to. She'd deal with it then.

Wilkes nodded, clearly sensing that Thea wasn't going to carry the conversation on. "All I'm saying is that we've got a good team here." Thea knew that was a lie, and she knew Wilkes knew it was a lie. He wasn't stupid, he knew the true colours of some of his officers. "Take the time to go for a drink with them. Integrate. I'm not saying pour your heart out now, just make sure you're ready to have someone around when you absolutely have to talk to someone."

Thea sighed, trying her best again not to sound petulant. "I will, just in my own time." She tried to make that sound like a request.

"That's all I'm asking. Go get some lunch or something, take an hour." Wilkes smiled.

Thea stood. "Thanks, sir."

"Crack on." Wilkes gestured for her to leave. It was his customary sign off.

Thea stepped back out into the main office. It was a tatty space, a dour green carpet, cheap desks and chairs, aging computers, paperwork strewn all over the place. The phone on one of the desks was ringing, the main line to the office. Another case. Thea had her orders, however, and she walked past it to her desk.

"You not getting that?" another Detective Constable on shift, Chris Randle, called at her. He was a guy fast approaching his forties who should have been a salesman, such was his lack of earnestness. He wasn't a cop. He was an embarrassment, and how he had found himself in a role such as this was beyond Thea.

"Got to head out," Thea explained, shrugging back in the general direction of Wilkes' office.

"Bloody hell," muttered Randle, not even attempting to mask his disdain at having to do some actual work.

Thea collected her phone and car keys from her desk, half listening in, picking up the thread of the conversation, as someone from uniform, no doubt, began to relate the details of a case to Randle. He sat there disinterested, not even taking notes. There was no way he was taking this case the moment the phone rang, that was clear. Thea had become used to it; she had allowed that to go over her. Someone in uniform would do the job, and she hoped they would do it well. She had almost stopped listening when he dropped the bomb.

"Listen," Randle said to whoever was on the other end of the line. "There's rape, and then there's proper rape."

Thea stopped what she was doing. She couldn't have carried on if she wanted to, the red mist descending on her in seconds, focusing her mind solely on DC Randle.

The office was empty. Just her and Randle. Wilkes couldn't see them from where he was sat. Randle kept talking on the phone, excusing himself from the crime, making his case for inaction as watertight as possible. He never saw Thea pace silently up behind him. She waited.

Randle hung up the phone. He still had no idea that Thea was standing behind him. The first indication he had was when he felt his chair begin to tip quickly backwards. His body braced itself, he pushed forward, a natural reaction to arrest the imbalance, but it didn't work. Thea had a firm grip, both hands, she was pushing down hard. The chair and Chris Randle tumbled backwards, slamming down onto the floor.

He gawped upwards in shock at Thea, who quickly placed her foot down on his face and pushed hard, squashing his head down and to the left.

"There's assault, and then there's real assault," she had snarled at him. She pushed her foot down a little harder for good measure, then snapped it up, turning and walking out of the office.

She had barely made it to the front door of the station when her mobile rang. She expected it to be Wilkes calling her back up to explain herself, but the number was from another station, Pickering, which was on the edge of the North Yorkshire Moors, northeast of York.

"CID," she answered and immediately felt annoyed at the despondent tone of her voice.

"How do," a proper Yorkshire accent came across the line, probably an older officer, someone born and bred, serving his local community. "This is Sergeant Rankine out at Pickering. I've got a lad here who came in last night."

"Pickering?" Thea asked, "Hasn't that got its own CID?"

"I know, I know," sighed the Sergeant, "but this lad's tale, well, I might just be airing on the side of caution, but if it's true, I wanted it to be outside the area who handled it."

"What's the story?"

"It's probably nothing," Rankine began, which Thea knew instantly meant it was something. "We ain't got much out of him, poor thing's proper shell-shocked, but he said there was a house he was being held in. I think for a long time, like years."

"Years?" Thea raised her eyebrows.

"He said he were five when he went in and he ain't five now," Rankine explained. "If his story is half right, it's bigger than us. It's definitely one for you lot."

"What do you mean?"

"Well, he said there were police officers there who were in on it."

"Where is he now?"

"We took him to Malton to the hospital to get checked out."

"I'll get over there as soon as I can," Thea said, hanging up, grabbing her coat, and racing out of the office.

The drive to Malton took less than an hour following the A64 through the rolling Yorkshire countryside. Thea hurried through the small hospital up to the ward and then on to a small side room where Sergeant Rankine was waiting for her. He was a small stout man, with thinning red hair and even redder cheeks. It made him look a little flushed, but the smile was genuine. He was definitely pleased to see her.

"How do," he repeated his greeting from the phone call as he offered a hand. She shook it.

"Where is he?"

"I've got him in a ward on his own. He's edgy when he's awake, but he sleeps most of the time. I've kept it off the records. What he said, some of the names, I recognised them."

"They're cops?"

"Yeah, some of them and a couple of other local faces."

"You believe him."

"It's a bloody cracking tale if he made it up, and I challenge anyone to go and look at him and not believe he's been through bloody hell." Rankine's voice cracked a little, and Thea wondered why. Was the story that heart-wrenching, or was it pulling at something buried deep in his past? Whatever it was, she knew in an instant that the boy had been lucky to find him. Another officer would have just followed protocol and put the boy in the system. Rankine hadn't wanted to take that risk. If there was any truth to the story, then that could have put him in real danger.

"The officers he named, we need them investigated, suspended straight away. If there's any proof, I want them in a cell." An obvious move, Thea thought, but one that was going to raise some eyebrows.

"I can get a call in to Office for Police Conduct, see what they can do," Rankine said in a tone that suggested he wasn't really happy with being the one to grass up colleagues but would do it all the same. Thea sympathised with him. It was never easy turning on people you thought you could trust.

Thea peered through the door into the side room the boy was in. He looked like he was asleep, but she could see already the obvious signs of abuse. His face was drawn, clearly undernourished, and he had visible bruises and cuts to his face.

"What did the medical report say?" Thea turned back to Rankine.

"Fits the story he gives. No major current injuries, but evidence of some old injuries, scars and so on. Just lots of cuts and bruises now, and he has been, yeah, he's been… assaulted," the Sergeant reported gravely, awkwardly spilling the final piece of information out as he struggled with the magnitude.

"Shit," Thea breathed, turning back to the window and looking at the boy as he turned over awkwardly in the bed, wrapping himself tightly in the sheets, eyes still firmly shut. He looked tortured, and Thea realised she had forgotten to ask the most important question. "What's his name?"

"Ciaran. He doesn't know his surname, just knows he's called Ciaran."

"Jesus Christ, what the hell have they done to him?"

"It's the others I'm worried about," Rankine said.

"Others?"

"Yeah, he said there were lots of kids in there, they came and went, different ones all the time."

"How many?"

"He didn't know, he can't count."

"Can't count?" Thea couldn't believe what she was hearing. "Where is this place?"

"Somewhere out in the countryside. A farm he reckons, something like that, which out here could be one of a hundred places."

Thea ran her hand through her dark hair and sighed.

"Are you going to get some specialists in on this?" Rankine asked.

"I need to talk to Ciaran first," Thea nodded. "Are there people in your department you trust who can watch him?"

"Absolutely, there's a couple of lads and lasses who I'd trust with my life."

"Good, one of you needs to be on this door at all times. And tell the hospital that they're to not give out any details if anyone calls," Thea ordered, before adding, "I'm going to see if he's awake."

She opened the door softly, creeping in, but all the same, she saw Ciaran's eyes shoot open and glance nervously at her.

"Hello," she said softly. "I'm Thea."

Ciaran shuffled in the bed, raising himself up on his elbows, his thin arms poking out underneath his hospital gown, showing further evidence of the attenuated figure he had now become. He looked warily at her, saying nothing, so she pulled up a chair and sat by the bed.

"I'm really sorry that they hurt you," Thea soothed.

Ciaran remained silent, not that Thea was surprised.

"I can help you. I can put them in prison."

Ciaran shook his head, slowly, timidly.

"What?" Thea asked. "You don't want them to go to prison?"

"You need to kill them." His voice was croaky and harsher than it should have been for a boy of his age. "They won't go to prison. You need to kill them."

3

There hadn't been many periods of peace in Jack Quinn's life. As a kid, he had always found trouble, or more aptly, trouble had found him. It all stemmed, he would argue now, from his upbringing. His parents had both worked, so he had spent his earliest years under the care of his maternal grandmother. She had been a throwback to a bygone age, where respect was the name of the game, and looking after your neighbours was second nature. She taught a young Jack Quinn that it was everyone's duty to do the right thing and to make sure they stuck up for their friends, so that's what Jack did.

Bigger than his peers, at school he would often find himself righting the wrongs of the playground, taking on bullies, and winning. As he got older, the arguments he would have with his teachers in his defence always spun around the simple fact that he had seen something unjust, tried to fix it, and found himself left with no option but to fight. No matter how many times his teachers extolled on him the virtues of telling them if he saw something happening and letting them deal with the issue, that simply didn't fly to young Jack Quinn. He saw far too many blind eyes turned, or far too many children too scared to come forward and finger their bullies. No, the teachers were wrong, and he was right. If detentions and suspensions were the price he had to pay for doing the right thing, then that's the price he paid.

Jack had set his heart on the army from an early age, and he signed up quickly. His goal had always been to get into one of the branches of the UK special forces, and shortly after his twenty-first birthday, he joined the SAS.

By this point, he had met Isobel, and they were rapidly falling in love. If Jack ever looked back on his life, ever had to pick a moment when he had felt bliss, felt indestructible, this would have been it. For eighteen months, his life had become what he had wanted it to be. He had been a lover and a warrior.

All good things come to an end, however. Soon cracks had appeared in his relationship as the stresses of deployments overseas had pulled at them both. First Kat, and then Calum, his two children, had helped to plaster over the holes that his job created, but it couldn't hold them together. Both he and Isobel realised something had to change. Their relationship ended little over ten years after it began.

Jack had always thought he would die a soldier. Like most young men, he didn't contemplate old age, but unlike most, that wasn't down to his own sense of immortality. Quite the opposite. Jack knew he was going to die, and he embraced that fact. As long as the cause was right, his life was worth expending.

Then the cause had changed.

The war on terror had been just, Jack knew that. He ardently believed that. Britain's allies had been attacked, and British lives had been lost. There was an enemy, and that enemy had to be found and eliminated. Jack had absolutely no problem with being a part of the operations. He had served with pride in Afghanistan, but it was in Iraq where he had begun to question himself.

Jack had been there at Abu Ghraib, the infamous jail where Iraqi prisoners of war had been abused and degraded by rogue elements in the British Army. Seeing his own soldiers, his own side acting like that and the contempt shown by the superiors who knew about it, the disdain shown for people who may or may not have been enemies was too much. Jack wasn't green. He knew that a real part of being a soldier was the ability to switch off that part of your brain that humanised the enemy, and that sometimes that slipped a little, but there was always someone there to help pull you back. That was how they knew they were the good guys, that was how he knew he was right. Now he wasn't sure.

The fire of dissent grew quickly, and before he knew it, Jack was out of the army, a whirlwind of circumstances and reactions that left him back home, jobless, and with a young family to provide for.

Jobs for a man of Jack's size had come easily enough. He was muscle, protection. There was money in that. Some of the jobs were good, honest trade, some not so much, although, by that point, Jack was beyond caring. When the first offer to do mercenary work came up, Jack took it, and six days later he had found himself in a cargo plane hold, heading for some war-torn part of Central Africa where country boundaries no longer mattered, hoovering up resistance groups who were hassling an oil pipeline system. It was a chance to do something, a chance to escape, plus the money was far too good to turn down.

He hated what he had become. He felt a failure to his wife, to his children. The world was an evil place, and despite his best efforts, he couldn't make it any better for them. Drink had followed. Many lonely, silent nights in the stupor of drunken contemplation, Jack had tried to work a way out of his rut, to find a way to make himself the man he wanted to be, but he hadn't.

One of those lonely nights, David Warner had found him.

The tall stranger had approached him in a bar and sat next to him, which Jack had immediately found strange. People weren't given to talking to Jack. His size was usually enough to intimidate most, and his scowl would certainly do the job if that didn't. The immaculately dressed black man with the cropped hair who was sitting at the bar next to him barely seemed to have registered him, although Jack knew he must have done. Already from the way he held himself, Jack was sure he was forces too. For a moment, he feared hearing another soldier's woes and war stories. Jack wasn't one for small talk, not anymore. Thankfully, the stranger ordered a drink and stared straight ahead, and for a minute at least, silence ensued.

"It's hard, isn't it?" the stranger asked. "When you first lose your way, it's hard to find a new path."

Jack said nothing, although the question was clearly meant for him and suggested that, whoever this guy was, he knew something about what Jack was doing. He had been piqued, he knew that. He felt the stranger shuffle and turn to look at him.

"I'll get to the point, Quinn. You're a good man doing shitty work for shitty people. I can change that."

Jack turned. "You are?"

"David Warner, and I want you to come work for me."

"A job?"

"A proper one."

"I don't do nine to five."

"Neither do we. We fight for what's right, and we do it all day, every day. You're going to join us."

"Does it pay well?"

"Money isn't an issue, but you don't want money."

Jack cocked his neck. "What do I want?"

"You want to make the world better."

That had been nine years ago. David Warner had been right, Jack wanted to make the world a better place, and for nearly eight years, he'd done just that, as a Regulator, a part of a vast vigilante network that crossed the globe, targeting people in power who skirted the law and evaded the system. Jack had brought many people to justice. For some others, he'd delivered justice personally. Now, however, he was facing the end of that chapter of his life.

When he had first been suspended, the anger he expected to feel had given way to relief. He had done the right thing, he had abided by the rules, he had expected reinstatement. As his suspension had dragged on, he realised that maybe his time as a Regulator was over.

The anger he had feared the realisation would bring wasn't there. He was tired of it all. Tired of killing, tired of hurting, tired of making the sort of decisions which changed lives forever. He knew he had made the world a better place, he had done his part, far more than most people could ever dream of doing, and he trusted that others would follow suit. He wasn't the only person who felt that way. Adam, David, Mo, and so many other colleagues in the Regulators and the Vehmic courts, which they acted on the behalf of, would fight the good fight. There were even people in the regular strands of justice, like the detective he had last worked with, Thea Watts, who were incorruptible, doing all they could to keep the world safe.

No, the world didn't need Jack Quinn's help anymore. He had done his piece, he would await his retirement, and then he would lead a quiet life.

He had sold his house, moved a little further from his Isobel, given himself that extra separation he finally realised he needed, and found a new place in the country, just outside the small town of Uckfield in East Sussex. A small, run-down, three-bed cottage, in need of extensive renovations, where both the kids could have a room and spend a week in their holidays, maybe even one day bring his grandkids. It was to be his project, something to keep him occupied as he worked out what to do with the rest of his life.

At least that was the plan.

Then the phone rang.

"Hello?"

"Jack?"

He recognised the voice instantly, which caught him a little off guard.

"Thea?"

"I'm sorry to call. It's just I think I need your help."

4

David Warner had agonised over how to approach this moment for a long time. There were many moments in his career when he had been forced to deal with awkward situations. He had presided over firings, condemned people to a life behind bars. He had read eulogies at friends' funerals, held the hands of newly widowed partners. He had been able to approach the enemy and engage them in conversation to find a solution other than bloodshed. He had found down-and-out former soldiers and offered them lifelines at their most desperate. All of those things he handled with ease. The one thing he struggled with was making introductions.

This one wouldn't be any easier. In fact, it may be one of the hardest. Right now, he was introducing Adam Morgan to a new partner. A replacement for Jack Quinn. It was something he had always known he may have been called upon to do, such was the nature of their job. He just didn't realise it would be in these circumstances. The one solace was that he truly believed that Adam's new partner was going to be good for both Adam and David's wider team.

"Emmie Weston, Adam Morgan," David introduced the two of them. "You're going to be partners," he added, despite being completely sure that the two of them had worked that out within seconds of being in the room together.

Now the three of them were sat around David's desk in his office. David behind the sleek mahogany desk, Emmie and Adam on the other side, their backs to the frosted glass doors and windows that looked out over the main floor of the Regulators London field office from their raised vantage point.

"Pleased to meet you," Emmie replied politely, offering a slender hand from her long and toned arm. She was only a couple of inches shorter than Adam and with them both sitting, the difference was barely visible.

"Likewise," Adam grinned back. David knew this would be a shock for him. Jack and Adam were close, a real double act. David had loved their passion for the job. It had been one of the reasons he had spent so long finding the right partner for Adam. He knew that no one would replace Jack, but there would be someone who could continue to bring out the best in Adam. Someone who could help transition him into being the senior member of the partnership. That wasn't to say he had been Jack's sidekick – they were quite clearly equals – but Jack had been the one to bring Adam under his wing when he came in. Adam now needed to take that responsibility on. Emmie would hopefully allow him to do that whilst keeping him grounded.

"Ms. Weston here just completed a secondment at the Manchester branch. She's been transferred here for her first full rotation. You're to show her the ropes."

"Not a problem at all," Adam would relish the challenge, David thought. "Where did you come from, Emmie?" Adam asked his new partner.

"Come from?"

"Before you were a Regulator," Adam explained.

"Oh." Emmie slipped her hand through her shoulder-length light brown hair. "I was at university. Oxford."

Adam cocked his head, and David saw the slight look of confusion on his face and decided to interject.

"She applied straight out of university."

"Applied? What? How? I didn't know we had adverts down the Job Centre." Adam looked even more puzzled.

David pulled a face. The answer was one he was proud to tell and equally ashamed to tell. "There was a server that we didn't secure properly. Emmie here found it and applied using it, whilst pointing out our security flaw."

"How did you even know to look?" Adam turned to his new partner.

"My grandad was a Regulator," Emmie explained. "He trained me from a fairly young age, said he could see something in me. Set me up for this life."

"Your grandad?" Adam's mouth hung a little open now. David was sure it was exaggerated. "That is absolutely nuts." Adam looked back to David. "You do pick them, don't you?"

"I wanted someone who at least had a chance to keep up with your boundless enthusiasm," David replied, not trying to hide the playful barb.

"I don't think it will be a problem, sir," Emmie joined in. David was sure it wouldn't be.

5

His hands worked quickly. They had to. Mo Younis was running out of time, and the program he had hoped would get him past this final hurdle was stalling. It was his fault, he knew that much. The program had simply been hastily coded, this was not his best work. He cursed himself silently and then cursed himself again for cursing.

Sweat began to form on his brow under his loosely curled hair. If it looked like it hadn't been washed in longer than Mo would ever care to admit, that's because it hadn't. There hadn't been time. They had been moving around from one location to another. Sometimes an abandoned factory, sometimes the house of a relative or friend of someone who knew someone, sometimes the rear room of a small business. Wherever it was, the three men on this mission would stay hidden the whole time they were entrenched, only ever venturing out, tentatively, to use the toilet. They ate, slept, prayed, and worked together with this one goal in mind: find the data, extract it, and get out alive.

They were in one such business now, above a local store that sold simple, day-to-day products, mostly local, but some imported from the sub-continent. One of the brothers, Ahmed, really appreciated that. He had been born here, in London, Dagenham to be exact, but he had spent much of his childhood growing up back in Pakistan and had a love for chocolate Barfi, a milky sweet of Indian origin. The proprietor of the store, a cousin of a cousin of the other man with them, Suleiman, had been only too happy to give his esteemed guest as many Barfi as he could stomach.

The shop owner had been the only person they were allowed contact with. They hadn't been told his name, and he hadn't been told theirs. The shopkeeper believed it was as much for his security as it was anyone else's, but he was wrong. His security wasn't even secondary to theirs, but such lies had to be told to get them access and to allow them to carry out their task. In the end, he hadn't really committed a crime, so he was probably safe if anyone ever came knocking.

His shop was on a main street in London's Ealing district, just a couple of doors down from Ealing Common tube station. It was a busy road, with people coming and going at all times, entering into many different cafes, bars, shops, and other establishments, many of them using phones, tablets, and laptops, pretty much all of them making most of the host of free Wi-Fi hotspots in the area. Just as the three of them were doing now.

They each had an account with a different wireless service that was being broadcast in the area, all of which were connected to burner phones, registered in made up names, living at addresses that led nowhere. Mo's account was registered to a cemetery in the Midlands town of Nuneaton. Mo had never been to Nuneaton. He was fairly sure he wasn't missing out. Perhaps someday, some law enforcement official would have to check it out. Maybe they'd like its charms. Maybe not. They certainly wouldn't find what they were looking for.

The problem with using a connection like this, however, was that it was slow and unreliable. Right now, that was causing Mo all sorts of headaches, just as he was within touching distance of their end goal.

He groaned, a long drawn out groan.

Suleiman looked up. "What's wrong, Mo?"

Mo's face was crumpled, his clothes tatty, his hair a mess. He'd filled out a little as well, his gut starting to push at his t-shirt. Living out of a suitcase on takeaway meals for three months would do that to any man, he had told himself. Here, they had been sending the shopkeeper over the road to a nearby Nando's for lunch and dinner. Mo had loved chicken before this week. Not now.

"I got in," he groaned, "but the bloody code is no good, I can't get a good enough connection to work through it in time. They're going to know we got in."

"You're in?" Ahmed exclaimed.

"Nearly, I mean, yeah, as good as," Mo exhaled. "But if I don't clear this up and hide myself, they're going to be able to shut it all down before I can find what we need."

Suleiman and Ahmed were now crowding round him. Their attempts hadn't been as fruitful on this occasion. True, over the course of the operation, the three of them had all contributed greatly, narrowing down a massive database of possibilities to find what it was they were looking for, buried deep in a dark corner of the government's servers. It had been forgotten, it seemed, but there was no doubt that someone would be monitoring their systems every second of every day. One wrong keystroke could lead to the data being deleted forever.

That simply wasn't an option.

The hunt for what they were after had taken them over a month. Mo knew that it had taken a lot longer in the run-up before that. The man who hired him, Ehab, had said as much, although he had never delved into the specifics, only talked about inevitable sacrifices for the greater good. Mo was fine with that. He wanted to do something that he believed was good, against people he knew were bad. This was definitely it, he knew it.

Now, though, the mission was in jeopardy because of bad code and a spotty connection. It was part of the way they had chosen to operate, going guerrilla as opposed to using multiple VPNs to try and hide their location. They were still hiding behind some VPNs, but using a connection that was public, in a place where they wouldn't be seen, gave them an extra layer. In a perfect world, there would have been the kit and infrastructure, but this wasn't the perfect world and the danger involved in getting this hack wrong, meant they had decided to be cautious. They were all prepared to die for their cause, something Mo had been shocked to realise in himself, but none of them actually wanted to die.

"Look, just don't worry about the trail, get the data first, man. We need that, or the whole operation is over," Suleiman insisted.

"I know, I know." Mo's brow was getting more and more furrowed. It went against his careful nature to leave any evidence, but if it was leaving a trail or missing out on the data, he knew which one had to give.

The data they wanted was encrypted and could only be accessed by someone who knew the correct key. None of the men in the room did, but they were hoping a program that they had uploaded to that very same server earlier in the week would do.

Mo was activating the program now, all the while waiting for his connection to be pulled, for someone at the other end to notice what was happening and close the port before deleting the information. By now, anyone watching would know what it was they were after, and they would probably decide that it was better forgotten than left where it was.

Mo's fingers stopped. He had done all he could. The program was activated, and it was now a question of waiting for it to work. All three men knew it and an expectant hush settled on the room.

Then there was a noise. A quick and subtle ping.

"It's downloading," Mo half gasped.

Ten more seconds and the data was on his machine, then quickly transferred onto three different hard drives, from which it would be later uploaded to different servers. The three men quickly packed whatever scant belongings they had into their duffle bags, including their laptops. All of those would later be dumped, according to the plan they had been given for escape, somewhere off-grid, never to be found. Before that, they needed to leave. They silently exited the flat above the shop they had been sharing and walked out onto the busy Uxbridge Road.

They split up, the three of them heading in three different directions. No one paid any attention to them as they disappeared into the bustling mix of pedestrians. No one in Nando's cared, no one in the betting shop next door cared, no one in the bar across the road cared. For all Mo and his partners knew, they were home free.

6

Jack was in Malton the day after Thea's call. He had packed light, just a couple of days' clothes in a backpack, a spare pair of boots, and a drab dark green jacket. He had bundled them into his car, a second-hand Audi estate that he had bought shortly after moving to the house, knowing that the reliability and size would serve him well during his remodelling. The drive had taken the best part of six hours, sweeping around London on the M25, up the eastern side of the country on the M11 and then following the Great Northern Road, the A1. He had stopped off twice on the way to give himself a break from the monotony of the British road systems, once pulling off the M11 near Saffron Walden, and another time taking a pit stop in an American diner on the A1 near Newark. Whilst there was a certain urgency to getting to Malton and helping Thea, he didn't see it as critical, and he wanted to make sure he arrived in a fair state, as opposed to strung out from sitting behind the wheel staring at brake lights.

He'd booked a room in a small B&B for a week. The owner, a small man with round spectacles and an equally round head, greeted him. He was quiet and disinterested in striking up conversation with his guest, it seemed, which Jack found surprising but welcome. He went to his room, dropped off his belongings, then phoned Thea.

"I'm in town," he said when she picked up. "Where are you?"

"At the hospital," she replied, more than a hint of stress in her voice.

"I'll meet you there," Jack volunteered. Once Thea had told him which ward to find her on, he was back out of his room, out of the B&B, and into his car.

Malton was a small town, so getting around anywhere didn't take long, and he was walking into the hospital less than ten minutes after walking out of his B&B. The hospital, like the town, was also diminutive, but it had clearly expanded over the years. An old Victorian-looking building took centre stage, with more modern wings having been added later, one which looked, by its architecture, to have been around the 1960s, another, much later. All the same, it was unmistakably a hospital. The signs all bore the same colour scheme as hospitals up and down the country, with wording typed out in the same font you would find at every NHS hospital. The wards all had names that Jack assumed had been derived from the local area, including Ryedale, which was where Malton was located.

He had been told that Thea and the boy would be in a private room. Thea had put a police guard on the door as well. She hadn't told him everything, just a brief outline of the situation. A kid had turned up, scared and hurt, clearly the victim of countless, heinous crimes. Then he had started naming names that had worried Thea, so she had decided she needed extra insurance. That was what Jack was there for.

He walked into a small reception area and quickly spied the sign pointing him in the direction of the ward he wanted. It wasn't hard, there were few options to choose from. He wandered through the corridors, all of which were clean, shiny, and well lit. Again, unmistakably an NHS hospital. He followed the signs up a small flight of stairs to the first floor and entered into a small crossroad between two corridors. For a moment, he was unsure which way to go and looked for a sign, not paying attention to where he was going, nearly barrelling into another man, who was coming around the same corner.

"Sorry," he said earnestly. The man looked up at him, a mixture of indignance, that quickly gave away to what Jack assumed to be shock, on account of his size, before scurrying off down the corridor Jack had just come down without even a word of recognition.

Jack shrugged and moved on. He was a big guy, with more than a hint of trouble about him. It was all over his face by way of old battle scars. The six-hour drive wouldn't have done him much good either. The room was just off the corridor in front of him. A constable sat outside on one of the dark blue plastic chairs that lined the corridor was a real give away. He stood as Jack approached.

"Jack Quinn. DC Watts is expecting me," Jack offered, and the constable nodded.

"Aye, she said you were coming. In you go." The officer grinned quickly and warmly, opening the door for Jack.

"Thanks." Jack nodded and walked into the room.

Thea sat on a grey chair next to the bed. She had cut her hair since the last time he saw her, he noticed, surprising himself. It suited her. She stood as he entered, but left her hand placed softly on that of the boy in the bed. Jack could see he was asleep or pretending to be. His face was pale, and he looked thin. Not quite gaunt, not quite starved, but definitely not healthy. He was tucked under a sheet in the bed, lying on his side, head to Thea, with one arm sticking out. There were bruises, and scrapes dotted all over his arm, that Jack knew were probably only a precursor of what was to come.

"Hi," he whispered as softly as he could, not knowing whether to approach or if Thea would come to him. In the end, she lifted her hand off the boy's, who wriggled slightly at the release, and then walked to him.

"Hi," she repeated. "Thanks for coming."

"No problem. You okay?"

Thea shrugged. "I've been better, I've been worse."

"Par for the course."

There was a silence.

"What happened to him?"

Thea looked back at the boy in the bed. She swallowed and then looked back at Jack. Already there were tears in her eyes.

"You don't...he doesn't need people knowing all the specifics, just..." She was struggling with this, Jack saw. For a moment, he wanted to tell her that it was fine, that he could handle it. Then he realised she wasn't protecting him, she was protecting the boy. She didn't want to spread his story far and wide, didn't want to make him feel that everyone knew what he had been through. She was protecting him from as much pain to come as she could because no one had protected him before.

He stepped forward and put his hand on her shoulder.

"It's fine. I get it. A line was crossed. What do you need from me?"

"I don't know, Jack. I'm just not sure yet. I want to do this, do it the right way, you know I do. But Jesus, if what he said is true, if some of the names he gave really are involved in this, then I need to make sure he's safe. I know you can do that for him."

"No problem," he said. "You need me to stay here?"

"If you could, for now. I've told my DI that you're a relative."

"You lied?"

"I didn't have a choice, Jack. The story this kid told me, if it's half right, we're all in danger."

"What is it?"

Thea looked back at the boy, then walked Jack to the corner, further away from the boy, and spoke in a whisper.

"When he was five, he was dumped at a house by his care worker. There were lots of other kids there, boys and girls, all different ages. He said that men would come, near enough on a daily basis, and do all kinds of things to them. Everything Jack, not just rape, not just the physical side, but the mental side too. He said that they killed some of the kids who tried to escape, or the kids simply got too old and they couldn't find another use for them."

"How many kids?"

"He didn't know, he can't even count properly, but going by what he's said, over the years, hundreds."

"How? How does that even happen?"

"The house was run by the same people all the time apparently. They used to warn the kids that if they escaped, that if they tried to go to the police, then they'd be caught because some of the people who came to the house were police officers. Not just police officers, judges, MPs, doctors, anyone who might be an authority figure, it seems. If that's true, then we're talking about some sort of conspiracy."

Jack cocked his head slightly, guessing the other reason that Thea had wanted him there. "You want to know if the Vehm or the Regulators had anything on this conspiracy?"

"In a word, yes."

"You know I'm out?"

"Out?"

"Suspended, indefinitely. I was supposed to tie up some loose ends on a job."

"And you didn't?"

"You're still here, aren't you?"

Thea shook her head in disbelief. "Reuben was right." Reuben had been a South London gangster who Thea and Jack had both been chasing. He'd ended up besting everyone, but at a considerable cost.

"Don't get involved with them, Thea. It's a road that leads one way only."

Thea looked him firmly in the eyes. "I don't have a choice. He needs someone to help him, and I'll do what it takes. Will you?"

Jack shook his head. "Even if I wanted to, I can't. I'm sorry. I'll stay with the kid, I'll be his uncle or something, but that's all I can do. Sorry."

Thea's face changed in an instant. Sadness swapped with determination. She put her hand on his arm and pulled him outside. He knew she didn't want to leave the kid alone, but he also knew he'd tipped her to a point where she was going to blow, and he was certain that she didn't want to do that in front of the boy.

"What do you mean you can't?" she hissed through clenched teeth, trying her best to keep her voice low, but still letting her irrepressible anger slip out.

"This isn't something where you just drop them a friendly call and get access to what they know. I was a part of a worldwide organisation that fought against corruption at some really powerful levels. They have enemies everywhere, people who would love to get access to someone like me, now that I'm out. They won't run risks if they think there is one. I start asking for information, they'll kill me, just on the off chance I'm working against them."

"They're that cutthroat?"

"I'm only alive right now because they didn't feel I'd technically done anything wrong. I'm a grey area, I disobeyed an order, but it was an order that contravened what they stood for. Killing me for that would have caused far more problems down the line. Best to put everyone in a corner to look at later, or never. Whichever comes first."

"That kid needs us."

"And my kids need me. Alive. I'll do everything I can, I'll help you in any way I can, but doing that won't get you anything positive. It's just not a smart play."

Thea looked up at him. He knew he wasn't the man she expected when she called him. The Jack Quinn she would have remembered had been happy to break rules, happy to do what was right, regardless of the personal consequences, but that Jack was gone.

"Okay," she sighed. "Maybe you don't want to risk yourself, I get that. I've seen what happens on that side of it all, but can you at least tell me how to contact them?"

"Why?"

"Because if this is something real, then it must have come up on their radar. They're fighting corruption in government, that's what they're all about. You told me that, so they must have at least looked into this. There's all sorts of batshit crazy stuff on the internet, after all."

Jack shrugged. "It was never an area that they got us looking at. I don't know any more than that."

"Isn't that strange?"

"No, not really. There are hundreds of different teams across the country. Different locations, different mandates. It simply wasn't mine at any time I was there. Could easily have been someone else's, I just wouldn't ever have known."

"So, who would?"

Jack took a second to think. "You told me you met a woman once; she warned you off. I think that was probably Lowri Graves. If you look for her, you'll find her, but I've got to warn you, she was the one who gave me my orders and the one who suspended me."

"Will she help?"

"She's your best shot. Doesn't mean she will."

There was a silence. Both knew this wasn't the outcome Thea had wanted, and Jack regretted not being upfront with her from the beginning. He had suspected she wanted him for his access to the group, but he had hoped that she merely needed his muscle. He was loathe to speak about the Regulators or the Vehm on the phone, as he was positive he was being bugged. He knew that he owed it to her to give his all where he could.

"Do you want me to stay here tonight with the kid?"

"Yeah. I'll introduce you both, see how he reacts, and then we'll go from there, try and build a relationship. For now, though, if you're okay with it, it might be best if you station yourself out here. Keep an eye on anyone coming and going, just in case they're scouting the place. It's a small hospital, and this is a quiet corner, so you shouldn't have anyone really wandering around, save the odd soul. Hopefully anyone suspicious should stick out like a sore thumb."

"I'm sure we'll be fine. If they've got this far, then they've had more sophisticated plans than snatching kids out of hospitals. Too many questions left unanswered afterwards. But I'll be here, as long as it takes. What's the long-term plan with him?"

"I don't know." Thea realised there wasn't one as she spoke. "He's got no one, but if he goes back into the system, then they'll be able to get at him."

"Then you need to find a way to stop them. Lowri will help. She's good at this. The best, in fact."

"Does she still want me…" Thea raised her eyebrows, not saying it.

"Dead? No, that's all the past now. You've stepped away from it all, they'll know that. The case is dead. No one else needs to be."

7

Mo had spent the best part of three days on the run. That had always been the plan. Lay low, take stock of the situation, avoid each other, and stay safe. Mo had felt a burst of exhilaration when he first left the flat. They had carried out their mission successfully, and he'd been the one to get through. This was his success, and while the adrenalin flowed, he felt pretty much invincible for the first time in years.

It hadn't lasted.

The come down from that high had been quick. Their security. The plan they had devised had been one that they were sure would mean they were near enough invisible in that sense. How could anyone possibly find them if they didn't know where to look?

But the more Mo held that notion in his head, the more he began to pick at it, the more he began to find vulnerabilities. That was what he did after all; look for a vulnerability in a system and attack it. Now, he was doing the same to his own security system, and he realised that there was no such thing as foolproof. Not even close.

They had all been obsessed with hiding where the hack had been perpetrated. Admittedly, they'd done a good job, but they hadn't figured on hiding the *when* it happened. Ultimately, they would be able to pinpoint roughly where. They might never know the exact location, but they would be able to put it within a small area. Then it was just a case of looking in that area for variances from the normal pattern. Discrepancies that would point to an anomaly.

That was their problem. Even though they had worked hard to ensure that their leaving the flat and splitting up wasn't seen by any cameras, the location having been chosen for the fact it was in a blind spot, as well as the welcoming nature of their host, there were still countless other ways that could have been caught and memorialised, be it on a dashcam, mobile phone, or god knows what else. It would be bad luck if that happened, but relying on pure luck was a strategy that got people in trouble.

So, Mo, the hacker, had run a debug in his head. He knew now that he had to ensure that he disappeared once more. The problem was, he was in one of the worst places in the world for someone to escape. London was littered with cameras, over half a million of them. If someone wanted to disappear in London, they had to find a way to navigate through the complex labyrinth of surveillance systems that seemed to be expanding with the second. They were everywhere, on the streets, in shops, in taxis, on buses, on the Underground, even now in some of the sewers.

But not yet all of the sewers. That was where Mo had to head.

There was a last problem. Using the sewer meant exposing himself further. He needed protection whilst he was down there. A protective suit for him and the drive. That meant heading into a shop to buy the requisite protective gear to allow him to be able to simply breathe down there, never mind traverse the four-mile route he had planned.

He'd made a list in his head of all the things he'd need. A thick, hooded overall suit, duct tape, goggles, and a thick plastic bag to place around his rucksack. Whilst his health might have been his first concern, he was as confident as he could be that compared to that pen drive, he was expendable in the eyes of his employers. That didn't faze him. There was a mission, and he knew that he had to complete it, come what may.

The store he bought the supplies from was a brightly lit tool shop, a high street brand that dealt with tradespeople on a daily basis, and Mo had to wait in line behind a couple of chipper builders who bantered back and forth with the smiley, middle-aged woman behind the counter as she supplied them with a small arsenal of tools and supplies they apparently needed for their job before charging everything to an account, no doubt paid for by their employer and monitored less rigorously than it needed to be.

Mo made sure he came across as relaxed and happy, trying his best to drum up small talk with the shop assistant as she picked up the items he requested. He knew what he was. He was a Muslim in London, buying equipment that an overactive imagination could easily link to all sorts of exotic, potential attacks. The last thing he needed to do was create a negative impression in this woman's head, so that an hour or two later, after playing the situation through in her head, she was calling the police, reporting the surly Asian looking gentleman who had just bought himself a DIY hazmat suit. To be safe, he spoke in his best cockney twang, dropping in the odd 'fucking,' 'shitting,' and 'bollocks' for good measure.

When she asked what he was doing, he told her the truth, near enough. He was heading down into the sewers, but in his story, he was part of a film crew doing a documentary on the sewer network, at which point she was far more interested in which celebrities he knew than anything else. She'd remember him, he couldn't escape that, but for positive reasons. Even if anyone did come here following his trail, this would be the penultimate stop before they lost him.

He walked a good half a mile from the tool shop before he found what he was looking for, an access cover to the low-level sewers running across London from east to west. It was obscured down a small back alley, behind a row of shops near a major road. He would have been seen on CCTV going into the street, there was no way of avoiding that, but the list of places he could have disappeared to was so great, he was hopeful that it would take anyone hunting him far too long to pick up his trail.

He pulled on the overalls, placed his rucksack in the bag, pulled the goggles over his eyes, and started to tape everything up. The last thing he needed was for anything to seep in and get on him. The stench of what he was about to wade through was going to be vile. He double-checked each seal. Finally, he was happy.

Fully protected, he quickly descended the rusty ladder into the depths of the sewer. It was twenty feet down to the bottom. Mo found himself in a nine-foot-high tunnel. A small stream of dirty water, no more than six inches deep ran beneath his feet. So far, so good, he thought to himself before setting off.

It was less than a quarter of a mile before things got worse. He reached a dip in the sewer where it nosed down quickly, the water picking up speed ahead of him. More and more pieces of debris pushed past. As he moved on, it seemed that the size of matter passing him in the flow of water was getting bigger and bigger. It wasn't going to get any better. He knew that. He was heading downstream, along with everything else.

Every footstep was treacherous now. The cobbled stone below him had been worn smooth by years of the flow of noxious materials in the sewer, leaving them dangerously slippy. Falling had many pitfalls. The water was getting deeper; he could feel it moving against his leg. If he fell and ripped his suit, it would quickly fill up, and there would be no escape. That could be fatal.

He stumbled on in the darkness, the resistance building with each footstep as the flotsam in the water got thicker and thicker. Mo felt his feet skid below him, his left leg sliding down under his right. He wobbled and teetered, then as he tried to correct his motion, he felt his right foot rushing forward with the flow of the water. Both feet kicked out in front of him, and his hands grasped hopelessly. He landed with a thump on his rear, the water surging around his body, chunks of God-knows-what crashing into his back, charging under his arms. For a horrible moment, he thought something had ripped. He clutched the bag to his side with his left hand, gasping for breath in the suffocating plastic suit. His right hand slipped against the wall, finally grabbing onto something solid, more through fortune than design. He propelled himself upright.

He breathed deeply. Could he smell anything? He wasn't sure. No. If he had split his suit, he would be retching by now. Taking a moment to settle his nerves, he berated himself for thinking this was in any way a good idea.

Slowly he moved on. There was no point in rushing. He picked his way steadily through the sewer system. It took another two and a half hours, but eventually, he found the ladder he was looking for. He hauled himself up out of the foul water, hanging on the ladder, letting the worst of the sewer's grime fall off him.

The last thing he wanted to do was slip off the ladder. He climbed up, opened the manhole, and was out.

Dumping the overalls did nothing to take away the foul smell from Mo, and he longed to get to the safehouse, where he hoped he'd get the chance to clean up. A long shower, a really long shower, was all he was thinking of as he hurried towards the address he'd been made to memorise for weeks.

The house he was looking for was a small terrace house near to the river, on the south bank of the Thames, in Barnes. There were good road links, with London's South Circular snaking it's way around the capital just a quarter of a mile away. It also had an access via a rear entryway, which could be reached by way of a dirt track that ambled up behind the two rows of houses.

It was up this track that Mo had been asked to walk, presumably because it meant he couldn't be observed entering the property from the street and there was no chance of anyone tailing him without being spotted.

The house itself was one of the furthest along the track, at the end nearer to the river. Mo had spied it from a good distance away, looking to see any signs of life. The windows upstairs had their curtains open, but there was no obvious sign of activity. Clearly, the surveillance was being done by camera, probably a number of them mounted to look in different directions to give an all-around view of anyone approaching.

Mo reached a sturdy, solid metal gate, that stood over seven feet tall, in the middle of a thick brick wall that rose up slightly higher than those of the neighbouring properties, but not enough to be completely out of place. It looked weathered, so it was clearly an addition to the property well before it began life in its current configuration, and therefore unlikely to attract suspicion from the neighbours.

Mo rapped his knuckles on the metal gate, hearing a dull thud echoing out, then he waited. Eventually, he heard the sound of footsteps on concrete and the sound of heavy locks sliding before the door opened slowly, and Mo was able to walk in.

"Mo Younis?" a tall man with thick arms and a stubbly beard, dressed in black fatigues greeted him before carrying on without waiting for a reply. "You're late."

"I had to take a different route." They stood in a small yard, a bare concrete floor stretching out to a thick-looking wooden door that led to the house. The downstairs windows had their curtains closed.

"Were you followed?"

"No, I just—" Mo felt a sudden rush of fear. Had his deviation aroused suspicion with his employers? "I didn't feel safe."

"The route was chosen specifically so you would be safe."

"I know, I just…"

"Come," the tall man butted in. "Nabil will want to speak to you."

The man stepped back, ushering Mo ahead of him and towards the door. Mo hesitated, then stepped forward. He hoped for a warmer welcome inside.

8

She had never admitted it out loud, she had barely even allowed herself to admit it internally, but Thea Watts had been bothered by the invasion of her property by Lowri Graves. Turning up to find a stranger in her home, sitting on her couch, drinking her drinks, and then giving her a thinly veiled threat made up to sound like a friendly warning had been something that Thea still hadn't moved on from. She wasn't scared by it. She didn't sit there at night worrying that Lowri would turn up again, far from it. Indeed, if anything, she had to prove that very point. She had allowed someone to assert themselves over her, now she had to level the score.

She knew Jack didn't want her getting involved with the Vehm, the shadowy underground court system that Jack had told her Lowri was a high-ranking member of, but she had persisted, and he had relented. Jack was different now. That tenacity and drive, so evident in him when they last saw each other, was now gone, replaced by something else. What was worse for Thea was that she didn't necessarily think it was a bad thing. He didn't look beaten or broken; he looked like a man moved on. Closure.

It hadn't been easy for her to find an address for Lowri Graves. That had been less than surprising, but ultimately, she had found her target after contacting a colleague in Parliamentary and Diplomatic Protection team, the PaDP. Lowri was still a civil servant at the House of Commons; therefore, they had access to her address details as part of their security procedure. Thea had explained, truthfully, that she needed to get hold of Lowri as part of an investigation into a potential paedophile ring. She left out the part about how she planned to break into Lowri's house before she talked to her, but she figured in doing so, she saved herself the issue of her request being denied.

From the outside, the house looked normal enough. A tall and imposing structure, not out of place in London, dating back to the Victorian era, and crawling up from a small basement level to three more floors above, the final one occupying a space in the loft. There was a door to the front, up a small flight of stairs, as well as a door to the rear, accessible from a gate that led to a small passageway that ran along the side of the house. Thea had ruled that out; the gate would be locked. Anyone stood next to that for too long would draw attention, but someone stood next to a front door, idly stood there waiting, especially a smart-looking woman, wouldn't draw the same sort of looks as, say, a six-foot-five man.

Jack had given Thea a small electronic lock pick that he assured her would get her in the front door, but he warned her that Lowri no doubt had employed an array of countermeasures inside her house. Even before last year, when she had been abducted on her doorstep, Lowri had been careful. Thea didn't want to be stealthy; Thea wanted to show she wasn't scared. Not scared to be seen, not scared to be there.

Thea walked up to the front door and knocked loudly. She waited. No answer. Good. The last thing she wanted was for Lowri Graves to be in and greet her at the door. She took out the small lock pick, stepped forward, reaching up with her left hand as if knocking the door for a second time, but with her right hand carefully sliding the end of the lockpick into the lock and activating the mechanism. She stepped back and watched, waiting for the lock to click.

There was nothing. She reached forward and went to pull the device out, only to find that it was jammed in place. Had she done something wrong? Jack had assured her that the device would work automatically, dealing with both the mechanical side of the lock, as well as scrambling the electronic brain of any more sophisticated system. He said it would be as simple as that. Was he wrong?

A resounding clunk suddenly stopped the tension. Thea pulled once more on the device, this time it came out of the lock easily, and she slipped it back inside her pocket before opening the door and stepping inside.

The moment she did, she had no doubt she would have been picked up on a camera somewhere. She scanned all the walls, looking in the corners, along the join between ceiling and wall, on the tables to her right where a pair of gloves and a small mirror sat, but saw nothing. She carried on inside the house, passing over the black and white tiled floor, past the stairs that led upstairs with their dark wood bannister, and to the first door on her left. She looked in to see a tidy and elegant living room with a light grey-coloured sofa and chair set arranged around a wooden coffee table. A large TV screen sat opposite, and a huge bookcase occupied another wall.

Behind that lay the dining room, more bookcases, a long dark wood table that seated eight with immaculate, slender chairs arranged around it, while to the right of that lay the kitchen, where Thea began her search. It was a modern affair, small by some standards, but still large enough for Thea to be able to move about with ease, opening and looking through the white cabinets before she found what she was looking for, a glass and a bottle of vodka.

She poured herself a drink, then went into the front room and waited.

It was a little less than two hours before she heard the lock on the door going. She felt herself tense a little, a mixture of excitement and a little fear. She wondered how long Lowri had waited before deciding to head home. Thea figured that Lowri wouldn't want to dash right over, for fear of giving away some notion of panic on her behalf. She would have waited a little while, let Thea sweat it out, then when curiosity got the better of her, when she realised her house guest wasn't leaving, she would come. Thea had expected to wait a little longer. Perhaps she had overestimated Lowri.

The door shut, and Thea heard the sound of a briefcase being put down, clothes – probably a coat – being removed, footsteps on the tiles, someone approaching the living room. Then Lowri was stood in the doorway. There was no mock surprise. That would have been patronising.

"Hello," Lowri said impassively.

"Hello, Miss Graves," Thea replied.

"You know, you should tell Mr. Quinn that getting involved in things like this will get him in even more trouble."

"He had nothing to do with it."

"Yes, because you happened to have the sort of device that can pick both my physical and electronic lock in your regular CID arsenal."

That stung Thea. She had thought she would be able to convince Lowri she had kept Jack as far out of it as possible, but she knew that even the slightest hesitancy before a reply would give away an attempted lie, and she hadn't prepared an answer for that accusation. She just kept quiet.

"Knowing Jack though, and I know Jack," Lowri looked hard at Thea as she said that, "he would have told you not to do this and, knowing you, you wouldn't listen to him."

"Why did you cut him loose? He's good at what he does." Thea's voice raised slightly as she spoke.

"I'm afraid I don't think you're at the requisite pay grade to be discussing our HR situation."

"I am when it comes down to a choice between my life and his job."

"So, you have your answer, but let's cut the horse shit shall we, Thea? I'm going to pour us both a drink, then we're going to talk about why you're here. I'll give you a moment to compose yourself before we get down to business."

Lowri bent forward and picked up the glass next to Thea, never taking her eyes off the CID officer as she disappeared into the kitchen. She returned a couple of minutes later with the glass refilled and another one for herself. She handed Thea her drink, then sat down, took a sip and nodded for the conversation to begin.

"A child turned up at a police station in North Yorkshire. A young boy. He doesn't know how old he is, only that he was five when they took him out of care and put him in a house somewhere. Since then, he's been bussed around the country, from place to place, along with a host of other children, and used as a slave, sexually and otherwise, by a whole host of men. Some of the names of these bastards lead me to believe there might be a paedophile ring working at the highest levels of our society. I'm talking MPs, Lords and Knights, high ranking officials, national bloody treasures, the works."

Lowri nodded. "You want to know what we know about it?"

"If something like this has been happening, it seems like it would have crossed your desk."

Lowri looked thoughtfully at Thea as if she was making a decision. *She's wondering if she can trust me,* Thea thought.

"We have looked at this, yes. There have been a number of ongoing operations. We have removed people in the past, and we have passed on information to the police in the past. Other times, we've simply not found what we've been looking for. There have been some big names, and there have been some smaller names, but most of them have been in isolation, or at the very most, a couple of men working together. Nothing on the scale that you've talked about."

"You don't believe the kid? I could bring him here, let you listen to him. Trust me, you'd believe him then." Thea didn't like the idea she was being fobbed off.

"I didn't say that," protested Lowri. "What I mean to say is that we have covered it before and we will cover it again if you can't make your investigation bear fruit. I assume that's what you came here for?"

"No, not at all. I want your intel, your files, I want it all. I want what you know, so I can build a case because, right now,

I'm starting from scratch on a case that revolves around the testimony of a child and nothing more."

"We're not really the sharing type."

"And I'm not really the asking type, but if this is true, it's bigger than my pride and it's bigger than yours. These are kids, just children, who are being used, prostituted, raped, killed, by men who see them as less than a commodity. Whatever I might think of you, and believe me, it's not much – I know that you only do this because you think you're doing good. You think you're serving the people, as am I. So, I'm going to make this one-time deal, and it is a one-time deal. You give me your info, then if I can't make it work, I give you mine back, and we crack this. Either my way or yours, I don't care."

Lowri sat back in the chair, taking a small sip of her drink and watching Thea take an even larger one of hers.

"Do you remember when I came to your flat last time? I told you that, one day, you would find yourself in a situation where you realised that you couldn't beat them your way, and you'd step over that line."

"We're not there yet."

"No, but we will be, and you've already made your promise. Fine, I'll share my information with you, Miss Watts. I hope you get your conviction. If not, I hope we get ours."

Lowri raised her glass, and Thea leant forward, chinking hers against it. Lowri sat backwards.

"Do you also remember, Miss Watts," she went on, "that when you offered me a drink. I refused? There's a good reason for that."

Thea looked at her drink, this time, real fear flushed through her. "What have you done?"

"This time? Nothing." Lowri smiled. "But next time, someone else might. Consider that your first lesson in how to survive in our world. Never let your guard down for a moment."

9

The plastic chairs weren't comfortable, especially for a man of his size. Sleep had been nearly impossible. At first, he had tried lining them up, a row of seven that he could try and stretch across, but the rise and fall of the seats dug into his body in different places, so that no matter how well he tried to pad his makeshift bed with his coat, he just couldn't find a spot that would allow him to relax and get comfortable.

In the end, he had switched to sleeping upright, rolling his coat up and around his neck like a travel pillow, to aid his posture and stop him getting stiff. It had been better, but not by much. The chairs didn't provide much support, and anyone walking down the corridors had his ears pricking and his defence mechanisms whirring, just in case.

Ciaran had slept. Jack had only spoken to him briefly, a quick introduction with Thea there, but the boy had seemed disinterested and distant. He had grunted, nodded, then turned his head slowly away and into his pillow, trying once more to descend into the restless sleep that seemed to make up the most of his days.

Clearly, the boy was traumatised, and Jack knew that the mental scars were just as big a threat to his long-term wellbeing, if not more so, than those who might seek to keep him quiet. He'd seen soldiers – good men, tough men, with strong, unflappable characters – come back from war zones and simply fall apart, their lives forever changed by what they had seen and experienced. Here was a kid, nowhere near as mature as those guys, who had lived through far worse, for far longer, and with no hope of escape. How he was still going, Jack didn't know, but he admired the kid's courage. It was the least he could do.

He had wondered whether he should be regularly checking in on him. His role, as he knew it, was to guard the door, make sure no one got in. That was a simple job, a soldier's job, but Jack wasn't just a soldier. He was a father, and he knew that in there was a kid who was scared and alone, who needed some sort of reassurance. The only problem was, Jack was pretty sure that he wasn't going to be the guy to give it. His own failings connecting with his own kids, no matter how hard he tried, still haunted him. If there was one area in life he hadn't succeeded, it had been his relationships with his wife and kids.

So, he sat in the corridor, on the uncomfortable plastic chair, and closed his eyes and tried to sleep.

The hospital was a small rural affair, which mostly shut down at night. There weren't really any inpatients, save for a couple of people on a side ward, all of whom Jack had seen the record for and all of whom were far too old to be likely to be hiding ulterior motives. None were seriously ill, just safer in a hospital than at home while they finished their recuperation and as such. There were no visitors in with them overnight. That helped Jack in keeping a count on who should and shouldn't be in the hospital.

The staff were a skeleton crew. A handful of nurses, two of which took turns at keeping an eye on the front desk, just in case anyone turned up, while there were another two sat in the nurses' office that looked after the ward where the other patients were situated. One of them sporadically came down to check on Ciaran. She was a calm and confident woman with a soothing voice, dark hair pulled back in a smart ponytail. She carried the kind of aura that made it feel like the whole hospital worked to her whims. Ciaran seemed at ease around her, and that made Jack feel a little happier.

He'd met Rankine earlier in the day. The friendly Sergeant had promised to come in first thing in the morning with a little breakfast for both of them. The hospital had basic catering facilities, not the best, so Jack didn't object. He didn't know what Rankine had in mind. He seemed like the sort who would enjoy a proper hearty northern breakfast, which would hit the spot for Jack. He was also sure that he would be thinking of the kid, and if there was a Mrs. Rankine out there, then she'd be aiming for something healthier. That was still a way off, however. It had only just gone half past ten at night. There was a long way to go before Jack could think about food. A ground floor vending machine was as good as it was going to get for Jack anytime soon.

As uncomfortable as it may have been, Jack had managed to shut his eyes and feel a little restful. He was on the verge of dozing off when he heard the sound of shoes on the tiled floor, somewhere out of vision still, but already Jack knew it wasn't one of the nurses. These weren't the soft-soled trainers that so many of them opted for, being on your feet for so long can take a toll after all. These were firmer and there was more weight behind them. A man, definitely. Jack eased himself up and looked around, ready and waiting.

Then the man appeared, coming around that very same corner Jack had earlier. He was tall, late thirties probably, a slight double chin, but a cheerful face with round glasses and curly hair that was now greyer than its original black.

Jack stood as the man approached and smiled. He put a hand out towards Jack. "Hello," he said with a cheery northern twang that chimed a relaxing note out around the corridor. "I'm Dick Shakespeare. Social Services." As he spoke, he pulled a wallet with some identification, raising it casually towards Jack.

"Jack Quinn." He shook Dick's hand and smiled back, taking a moment to scan the identification. It looked real enough. "Ciaran's asleep."

"I was worried that would be the case, but I wanted to come up on the off chance," Dick sighed. "We only got the Police Protect paperwork through this evening, so we're playing a little bit of catch up?"

"Police Protect?" Jack didn't know what that was.

"The force has authorised us to take him into care, once he's been discharged. Sorry, but who are you?"

"I'm his uncle. Maybe. We're not sure," Jack lied quickly.

"His uncle? I thought we didn't know who his family was?" Dick raised an eyebrow.

"We don't. I had a nephew in care who went missing five years ago. His name was Ciaran. We just thought the system had swallowed him up, that he had moved on and his paperwork had got lost. His parents didn't care; they weren't allowed to contact him, so we had just let him go. The call came out of the blue. I still don't even know if it's him. He looks like him, a little." The lie came easily, years of conducting cover stories often off the cuff.

"So, what are you planning to do?"

"We're going to do some swabs, DNA, see what happens. Then, I don't know. I guess you will know more about that than I do." Jack shrugged at the social worker who nodded thoughtfully as he studied Jack.

"Yeah, let's cross that bridge when it comes to it. He's asleep you say?"

Jack stepped forward quietly, then silently opened the door so Dick could look in. Ciaran lay on his side in the bed, eyes closed, mouth open, asleep. Jack closed the door. "It's pretty much all he's done. He's been through a lot, apparently."

"So, I've heard. Are you staying here?"

"Someone should. Can't leave him all alone."

"On the chairs? Doesn't look too comfortable," Dick chuckled.

"I've slept in worse situations. Ex-forces." Jack smiled. He didn't know whether he could trust this guy yet. Someone in the social services had sold this kid out once before, and as amiable as Dick was trying to be, Jack had never been one to let his guard down.

"I don't doubt it." Dick nodded. "Okay, well, I'll pop back tomorrow. They've not said anything about discharging him yet, have they?"

"No, I think they need to work out where they'd discharge him to first. The hospital has been really good about it all, though."

"Yeah, well, we like to extend a warm welcome up north," Dick explained breezily. "I'll be on my way, though. I'll see you soon, I'm sure."

He offered his hand once more, and Jack shook it. "Take care," he said as Dick turned and walked away, his feet thudding on the tiles, the sound slowly diminishing as he got further and further away until they disappeared behind a closing door.

Jack waited till the silence returned and then sat down. No sooner had he, then he saw the door to Ciaran's room open a crack. Ciaran's face peered through.

"Thanks for sending him away," he croaked.

"No problem. He wasn't someone who hurt you was he?"

"No, I don't think so," Ciaran said timidly.

"Okay. Well, if anyone else comes, I'll send them away too until someone comes who you do want to talk to."

Ciaran stared for a moment. "Do you have a gun?"

"A gun? No." Jack tried to put a lid on his shock.

"Get one, then when the bad people come, you don't have to send them away, you can just shoot them. Then they won't come back," Ciaran said in a hushed but firm voice. Then he closed the door, and Jack heard him climb into bed.

10

Nearly twenty years as a Regulator, five as a judge of the Vehmic court system, and over thirty years as a civil servant meant that Lowri had heard numerous cases and allegations involving supposed and proven paedophile gangs. There had been stories that had affected her deeply, some that stayed with her even now, but as she began to pore over the statement Thea had taken from the boy in Yorkshire, she began to realise that this might be bigger than all of them put together.

Helping Thea hadn't been something that sat right with Lowri, but she had to admit, she admired the woman's determination and her guts, but more than that, the story that she had told worried her.

The Vehm and the Regulators had heard about such stories in the past. It was something that had been documented on some of the more elaborate conspiracy theory websites out there, with the names of celebrities, politicians, and many other prominent people being bandied about as possibly being involved in such a setup. The problem was that whenever they had investigated it, whatever evidence they thought that they had found, it always seemed to lead nowhere, other than to an overactive imagination or a fantasist screaming for help.

At least, that was how it had seemed. Now that she was digging deeper into the report that had been filed surrounding the appearance of this child, Lowri was having her doubts. The stories that they had heard elsewhere often came from adults, most of whom spoke only of a passing understanding of the system. There had never been a report from anyone credible that had claimed to have been a victim. Certainly not from a child who had just escaped.

This changed everything.

There was a knock to her office door. She was still working out of her office at Westminster, where she worked her day-to-day role as a civil servant, reporting to the Home Secretary, a job that linked her into a whole host of people that were both beneficial to work with, as well as to keep tabs on.

"Come in," she called, not looking up from the notes she was reading.

In walked a well-dressed man in his early thirties, Nick Poole. Nick served as her general caseworker, a role that was commonplace in the civil service and gave Lowri free reign when it came to assigning him different tasks. That was doubly helpful, as Nick Poole was also a field agent for the Regulators.

"Morning, Ms. Graves." He smiled as he entered holding two take away cups of coffee, one of which he placed in front of his boss. "Anything of note?"

"It's going to be a long day, Nick," Lowri warned.

Nick sat down at the chair opposite, taking a sip from his cup as he settled. "I didn't really expect anything else, hence the coffee."

He raised the cup as if to offer a toast, and Lowri reciprocated from her side of the desk, the two cups never coming close to contact. "Hence the coffee," she saluted back before explaining what lay ahead. "We've got a situation I'd like you to look into. A former operative of ours, Jack Quinn, seems to have stumbled across a plot we've heard rumblings of for years. I'd like you to be my eyes and ears here in the palace. This is going to link back to a lot of people in this building, visible and not so, and if there is something going on, I want to know names."

"Of course." Nick nodded. "Is there anywhere you'd like me to start?"

"The archives. All we have so far is a name of a child and a town he was found in. There's a long list of suspects I'd like you to cross-reference. See if there's anything in there that links to anyone here, no matter how tenuous. Discount nothing, then report back to me as and when."

"You'll get real time updates, but, if you do pardon my bringing it up, isn't Mr. Quinn a persona non grata?"

"He's been off the Christmas card list, that would be fair to say, yes; but for this, I think we need to be a little bit flexible. I don't want to use him if I can avoid it and it appears that the local police up there might be able to get a handle on everything if they work fast. However, there is the possibility that this goes way beyond one isolated incident in Yorkshire. If that's the case, it might be useful to have someone in play up there who knows our systems."

"Can I be frank?" Nick leaned forward.

"Please." Lowri opened her palm out to signal that the floor was his.

"I wouldn't trust someone we've cast out."

"Nor would I, which is why I intend to send someone up there to get a little bit of a lie of the land, perhaps find out a bit more about where his head's at."

"A field report?"

"Quite."

"Would that be a job you'd need me to fulfil, ma'am?"

"No, I'll handle that another way." Lowri didn't have to explain to Poole who it was; she didn't have to explain to him why she wouldn't tell him that either. Things worked best when they were compartmentalised. Poole would respect that. His background was the Secret Services, a few years in Mi6, or Six as it was colloquially known. Their mandate was dealing with threats abroad. Poole had been a young but well-regarded agent before he'd been let go in the wake of the rendition scandal, where foreign terror suspects were sent to the US whilst the UK turned a blind eye to their torture.

He had been one of the sacrifices made to keep the politicians happy, but as far as Lowri had been able to ascertain, his involvement on it was minimal at best, confined to handing over suspects on airport taxiways. That had made him the perfect candidate for recruitment to the Regulators, and already, a stellar career was being mapped out for this rising star. There weren't many ex-spies of his age that became available, and it was hoped, under Lowri's tutelage, he would become a real asset.

Poole stood up, drink still in hand. "I assume the relevant files will be available for me, as and when I'll need them."

"Everything will be uploaded to the server. Start your work from the Lords, , anyone with any connections to North Yorkshire would be a start. Anyone with land, a freeholding, even a holiday home. Put all that together and work your way out from there."

"No problem at all, ma'am."

"Thank you," Lowri said, dismissing Poole.

Alone with her thoughts, she tried once more to put this together. It had to be a honeypot-style operation, something which could be used to exert influence over and control members of Parliament, Lords and Ladies, influencers of all walks of life. The question was, a honeypot set up by whom? Foreign powers? Private individuals? Members of Parliament? Each one had its own specific threat. She had to find out which, though, to stop it.

11

It had been an intense morning working their way through the open cases that, up until now, had been solely under Adam's jurisdiction, but Emmie had proven herself to be a quick learner. She listened intently as Adam laid out the bare facts of the cases. She studied the supporting materials at the same time, and she hadn't been afraid to chip in with her own input when she saw fit. Adam had been impressed.

Finding a new partner had been something that Adam had been wanting to do for a long time, but crossing that threshold into David's office and asking the question had been something that he hadn't ever been able to muster up the courage to do. At first, there had been the lingering hope that maybe, just maybe, Jack's suspension would be revoked. Then when it had become clear that it had become a permanent solution, Adam had been waiting for the perfect moment. He'd wanted a lull in the incessant flow of cases, a chance for him to take stock of whoever came in. That too had never happened.

Now, however, seemed like the right moment. Emmie seemed like the right person as well. There was still a lot of work to form a proper partnership. A really long way to go before they could even begin to think of being friends. It was probably impossible that she would ever replace Jack. That was a once in a lifetime friendship. A brotherhood. Yet she was smart, she was determined, and she was here. He would make it work.

"Your granddad was a Regulator then?" he asked, desperate to know more about her unusual route into the group. Everyone he had ever spoken to, every other Regulator he had ever heard of, had been approached, scouted, just as he had. No one applied.

"He retired just after I was born. I spent a lot of time with him. Something must have rubbed off," she replied.

"No doubt. Where was he based?"

"He worked London, although I don't think this office was here then. It was all a little different in those days."

"I have no doubt."

"What about you? What's your story?" Emmie looked up from the stack of papers she had been reading.

"My story? Ex-cop, current Regulator," Adam shrugged.

"There's more to it than that, surely?" Emmie raised an eyebrow.

Adam made himself comfortable. "I'd had enough of being in the police. I was fed up of chasing down criminals I couldn't catch, those that wanted to hide behind muscle, fear, extradition treaties, god knows what. There was one case, and it really got me. A truckload of people coming over from Azerbaijan. The driver said he didn't know they were there until he pulled over on the A5 somewhere just north of Rugby. Forty-four people had got in somewhere between there and Bucharest, twenty-eight got out. Turns out they'd paid to a people-smuggling gang for that privilege. We knew who they were. We knew where they were. Thing is, we couldn't extradite them."

"So, you quit the force?"

"No," Adam admitted with a sigh. "I let it fester. I got angry. I started messing up, breaking rules, cutting corners. I was in trouble constantly. I was done. If things hadn't changed, I'd have been an angry man out of a job, but then David approached me. Met me in a restaurant. Told me I could get the people behind the gang if I jumped on a transport plane with him that night. I did. I never looked back."

"What happened to the gang?"

"We got them. Picked them up, those that gave us that option, took them back here and tried them."

"Did it make you feel better?" Emmie asked the question.

"It made sense," Adam replied earnestly. "It made perfect and complete sense. We have rules that stop innocent people being hurt, but there are those who will always find a way to make words on a piece of paperwork for them. No legal system is infallible. So, sometimes we need to ignore it and just do right."

"Yeah, but how did you feel?" Emmie insisted. "I've never done this, not actively put someone away start to finish. What was that feeling like, taking their liberty away personally?"

Adam thought for a moment. He'd never reflected on how it had made him feel. It was all so long ago.

"I guess I felt exonerated. All the anger I'd felt when I walked through that trailer, all the sadness for those people, I finally felt like I'd been able to give them something back. Give them a little justice so that they didn't die in vain. The people who cost them their lives wouldn't cost anyone else. I felt like I'd done the right thing and, in truth, I felt exhilarated. I'd broken the law for the right reasons and got away with it. That feeling, it never gets old."

"You like breaking the law?"

"When it needs to. As I said, laws are made by men, usually powerful ones whose only motivation to look after those below them is to make sure that they can retain their level of comfort. They've no interest in stopping their own, no interest in saving the most needy. I'll break those laws any day of the week for the right cause."

Emmie must have been happy with that because she looked back down at the papers. "It's good to know what makes you tick," she stated.

"What about you? What are you going to get from this?" Adam returned the compliment.

"I guess I'll find out when the time comes."

Adam knew that she probably wouldn't have long to wait.

12

It was cold in the cellar. Plasterwork had fallen off in chunks exposing the brickwork that made up the foundations of the house. Patches of damp could be seen collecting on the walls. In some places, the damp was so prevalent, Mo could see the glisten of water as it seeped through the pores of the masonry. It was a room that had clearly been forgotten by the home's previous owners and tenants, but the current occupiers had plans for it.

A large metal filing cabinet had been placed against one wall. It stretched to just below the ceiling of the cellar, over six feet tall and more than that wide, bolted to the wall. The doors were shut, leaving Mo with no idea what was inside. There were a few other metal shelving units, sturdy enough looking racks that were placed around the room. Some had empty Peli Cases, which Mo knew would have been used to transport the vast array of computing power they had upstairs, as well as the web of cameras that had been erected all around the area to keep the house secure. Others, the smaller ones and the longer ones, looked like they might have been used for weapons. Pistols, rifles. Mo hoped that he wouldn't be around when the contents were used.

The last two items in the room, other than the light that buzzed from a worn-looking cable overhead, were two wooden chairs. Garden chairs in another life. Mo couldn't believe that they would have been the sort of thing his employers would have brought with them. More likely they were a lucky find left over by the previous occupants. They didn't look like they'd seen the sun in a while. Mo sat in one. He was free to move around the room, but he knew there was a man guarding the door at the top of the stairs. He wasn't going anywhere. He patiently sat in the chair, opposite the second one, as if awaiting an interview.

At least an hour had passed now. Maybe they were in the middle of something? The tall man who had greeted him certainly seemed on edge. Something wasn't quite going according to plan. Mo thought back to the question about his route. They had clearly been watching out for him, at least on some points of the way. He regretted that now. The others would be able to vouch for him though. They had struck up a bond. They were brothers in arms.

The door at the top of the stairs opened, creaking on its hinges and illuminating the wall, spotlighting even more dark patches of mould that had been unseen till now. A shadow passed over as a man came down the stairs, reaching the bottom and staring grimly at Mo. He was older than Mo but had clearly kept himself in incredible shape. His thick arms stretched the green-checked shirt he wore, the top two buttons undone to accommodate broad shoulders that held a wide neck. His hair was thinning on top, and he wore a moustache, both of which served to make him look older than he would otherwise. He wasn't anywhere near as tall as the man who had greeted Mo, average height at best, five-eight, five-nine. It all made him look stronger.

He walked slowly and purposefully towards Mo, his motions fluid. He exuded strength and power. As he sat, he locked eyes on Mo, never breaking the gaze. Mo had met him before, but he had never seen this level of intensity. He was Nabil, Mo's handler inside the Brotherhood. A passionate man who believed firmly in the righteousness of what they were doing.

"Why did you do it?" Nabil asked curiously.

"Do what?" Mo's mind raced, trying to put together a list of possibilities. What was Nabil talking about?

"Sell your brothers out," he answered Mo's unasked question.

"I…" Mo stammered. "I didn't."

"They killed them. Did you know they were going to do that, Moeen?" Nabil used Mo's full name. It made him feel like a child being accused by a teacher or parent.

"What, no? Sully? Ahmed?"

"Dead. They followed their routes. Now they're dead. You, however, Mo, didn't. And you live."

Guilt washed over Mo. He had felt that he should go his own route, something had nagged at him, but he hadn't shared that with the others. He wished he had. "I just didn't feel safe. I can't explain it."

"Can't explain it," Nabil mused, rubbing his chin. "Do not lie to me, Moeen!" Nabil shot up from this chair, shouting loudly and directly in Mo's face, forcing Mo to cower backwards.

"I'm not!" Mo exclaimed back sharply.

"Then explain to me what happened? Where were you, Mo? How did you get here?" Nabil was seething. Spit flew as he shouted at Mo.

"I was in the sewers. You can still smell it on me."

"I smell your deceit," Nabil growled.

"Nabil, I swear to you, man, I didn't do anything. I believe in this, I believe in you. What we're doing, all of it." The words were blurted out as he desperately sought to make Nabil believe him.

"You came from a world of lies, why should I believe that you're different to them? To the Vehm, to the Regulators. You're still one of them."

"I'm not."

Nabil's eyes were bulging as he pressed his face closer and closer to Mo's. There had to be some way to prove his innocence, Mo thought desperately.

"The data on the drive you gave us. It's not real, is it? This is a trap."

"No, I swear to you. That's what we pulled from the server. Your team can verify that."

"Then where were you?"

Mo searched through his route. Was there a way he could prove his story? "I was in the sewers. I bought some gear to keep me clean. I dumped it near where I came out. You can find it, find my overalls."

Nabil sat back. His voice became softer. "Where?"

"They're on some wasteland, near the station at Barnes. Get me a map, and I'll show you exactly where. Send someone to get them."

Nabil said nothing. He looked over Mo's shoulder, towards a corner of the room where it met the ceiling. Mo had seen nothing there when he had first surveyed the room, but there must have been some sort of hidden camera. Nabil nodded. He turned back to Mo.

"This does not absolve you of anything, but it does add credence to your story, if we can find the clothes."

"I swear to you Nabil…"

"Do not swear to me. You owe me nothing. Swear it only to Allah."

"Wallah, I do."

Nabil looked at Mo, shaking his head. "Moeen, I have spent many hours with you. Prayed with you. So, I believe I know you and know the faith you carry in your heart. You are either a good Muslim, or an even better liar."

13

Ciaran's request for Jack to get a gun had unsettled Jack more than he could have ever predicted. That a kid so young would be so cold and emotionless about the idea of killing someone had shocked him.

Jack wasn't completely naïve to the idea. He'd been in war zones where child soldiers had been used, but those kids were often drugged, drunk, and brainwashed by their seniors. This was different. This was a kid that had been through so much that he simply didn't care anymore.

What had they done to him?

Ciaran had fallen asleep again fairly quickly, leaving Jack alone with his thoughts. He had tried to sleep himself, but the combination of chair and Ciaran's request had rendered any rest broken at best.

Jack reached into his pocket, pulling his phone out to look at the time. Just after 7 am. No doubt Rankine would be here soon enough with the promised breakfast. That would help. Jack peered through the door. Ciaran was still asleep. He closed it gently and then dialled his son, Calum.

"Hello?" came the response from the other end. Calum sounded dazed, as if he had just been roused from bed.

"Hey, son."

"Dad. What's up?"

"Nothing, I just…needed to hear your voice, son, that's all."

"What?" the concept was lost on Calum, it appeared.

"It's alright. You okay, son?"

"Yeah, you woke me up," Calum protested.

"Sorry about that. It is a school day, though, you need to be up," Jack explained.

"Uh-huh." Calum wasn't the most talkative kid at the best of times, never mind unscheduled wake ups.

"I won't keep you." Jack realised he had nothing really of substance to say. "I just wanted to tell you that I love you, Calum."

"Are you okay, Dad?" There was more energy in Calum's voice now, and Jack suddenly felt guilty in case he had alarmed him.

"Yeah, I'm fine. Just visiting an old friend up north and it got me thinking about family. You."

"What friend?"

"A woman I used to work with. A cop. I thought I might be able to help her with something. Now, I don't know." Jack found himself unexpectedly blurting out his fears to his son. It was not what he called for.

"Is it legal?"

Jack laughed. "Of course, she's a cop."

"Then just do what she asks. It's probably for a good reason if she's a cop."

"Thanks, Cal," Jack said.

"That's alright, Dad."

"Get five minutes more before your mum starts hollering at you to get ready."

"I'll try."

"Love you, Son."

"Love you, Dad."

Jack hung up. He would do what was asked of him. He would do it as if Ciaran was his own. He would find the people who did this, and he would make them pay.

Rankine didn't disappoint with the breakfasts. He arrived with a plastic bag containing three bread rolls, or baps, or cobs, or batches, whatever they were called in this part of the world. Each one was stuffed with bacon, sausage, mushrooms, and an egg then tightly wrapped in silver foil to keep them warm and just ever so slightly moist. Maybe there wasn't a Mrs. Rankine.

They were packed so well that Jack had wondered if Ciaran would want something so daunting, but the boy had devoured it quickly while Rankine and Jack still made their way through theirs.

"That was good." He beamed. It was the first time Jack had seen the boy smile. "What was it?"

"Breakfast, lad," Rankine answered. "The works. Bacon, sausage, eggs, and mushrooms. Didn't think you'd fancy black pudding just yet."

"Do we have that every breakfast?"

"Sometimes. Special occasions maybe, or if you've got a big day ahead and need lots of energy."

Ciaran looked at the silver foil on his lap where the roll had been. There were still a few crumbs scattered in there that he picked at idly as he thought. "I want lots of energy," he said resolutely. Rankine seemed to bring out the best in the kid. Jack had noted that he always seemed more at ease around the sergeant.

"You'll get that from that, lad, that's for sure." Rankine smiled. There was something about the innocence of kids, Jack thought to himself.

"Me and the sergeant need to talk outside for a minute. That okay, pal?" Jack asked.

Ciaran nodded. "You're not going too far, are you?"

"Right outside the door. If you can't hear us, you come look. We'll be there."

"Okay."

Rankine and Jack stepped out into the corridor.

"What's up?" Rankine asked.

"I had a visit from a chap who said he was from Social Services last night. Dick Shakespeare."

"Yeah, he called the station this morning apparently. I've checked him out, he's real."

"That's as may be, but someone in Social Services has to be facilitating this, so treat him with caution. Don't let him disappear with the boy or anything."

"I won't. You think he's a bad 'un?"

"I don't know. I didn't really get much of a handle on him at all, but I'd rather be safe. I told him that we suspected I might be the kid's uncle. If needs be, I can get a DNA result knocked up, in case they want to put him back in the system."

"He'll be your responsibility then."

"I'll cross that bridge when I come to it." Jack was concerned about where the kid would end up. No option seemed safe. "I also want to tap into your local knowledge."

Rankine raised his eyebrows, flattered a little by the compliment. "Go ahead, what do you need to know?"

"If they were holding a load of kids somewhere, a place like that would need some level of protection. You wouldn't want prying eyes. You'd do whatever it takes to keep that hush-hush."

"I think armed guards swanning about the York Moors would have some backs up," Rankine protested.

"I don't. Gamekeepers, beaters, people who work the land can often be found wandering around. Armed with a shotgun. If I was trying to keep a covert guard on my property, that's the sort of person I would use."

"That's a bloody good point. We've got a few of them around here. They have to come to us for their licence."

"Great, you have a list of potential suspects. Get it to Watts. Just you and her."

"Okay, I will do. What are you going to do?"

"I'm going to stay here. I'll stay here till it's safe. You don't need me in your way."

"No, you're not in the way. You're doing a grand job so far," Rankine said with his typically pleasant delivery.

"Not yet," Jack laughed. "Give it time."

14

Lowri's fingers drummed on the bed nervously as she waited. That was fine. That was acceptable. She had to get that nervous energy out of her now while she was alone. Everything Lowri did hinged around being in control, around not letting her base fears get in the way of her decisions. That was near enough impossible for anyone, even someone like Lowri Graves and the years of experience she had; but yet, she did everything she could to let people think otherwise.

Right now, she was feeling it more than ever. Lowri believed in very little. She believed that people would strive, that some would succeed and some would fail. She believed that the system was fallible, but it was the best they had. Finally, she believed in the Vehm and the Regulators as a power for good.

Now she had her doubts. That made her more nervous than she had ever been before.

The hotel room she was in was sparse. Just the way she wanted. When she arrived, she had spent the first fifteen minutes in the room unplugging everything electrical, removing the phone from the phone line and checking in all the drawers and cupboards, under the mattress, inside the toilet cistern. Anywhere someone might have placed a bug.

She didn't think they would have done. The message she had sent to David had been coded, a system that the two of them had worked out for themselves a number of years ago when they had first embarked on a short-lived but tempestuous relationship. Only they knew the code, anyone else wanting to work out the exact location of their meeting would have to follow David to the door of the hotel room, then get into place themselves to monitor their conversation. Plausible, she would just have to cut to the chase quickly.

The sharp sound of someone knocking on the door stopped her finger drumming. She composed herself in an instant.

"Come in."

David Warner walked into the hotel room. Smartly dressed as ever and right on time. Lowri saw his eyes scanning the room. She knew he would quickly notice that she had unplugged everything. Phone lines, power sockets. Everything had come out. He didn't mention it.

"Ms. Graves." It was the standard greeting he had always given her, even when they were seeing each other. They had both found it mildly amusing at the time. Now it spoke more of the division their union had caused once it had ended.

"Thanks for getting here quickly."

"I didn't really have a choice."

That wasn't strictly true, Lowri thought. Everyone has a choice, but the coded message she had sent him had suggested the highest level of urgency, and she knew full well he would come as quickly as possible. Still, she moved on. "I had a visit from an old friend. Thea Watts."

"Hmm," David sounded mildly surprised. "What did she want?"

"She's stumbled onto something. Something we've looked at before."

"What is it?"

"Do you remember a couple of years back, when Yewtree was over, we started an investigation into supposed paedophile rings operating throughout the UK. We had a list of suspects that read more like a who's who of the British elite." Operation Yewtree had been a police investigation into historical child abuse claims that had been sparked by an exposé into a dead celebrity. What had been revealed in the documentary turned out to be the tip of the iceberg. The floodgates had opened, exposing a shocked British public to a horrific truth that had been hidden for years.

"Operation Malice. I remember it well. We nailed a few to the cross as well."

"Some. Yes." Lowri knew she sounded less than enthused by the result.

David cocked his head and narrowed his eyes. "What aren't you saying?"

"I'm not, not saying anything." Lowri sighed hoping David understood her use of the double negative. "I'm just worried we missed something. I want to ask you a favour. Off the record."

"Of course."

"Go there and take these files." She passed him a hard drive. "Jack Quinn is helping her, so I just want someone I know in play. I need to know what's happening, so I can bring this all together."

Lowri found herself looking at the floor as she spoke. So much for maintaining the image of calm and control, she thought to herself. David stepped forward and put his hand on her shoulder.

"Are you okay? What's happening?"

She brushed his hand off. "A lot of things are happening, David, but all I need you to do is make sure we didn't miss anything last time. Help the police. Get to the bottom of this, and if someone has a case to answer, make sure they do."

David nodded, stepping backwards, and Lowri felt awful. He had only meant to console her, but she didn't want him to see a weakness.

"I'll hit the road this afternoon. Anything else that comes up, you can forward to me *en route*." He turned and headed for the door.

"David." Lowri stepped after him, and as he turned, she pushed herself forwards, kissing him hard, her hands grabbing the back of his neck and pulling his body into hers. He didn't resist. His hands slipped down to her blouse, grasping at the buttons on the front of her blouse, pulling it open with eager ease.

She pulled him back into the room, the two of them tumbling to the bed. It had been a long time since they had been with each other, but quickly, they fell into their old intimacy. His body was exactly how she remembered it. Age hadn't caught up with him, his skin was still taught and dark over his chest, the desk job clearly hadn't got in the way of him exercising. She felt the power of his body as he eased on top of her.

Her nervousness now was gone. Why didn't she think of doing this before she started talking to him, she wondered?

Twenty minutes later, David Warner stepped out of the hotel room. Lowri watched him leave. She still didn't believe in many things, but one thing Lowri believed was that she could trust David Warner with her life. She just hoped she hadn't just sent him into harm's way.

15

Compiling a list of likely suspects hadn't taken Rankine long. By the time she was at her desk that morning, Thea had a printed copy in front of her. Names, addresses, photographs. A very useful starting point. She'd bought Jack up here simply as muscle to protect the kid, and so she could tap into his connections, but already she knew he was going to play a bigger part in this, whether she wanted him to or not.

"What's that?" Wilkes was behind her.

"List of people we want to talk to about this kid in Malton. People who work the land, who might have seen something going on." It was sort of the truth. Most of them would fit that description exactly, but one of them could be more than a witness. Thea didn't want to say that just yet. If there was a conspiracy, it could reach far further than that small pocket of rural Yorkshire.

Wilkes came around her and sat on her desk, forcing her to look up at him.

"You know I'm getting it in the neck from the boss, right? The suspensions are causing all sorts of trouble, especially when it's not even our patch."

"I can imagine."

"Good. Just make sure you get a result. A good one. If it starts looking like a chicken chase, I'll have to pull you."

"Understood, sir. What about a witch hunt?"

Wilkes stood up and looked around the office, then back at Thea. "I've never been a big believer in the occult. Feel free to prove me wrong, though."

Thea smiled, and Wilkes walked away. She liked his management style. Do your job, and he looked after you. It was true, he was bound to be getting some heat from further up the chain of command, whether they were people involved or not. The local CID would be more than a little put out that they weren't involved in a case on their own turf. Again, whether they were in on it or not.

It was going to make things harder as the investigation progressed. Resources would be harder to come by, especially manpower if they needed to act quickly. She knew she would have to plan for a number of contingencies. She also knew that meant she was going to end asking Jack to do a lot more.

She got up. "I'm heading out," she shouted to no one in particular.

She was in Malton a little later that afternoon. Jack was where she had left him, attentively guarding the boy's room.

"You look like shit," she greeted him.

He laughed. "These chairs aren't exactly Memory Foam."

"You should head back to your room. At least just to freshen up. I can have a chat with Ciaran."

Jack mulled the suggestion over. "Yeah, I think a shower and a quick nap wouldn't go amiss. Anything new come to light?"

"I've got that list of names, the gamekeepers and all that. Thanks for that, it was a smart idea. When I get Lowri's information, I'll cross-reference it, see what I get."

"Makes sense." Jack shrugged. "Mind if I take a look? Might be I recognise a face."

"Yeah, be my guest. There's nothing in any of their backgrounds that immediately stands out. I mean, they wouldn't have the licences otherwise. Few ex-forces."

"Obviously. Both good jobs for people being out and about." Jack took the paper and scanned it.

"Anyone?"

"No one I've seen, but good to have some faces in mind, just in case anyone came around." He took one last look as he handed it back to Thea.

"Yeah, speaking of which. I did some digging on our friend, Mr. Shakespeare."

"Let me guess," Jack cut in. "He's written a book?"

"No books, big ska fan. Couple of previous for possession of cannabis in his youth, nothing that sticks out. Normal family, proper leftie, vegetarian. Been a social worker for a number of years now. All the case reports I've seen of his seem pretty thorough, on the mark. I like him as a good guy."

"That's reassuring to know."

Jack stretched, sighing as he did so.

"How are you finding it up here?"

"What?"

"The quiet life. Yorkshire. Is it working for you?"

Thea pulled a face, feeling uncomfortable. The thought of failing in the way she did still hurt her. The thought that she had run away even more so. "I'll make it work. Don't really have much of a choice."

"I don't know about that," Jack mused. "You know you could have stood your ground. You didn't have to walk away."

"I did, though," snapped Thea. "I couldn't beat them my way. I wasn't playing their game. Do you know how long Bowen lasted for inside?"

Bowen was the man who had orchestrated the plot that first brought Thea and Jack together. Back when she was an NCA officer and he was still a Regulator. Thea had ultimately arrested him for the murder of her commanding officer, Frank Knight.

"I heard they got to him within three days," Jack replied grimly.

"Three days. Three days inside a maximum fucking security prison. They still got to him. No one even knows how. Coroner called it natural causes. Can you believe that?"

Jack looked at her in a way that sort of suggested that, sadly, he could believe that quite easily.

"Yeah, of course you can," Thea continued. "You're part of that world. You know the games they play."

"Not anymore." Jack shook his head.

"But you know it. It's all rationalised for you, and it never was for me."

"Which is why you should have stayed to fight them." Jack reached out, putting his arm on her shoulder. "People like you, they're few and far between. Too many people get cowed, walk away, or worse, take the money and turn a blind eye. You're different."

"I'm clearly not. I walked away, remember."

"And yet here you are again. Another conspiracy, another chance to take the easy route out and do nothing, but what have you done already? Took the case on, contacted someone who could have you killed for looking the wrong way at her, brought me into the fold. You want to get it done. No matter how hard you beat yourself up for walking out of the NCA, that fire is in you, it's not gone away. You're Thea Watts. You won't ever change."

Thea shifted uncomfortably. She hadn't thought anything of her decisions so far. She had simply gone on autopilot all the way. Doing what she thought was right and what she thought was best for the case. Jack was right, though. She was standing on the brink of something big again. She knew she should feel scared, feel anxious, but she didn't. She was exhilarated. There was no hiding it. It felt good to be doing the right thing.

"What about you? Why are you still here?"

"That kid needs help." Jack said it with such simple earnestness, like it was a complete no brainer.

"He does, but why you?"

"It's always me, Thea. Whenever someone needs help, I help. That's the way I'm programmed. I can't walk away, no matter what. It got me kicked out of school. Made me leave the army behind. Made me a bloody Regulator, a vigilante, because I had to go and do the right thing and not just what the law says is right. Cost me my wife. Probably one day it's going to cost me my life. While I'm standing, though, I do the right thing. I'm insignificant on this earth. My actions aren't."

Thea couldn't help herself. She laughed.

"What?" he asked, sounding a little hurt.

"That is a bit of bullshit right there. I mean, you know that, right?"

Jack looked at her, and she could tell he was trying to figure out whether or not to take her seriously. Slowly she saw it click in his mind, and he shook his head in mock disbelief.

"Are these your only settings? Angry and taking the piss?"

"Taking the piss keeps me from being angry all the time." Thea shrugged. She and Jack had never been close when they met before. There wasn't a pre-existing relationship at all. Maybe it was the loneliness she felt being here alone, but something about him felt familiar and reassuring. It made her feel at ease in a way she hadn't felt for a long time.

"Well, beats you being angry off at me."

There was a moment's pause.

"Go," she urged. "I'll be here for a few hours at least. Take a nap, eat some dinner."

He nodded. "Okay, I'll see you shortly. Any problems, call me."

Jack bent down and picked up his jacket before easing past her and heading out of the corridor. Thea watched after him till his footsteps stopped echoing. She turned and walked into the room to talk to Ciaran.

16

They had made him wait a long time now. Probably all night. They had brought him an airbed, and Mo had managed to get some sleep. It hadn't been easy, there wasn't really anywhere comfortable, but he was exhausted. His sleep had been a dreamless, restless affair. When he woke, he had no idea how long he had been out, only that he hardly felt any better for it.

Eventually, someone had come down with a simple breakfast of roti and some scrambled eggs, alongside a cup of green tea. He ate them quickly and eagerly, feeling much more alive when he had done.

More waiting followed. He wondered what was taking them so long to verify his story. He had gone to sleep last night feeling confident that they'd believe him, but as the time ticked on, more and more doubt spread. Every second he spent waiting in the cellar allowed new tendrils of apprehension to creep through his brain, making every creak of a floorboard above send tingles of fear through him as he awaited the judgement.

The door opened.

Nabil walked slowly down the stairs. His face was expressionless. He sat opposite Mo.

"Well," he began. Mo inhaled. "Your story checks out."

Mo felt a blast of relief, the tension falling from his body. "Thank you," he croaked, becoming acutely aware of how dry his mouth had become.

"We found the overalls, just where you said they would be. There was little doubt they'd been in a sewer." Nabil smiled at last.

"I swear, I would never turn on you or our brothers."

"I know that. I always knew, I just had to be sure."

Mo wasn't too sure he believed his innocence had never been in question, but he was happy enough to take Nabil's word for it. "We need to work out what happened to them."

Nabil raised a hand. "That's for the field teams, not for you, Moeen. You will have other tasks."

"I can help with the field teams, you know I can."

"The field team is already out and looking. They've gone to the location to see if there is any way that we were sold out there."

"See if we were sold out? That guy looked after us. He had no idea that we were even leaving. We told him nothing."

Nabil looked sternly at Mo. "Okay," he said. "Let's see what's happening. You can talk to him if you'd like." He pulled out a phone.

"Of course, anything," said Mo eagerly.

Nabil was already dialling. There was a brief pause, then the muffled sound of someone answering on the other end.

"Tariq. The old man, have you spoken to him?"

More muffled sounds. Nabil's face took on a concerned expression.

"You're sure?"

Mo wondered what was being said.

"Okay. Find out what you can, then get out. It might not be safe still."

He hung up.

"What happened?" Mo asked.

"The shop was closed. No one there. Tariq is trying to find out what happened. Apparently, it's been closed for a few days. No one seems to know what happened to the owner."

"Oh my God!" Mo felt a new panic. Not for his story, or a danger to him from Nabil, but for the kindly shopkeeper who had looked after them, not to mention the rest of the team, and the whole mission itself. "How did they find us?"

"Maybe we weren't as careful as we hoped with hiding the location of the hack. We always knew it was a possibility, but we did all we could." Nabil shrugged.

"That might be why they got the shop, but the other two, Suleiman and Ahmed, we were all out of there so quickly. There was no way they could know it was us."

"Something is wrong here, something is very wrong," Nabil said.

* * *

Tariq was on edge. More so than normal. His job required him to be hypervigilant on a daily basis, but now the danger was very real. He didn't want to stay in the area much longer, but he knew he had to find out more about what happened to the shopkeeper. The trouble was, no one seemed to know. There was just one last place he had to check, a dive bar that sat opposite the shop. An old rundown concrete affair, which proclaimed to be an Irish bar but looked as Gaelic as he did. The doors were dirty and tatty, two dark brown, thin pieces of wood with round porthole windows, one in each. A thick padlock sat on the door, but it was unlocked. Someone was in. Grimacing, he made his way to the door. If they knew nothing, he would have to leave emptyhanded.

He pushed the door open and walked in. He was about to make his way to the bar when he stopped. The barman looked up at him, thinking of something funny to say no doubt, but Tariq didn't give him time. He had already turned and left, taking his phone out.

"Nabil, it's me. We missed a camera. There's one in that bar. Brand new it looks like, looking right out across the way to the shop."

* * *

The phone call sparked a flurry of activity back at the house. They had to get out of there and they had to do it quickly. If the camera had been used to find the three of them leaving the house, there was every chance that Tariq would have also been picked up on it, canvassing the area, talking to people. Working backwards, they would have seen him arrive at the shop, trying the door to the flat. Working backwards from that, they would have seen him walk from around the corner onto the street. Then they would have been able to use a myriad of cameras to work backwards even further to find where he had parked his car. To find its number plate.

ANPR was a great piece of technology for keeping tabs on people, and very quickly, they would have been able to create a map showing the locations where that particular vehicle had been seen. It would lead them to a small area of Barnes, South London. It wouldn't give them an address.

What would give them an address would be a cross section of things. They would be looking for a rented house, one that had a high-power usage and no registered residents. A selection of addresses might be found at that point; that's when the physical sweep would begin. Drones with thermal and electromagnetic imaging, followed up by foot patrols and driveby reconnaissance, looking for closed curtains, cameras on houses. They would pinpoint a few houses, then search through nearby CCTV footage to confirm their suspicions.

It would not take them long.

Everyone in the house knew that. They knew that time was against them. They had to get out quickly. Mo found himself a spare wheel in the chaos. He had no role here, his job already done, meaning that he should have been released and out into hiding well before this point. He waited in the cellar, which all of a sudden seemed a place that offered a sanctuary from what was to come.

Upstairs he heard the sound of equipment being broken down, of shouted orders, and of feet thumping on the floorboards. Every now and again he would be able to make out Nabil's voice shouting an order. Always calm but firm. Always in control.

"Moeen!" Nabil opened the door and was shouting him from the top of the stairs.

Mo came to the foot of the stairs to see Nabil coming down.

"What's up? Can I help."

"I believe so. Here." Nabil returned the USB drive that Mo had delivered. "Take this. We have brothers elsewhere who will know what to do. You know you're the fall-back plan?"

Mo nodded. He had a phone number written down in code across three pieces of paper that he was to either use in an emergency or swallow in the event of capture. Hardly the highest tech of methods but effective all the same.

Nabil smiled. "Good, you have done well, Moeen, but now you have one last job. Get this message to the world. Let the people know what is happening."

"What are you going to do? You're not going to fight them?" Mo asked worriedly.

"We will give you the head start you need. Just be sure, we will not hurt anyone. It is not what we are permitted to do, you know that." Nabil put his hand on his shoulder. "Come, it is time for you to go."

They started to walk up the stairs. They hadn't even got half way up before a shout came from somewhere upstairs, a mixture of excitement and fear. "They're here!"

"We were too slow. Come on." Nabil turned and pulled Mo back down the stairs.

"Where are we going?"

"This way." Nabil's voice was urgent now.

They approached the metal cabinet that Mo had seen earlier. Nabil grabbed an electric screwdriver that sat on one of the metal racks as they went before opening the door to the cupboard. "Wait," he cautioned tersely.

Mo watched as Nabil began to use the screwdriver to unscrew the back of the metal cabinet. What was he doing? There were people approaching the house, people who would at the very least want to lock them up and throw away the key. All he wanted to do now was get out.

Nabil moved quickly, saying nothing, as the screws fell to the floor, each landing with a sharp "ting" on the floor by his feet. There were ten in total that held the panel in place. As the fifth one fell, the panel sagged forward, and Mo saw what was behind it.

Nothing.

The final screw came out, and the panel dropped, Nabil catching it and sliding it across. A tunnel. Mo had no idea they had dug one, but where did it go?

"Follow it for a hundred feet, and you will find a wooden hatch above you." It was as if Nabil had read his mind. "The house there is empty. You will find a mask, it will cover your skin colour, at least from a distance. Walk straight out the front door to a factory on the river. There will be a boat there, Blue Boy. Instructions are inside it. Here." He handed him a set of keys that looked like they would start the boat and open some small locks. "Now go."

As he said it, Nabil pushed Moeen through the hole and into the tunnel. There wasn't even time to say goodbye before the metal sheet was slammed against the back of the cabinet. Mo stood for a moment, listening to the sound of the small screwdriver fastening it in place. Then, remembering the need for urgency, he turned on the light on his phone and made his way as quickly as he dared along the tunnel.

It was a thin tunnel and barely six-foot tall in its highest points. There was no wall or roof to speak of, just the clay of the earth and some timbers for supports. The uneven nature of the surfaces meant that Mo was constantly scraping against the walls and ceiling and being forced to duck to avoid the shallower depths of the tunnel.

After what he thought was a hundred yards, he began to scan the ceiling for the promised panel. Nothing. He went on and on, and still he found nothing. Had he gone too far? Was the tunnel built longer to confuse someone who found it? He was just about to turn back when he saw it.

Gripping the phone in his teeth, he was happy to find that foot and handholds had been cut into either side of the tunnel wall, helping him to scramble up to the panel and holding him in place as he pushed it upwards.

His hands grasped into the house and pulled him through, sliding in on his belly as he went, rolling over and casting his head around quickly, looking for any signs of life. There seemed to be none. The house looked to be deserted as Nabil had promised. He pulled his legs through and then quietly placed the cover back over the hole. Just in case.

Softly he began to creep through the house, looking for the mask Nabil had promised. He hadn't told him where it was, so Mo assumed it had to be somewhere obvious. The kitchen was empty. Nothing on the worktops, save the usual things you might expect to find on kitchen work surfaces. Toaster, microwave, kettle. All as it should be.

The dining room provided similar disappointment; the living room did not. There it was, in the centre of the coffee table, looking at the TV like some sort of ghoulish resident, mouth agog as the latex sagged without anything to support it. Mo reached forward to pick it up.

CRUMP!

A loud but flat sound shook the house, instantly followed by a chorus of car alarms that shrieked as if scared by the noise. It could only have been one thing. An explosion.

Mo grabbed the mask and ran upstairs. He needed the back bedroom window if his geography was correct. Top of the stairs was a bathroom, to the right was the bedroom. It was empty, not even a bed, only a set of thin, beige curtains, closed, allowing only a dull light into the room. Mo ripped them open and saw what he feared. The house he had been in less than five minutes before was gone. All that was left was a smouldering pile of rubble, shrouded in a rising cloud of dust, already being swarmed over by a team of men and women who looked like they belong to some form of law enforcement. Black stab vests, gloves, sturdy boots, but no obvious identifying logos that would attribute them to any one organisation.

Had they really sacrificed themselves so he could escape? His stomach turned, and he thought of the small cargo he carried. Was it really worth their lives?

Mo quickly pulled away from the window and looked at the mask. He hoped it would work. If he was captured, there was a good chance he would be the only one able to answer anything now. He briefly considered staying in the house, hoping that the tunnel wasn't discovered, but he knew that this was the best chance to get out without being spotted. There was so much going on that he had a chance to slip away quietly.

He swallowed, placed the mask on, pulled his hood up and went downstairs and out the door.

17

Going back to the hotel would have been a welcome choice for Jack. He was tired, and his body ached from the uncomfortable plastic chairs in the waiting area, but he didn't have a choice. Not now. Not since he had recognised one of the faces in that list.

He almost hadn't. His eyes had darted back up as he scanned down the list, and for a moment, he felt sure Thea would have seen his reaction, but clearly, she hadn't. He'd only seen the guy for the briefest of moments, but years of training to be hyper-aware of his surroundings, especially when walking into a new location, had meant that when he had first entered the hospital, every single face had been processed and logged.

Including the man he had spooked in the corridor outside Ciaran's room.

At the time, he had just written it off as being someone surprised by his being there. It happened. He had admonished himself silently for that on the walk out of the hospital. From now on, he was going to suspect everyone.

He hated lying to Thea, but he didn't have a choice. While he was sure that she wasn't compromised, it was clear that someone was. How else would they have known where Ciaran was? Telling Thea would have put her in a difficult position. Her job would dictate that they had to make a move on the location, but Jack knew that wasn't the right play. The word would have been out, that might have put the children in even more danger. If they felt that the net was closing in, they may have cleaned house.

So, for the sake of a few hours, Jack wanted to do some reconnaissance. Before he could, he needed to work out where his target might be. All he had gleaned from the sheet was a name. John Braun.

He had a couple of options. He could trust in Rankine to keep Thea out of the loop. The man was clearly extremely keen to help however he could, and there was no doubt that Jack believed this was for the right reasons. After all, he had been the one to call in Thea and to take it out of local hands.

As he walked back to his car, he thought about his second option. Contacting the Regulators. They would be able to access the information, and if he was going to trust anyone, it was going to be them. But it was a risk, a risk that could cost him his life, as well as have potentially grim repercussions on whoever he picked.

He approached the car and reached for the door handle.

"Quinn." The voice was firm, authoritative, but above all that, it was familiar.

Jack turned smiling to see David Warner.

"What the hell are you doing here?" he asked, stepping towards his old boss and embracing him warmly.

"Would you believe Lowri sent me?"

"To kill me?"

"You'd be dead already." David grinned. "No, your friend made an impression on her. She sent this." David passed the hard drive to Jack. "It's the intel she promised Watts. Think she'd ever switch careers?"

"I doubt it. Is that why Lowri is being so accomodating?"

"I don't know. I think she's worried about whatever this is you're getting into. Something has her rattled."

"Lowri Graves? Rattled?" Jack didn't even try to hide his amazement.

"I know. Which worries me and should worry you as well," David warned.

"That bad, huh?"

"Could be. So, what's the situation?"

"Let's talk in the car. You can drive while I explain." Jack ushered David back towards where he had come from.

"Where are we going?"

"You're going to tell me."

Once in the car, Jack explained how he had identified a prime suspect, and David quickly got on the phone to Raf, asking him to pull up everything he could on John Braun. Raf took less than five minutes to compile a huge swathe of data on Braun. Age, education, previous addresses, his military record that included the Falklands and first Gulf Wars, as well as his current occupation. Gamekeeper for one of the local landowners, Lord Brier.

"A Lord. No wonder this has got hushed up," David said.

"I don't think it's going to stop there either from what that kid has said."

"What's your plan?"

"Originally I was going to go and reconnoitre his patch, see if I could find anything that might point me to where he might have the kids holed up."

"And now?"

"Well, the problem is he's seen me, and he also knows the land, so I'd have to be incredibly cautious."

"But he hasn't seen me." David read his mind.

"Still got enough in the tank for some field work?" Jack teased.

"I'm not dead yet."

Jack laughed. It felt good to not be alone anymore.

They found a public carpark on the edge of Lord Brier's land. As with most of the North Yorkshire Moors, paths crisscrossed the landscape allowing walkers, ramblers, joggers, and riders to navigate their way through the spectacular countryside. David was pulling some waterproof walking trousers over his suit trousers. A warm walking jacket lay smartly folded on the parcel shelf, whilst walking boots sat in the boot of the car, in front of three black plastic boxes that Jack was sure contained a host of other useful bits of equipment. Jack had never seen David in any other outfit other than a smart, sharp suit.

"Planning ahead, were you?"

"I was hoping it was all a wild goose chase, and I might get some fresh air while I was up here."

"Halfway there," Jack mused.

"What are you going to do?" David asked.

"I'm going to take the car for a spin, see what I can see from the road. I still might get spotted driving through, but it's far more plausible than me taking a stroll in their back garden."

"Okay. Let's try and keep our phone lines clear, just in case we need to report anything in."

"You got it." Jack found himself going to say "boss." Old habits die hard.

"I'll aim to make it back here in three hours. That's a long enough stroll for me. I'll see you back at the bed and breakfast."

"You don't want me to pick you up? Are you sure you can handle the walk at your age?"

"There's life in the old dog yet," David laughed. He went to leave and then turned back. "And Jack."

"What?"

"Get some bloody sleep. You look like shit."

18

Ciaran hadn't recognised any of the men Thea had shown him in the photographs. She had feared that might have been the case. Any public facing front of the operation, someone who had to bed in with the local community, may well have been insulated from those being held captive. After all, if the person on her list was guarding the perimeter, there was every chance that he never set foot in the house, especially if he wasn't into getting his kicks from kids. Even the most hardened person, seeing it in the cold light of day, might have their doubts. Anyone running such an operation wouldn't take that chance.

Ciaran had been more awake than previously. A healthier diet had given him more of the energy a young boy would normally have, and as his wounds had begun to heal, he had spent longer awake, becoming more restless. Thea didn't know how to fill the time. She had asked her procedural questions, then ran quickly out of things to say. Rankine's arrival had been greeted gladly by both of them. It was clear that Ciaran had taken a shine to the officer, who in turn had made as much effort as he could with the boy. Thea was about to make her excuses and leave when there was a polite but firm knock at the door.

Wilkes walked in. "Hello." He smiled politely before looking to Ciaran. "I'm Sergeant Wilkes, I'm Miss Watt's boss."

Ciaran nodded hesitantly back. "Hello," he murmured.

"It's alright, Ciaran. He's one of the good guys," Thea soothed.

"I try to be. Can I get a quick word, Thea?"

"Sure. I was just about to head back to the office anyway." She stood up, putting her hand on Ciaran's. "Rankine's here now. I would say he's in charge, but we all know you are."

Ciaran smiled.

"I've never been in charge of owt as much as a cuppa," Rankine moaned playfully.

"I'll see you all later."

Wilkes backed out of the room. "Bye. Pleased to meet you, Ciaran," he added as he went. Thea followed him out.

"What's up?" she asked once they were out in the corridor.

Wilkes sighed, placing his hands on his hips. Thea was trying to work out if he was angry or exasperated. "Have you got a penchant for self-destruction?"

His tone wasn't scalding, more disappointed. He didn't want a fight, Thea could tell, but he clearly wasn't happy.

"What do you mean?" She was sure she probably didn't want to know.

"I had the old man in my office earlier." The old man was Detective Chief Inspector Graham Hayes, a dour and humourless man from Northumberland who headed up the whole CID operation at York. "Apparently someone has made a complaint against you."

"Who?" Thea asked. She knew the list of potential suspects would be long.

"Randle."

"Oh, for fuck's sake, that waste of space? Did he tell you what happened?"

"He's alleging you assaulted him."

"And I'm alleging, no, I'm insisting, that he's a fucking embarrassment to the bloody badge we carry. There's rape and real rape apparently, according to that fat slob. Sorry, but no, that doesn't wash. He got his arse tipped out of his chair, and that's that. If he doesn't like it, he should work harder at not being a dickhead, then things like that probably wouldn't happen to him."

"Jesus, Thea, take this seriously. They want to suspend you pending an investigation." Wilkes was scalding her now, which did little to quell her own anger.

"For that? You're going to let them do me for that?" She couldn't believe it. It was ridiculous. It was preposterous.

"It's not my choice," Wilkes pointed out.

"Fucking hell." Thea sighed. Then things fell into place. "Jesus. They're trying to get me off this case."

"What?" Wilkes looked at her. Thea had entrusted to him a lot of the information she knew, but not everything. He had no idea that Jack was working for her, no idea that she had been to see Lowri and no idea that this might be a national scandal. Thea didn't disbelieve Wilkes' intentions, but bringing him into the fold would make things less controllable. He would have to tell someone. He would want to push some buttons.

Thea thought fast. "Randle. He wants me off the case because he wants to sabotage my career."

"That's as may be, but he may well get his way," Wilkes responded cautiously. "I told Hayes that I would try and sort this out myself. My team, my issue. I need you to go and kiss Randle's arse and say sorry."

Thea went to fire off an angry retort, but she caught herself, thinking of the boy in the ward and knowing she needed to be there to help him. If someone was trying to get her out of the way, they were going to have to come at her in a far less subtle way than that.

Their problem now was that Thea Watts was on notice and she would be ready for them.

19

Blue Boy bobbed nonchalantly up the Thames. Inside, Mo felt anything but nonchalant. He had made his way as quickly as possible to the riverside after leaving the house and found the boat exactly where it was supposed to be. No one seemed to have seen him, at least certainly not in a way that might have alerted them.

He pushed the boat off from the side, then eased out into the middle of the river, away from the banks, where he might easier be spotted, heading for the pre-determined rendezvous at the marina in Shepperton. Mo didn't know Shepperton. He'd heard of the film studios, but that was as far as his local expertise went. He wasn't planning on doing any autograph hunting when he got there.

Everything had been set up as he had been told to expect. There had been a phone, still in its box, unopened, a prepaid burner, that he would have to use when he arrived at his destination in order to get his next set of orders. Next to it was a zip-up plastic pouch. Flexible but sturdy enough to ensure that if something needed protecting from the elements or keeping dry should he have to bail into the water, it would do the job. Mo placed the drive into it, then folded it before slotting it into a zip-up pocket on his jacket. As safe as he could make it right now.

Idling down the Thames in Blue Boy was slow going. Painfully so, Mo lamented. There was an eight-knot speed limit on the stretch where he had cast off, which dropped to nearer four once he passed Teddington Locks. Anyone watching for him wouldn't miss him. However, going at such a leisurely pace would surely disqualify him from any random search, or so he hoped.

It was grey and cool outside, and the wind whipped at him on the boat, channelling itself down the river between the trees as the boat bobbed onward. There was an assortment of other boats on the river, all of which got smaller and more sedate looking as he went on. Barges and pleasure cruisers mostly piloted by retirees on holidays made up most of the other traffic, as well as the odd tourist boat taking in the sights. The river eased through London's finer parts, passing Ham House, skirting Hampton Court Park and it's Palace, and coasting through some of the more affluent suburbs, including Twickenham and Walton, near to which he found the marina.

Mo was no seafarer, but he had driven boats. Speedboats mainly, whilst on a holiday to Greece when he and some friends had been trying to impress a couple of women they'd met on the beach. Blue Boy didn't have the power, which had made the river cruise relatively simple, but as he entered the marina, Mo remembered that back in Greece, he had subtly stepped aside from parking the boat at the dock for fear of messing up. Blue Boy may have been a plodder, but the marina was packed with other boats and all the spots he could see to moor in looked incredibly tight. He didn't want to draw attention to himself, that was a given, so ramming into a pontoon or a neighbouring vessel was to be avoided.

The marina spread to the left and right with what looked to be an office area on the right. That sent Mo left. Less people. He eased back on the boat's throttle as he neared a space he deemed wide enough to give him the best shot at getting docked without damaging anything.

He carefully tweaked the throttle, edging the boat into position. The water was calm and made the job easier, and soon Mo had Blue Boy bumping against the boards of the dock. He cut the engine, grabbed the packet containing the drive and the burner phone, and then hopped onto the dock. There was a rope that was attached to the front of the boat, and Mo used it to tie Blue Boy in place.

"Thanks, pal," he said to the boat quietly, once he'd checked the knot was secure, then he walked away, heading for the exit.

Turning right out of the marina, he spotted a modern hotel, part of a big brand group, the sort that cropped up in every town in every county in the UK. London had a host of them. They were the sort of place that straddled the line between cheap and business, meaning they attracted a whole host of transient visitors, from those in town for work, conferences, or meetings, to leisure bookers looking for a night out or a night in. Whatever your pleasure. Mo beelined for it. Standing outside and making a call near the hotel entrance would add a layer of camouflage. People expected to see that.

As he got near the doors, he was pleased to see there was no one else there. No doubt that wouldn't last forever, so he took the phone out and dialled the number he had spent the best part of the last month remembering.

"Hello?" a gruff voice answered.

"It's Mo."

"You're okay?" The voice was surprised. News of the explosion must have reached them.

"Yes, for now. I need picking up. I can carry on the work."

"You're where you should be?"

"I'm on my way."

"Good, half an hour."

The line went dead.

Where he was meant to be was an under-construction business park just north of where he had landed. Half an hour was just enough time to get there on foot. He took the SIM and the battery out of the phone, shoving all three back inside his coat pocket. Then, with head down and collar up, he walked as quickly as he could to the rendezvous.

There was no sign of life at the business park when he got there, but still, Mo was counting the cameras that were installed to protect the construction equipment, and that made him feel more than a little uncomfortable. The site had been chosen due to the reliable nature of the security team onsite, meaning that some, if not all of them, were on the payroll. All the same, it was a record of where he had been, and Mo wasn't keen on leaving too long a trail.

The light was fading, and Mo decided to hide himself in the treeline that ran alongside the road. On the other side of the street was a golf course. Mo could see lights from inside the clubhouse, but any view of where he hid was obscured by the hedgerow that dotted the perimeter. He stepped off the pavement, forcing his way through the thin branches that tugged and scratched at him. Behind the first line of trees was a small hollow, and Mo settled there, crouching down on his knees, watching the road.

He hadn't been there five minutes before a car turned up. It rolled slowly down the road once, watching the site, before returning again on the other side of the road and pulling up. A nice-looking estate car, a tourer, built for comfort and performance combined. Mo waited. He wanted to be sure that this was his ride.

No one got out at first. A minute passed. Mo wondered if he should put the phone back together, but he knew the instructions he had been given. Radio silence at all times unless critical. The team in the car knew how to make contact, that was their job, not his. A system designed to keep him safe. Mo liked it.

Both the driver's and passenger's doors opened in unison, and two men got out. Both Asian, dressed in dark jackets and jeans. It must be them. Mo went to stand, but then stopped. Another car was approaching. He'd wait until it was gone, then make his move.

The two men from the car walked towards each other, a low muted conversation taking place. Mo couldn't hear it from where he was.

The other car approached, it's speed normal, consistent, Mo noted. No interest in what the two men were doing. Almost time. Mo braced himself to stand.

The screech of the brakes from the second car stopped him. It ground to a sudden halt just in front of the estate car, causing the two men to turn around. Mo saw before they did that the passenger window was open. He saw the flashes of muzzle fire from inside the car but didn't hear the sound. Silencers. The two men fell, and Mo stumbled backwards.

Cowering down, he watched as all four doors of the other car opened. More men, again all dressed in dark clothes. This time, however, they were different races. Three white, one black. Not his ride. He crept as softly backwards as he could, further into the treeline. He had to escape, he had to get out of here, but he needed help.

His fingers grabbed inside the pocket for the phone. He pulled it out and hurriedly put it back together in the gloom, glancing between phone and the four men who were currently stooping over their victims. It looked like they were taking photos of their faces, scanning their fingerprints. IDs. Would they know that he was there as well?

"Unless critical." The proviso for using the phone rang in his head. Could it be any more critical? The phone powered up, but Mo didn't make a call. He went to a website that he had created years ago for just such a situation. Embedded on a hidden page, there was an encrypted file. Within seconds, he had entered the encryption key and was downloading an app to the phone. It was the app that he hoped would save his life.

20

The light was growing dimmer with every second, and a light rain had started to fall, causing specks of rain to cling to the windows of the dark grey BMW. In the distance, the leading lights of airplanes landing and taking off at Heathrow cut through the murk. Adam and Emmie watched out of the windows, an uncomfortable silence between them. The sort of thing that happened when two people were forced together unexpectedly and had quickly run out of small talk.

Emmie was still trying though, Adam had to give her credit for that.

"Your wife, what does she do?"

Adam shifted uncomfortably. He had tried to keep Laura and work separate. Not just Laura, his whole family. With Jack, it had been different. They had built a bond that had allowed conversations about partners, kids, life, and love to become commonplace, but hearing this stranger whom he didn't know asking him about the most important person in his life made Adam nervous. Something he hadn't felt in a while.

"She, uh…" He struggled to find a way to avoid the question without being rude. "She works, part time, looks after our kid the rest of the time."

"Jasmine."

It was a statement, not a question. How did she know that? This girl was well read, had done her homework. Adam knew he should be impressed, knew that was what she was trying to do with him, but all he felt was unease.

"Yeah, Jasmine. Listen, family and stuff, have you got one of your own?"

"No," Emmie shook her head. "This was what I wanted now. Maybe the future."

"Well, it's just, work and family, especially this game, they don't mix. They can be your weakness, your undoing, so I don't like to talk about it. I don't mean any offence or anything," he explained.

"It's fine." Emmie smiled. She was unflappable. Did she even realise how her questioning had made him feel? "I'm not trying to pick out your vulnerabilities though. Well, not to exploit them, but I suppose it is useful to know where my partner might need some support, in a fix."

Adam felt his eyebrows raising. "You're blunt, you know that, right?"

There was no time for Emmie to reply. The centre console of the car, which normally worked as a sat-nav system but in this car doubled as an onboard computer, suddenly lit up and a harsh alarm set off two short, sharp bursts that repeated once more before Adam had reacted and pressed the screen.

"That's a personal alarm, someone's in trouble." His attention was on the screen, and he knew Emmie's was too as she moved forward slightly in her seat to look at the screen.

"Who?"

Adam paused. The computer showed Mo's face. He hadn't seen his former colleague in over a year. Not long after Jack had left. How had he accessed their system?

"It's Mo." If anyone could access that system after leaving the Regulators, Adam reasoned it would have to be Mo.

"Where is he?"

"About ten minutes from here. Come on, we need to move."

"We're going to help him? I thought he left."

"Yeah, well, he might not be on the payroll, but he's still a friend." Adam was already turning the key to the ignition, firing the car to life. He slipped his seatbelt on with his other hand, then put the car into first. The wheels slipped on the damp dirt beneath them, then found traction, catapulting them forward. Adam nodded to the screen. "Try to get him on the comms."

Emmie pressed on Mo's face on the screen, and a symbol appeared next to it, four dots, like an extended ellipsis, appeared and disappeared in sequence showing that the system was trying to connect to Mo. Seconds later, the dots all came on together.

"Mo?" Adam's voice was composed, clear and calm.

"Adam?" a harsh whisper came back, but still Adam knew it was Mo.

"What's up?"

"Mate, I am in real trouble, I got four guys just took out my extraction team, now I think they're looking for me. I don't know where else to turn, man." Mo was scared, as he should be. He had to be if he had been brave enough to reach out like this.

"Where are you?"

"I'm in the southwest corner of the business park that they're building up by Shepperton Marina, trying to keep my head down."

"Can you see the hostiles?"

"I can see two of them. They split, the other two went off north, out of my sight now."

"Okay, find a spot you like and stay there. Can you still access the secure comms grid?"

"I can if you give me a couple of minutes."

"We're a couple of minutes out, so that works for me. Hang tight, buddy. We're coming to get you." Adam pressed the screen, and the line went dead. "Dial Raf," he ordered the computer.

Raf's face appeared next to the same symbols. He was connected almost instantly, clearly monitoring the alert that would have been flashed to all the Regulators channels. This time a video displayed Raf in real time.

"You heading to Mo?" Straight to the point.

"Yeah, I need a drone up here. There's four hostiles on site, maybe more. We've got no eyes on the ground, so we need them in the air."

"I'm sending one into the location. What's happening?" Raf had to have been curious about this, and whilst Raf was known for being a stickler for protocol, he was also Mo's friend.

"I don't know. Let me know when the drone is in place. I'm going to get Mo on a secure line as well, so you might have to help him find a path out of there."

"All over it." Raf hung up, and the screen went blank.

Adam slung the car across the roundabout, glancing quickly to make sure there was no traffic coming towards them, briefly, but enough with his advance driver training. The car bounced across the lanes as it joined the Staines Bypass and headed for Mo.

There was silence in the car. Adam had half expected Emmie to be full of questions – it was the first time the two of them had been in the field together – but she sat there silently. He risked a quick glance her way and saw her eyes focused on the road ahead. Calm and in control. It reminded him of the many times he and Jack had ridden into action. A controlled silence had always marked the build-up to a mission. Both of them knew their roles, their skills and strengths, and both of them trusted each other. Adam didn't know Emmie, he didn't know her skills and strengths, but something about the way she sat there now told him he could trust her.

As they got closer to the location, they came off the bypass and onto more residential roads. Adam eased up on the throttle, for the safety of those around and to help mask their approach. He touched the screen on the computer again, and Raf reappeared.

"Drone is thirty seconds out," Raf said, reading Adam's mind.

"We're just behind. Let me know the lay of the land when we get there," Adam said, before adding, "I'm going on comms, get me there."

He tapped the screen again and swiped the display right, bringing up Mo's face. There was a brief wait to be connected, but then Mo's voice came through, even more hushed than before.

"I'm inside the building site. There's a small metal container being used as an office on the northeast side."

"Got it, stay low." Adam hung up the call. Mo needed to keep himself invisible now, and Adam wasn't going to jeopardise that.

He swung the car left, onto the road the business park was situated on. It was deserted. He cut the lights and the engine and let the car roll to a stop.

"Look." Emmie pointed. Ahead of them were two cars, both now with lights off and parked at the side of the road. There was no sign of any bodies if this was where Mo had seen the shooting. Just two parked cars.

Adam hit the brakes fifty feet shy of the other cars and with their vehicle still hidden from the business park by the treeline.

"You ready?" He felt he had to ask.

Emmie nodded eyes on the road ahead of them, even while she checked the safety on her pistol.

"Raf?" Adam tapped his ear, turning his comms unit on.

"We've got four people circling the premises on infrared. They're coming in and out of the buildings so I'm losing them for periods. Seems to be a pretty standard sweep procedure."

"Can we get Mo out without engaging?" Adam decided that the best choice was stealth.

"Where is he?"

"Northeast corner."

"I think so, they seem to be congregating around the main building site at the moment, but I wouldn't expect that to last forever."

"Understood." Adam opened the door and turned to Emmie. "Let's go."

The two of them exited the car and made their way into the building site. By now it was almost completely dark and that helped mask their approach. All the same, they tried to make sure they always had something between them and those stalking the premises.

To their left, the main building site rose up into the night sky. A tall and imposing metal warehouse that seemed to stretch on for far longer than was necessary. It stretched up high into the sky, towering like a giant aircraft hangar. To their right was a selection of ramshackle metal containers, most of which looked to have been used for storage and were surrounded by the furrows made by tractor tracks that were now beginning to pool with water as the light rain continued to fall. The main building was dark and unlit, but the area near to the containers was bathed in floodlights, presumably to help protect any equipment that might be stored there.

Adam and Emmie crept towards the containers. Putting as much between them and the others was paramount, especially in the glare of the floodlights.

"One of their teams went off my scope, into the building," Raf's voice hissed into Adam's ear. Neither he nor Emmie acknowledged it; they didn't need to. Raf would continue to provide commentary throughout.

"Mo?" Adam breathed hoping that the analyst would hear him on the comms. There was no response.

Slowly they picked their way towards where he said he was holed up. Adam could see the office he was referring to. A metal container raised up on top of another one with a hastily constructed wooden stairwell leading up to it. The wooden steps were a blessing and a curse at the same time. The wood would make less noise than metal. However, they were placed on the side of the building that was in direct line of sight to the main complex, lit up by an overhead security light. At least it seemed to be permanently on, not motion sensitive. Small mercies, Adam grimly observed. It was going to be so hard to get in and out of there. If only Mo would answer the comm, it would eliminate one trip in.

"The second team is back out, heading southwest, away from you." Raf's reports kept coming.

Adam and Emmie closed on the building.

"Adam?" Mo's voice rasped through the intercom. Adam and Emmie both stopped and dropped on one knee next to the container they were walking past.

"Go ahead."

"That you by the container to my south?"

"That's us," Adam answered. He looked up at the container windows. He couldn't see much, but he convinced himself he saw the movement of someone darting around, trying to get a look outside while staying as hidden as possible. "You need to come out."

"Where are they?"

Adam knew who Mo meant. "They're over by the main building, but they're not going to stay there, which is why you need to go."

"I need to find a way to shut the light off."

"No!" Adam snapped. He could hear the fear in Mo's voice, and he knew that he was wavering. "You do that, it's as bad as coming out shouting. They'll see it, and we'll all be in the firing line. You need to open the door quickly, quietly, and then get down those stairs."

Silence.

Finally, a one-word reply. "Okay."

Adam and Emmie tensed. "Raf, keep us posted on the hostiles," Emmie spoke to the consultant now, taking some control. She was really growing on Adam.

"They're still happy over the other side. Lot of places to explore," came the reply.

Raf was right, there was a lot of places over there for them to check out, all dark and hidden, not lit up like where they were now. A far more obvious place to hide. If Mo had made his choice of hiding spot based on that little bit of reverse psychology, it was a piece of genius. He'd have to ask him. If they got out of here.

Adam fixed his gaze on the door. The handle slowly began to turn, then the door edged open. Just a crack at first, pausing for a moment as no doubt Mo gathered his thoughts.

"Come on," Adam quietly urged his friend to come out.

The door flew open, and Mo lurched out, racing down the stairs as quick as he could. Too quick. His left foot slipped on a damp step and shot out in front of him, bringing him down onto his rear, bouncing off the steps as he tumbled, undignified and noisy.

There was a shout from the other side of the building site.

"Shit!" Adam swore as he stood up and began to run around to where Mo had fallen, Emmie matching him stride for stride.

"You got company!" Raf called out. "Three of them heading your way."

Mo was on the floor, pushing himself up out of a muddy puddle as Adam and Emmie reached him. "We need to go!" Adam shouted.

They turned to run just as the first shots were fired. There was a metallic twang as a bullet ricocheted off one of the containers, but no sound of gunfire. Silencers, naturally. A small win, Adam thought. The long barrel of the silencer would slow the speed of their aim down, especially if they got in close quarters. Not much, but maybe just enough to make a difference.

There was only really one way out; the way they had come in. Where they were on the periphery of the business park was surrounded by open wasteland that offered little cover, other than darkness should they get to it, but such was the reach of the floodlighting, they would be lit up for so long that they would present pretty favourable targets to their pursuers.

"Take Mo," Emmie ordered. "I'm going to try and flank them."

"Flank them?"

"Just go!" she urged.

Adam nodded, scooping an arm under Mo, hauling him to his feet. The two of them sprinted for the exit.

More bullets pinged and tinged off the metal containers around them, fired more out of hope than expectation, designed to try and pin them down, stop their escape and allow those chasing them down to get in closer for the kill.

"Don't stop," Adam urged, knowing the ploy, putting his hand on the small of Mo's back, pushing him on through the rain and mud.

Something moved on Adam's right. A figure. Instinctively, he turned his head and weapon towards it, using his spare hand to move Mo to the other side of his body, putting himself between the figure and Mo.

Three flashes from a muzzle. Two pings of bullets hitting the container and one sharp sting at the back of Adam's shoulder. He'd been hit.

He stumbled but caught himself, firing back. The figure darted behind a container.

"Get down!" Adam pushed Mo behind a pile of breeze blocks.

The two of them tumbled down, both breathing heavily. Adam placed his left hand on his right shoulder, feeling the wound.

"You're hit?" Mo's eyes widened.

"It's okay," Adam said, reassuring himself as much as Mo. "Just grazed my shoulder. I'm good."

He pushed himself up against the breeze blocks and assessed the situation. The shooter couldn't see them, but they could be easily flanked.

"Raf, where are they?"

"You got one coming in from your northwest," Raf warned.

Adam levelled the nose of his gun at where he expected the man's chest to appear. He was right. Two quick squeezes of the trigger dropped the attacker a split second after he rounded the corner into Adam's line of fire. One down.

"Where's Emmie?" Adam asked.

"Lost her, she went into some containers. I've not got her back on my scope yet."

"Damnit," the last thing Adam wanted was some friendly fire, but could he allow himself the luxury of IDing his targets? Probably not.

"The one who stuck around is holding his position, the other two are working their way towards you, but they're taking no chances."

"Emmie, where are you?" Adam asked.

Nothing. Was she okay?

Adam peered above the breeze block.

CRACK.

The sound of a sniper rifle came echoing through the business park, and Adam heard the dull thud of the bullet going through a container behind him as he ducked.

"The hell was that?" Mo was panicking. He bounced where they crouched, desperate to escape as quickly as possible.

"That would be why the last guy held his position," Adam was berating himself silently in his head, but also counting his blessings. Now he had his range, the shooter likely wouldn't miss twice. Had he taken the time to line up the shot, well...

"Sniper?" Mo had worked it out.

"We're pinned down," Adam explained. Mo's face dropped as he saw Adam's grim expression. "All on Emmie."

"They're closing in on you." There was a real urgency in Raf's voice now. Adam knew that they had seconds to decide.

"How fast can you run?"

"I ain't Mo Farah," Mo answered. "But I'll move if I need to."

"You need to. When I start shooting, go for the exit and don't stop."

"Shit, dude, really?"

"Really."

Mo nodded. Adam swallowed.

He closed his eyes for a second, visualised the scene, then opened them and acted. He rolled out on his belly, gun pointing in the rough direction of the sniper, firing four shots into the darkness, praying for a hit, but hoping at least to put the shooter off his stride. He felt Mo get up and heard the sound of Mo's feet crunching in the wet gravel as he ran.

The now all too familiar metal pings came back, a volley of shots in Mo's direction but not at him. He only had seconds before the sniper found him, if he could clear just one of them, it would be a start.

"On your eleven," Raf guided him to where he needed to look, interpreting the tactical situation through his screen back at the office.

It was enough of a heads up for Adam to see the figure of a man reloading. Two shots and the man fell, just like his compatriot had. Two down.

Adam rolled back behind the breeze blocks just as the crack of the sniper rifle came again. He saw the cloud of dirt and water rise up as the bullet dug deep into the ground where he had just been lying. A second or two in it. Fine margins.

"That made the other guy think – he's holding position, twenty yards from you, near enough dead ahead, behind a portable toilet."

"Where's Mo?"

"He's hiding behind the last container. Stopped there."

"Is he okay?"

"I think so, looks intact on my screen." Raf's words were a relief to Adam, although he had hoped Mo would keep going. At least, for now, he was safe. If they could just clear that sniper.

"Adam." It was Emmie.

"Where are you?"

"I need you to go for the third guy down by you. Rush him, whatever, just make sure that you're seen."

"Great plan!" Adam replied incredulously.

"Trust me."

Adam knew what she was doing. He was the bait. If he gave the sniper something to think about, she could get close enough unnoticed to take him out. It wasn't his favourite plan, but it was the best on the table. It was the only one on the table.

"Fine."

Adam put all thoughts of the sniper out of his mind. He had to focus on the third guy. If they were all communicating, which he was sure they would be, then the third guy would know Adam was coming almost instantly thanks to the sniper. If not, then he might have time to get to the position and surprise him. That seemed unlikely.

129

He checked his magazine. Eight rounds. Put six into the portable toilet, and hope they find a way through the plastic to something fleshy and breakable, then save two just in case he had a better shot.

Time to go.

He breathed in.

"Don't mess this up, Emmie," he muttered.

His gun led the way out, and he followed, the first shot going into the portable toilet just as he straightened up into his sprint. He fired once more and then jinked left, just in case there was a shot coming his way. Two more shots, then the noise of gunfire in the distance, the crack of the sniper rifle. He didn't know where the bullet landed, only that it didn't land in him.

The third guy lurched out from behind the portable toilet, gun in hand, then stumbled, his left-hand clutching at his leg. Something fleshy and breakable. Adam fired again, twice more, missing both times as he ran. He was less than ten yards away now.

The third guy, realising he had only one chance, tried to compose himself to return fire. Adam didn't let him. He dropped down to his knee, locking his grip despite the burning pain in his shoulder and fired his last two rounds. The man fell backwards, twisting over and coming to rest in a puddle looking at the sky with empty eyes.

"Emmie." Adam struggled to his feet. If she had failed, he was a sitting duck. "You get him?"

"Sniper down," came the reply. Cool as you like.

"Good job." Adam breathed heavily.

"We good?" Mo spoke up now.

"We're good, we're all good." Adam wobbled a little as he walked towards his friend who was now peering out from behind the container where he had been sheltering. "You need to tell me what the hell this was all about though."

21

When he woke, Jack felt far better. Sleeping in an actual bed, not the plastic chairs he had been using the last few days, had made the world of difference. Where there had been aches and stiffness in his joints before, now he felt loose and agile again. He wasn't at full capacity, the one drawback of a good sleep was that he'd awoke with cobwebs in his head, but a quick routine of sit-ups, press-ups, planks, and twisting crunches, followed by ten minutes meditation, soon had him focused on the job at hand.

David hadn't checked in, so Jack decided to give him a call. He wanted to check in with him first before Thea, mainly because he'd been in out in the field. David could handle himself, Jack knew that, but making sure you had the back of anyone you worked with was a fundamental for Jack.

"Jack." David sounded happy, the fresh air clearly doing something for him.

"How did it go?"

"I think I made contact with your main man."

"Did he make you?"

David let out a snort. "Come on, no. I asked him for directions to a local landmark. He was a little guarded but nothing over the top. Certainly not that would have drawn suspicion from your average punter. Just a little standoffish with the townie."

"What was he doing?"

"Patrolling, I'd say. Had a couple of gun dogs on a leash with him, rifle slung over his back. Looked just like a man working the land, blends right in."

"And it was definitely Braun?"

"No doubt about it," affirmed David confidently. "We're in the right area. We just need to narrow down where the kids are being held and then decide how best to move next."

"We? I take it this is becoming an official interest now?"

"Reckon you can do it on your own?"

"No, but North Yorkshire's finest might well be able to."

"That's if they're not already compromised."

Jack wondered the same, although he wasn't prepared to admit it. Whilst the help from David, Lowri, and the whole Regulators and Vehmic system was welcome, he wasn't happy with the thought of them coming in and riding roughshod over due process. It was the issue that had led to his suspension from the Regulators, and it was still a sore point.

"You got to give me your word that, if they're not, you guys step aside. I can't see this go wrong. This is kids' lives at stake, not the willy-waving of some underground organisation."

"You've got my word, Jack. We'll do this right. You know I want the same thing as you on this."

Jack did believe that. David was a good man, humble enough. It wasn't really him he was worried about though, not that he intended to get into that discussion now. "Thanks," he said, before adding, "What are you going to do now?"

"I'm going to report back to Lowri, give her a chance to formulate a plan by the time I'm back, then I'm going to head back to base. There's a number of things I can do there that I can't do here for you."

"That's true. You reckon you'll be sending in the cavalry?"

"I'm going to task a couple of drones to sweep the area, see if we can't spot anything out of the ordinary from the air. As for boots on the ground, that all depends on what the police do. It's all on them."

"That's a big help," Jack replied earnestly. Having drones to scan the area would drastically shorten the amount of time it might take to find the location. That could be the difference maker when it came to saving lives. Whoever had been holding these children would be going through a contingency plan right now, with Ciaran now in police custody.

"No problem. How are you feeling now?"

"A bit more rested, bit more human. Not sure how long that will last, I'm sure there will be a few more nights on those plastic chairs."

"You need to get that kid out of that hospital as soon as possible. Is there anyone up there you can trust?"

"Thea, for sure, but I don't think she's in a position to help. The only other person I've really met is a Sergeant, Rankine. He seems decent enough, but I don't know that much about him. Certainly not to be putting that level of trust in him."

"Get to know him. That hospital isn't going to work for long if they're going to come after the kid. You can't be there all the time; you need to be taking the fight to them before it's too late."

Jack acknowledged the truth in what David was saying. He was being passive. Not his stance of choice. "Yeah, you're right. I'll talk to Rankine. If you can pull his file as well, make sure there are no red flags, that'd really put my mind at ease."

"I'll get Raf on it straight away."

"Cheers, safe journey, pal."

"You too, happy hunting."

The line went dead.

Jack got dressed and decided to make his way back to the hospital. He wanted to show his face to Ciaran, make sure he knew that he was still around. He also needed to get a feel from Thea about how the police investigation was progressing. If he could find a way to get the Regulators and Vehm to support a police investigation rather than taking it over, he knew it would make him feel a lot more comfortable.

It was getting later in the day, the sun was almost completely set over Malton, and the already quiet roads seemed even quieter now. Barely a soul about. That suited Jack just fine. Anyone out there watching him would find it even harder to conceal themselves here, even with local knowledge.

Jack made the by now very familiar stroll in less than ten minutes and was outside Ciaran's door. A quick knock and he made his way inside. Ciaran was alone.

"Hey." Jack tried to conceal his surprise from the boy. "Where's everyone else?"

Ciaran shrugged. "The policeman was here, but then he went away."

"Where's Thea? Miss Watts?" Jack kept his voice calm, so as not to spook the boy, as he made his way to the window and took a cautious glance around.

"Not seen her for a while." Ciaran sniffed with indifference. Jack didn't like that.

"Okay, no problem, I'm here now. The officer outside didn't mention it, that's all."

"Outside?"

"Yeah," Jack carried on the lie. "We've always got someone watching you to make sure you're safe." *We damn well better now,* he thought.

It all seemed to work. Ciaran seemed nonplussed. Jack wandered to the window and looked out. Everything looked as it should. There wasn't a lot to see: a couple of houses across the road shielded by trees that were thick and full of leaves, barely leaving anyone enough room to squeeze a glimpse into the window of Ciaran's room, and even if they did, the blinds were almost always pulled at least part way across.

"You need a drink or anything? It's hot in here." Jack turned back to Ciaran.

"Can I have a pop?"

"A pop? You allowed pop?"

Ciaran shrugged.

"I guess you are," Jack conceded. "I'll get you a pop."

He smiled once more at Ciaran and headed out into the corridor. There was still no one around. Jack didn't know whether to be angry or worried. He shut the door softly and waited outside the door for a moment. The hospital was quiet, save for the normal background hum of the ever-on heating system and the lights above his head. In the distance, doors creaked open and closed, and people carried on their normal business.

Reaching into his jacket, he took out his phone and dialled Thea. Surely, she didn't know what was happening. She answered almost immediately.

"I can't stay on long, is everything alright?" she asked, which meant that she knew things weren't alright.

"There's no one on the door at Ciaran's room. Where are you?"

"Shit," she sighed, it sounded almost resigned. "I tried to get someone from uniform down there, but I guess they pulled them. I'm being investigated by the office, I'm being kept off all active duties."

That explained a lot, Jack thought. "Why? What happened?"

"A disagreement with a colleague, one that shouldn't matter but apparently now does."

"What did you do and to who?"

"I had a falling out with a guy in the office, a proper waste of space called Randle, over how he handled a call. Tipped him out of his chair, nothing more. Shitty stuff."

"A mountain out of a molehill. Someone has put him up to this to clear a path. Can you get in touch with Rankine?"

"I don't want to run the risk of getting him in trouble. I'm poison in here, again."

"Fine. I'll get in touch with him myself. Can you clean this up yourself?"

"I'll find a way."

"Okay."

Jack hung up. He needed to get Rankine in place, but he needed to do a lot more than that. It was time to pick up the pace, and he knew it. He walked to the window that looked out from the corridor over a small courtyard in the centre of the hospital. It was dark outside. Pitch black. No stars, no moon.

No lights in the courtyard.

Jack thought back. Had he looked out there before at night? He must have done. Had there been lights? He let his mind build up a visual picture, trying to remember exactly what he had seen and what he had expected to see. There was a pond in the courtyard, he remembered that, a small concrete-lined square one covered over with lily pads. He had seen it in the day. It had reminded him of one he had seen when he was a child at primary school. They'd counted tadpoles in it, that memory sending him back to a time when he had been Ciaran's age and he had been happy. A memory Ciaran had been cheated of. That's why it had stuck, but that was in the day, not at night.

Then he remembered looking out earlier, seeing the pond reflecting the yellow light of a lamp, seeing the black spots where the lily pads stopped the glistening colours being bounced off the water. It was a small light next to the pond. The sort of thing used to pick out features in a garden. It was definitely off now.

Jack scanned the courtyard. No movement. His eyes adjusted more each second. He looked at the door at the far end of the courtyard. It looked closed from a distance, but Jack wasn't so sure. The door nearest to him could have been just slightly off the latch, leaning on the locking mechanism, not quite closed, allowing someone a quick escape back through it.

Jack stepped away from the window and looked back down the corridor. If someone was coming, he had to be ready. He didn't have a weapon with him. He wished he'd taken Ciaran's advice now.

He looked around. There wasn't much to hand. He didn't fancy going back into Ciaran's room and spooking him any more than he needed to, so he would have to make do. He reached down and picked up one of the plastic chairs, moving it up and down to feel the weight. It wasn't particularly heavy or sturdy, but given the right momentum, it would do the job it needed to.

Jack stepped forward to the intersection of the corridors that approached Ciaran's room. He glanced slowly and cautiously left. No one coming. He stepped back in. Then he looked slowly, tentatively right.

Two men. Dressed in black, armed with small, silenced pistols. He saw them; they must have seen him. He was at a clear disadvantage now, but at least he knew the odds.

He stepped backwards into the corridor. He needed to do something to take away their advantage. He scanned the walls, chair still in hand. A fire alarm and fire extinguisher hung on the wall opposite Ciaran's door. They'd help. Jack took the fire extinguisher off the wall, took a second to compose himself, then with his free hand, smashed the alarm, the shrill ring of the bell echoing through the corridor. Ciaran would be spooked now, but that couldn't be helped.

He was already moving, racing forwards to the corner. The chair was in his left arm, which he swung back, then brought forward in a large arc, the chair releasing just as his arm came out into the corridor, sending it sprawling forward towards the attackers. It wouldn't do much more than slow them down, but that's all he needed.

There was a clatter and a shout, but Jack wasn't waiting for that. He was already around the corner, left hand now grabbing around the nozzle of the fire extinguisher. He fired it into the already confused attackers, the white cloud enveloping them, causing them to shout and stumble. One attacker alone would probably have been able to loose off a few rounds, hoping for the better, but these two were too well-drilled, and they knew the risk of hitting each other.

Jack went for the first man, bringing the fire extinguisher up with his right arm, another big swing, that caught the man at the top of the chest, not quite where Jack was hoping but more than enough to incapacitate him, knocking him backwards. The second attacker was regaining his composure now, his eyes clearing from the fog that had temporarily blinded him. He was looking for Jack, but all he had time to see was the bottom end of the fire extinguisher slamming straight into his face with a grotesque crack of bone and tissue as his face took the full weight of the blow. He wasn't getting back up.

The first man was scrambling on the floor, clutching at his chest. Probably a broken sternum. His day wasn't going to get any better. Jack spun, dropping the fire extinguisher and launched himself at the first attacker. He grabbed both hands onto the man's collar, lifting his head up and smashing it down on the hard floor. Once, twice, three times. The man was limp.

Jack picked himself up, glancing over both shoulders in case anyone else was about to attack him. All he saw was Ciaran's face, peering wide-eyed around the corner. When he saw Jack, he disappeared quickly around the corner. Jack heard the door to the room slam.

22

Narek Voskerchyan looked at the brown paper bag in the man's hand. Was this guy being serious? That was a lot of money right there, as well as a hell of a lot more to go to his family back in Yerevan. It could change everything.

Narek had always dreamed of changing everything. Life had been hard growing up in Armenia. It was hard for everyone, but he had applied himself, found himself a trade and was, in a relative sense, doing well. Driving his articulated truck across Europe earned him a decent wage, kept his family under a decent roof, gave his children the best possible start he could have hoped for.

Until now.

"How much?" he croaked. His mouth had gone suddenly dry.

"Ten million dram," the man replied coolly. "A million up front, the rest wired to your account back home."

The man was well dressed, smart. He looked like ten million dram wouldn't even be a drop in the ocean to him, but it was to Narek. What even was ten million dram in British money? Ten thousand? Fifteen thousand? Narek tried to do the math but gave up quickly. It didn't matter what it was worth here. He wasn't going to live in England; he could go back home, be with his family.

"Okay, tell me again what I got to do?" No going back now, Narek thought.

"Our man will be driving a car with a communication's device in it; we'll give you one as well. When he pulls alongside, at a safe point, he'll tell you to swerve. You'll veer right, cut him up, and then we'll just put it through the insurance. No one will get hurt, he'll keep his distance. Just remember to drop the earpiece into the side of the road when you stop and to take the pill. It'll make you feel a bit nauseous, which means you won't get blamed for the crash. We don't want anyone getting in trouble." The man's tone was reassuring. It seemed like a slightly over the top way to make some money on an insurance scam, but he had already explained to Narek that the car would be carrying disk drives that were insured for thousands in the event of a crash. Flimsy bits of plastic that wouldn't deal with a bump.

"Sounds great," Narek beamed at the man.

The man reached out a hand, and Narek took it, shaking it, feeling him press a small plastic case into his hand. Narek clasped it as he withdrew and the man stood up.

"A pleasure, Mr. Voskerchyan." The man straightened his suit jacket.

Narek went to return the compliment but realised that he didn't know the man's name. He'd insisted he couldn't tell him, just in case there was a problem later down the line. That made sense, Narek reassured himself. "You too," he replied.

Narek made his way back to his truck, clambering into his cab and turning on the heating. It was cold outside, although it was no doubt a lot colder at home right now. Yerevan got extremely cold in the winter months, but the rest of the year it was much warmer than this country.

Behind the front seats of the cab was a pull-down bed that folded out from the wall. He lowered it and climbed in, staring at the ceiling. He had the earpiece in now, waiting for the instructions to get out on the road so that he would meet the target car at the allotted point, where it would be safest for them to have their collision.

How long would they make him wait? Did he have time to turn on his laptop, watch a film? Sleep felt beyond him; he was far too excited. He thought of the stack of money he had in his pocket. He should put that somewhere safe, before the crash.

He pulled it out of his coat pocket and looked at the notes again, his fingers flicking through the paper bills. This would change everything. He placed it down next to him on the bed. When he folded it back up, that would be as safe a place as anywhere in the cab.

A chance encounter in a service station near Blyth, just south of Doncaster. He could hardly believe his luck. He closed his eyes and pictured his family's faces when he told them. Maybe he should call them now? He dwelled on that idea for a moment, imagining the excited tones of his wife, Husine. He knew that he shouldn't, that he couldn't. The man in the cafe had been very clear. Don't tell anyone until you're back home and safe in Armenia. Not even on the phone. Apparently, the British police had new powers that meant they could listen in to people's calls. Narek had no idea.

It would be better, he consoled himself, to see them with such incredible news. They would be ecstatic. Husine would be cautious, as she always was. She would know that the money came from less than legitimate sources, but she too would be happy just to see her family thrive. It would all be alright.

He closed his eyes, trying to let himself drift on those happy thoughts.

"Narek." A hoarse sounding voice came through the earpiece, and Narek's eyes shot open. Had he been asleep? His mouth felt dry and fuzzy. He must have dozed off for a little while.

"Yes?" he answered, staring straight ahead.

"You need to be on the road within the next ten minutes."

"Okay, then what happens?"

"Just get on the road. You will be told more at the right time."

Narek shuffled off the bed, climbing over into the cab. Easing into his seat, he twisted his body and looked backwards one more time at the small wad of notes, then pushed the bed so that it rose upwards and into the wall, hiding it from view.

His hand rummaged in his pocket looking for his keys. It brushed past the small plastic case that still held the pill he had to take. He told himself not to forget. He was so close, he didn't want to get a single detail wrong.

His truck rattled into life, the cab shaking as the large engine underneath it spluttered back to life. It was an old truck, nearing the end of its useful life. He had dreaded having to repair it, or worse, replace it.

Such good fortune.

The roads were dark and relatively empty. It was past midnight now, and all that remained were other lorries heading north and south to deliver their loads. There were precious few cars on the road. Out here there wasn't much to be getting to and from for most people at this time of night. After Doncaster, the next real town of note was Newark-on-Trent, and that was a small town as far as he had seen on the few occasions he'd driven past it. It was doubtful that people were coming from all around at all hours to see it.

His orders, if you could call them that, were to drive south and wait. Sooner or later he would get the message and then he just had to jerk the wheel to the right. A minor impact, nothing more.

Narek's truck had cruise control, and he decided to set it at a nice, leisurely 52 miles an hour. A steady, constant speed should make the timings far easier, and setting it so low would make it so that he wasn't overtaking other vehicles.

The truck trundled on.

"Be ready."

The voice made the hairs on the back of his neck stand up. He looked in his mirrors. He couldn't see headlights yet.

"Where are you?" he asked back.

"Sixty seconds."

Narek looked again in the mirror. There were the headlights. In the distance. A car.

He did a quick check of his speed. Still 52. He cautioned himself not to touch the cruise control. He didn't want to mess this up. It was the opportunity of a lifetime.

Another glance. The lights were getting closer. Behind that was another car. Narek suddenly had a dreadful thought.

"Which car are you?"

"The front one," came the reply.

Narek looked again. The second car was well back on the first. If there was an accident, they would be able to stop. All the same, he felt his heart racing in his chest. This was it.

"Thirty seconds." That voice again. Narek couldn't believe the voice sounded so calm. He had been told it would be the driver. He knew how nervous he was right now, moments before the crash, but the driver sounded as if he didn't have a care in the world. Certainly not like he was about to collide with a juggernaut.

Narek looked again. The car seemed really close now. *"Any second,"* he told himself.

Time seemed to slow down. The car got closer. Narek's eyes darted from road to mirror, then back to road.

"Ten seconds."

Narek began to count down in his head. *Ten... nine... eight...*

He risked another look at the car. Was it already moving level with his wheels? Surely not. It must be a trick of the mirror.

Four... three... two... one...

Narek went to jerk the wheel, but still no word. Where was the call?

"Now!"

Instantly his arms snapped the wheel right as if controlled by the voice.

Then it all went wrong.

There was a huge thump, the sound of metal on metal and his truck lurched as the trailer it pulled bounced upwards over something. A vehicle. He felt the cab being pulled around as the trailer began to topple and jack-knife and he grabbed onto the wheel hard, holding himself in position, bracing himself against it.

The cab spun with the momentum of the trailer pulling on it. Narek saw the central reservation out of the front window, the truck slowly starting to come back down towards the ground, the tipping motion wasn't enough to take it over on its side. It bounced off the tarmac once, twice, then juddered as it ground to a halt, Narek's chest being beaten from underneath by the steering wheel that he still clung to.

Then it was over. The truck stopped.

Narek gasped for breath. The hiss of steam escaping from the radiator made him focus. Pushing himself up from the wheel, he looked back across the cab out of his passenger window. He couldn't see the car, just a trail of debris. A broken bumper. Shattered lights. Papers from the car.

Narek pulled himself across to the passenger seat and went to open the door. Then he remembered the pill. He knew he *had* to take it now. His shaking hand dove into his pocket, pulling out the plastic case, popping it open, and tossing the pill into his mouth.

What was he going to see when he opened that door? Narek wasn't sure he wanted to know the answer. What had gone wrong?

"Is anyone there he whispered?" hoping for someone to speak to him through his communication device.

Nothing.

His heart was racing even more now.

Looking at the car, he knew why. The roof of had been completely sheared off. Bent and twisted metal contorted out behind the mangled chassis. It had probably come into contact with one of the metal runners underneath his trailer, looking at the height of it. The car itself was twisted and mangled at the back where the wheels had first ridden up on it as it had been spun around, whilst the engine compartment had been gouged along the central reservation, cascading parts of the engine block along fifty yards of the road.

And there, in the middle of all that carnage, lay a man, a tall, athletic-looking black guy, in his late forties perhaps, blood gushing from a wound on his head, eyes rolling, his breath rasping above the steam. He wasn't looking at Narek, just staring into space, as if watching his life ebb away from him.

Narek could hear his own heart now. Actually hear it, pounding in his chest, ringing in his ears. He reached up and fished the earpiece out, throwing it on the floor. He looked around, beginning to feel a little nauseous. Like they said he would. Where was the other car he saw? Why hadn't it stopped?

Looking once more at the man, Narek knew he had to phone for help. He went to turn and go back into his cab, but his legs wouldn't move. It was like he was stuck in mud. He toppled forward, into the side of his truck.

His heart raced even faster.

What was happening? This was supposed to risk-free. An easy way to make some money. They had told him they had it all mapped out.

His heart raced even faster.

It wasn't supposed to be like this.

A searing pain ripped through his chest. Narek felt his heart stop pounding, and he tumbled to the tarmac.

23

Ciaran was under the bed when Jack had found him. No matter how much he tried to coax him out, the boy remained curled up in a ball under the bed, refusing point blank to come out.

"It's only you on your own," Ciaran had protested when Jack told him they were safe. "What if more of them come?"

Jack hadn't had an answer that didn't sound less than convincing at best. True, he had beaten two men, and it seemed unlikely that any more were going to turn up any time soon, but he didn't like making promises that might not be kept. Certainly not to a frightened little boy. In the end, he'd mumbled a weak suggestion of how he wouldn't let anyone hurt him, but it hadn't worked. It was only when Rankine arrived that the boy started to look a little more settled.

By that point, the place was awash with officers. The two would-be attackers had been arrested and removed. Both would require medical attention, Jack was certain of that. He hoped there was some delay in finding pain relief.

Jack sat on a plastic chair watching the scene unfold. One officer had politely requested he leave the scene, but Jack had insisted that he didn't leave the area while Ciaran was there. The officer had given a brief argument to the counter but had soon given up.

He knew it would have been a lot easier if Thea had been there. Whatever trouble she had found herself in was keeping her away from the scene. It meant that Jack was operating on his own, and the longer he stayed there, surrounded by all these officers, being asked small, seemingly innocuous questions, the more he felt that he was likely to make a mistake and slip up.

Getting up, he walked over to Ciaran's door and gave it a soft rap. He waited for a moment, then the door opened a crack. It was Rankine.

"How is he?" Jack asked.

"Getting there," Rankine said quietly. "Just trying to get him to settle, get some kip. Not easy."

"Sorry." Jack felt guilty for the interruption. "Has anyone said anything to you about who they were?"

"Not yet, no. They're not faces any of us know. I'm sure they'll work out it sooner or later. You got any theories?"

"Ex-forces, I would reckon, but not the best. Infantry at best, I reckon. Certainly not the sort who were used to covert operations."

"Take it that's why you got the upper hand on them?"

"Just lucky," Jack said calmly. Last thing he wanted to do was get overconfident.

"Well, luck or not, I'm glad you were here, for the boy's sake."

"Yeah, I wish someone else had been too. Do you think you can find out who put out the order to take the officers off the door?" Jack was keen to know who was behind that.

"I've no idea, but I can try find out. Might be above my pay grade though."

"I get it," Jack acknowledged. "But if something reaches your ear?"

"I got to be blunt, Mr. Quinn. As much as I'd love to tell you, I worry what you'd do with that information. Looking at them two lads they just carted out of here, that is."

Not everyone liked violence. Jack knew that much. Not every situation needed it, however. "I won't cross the line, I promise. We need to know who the enemy are though."

Rankine sighed, a sign of agreement, but also something else, Jack thought. "Fine. I heard the name Randle or something," Rankine confessed. So, he had known, but he didn't know if he could trust Jack. That hurt Jack a little.

"It's a name I know," he replied grimly. "He's the one who got Thea suspended."

"You reckon he's in on this?" Rankine's eyes widened.

"He could be, or someone could just be pulling his strings."

"I take it you're going to try and find out."

"I won't cross any lines."

"Good. Don't make me regret this, Mr. Quinn," Rankine said firmly. "I want to hold my head up high when this is all done."

"You will," Jack assured him. "I'm certain of that."

24

The door to the private ward flew open, and Lowri burst in, stopping just yards into the room. She knew what she was likely to see, it wouldn't be the first time she'd found herself looking down on someone hooked up to a host of machines in an intensive care unit. This time, however, it was different.

This time it was David.

A nurse stood over him, making a note of some data displayed on the monitor. Oxygen levels it looked like, to Lowri's untrained eye. The nurse turned and nodded a slight but not solemn greeting to Lowri.

"How is he?" she gasped.

"Haven't you spoken to anyone?" The nurse raised an eyebrow as he responded. Lowri shook her head, so the nurse went on. "He received a major trauma to the head. It looks like the tyres of the truck missed him, but he was hit by the roof of the car during the accident."

"Will he be okay?" Lowri stepped to the other side of the bed from the nurse, her hand reaching out towards David's but stopping short.

"The doctor will be along soon," the nurse cautioned.

"That means it's serious," Lowri extended the answer to her own question.

"This sort of head injury is always serious. We've induced a coma to help with the swelling. He's in good hands." The standard reassurance. It didn't help Lowri one bit.

The nurse took one last look at the monitor, noting something on a clipboard. "I'll leave you two alone. If you need anyone or have any questions, we're just outside."

"Thanks," Lowri whispered, hoping she said it loud enough so the nurse heard. She really meant it.

Alone in the room, the noises of the machine seemed to get louder and louder. The ping of electronic monitors, the hoarse wheezing and whistling of the breathing apparatus that was feeding oxygen into David, the hum of the background noise of the small private hospital itself all seemed to be unbearable. It made Lowri want to turn and run, something she wasn't accustomed to.

David didn't look like David. His head was wrapped in a thick swaddling of bandages, his eyes taped shut. A tube protruded from his mouth, again, held in place with tape. What little of his features she could see looked battered and bruised. Around his eyes was swollen, his nose looked as if it had been flattened, and his nostrils were ringed with a crust of dried blood, as were his ears. His left arm was encased in plaster, broken it appeared, although Lowri didn't know why. Perhaps he had been trying to protect himself from the collapsing roof of his car as he had crashed. A futile but reflex effort.

David looked anything but the man she knew, the man she had seen only hours earlier. Gone was the strong, proud, and decisive man that she had watched walk out of the hotel room, replaced by a shell that contained a million broken pieces that may never be put back together again.

Never had she felt more helpless.

All Lowri's life she had made decisions that had changed the world, her world or someone else's. She had worked and grafted to put herself into a position whereby she wielded a power that very few others in the world could even imagine. She made careers, destroyed lives, all with a quiet word to a subordinate or an encrypted email.

None of that mattered here, however. For everything her career had done till this point, she couldn't save the life of one of the few people that she could truly call a friend, and if nothing more, David Warner was that. He had been loyal, he had been fair, and he had been honest. What more could she need in someone?

She heard the door opening behind her. She didn't turn, expecting the doctor. The person stood on the opposite side of the bed, looking down at David. It wasn't the doctor, but it was a face she was relieved to see all the same. Eamon Grant didn't look up but spoke all the same.

"I'm really sorry."

"Me too." Lowri looked up. Grant was looking down at her, at them both, with a look of genuine sympathy and sadness.

"I only spoke to him earlier." Grant shook his head in disbelief.

"Me too." Lowri turned back to David, not wanting to let it slip that they had done more than talk. Grant must have realised that the time for pleasantries was over.

"The driver of the lorry collapsed and died at the scene. Heart attack. An Armenian national. They found a substantial amount of cash in his cab, for his line of work. NCA say they've been monitoring his potential role as a drug mule. Working theory is that he got high on his own supply and crashed into Warner. Funnily enough, for a man that deep into drug running that the NCA were watching him, his family back home certainly haven't reaped any rewards."

"A targeted hit?" Lowri was all business now.

Eamon looked up at her. He was tall, broad shouldered, his red curly hair starting to fade to grey, but his cheeks hadn't. They still looked as fresh and red as the day she had met him, a young recruit to the field ops team at the Regulators. An excellent soldier, an even better vigilante. Eamon was more than just brawn, he was a cerebral soldier who needed to understand his enemy and their motivations. It made the game personal, which gave him an extra level of focus that had seen him move from solely frontline to a more hybrid role as his career progressed. Lowri wouldn't call him a friend like she would David, but she knew he was dependable, and that's why he was standing there.

"I'd say so. We've dug into his previous route, found where we think the contact was made, a truck stop not far from the crash site. We've got him on camera for most of his stop there, but he managed to find a black spot for half an hour. A camera went down earlier in the day, as luck would have it."

"Have we got a suspect?"

"No. There was a corridor that led to a door, that led to a field, that led to some woods. A ghost."

"The money?"

"Small bills, non-sequential, not going to be able to trace that."

"Anything?"

"At this point, no." Eamon looked down at David again. "But there are a lot of holes in my investigation still."

Lowri knew what he meant. She had kept David's trip to Yorkshire off the record for this very reason, but now it had blown up. This clearly wasn't a coincidence. David had been made somehow, clearly had rattling someone's cage.

"He was following up a lead from Jack Quinn." She had to bring Eamon in. She had no choice. She couldn't do it alone.

"Quinn? I thought he was out."

"Suspended. Indefinitely."

"Don't mess with me, Lowri, we know what that means."

"He came across a thread that might lead to a paedophile ring that's run by and frequented by a number of senior figures in both politics and the public eye."

"That does paint a target on the back of anyone getting involved."

"Problem?"

"Not for me," Eamon replied calmly. "How much reach do I have?"

"As much as you need. I want you to take over the West London office, do David's job as well. You'll need some of your own people but only those you can absolutely trust."

"Ms. Graves, thank you." Eamon looked humbled. "I'll do my best."

"Good. I'll be working out of Westminster, running down what I can."

"What about Quinn? I don't really have much of a rapport with him."

"You worked with his old partner, Morgan, right?"

"We did a couple of jobs together, but I'm not sure if bringing him in is the right call."

Lowri paused for a moment, noting Eamon's objection. Finally, she spoke. "He's loyal, but he also loves his old partner. He'll give us the connection to Quinn we need."

"Fine, it's your call, you know the two of them better."

"Thank you."

"I won't let you down," Eamon promised.

"It's not me you need to worry about letting down," Lowri cautioned. "It's David. Let's get the bastards who did this."

25

Adam and Emmie sat on the small sofa of her one bedroom flat in east London, looking across at Mo. He had his eyes closed, head pointed at the ceiling, as he had done for the last five minutes straight.

"Mo?" Adam asked.

Mo said nothing.

"You gotta talk to me, pal. We put our lives on the line for you here, buddy. We deserve to know why," Adam went on.

Mo slowly opened his eyes and lowered his head. "Come on, man. You know the score. If this was you sitting here and me asking, you couldn't tell me, could you?"

"With all due respect, you broke into our comms system. You can either explain that to us here or to someone else back at the office," Emmie butted in.

Adam looked at Mo, knowing that Emmie had pulled a great move there. She had cornered Mo, and he wouldn't like that. Certainly not from someone he didn't know or trust.

"Emmie's right." Adam decided to placate Mo. "You know I don't want to go down that route either, but if I go in having picked you up with no reason why, I'm in a world of trouble too, and I might not get as lucky as you. I might not find someone else to work for."

Mo's eyebrows raised. "How did you know I was working for someone else?"

"Educated guess," Adam replied. "I mean, you're not the sort of person who in your day-to-day life finds ways to get hunted by four blokes with guns. This is definitely an occupational hazard."

"Nah, that's fair, man. You got me there." He sighed, then went on. "You know why I walked out on the Regulators?"

"No."

"I want to make a difference, man. I want to make a change, save the world and all that, but I need it to mean something. I need to be able to wrap my head around what we do and find a grounding for it. Something bigger than me, bigger than you, bigger than all of us. I mean, my religion, man, it's my everything."

"Not two things that go well in our line of work," Adam noted.

"No, and it tore me up, man. There was one thing, though, one thing that broke me. When we took down that nuke, the girl we pulled in, Annie, she told me that we were as bad as the other side because we wanted to preserve a system that screwed over so many people."

"I thought we wanted to preserve whatever the people had chosen?" objected Emmie. "We don't dictate the politics of it, just make sure no one subverts it."

"Maybe so, but I couldn't shake that, no matter what I tried. I needed to find a way to do this, but that I could find a grounding in. I found the Brotherhood of Uṣūl al-fiqh, a vigilante group like you but based around the Islamic principles of jurisprudence. Something I could believe in."

"I've never heard of them." Adam found himself at a loss. There were a number of different vigilante groups out there.

None as organised and effective as the Regulators and the Vehmic Courts admittedly, but here was a new name.

"You wouldn't. An Islamic group fighting on a doctrine based around the Qu'ran is hardly something that's going to go down well in this day and age, is it? Doesn't matter that one of our tenets is that we can't supersede the law of a sovereign nation, nor harm any innocent party. We're Muslims, we wear a target straight off the bat. So, we keep the lowest of profiles before we get labelled terrorists."

"What were you into?" Emmie inquired.

"This." Mo reached down into his jacket and pulled the hard drive out, still in the plastic wrapping he'd used to keep it safe whilst on the boat. "Don't know what's on it, but I know that eight of my colleagues blew themselves up today to make sure I got away safe with this thing, whilst making sure that no one else got harmed. I ain't ever seen sacrifice like that before."

"And you don't know anything about what's on it?" Adam pressed on.

"It came off a government server, something hosted inside the houses, man, so I know it's some serious shit. Took a lot of digging and a lot of work to find it. They killed the other two lads who did the hack with me?"

"Who did?"

"I don't know. Whoever wants this buried."

"You need to open it. You need to know what's on it." Adam tried hard not to sound too insistent.

"You mean *you* want to know what's on it." Clearly, he had failed.

"I do, of course. I just put my life on the line for it as well."

"There's the thing though, man, this is bigger than all of us, and I don't just mean this case, I mean the whole principle that we live by. I do this, and I die by this. I don't do this for me, I do this for the world. That's what I've been searching for, and it didn't really hit me till I looked and saw a house I was in just minutes before turned to rubble and burying my colleagues, killing them so that I could escape, this data could escape. I didn't call you to save me earlier; I called you to save this." He brandished the hard drive up in front of him, parading it to Adam and Emmie as if it were the most precious jewel in the world.

"And if you had died, what would have happened then? What would you have expected me to do if I had got my hands on this?" *Checkmate*, thought Adam.

Mo let out a wry laugh. "Mate, you'd have tried to look at it, but you'd have seen nothing. The thing is completely encrypted. Someone smarter than you would see it and do the right thing though, of that I'm sure."

"How did they find you?" Emmie again piped up, always moving Mo on, Adam spotted. Always keeping him from getting too far into his comfort zone. Indeed, Mo's smile turned to a grimace.

"That's the million-dollar question. Were we compromised? I don't know. Did they track me? I don't know. Something gave somewhere, and I know it puts me back under a spotlight."

"Back?" Adam was concerned for his old friend following that revelation.

162

"Yeah, like I said. There were two more guys who helped me on the hack, and I'm the only one who made it out. Then my whole team kills themselves to cover my back, now the guy who comes to pick me up is dead. I keep surviving where others keep falling. You know coincidences don't exist in our line of work. Even if they do."

"You've just been lucky, or smart, or both. Probably both, knowing you."

"But if he's not been lucky or smart, they could still be tracking him," Emmie pointed out. "Which means it's imperative we get that data into our system now so we can make sure it gets acted on. As you said, Mo, the data is what this is all about."

"Who is this girl, bruv?" Mo gestured at Emmie as he looked at Adam. "She's proper on fire today. I like her."

"She's my new partner. I think she's going to do just fine." Adam grinned, seeing Emmie smile, just slightly, out of the corner of his eye.

"You've got me right in a corner, Emmie," Mo admitted. "Tell you what, let me do this right. Let me call my people and see what they want me to do next. If it means I can share, I will."

"Have you got a way of reaching them?"

"I've got a last chance saloon number I'm to call in the darkest of hours. I've exhausted all other options with them, so I guess this is that moment."

Adam slid a phone across the table, the burner phone Mo had used before having been discarded before they left the construction site.

"Thanks," Mo said. "Let me make this in private though, yeah?"

"We'll go into the kitchen," Emmie offered, standing as she spoke.

Adam followed her up, leaving Mo on his own with the phone. The two of them walked into the neat but small kitchen.

"You trust him, don't you?" Emmie tried to pose it as a statement, but Adam knew there was a hint of a question in there.

"Mo has always, *always* been one of the good guys. I can't see him ever being anything else."

"The trail of dead behind him, it doesn't help him."

"No, his employers might have questions, but I don't. I mean that. Mo couldn't hurt someone. Not like that. That's why he walked out on the Regulators."

"We do things right though, we only target the people who cross the line."

"We like to think so. I guess Mo just needed a set of rules he could understand better. I don't do religion myself, but if I did, it might make it harder for me to do this." Adam wondered if he could do even a percentage of the work he did if he was a Godly man. How could he? It must be near on impossible. He had never thought of that before, certainly not when Mo had left. At that time, all he had felt was disappointment in Mo. He'd thought that the former analyst had just given up. He felt ashamed now that he hadn't given him the credit he deserved.

"Believing in God and believing in doing the right thing can go hand in hand. It all depends on your interpretation of the Bible, or the Qu'ran, or whatever. Believe me, there are going to be a million more Muslims who find what he's doing abhorrent. It's just the way it is, I guess."

"You talk like you've been here for years."

"My grandfather probably got me more prepped for this than I needed to be." She shrugged.

"He recruited you, didn't he?"

"I don't know if I would use the word recruited, but I guess he prepared me for this life as best he could."

"He recruited you," Adam countered. "And he did a good job. Getting your head around that, it's a big part of what we do. A lot of new recruits fall by the wayside on this issue."

"Well, I'm glad you think I won't." Emmie looked down at the countertop, maybe just a little embarrassed, Adam thought. "But it's still a line that your friend in there is going to fall foul of sooner or later. His religion, his personal interpretation of it, isn't going to match with everyone else's. It can't, and sooner or later, there will be a line."

"Let's hope it never comes to that."

There was a sound from the living room, someone getting up and walking towards them. The door opened, and Mo joined them in the kitchen, making it even cosier.

"They're going to let me crack it, share it with you, but we need to give them access too. Whoever has the best assets to deal with the next step, we go from there."

"Do they know what's on it?" Adam asked.

Mo shook his head. "The way we work is so compartmentalised. We don't let the different cells cross. This will only be known by one or two other people now."

"How long will it take you to crack the data?" Emmie asked.

"Not long, a few minutes at best. I just need a laptop and to make sure the Wi-Fi is off. Just in case."

"Mine's in the front. I'll unplug the router as well," Emmi said, heading out of the room.

Before Adam could speak, his phone started to ring. "It's Lowri," he said to Mo, knowing that, in all likelihood, she was going to want answers to why Mo had utilised the emergency call system.

"Tell her what you have to, man." Mo shrugged. "I got nothing to hide."

Adam answered. The call was not what he was expecting.

26

Chris Randle's problems with sleep had been something that had plagued him for a long time. The doctor had told him that it was a combination of him being overweight and his longstanding asthma. The asthma Chris could accept, but he took offence at the notion that his weight had any part to play in it. He might well be a few pounds over what he should be, but that was all.

Even now, as he tossed and turned, watching the light from yet another dawn begin to creep in, as his sinuses struggled to stay wide enough to drop him into a deep sleep, he wouldn't accept that this was in any way his fault. This was all down to his asthma, and you just *got* asthma. You couldn't catch it through anything you did. It wasn't his fault.

Tonight though, he knew that, despite his constant struggles with sleep, there was another thing keeping him awake: the feeling of exhilaration of finally being able to screw over that bloody Watts woman.

Thea Watts had become his nemesis very quickly. She was far too eager, far too forthright in her opinions. Since she had come in, all she had done was stick her nose into his business, criticise his working methods, the way he did things. How dare she?

Chris Randle had got to where he was through being Chris Randle. There was no other explanation. His way of doing things had worked so far, so why should he change for her? It was fair to say his career had been unexceptional, but it had been steady. He got results when he needed to; he did the job to the expectations that people had for him. That was all anyone did. Anyone but Thea.

It was hard to say what motivated that woman. She was a law unto herself, angry and confrontational pretty much every time she came into the office. It was no wonder she'd been turfed out of her old job, but it puzzled Randle what she had expected to find up here. Perhaps she thought she'd be able to run away to the Moors and live the life of a nomad? Well, bad news, Miss Watts. York wasn't the back of beyond, despite what some people in London might think of anything north of Watford.

The tension between the two had been simmering for a while now, but all the same, Randle had been surprised when he found Thea tipping him out of his chair. That had been completely uncalled for. That had been assault. He had known it at the time, and he had wanted to act on it, but he hadn't.

Looking back, he wasn't sure why. Now, as he lay staring at his ceiling, having made his complaint, he felt much better, like a huge weight had been lifted off his shoulders. And it was definitely down to having made the complaint. It certainly wasn't down to the man who had visited him the night before, outside his house, pretty much ordering him to make the complaint.

That had spooked him a little bit, the appearance of a man in a smart and most obviously expensive suit, immaculately groomed, almost James Bond-esque, at his door, asking for a quick word regarding his "problem at work." Randle, of course, had pointed out he had no problems, but when the man had mentioned Thea's name, he suddenly became a little more interested in what he had to say.

The premise had been simple. Complain about the incident where Watts had tipped him over. Nothing more. They would ensure she faced the maximum possible sanction and that she would soon be out of his hair. That had all been appealing enough, and Chris was only to glad to accept, so much so, that he had been surprised when the caveat had been added at the end.

"If you mention this conversation," the well-dressed man had said, leaning in and whispering quietly, placing a hand on Randle's shoulder, "you might have to disappear yourself."

Randle hadn't been able to process what had been said before the man was giving him a polite smile and walking away, back up Randle's drive and into the street. For a moment, Randle had been spooked. In fact, that feeling had lasted far more than a moment. It had been with him until he had walked into Wilde's office and made the complaint, but the moment he had set foot outside, the deed done, he had felt much better.

"Struggling to sleep?"

Randle jerked up in bed. There was a man in the corner of his room, leaning idly in the doorway. A big man, dark hair that was just a little over crew cut, with stubble that looked around the same length.

"Who the fuck are you? I did what you told me!" he protested, knowing the intruder must have been sent here by the well-dressed man from yesterday.

"I've not told you to do anything." The intruder shrugged. "Yet."

"Who are you?" Randle was confused now, and the man smiled at him.

"I'm guessing your complaint against your co-worker was inspired by someone, am I right?"

Randle said nothing. He didn't want to disappear.

"Doesn't matter, you already told me that. Well, seeing as you're in the mood for doing favours, I'm here to ask one of you as well. Drop the complaint."

"I can't."

"They threaten to kill you? Make you disappear?"

Randle said nothing, but he nodded slowly. Maybe this guy could help? His tone seemed softer when he asked.

"Thought so. Now, here's your problem. If you don't drop the complaint, I will do far worse. I want to do far worse. I know you were the one who pulled the officers off the ward."

Randle went to say something, but his mouth just hung limply. What could he say?

"I know, I know," the man went on. "You're stuck between a rock and a hard place here, so let me try and explain how things will go down. If you don't help me, don't drop the complaint first thing tomorrow, I'll have nothing better to do but come and deal with you. And believe me, there's nowhere you can hide from me and my friends. However, if you do drop the complaint, it's true, they will come for you, eventually, but they'll have a bigger problem on their hands: me and your colleague. They'll need to deal with us first before they can even think about cleaning up loose ends like you. See, we're a time-sensitive problem for them, something of a priority, so they'll tie themselves up trying to take us out. If they fail, you're safe, so you best start rooting for us, because right now, you just joined the winning team, didn't you, Chris?"

Chris nodded. Jesus, what the hell was going on? What had that Watts woman got him into?

"I knew you were a smart man," the intruder registered the nod. He stared for a moment at Chris, then turned, stepping out of the room silently. "First thing tomorrow."

Chris sat watching the door, listening for the sound of him leaving the house. He heard nothing. It was an hour before he dared to get out of his bed and carefully check the house. It was empty. No sign of any one having been there.

Chris spent another hour sat in his living room, staring at the blank TV screen, pondering his next course of action, playing the two options through in his head. In the end, he had no choice. What the intruder had said made perfect sense. He had to root for him, root for Watts, no matter how much he hated her.

The weight was back on his shoulders. He knew it wasn't going to go away any time soon.

27

Mo looked ashen-faced when he had heard the news. Adam knew that he held David in high regard, just as he did, so the news had been a huge blow to them both. Adam had done his best to hide his emotion, but Mo wasn't even trying. Given the day he'd had, Adam felt that was fair enough, so he was more than pleasantly surprised when, two minutes later, Mo was concentrating hard on the computer in front of him, doing all he could to crack the code. He wasn't the same guy who had walked out of the Regulator office all those months ago. He'd toughened up, more than Adam had ever imagined he could.

There was a tense silence. Emmie, whilst shocked by the news of David's accident, didn't have the personal connection there. Her first question had been to ask how Adam was doing. It was appreciated, and it was a good question.

Adam's mind was split now, one-half on the job in hand in front of them, the other on his boss, although to call David just a boss was doing him a great disservice. He was the reason that Adam was here now. He had recruited him directly, brought him into the fold and nurtured him every step of the way. Now he was hurt and helpless in a hospital somewhere.

He looked again to Mo, watching his fingers working quickly on the keyboard, his eyes darting from side to side as he watched characters and code scrolling across the screen in front of him. Adam envied that focus. He longed for something to get his teeth into, if only to take his mind off it. Sitting and watching someone else working wasn't doing him any good.

"I need to step outside for a minute," he said standing.

"There's a balcony, out the bedroom," Emmie offered.

"Thanks," Adam replied. "I'll be back in a minute, I just..." He trailed off and turned. No one waited for him to finish.

The balcony was outside of two tall French doors that were beginning to light the bedroom. They were locked, but the key was still in, and Adam turned it silently, stepping outside onto the small strip of concrete bordered by a three-foot-high metal railing.

It was much cooler outside than in the cramped flat which had begun to feel quite humid, although he knew that he wouldn't have helped his cause by keeping his leather jacket on. He placed his hands on the rails and let his body lean forward slightly, looking out over the London rooftops. Slowly, the city was coming to life. In the distance, the sound of trains, buses, and cars began to echo through the stillness. Life was going on, as it always did.

His mind turned to David, lying in the hospital bed, completely unaware now of the world around him as it began to shudder back into full swing again. Would David ever see another morning like this? Shit, how many more did he have himself? He thought of Laura and Jasmine, imagining them in a silent vigil over his bed. He let himself dwell on it for a moment. There were those who said that you needed to block such thoughts out of your mind in this game, but Adam wasn't one of them. Laura, and now Jasmine, were his motivation. They kept him wanting to make the world a better place, but more importantly, they kept him assessing the risk.

"Hey!" A shout came from inside the house. Mo. "I got it."

Adam took one last look at the cityscape in front of him. London was ready for another day. So was he.

Back in the living room, Emmie was standing behind Mo, looking over his shoulder at the laptop screen.

"What have we got?" Adam asked.

"It's a list, a database of some sort. Names, locations, dates, times, photos of people going in and out of places."

"What sort of names? What sort of places?" Adam came around the other side of the two of them and looked at the screen.

"All sorts, man, look at this." Mo had that excited tone to his voice again, the one that he always got when he knew he'd cracked something important. Adam looked at the names. He recognised plenty. Politicians, for the most part, it seemed, but there were prominent business people, celebrities, people from all aspects of the public eye.

"The locations are all over the place. Flats and apartments in London, private estates up and down the country." Emmie leant forward, pointing towards a small folder on the screen that said "Deeds." "Can you open that?"

Mo duly obliged and a new window opened. Inside were a host of files with the names of properties. Mo opened one, and they all scanned it.

"Looks like the deeds to some of the properties in the list. They all seem to be privately owned," he explained as he opened even more of them.

"Why would someone need a list of who goes to a building and who owns those buildings?" Adam thought out loud.

"Surveillance of some sort," Emmie replied. "What's on the photos?"

Mo's fingers typed quickly, and more windows popped up. Pictures of people heading in and out of the buildings, all time and date stamped.

"Is there any more? Transcripts? Evidence?" Adam knew there was something more to this. No one went to all this trouble just to protect a list of names and places.

"Give me a second," Mo replied calmly. It was barely a second before he found something. He shook his head and sighed, highlighting a folder on the screen. "Someone doesn't want this one opening."

"It's encrypted?"

"Yeah, but not for long." Mo was already slotting a USB drive into the side of the laptop. A few swift keystrokes and a progress bar appeared on screen. Adam noticed the grin on Mo's face as he spoke. "You're in luck."

"Why?" Emmie took the bait.

"The encryption on this is near-enough invincible. It's a self-generating code that changes every hundred thousand Nanoseconds." He looked up at them both. "That's like a ten-thousandth of a second for the uninitiated. Now, something like this, you don't crack, not without knowing the backdoor in. Thankfully, as the guy who created this, I do."

"This is your code?" Adam was a little alarmed by the implications. "How the hell has it got here?"

"That's a question for later. This little bad boy got around though, things like this always do. We used it, the government used it, I'm sure plenty of other governments did as well. That's just the nature of the beast."

"You let them?" Adam still wasn't happy with the explanation.

"Adam, man, I'm a hacker. Sometimes I need to be able to get into things that others don't want me to. One of the easiest ways to crack someone's lock is to make sure you have their key."

The screen went black for a second, then a list of folders appeared. Mo slipped the USB out, holding it up.

"This is my key," he said proudly.

Emmie was still looking at the display. "We've got video files, some spreadsheets."

"Let's see a video," Adam ordered.

A quick double-click on the trackpad and a video loaded. It was taken from what was clearly a small, CCTV style camera, with a fish-eye lens, placed in a corner of a bedroom. The picture was grainy, but again had a time and date stamp in the bottom right corner.

"I bet they've got them on camera with mistresses, hookers, and shit," deduced Mo.

"Play it," Adam said grimly. He wasn't so sure.

The video began to roll, but nothing happened in the room. The timecode in the corner ticked over, but other than that, there was no way of telling the video was playing.

"Spin it on," Adam said gruffly. He saw Emmie look at him out of the corner of his eye, clearly picking up on his growing anger.

The video played. The room remained the same. The timecode ticked over even faster.

Then the door opened.

"Stop." Adam had seen enough. "You fucking bastards."

He stood up and walked away.

Mo and Emmie both took a moment to process what they were seeing, to understand the implications, but he had known from the moment he had seen the room. He knew what it was that was such a dirty secret that it had to be kept hidden at all costs. He had known long before he had seen that image on the screen, the image of a former member of the cabinet walking into the bedroom, holding the hand of a young girl no more than seven or eight years old.

"Son of a bitch," Adam heard Mo exclaim. Emmie said nothing.

Adam turned back to the two of them.

"I want every single name on that list."

28

"Get yourself back where you need to be," Wilkes said. "And I'll say the same thing to you as I said to Randle. I don't know what's happening between you and him, just keep out of each other's way. It's that simple."

Thea was relieved. Confused, but relieved. She was back at work, able to help Ciaran, so all was right with the world on that front at least. Helping him had been all she had thought about since she had been suspended, and now, sat in the carpark of the hospital, where she had set up an unofficial stake out of the front door of the building. Not being able to get involved in the aftermath of the attack had been incredibly hard for her. Now she could get back in the game.

The time alone in the car had been time to contemplate what had happened. Jack was right. Randle had clearly been put up to this. The spineless slug had no appetite for a fight with her, she knew that much, and his lack of fortitude had put lives on the line. There would be time later for her to settle that score, however. What she needed to do now was to get Ciaran out. She had to find somewhere else for him to hide, somewhere where he wouldn't be found, at least not before she had whoever was behind this in custody.

Where would a young boy be safe? Thea had thought about placing him into the care of social services or even witness protection, but there was no way of knowing who could be trusted, especially as the circle of people getting involved in the case was getting wider and wider.

"Shit," she hissed, cursing for a moment the complete isolation that she had made her life. She had no family, none she could call on anyway. Her mum was a mess, self-involved and unreliable, her dad, sadly, long since passed. He would have known what to do. He had been one of the old guard, a bobby with his finger on the pulse of his beat. He knew the people he served, knew how to keep them happy, how to keep them safe. Finding a place to hide Ciaran would have come second nature to him. Royce Watts had been Thea's inspiration to join the force. How on earth had she got it so badly wrong?

Her dad reminded her in many ways of Rankine. Both of them were completely at ease with people, both of them dedicated to doing the right thing. That was her answer. She might not know a place to hide Ciaran, but Rankine would. He knew this town, knew the people. He would have the answers.

"There's a lot of good folk, least what's what I always thought," Rankine lamented when she put her plan to him. Rankine's house was a traditional English bay-windowed semi, in a quiet street on the west of Malton. The dining room they sat in now felt quaint. The furniture was all dark oak, whilst the whole room was adorned with an assortment of photos of Rankine and his wife and children dotted on different walls, ledges, and mantlepieces. It was the perfect tapestry to tell the story of their lives. Christmases, family get-togethers, caravan holidays. Rankine's children had clearly long since left. Graduation photos, wedding photos, bookmarked the end of the story, although Thea noted there were no pictures of grandchildren. Rankine went on.

"Problem is, now, I don't know who I can trust. I mean, I'll think of someone, think of something."

Thea knew he was right. There was a small group of people she trusted at the moment, especially for a job as important as this. She looked around at the room of photos once more. "You could take him. Take the caravan, pitch up somewhere, hide out."

"Me?" Rankine seemed genuinely shocked by the idea as if he was the least capable person in the world. He took a moment to mull it over. "The wife does always say we should be getting away more."

"You should. If anything, at least Ciaran will be out of the bloody hospital."

"Would he be safe though? I mean, I'm no bodyguard or anything, and the missus, as fierce as she can be when I leave the kitchen in a mess, she's not really up for secret agent stuff."

"I can give you a map of where all our ANPR cameras are. If you steer clear of them, then they're never going to find you. Not unless you get really unlucky."

"You want to talk about bad luck, you should see me down the bookies picking horses," Rankine laughed before remembering the gravity of the situation, a more sombre look spreading across his face as he decided whether or not to commit to the idea. "Bugger it, we need to do something. Lad must be going stir crazy in there. Bit of fresh air do him good."

"Don't tell me where you're going." Thea raised her hand quickly, stopping him before he revealed his plans. "Just phone and check in after a week. We can reassess then."

"And the office?"

"You're already working for me. I'll cover for your absence if anyone asks."

"They'd bloody better ask, I don't want to end up forgotten," he grumbled.

"I'm sure there's no danger of that."

29

You need to remain focused.

The voice that came again in Lowri's head was her own. It wasn't the first time she'd heard it, but she knew she needed to keep repeating that mantra. It was serving her well, keeping her mind on track. Off David and on the job in hand, which was where it needed to be.

Her bedside vigil for David had been anything but peaceful. Grant hadn't stayed long, tactfully disappearing with minimal fuss, only a short promise to do everything he could to the best of his abilities. For five minutes, there had been a calm in the room, other than the sound of the machinery that was helping to keep David alive. It hadn't lasted.

The first phone call she made was to Poole. She had wanted to apprise him of the situation.

"Hello? Ms. Graves?" His voice was rough, and he stifled a cough. Just waking up. Of course he was. It was still early in the morning.

"Poole, there's been an incident. I need you back at the office as soon as you can." Her voice was calm and monotone. She wasn't going to let the emotion show.

"What sort of incident?"

"David Warner was hit. He's alive but critical. They tried to make it look like an accident, but it was a targeted hit."

"Shit. Do we have any suspects?"

"No. Get in the office, chase what you can. Raf will have the details and a terminal for you."

"Understood. I'll be in shortly."

David's condition hadn't changed. The doctors didn't expect it to for some time now. There was excessive swelling on the brain, so for now, he was being kept in a medically induced coma, something that would give him the best chance to heal long term. What damage had already been done, they wouldn't know until he was conscious again. Which he would be, Lowri reassured herself as she looked at him. He would be.

Mo's rescue had been communicated to her. Now things had quietened down, Lowri began to let herself become more involved in what was happening. Like all former Regulators, Mo had enjoyed some level of surveillance since he had been let go. At first, he had disappeared into himself. He had been a mess, which was what the psychologists who had interviewed him a year ago had concluded would happen. The liability he was meant to become was a reality. But then something changed. He had made links to another vigilante network, one based on the tenets of the Muslim faith. The Brotherhood of Uṣūl al-fiqh was a group low down on the Vehm's radar, but Mo's involvement had led to Lowri at least stepping up her education.

Then he had disappeared altogether, something that had inspired newfound admiration in Lowri for both Mo and his new organisation. Not many people found it easy to disappear completely from the eyes of Lowri's network, but somehow, Mo had.

Now he was back, scrambling for help from her organisation, and Lowri had wanted to know why. When she found out, Lowri had dismissed the idea of coincidence completely.

David had always liked Mo. He was a far softer touch than Lowri when it came to his personnel. He got involved with them.

She looked at David again, catching herself in her own little lie. The idea that she didn't get involved with her staff was something that Lowri had allowed to be a part of her façade for years but was now completely laid bare upon the bed in which David lay.

The question of what had happened had started to run around in her mind more and more as she sat there. The preliminary reports from the investigating team suggested that this had indeed been a tragic accident, brought on by a medical emergency, but that was something that Lowri would only accept once every other avenue had been closed. Hearing what Mo had unearthed had opened up so many more possibilities. She knew it was impossible she would ever accept that verdict now.

She looked down at David once more.

You need to remain focused.

It was sage advice indeed. Lowri knew right now that she could let her emotions run away with her if she wanted. Let the anger she felt inside consume her and set her on a path of vengeance, forsaking all others, forsaking herself. That would be the dumb play, however, one that, in the long term, would cause more pain, more hurt, for so many more people. She had to keep herself in check, keep it all under control. There was evidence that needed to be followed, need to be worked to uncover those responsible for what was happening.

Mo's discovery, Jack's work in Yorkshire, David's accident, all of them revolved around one thing, powerful men using children for their own gratification. That was abhorrent enough. It made Lowri's stomach turn, but what made her even angrier was that she had already worked out the truth of what Mo had uncovered, and now she needed to get back to work and share that with her team.

You need to remain focused.

She looked down at David one more time.

"I'll be back," she promised, placing her hand on his.

Lowri stood, turned, and walked out of David's room.

30

It had been a year since Mo had left the Regulators office for what he believed, what he hoped, would be the last time. There had been no card on his desk from his colleagues, no farewell drinks, and although he had built some friendships, some rapport, as he had walked out those doors for the last time, he knew he had made the right choice. Nothing was going to bring him back in those doors, nothing at all.

Mo, however, hadn't planned for this. Things changed, he lamented as he got out of the car in the underground parking lot. Adam and Emmie stepped out in front of him, heading for the entrance. He knew which way to go, but all the same he hesitated for a moment. Going through those doors could well mean no going back. He took a breath and followed. He would not be a Regulator again, he told himself. Never again.

Walking up into the office floor, it felt like everyone was watching him. Mo saw faces he knew, people he liked, people he wasn't so keen on, and a host of new faces he had never seen before. Everything seemed familiar but just subtly different enough to be new and intimidating. Doubly so for a man who had turned his back on one of the biggest secret organisations in the world.

Grant walked over to them all. Mo had never really had much contact with him, but his reputation as being blunt and unforgiving came before him. He scowled as he approached them.

"I'm not happy," he grumbled looking directly at Mo and letting it be known quite clearly what he meant. "But what Ms. Graves wants, we do. We know the score."

"I'll be watching him at all times," Adam vouched for Mo, although that in itself made Mo feel uncomfortable, hearing someone he trusted saying he needed watching.

"You will," Grant affirmed. "I need you all to work on cracking this. I need a list of names on my desk by the time Lowri is back here."

"She's coming back?" Adam sounded surprised.

"Yeah, she just called. Nothing she can do for David, so she wants to be here. She's working on the assumption that everything is linked."

"Do you believe that? I mean, could she just be projecting her guilt for David onto this investigation," Mo blurted out his objection, instantly regretting it when he saw Grant's snarling face twist in his direction.

"I don't answer to people without the balls to stick this out," he sneered.

"Will you answer to me?" Adam butted in.

Grant looked back to Adam and Mo could have sworn he could see his nostrils flaring. There was a clear pause as Grant stopped himself from saying what he was thinking. "This is a highly emotive, high-pressure situation, so let's take a moment to remember where we all are," he finally warned. "Get yourselves set up, work that list, and be ready to report in when Lowri gets here."

"Sir," Adam accepted the order, and Grant was gone.

"He's a friendly guy," Emmie said softly.

"Lots going on, like he said," Adam conceded. "Probably should have let it go."

"Thanks though, pal," Mo said earnestly.

"I figure it's got to be hard enough coming back here without the boss being on your case," Adam explained.

"I'll be alright. We've got work to do." Mo found that he was desperate to get started. All he could think of was getting the list of locations finalised so that someone, somewhere, could go and get those kids. His discomfort about being in his old office, Grant's less than friendly reception, none of that mattered. It was all noise, he told himself.

Adam and Emmie took Mo to one of the side rooms away from the main floor. With the door closed behind them, the noise of the office was all but blocked.

"I want these bastards," Adam said as they sat down at the oval wooden table that dominated most of the room. "I want them hung. We've got to get this right."

"Do you really think it's linked to the hit on David?" Mo asked.

"If he was involved in the investigation, I figure we've got to view it as a real possibility," Emmie said.

"A certainty," Adam added. "I don't like how quickly they acted though. How could they even know we were involved?"

"It was the same with us," Mo added. "I mean, I can guess how they found us when we did the hack, we were sloppy, but there was no way they should have been waiting for me when I got to the extraction point. That was known only be people within our group."

"Two groups, both haemmoraging information," Adam pointed out.

"Two moles," Emmie added, "which means whoever set this whole thing up has power."

"It came from Westminster," Adam said. "Does it get more powerful than that?"

"That is where it came from, but what if someone just had the list there. What if they didn't make it." Mo barely believed it could be someone in government who could be so callous.

"How do we work that out?" Emmie wanted to know.

"You could try that server again, but chances are it doesn't even exist anymore. If it was my server, it wouldn't. Best bet is going to be boots on the ground," said Mo.

"We best hope there's something in this file that points to an author then," Adam said. "Because otherwise, that sounds like a long drawn out investigation."

The three of them looked at each other.

"No pressure then," Mo said as cheerfully as he could manage.

31

"What's the latest?" Lowri was back at work, addressing the small meeting room at the Regulators London field office. She was at the top of the mahogany table, looking down on Adam, Grant, Raf and Poole, doing what she did best. She was focused solely on the job in hand.

"We've identified a number of the sites where children are being held. We've already started leaking information to people we know we can trust. I'd love for us to be leading this operation ourselves." Grant was almost apologetic in his tone. "But we just don't have the resources for this."

"Leaks?" Raf sounded unsure, not quite incredulous but not far off. "Why are we leaking this? Have you seen some of the names on this list? Three current members of the cabinet, including the home secretary. The leader of the opposition. I mean, we put this out there, we better take some time to think of the fallout because we're going to be ripping apart the fabric of British politics."

Lowri nodded as she listened. What Raf said had merit. This was career-ending for those implicated. It was most likely going to end up with them spending the rest of their lives behind bars. So far, they had been able to verify one hundred thirty-three people who had been involved in some way, shape, or form with the crimes against these children. There were eighteen sitting members of Parliament altogether. That was enough to form a small party, certainly enough to be able to put enough pressure on any ruling party. With one rising as high as Home Secretary, another Leader of the Opposition, Lowri couldn't even bring herself to think what would happen if one made it to Prime Minister. That was why they needed to stop it. It might damage British politics in the short term, possibly even longer, but if it meant that they stopped an outside force from controlling the government, well, what choice did she have?

"You have a point, Raf." Negotiation was always a good idea. "But we can't sit on this. It's not what we do, especially with these people being so far up the food chain. God knows what they're susceptible to doing."

"And who they're susceptible from." Grant was leaning back in his chair arms crossed. "We have to tread very carefully here. Whoever put this together isn't going to be very happy we're pulling it down."

"That's why we need to close ranks." Lowri looked over at Grant. He looked dishevelled as he sat there, shirt not completely tucked in, tie crooked. It had been a hectic few hours, but he was filling David's role, and David wouldn't have looked anything other than immaculate. It was almost a betrayal to David's legacy, and it made her angry. Needlessly angry, she knew that, but right now she wanted someone to be angry at. Anyone. "We need people we can trust here, in a small bubble. We have to control this as best we can."

"Only we can't. The Brotherhood are all over this as well," Adam piped up now. "They know what's happening; they were the ones looking for this. They might know even more about who is behind it."

"What do you suggest?" Grant asked.

"Send Mo to talk to the Brotherhood, to see if they're willing to share with us on this. There is no doubt that they're doing this for the same reasons we are."

"They could have been protecting the data," Poole objected. "We know nothing about them."

"If they wanted to protect it, they had plenty of chances to get destroy it or hide it before we got involved. They were trying to decrypt it. Mo even said so himself," countered Adam.

"How big would you estimate an operation like this would have to be, Grant?" Lowri asked. "To put this sort of thing together, to keep on top of it? What sort of resources would it take?"

"They're professionals, and they're inside the government, inside the civil services already. I mean, it could be an inside job, someone on the staff, a group of people, working to keep rogue MPs in line. Could be our intelligence services, or it could be a foreign intelligence operation, even something more malign. It's big whatever it is."

"What branch of the authorities would you trust to get it cleared up?"

"I wouldn't trust any at the moment. Certainly not to find out who was behind it."

"Nor me." Lowri knew that would make a coverup so easy for anyone pulling the strings. "But it's a huge job. It could take months to unravel. We need to work the data, find out if there are any patterns in what these people were being made to do, see if there are any common threads. It's going to require a huge amount of resources, so if we can share that workload and still be able to maintain our current operations, I think we should.

After all, if this is the number one threat we need to deal with, it doesn't mean it's the only one."

"I'm really not happy with giving this to anyone else, especially not a group who picks up our offcuts." Grant moaned.

"Mo's a decent man," Adam snapped. "He's honest and straight."

"And he walked out on us when the going got tough."

"He found something he could believe in. I'd say that's an admirable trait."

"Admirable? Jesus Christ, Adam, he pinned his hopes on his fairy tale."

"Enough!" Lowri's voice cracked through the room, stopping the two bickering men in their tracks. They both looked at her. "The Brotherhood can play a part, but we will control the flow of information, for now. Mo can liaise with them and us for the time being."

"I don't like it," Grant said. "The Vehm won't like it."

"They won't like a lot of it," Raf chimed in. Why was everyone so intent on undermining her?

"Don't worry." Lowri waved her hand at them. "I'm going to see them next. I'll be the one dealing with the flak from the Vehm. I'm also going to share this with Thea Watts. I want law enforcement to have their say. If we give them the data, combined with the press story, we can secure these sites and save these kids. We've already agreed we don't have the reach, right?" Lowri looked around. No one disagreed. "That's settled then," she added.

Adam stood up. "I'll go prep Mo."

"Thank you, Morgan," Lowri said as Adam left.

His departure was a cue for the others to go, all bar Grant who sat and waited for everyone else to vacate the room. He looked at Lowri, head cocked to one side.

"Are you sure?" he asked.

"No. I think we're being played. Correction, I think we've been played for a very long time."

"What do you mean?"

"Operation Malice. It was our biggest case regarding the world of paedophile rings."

"And we got results, not many, but some. You and I both worked it. We worked it together."

"What if we were lied to?"

"Lied to?"

"What if someone in our ranks, or above us, fed us the wrong information to keep us off the scent. This thing has been going on for so long, we would have found it," Lowri said confidently.

Grant nodded. "We had a great team. If this is true..." He pointed to the tablet that sat in front of him.

"It is true," Lowri cut him off.

"Well, then we should have found it," Grant agreed.

"So, we either missed it, or we were played."

"We don't miss things," Grant said. "I'll get a list of everyone who ever worked that case."

32

"I like it," Jack nodded. "It's the right play."

Taking Ciaran out of the immediate area was the best move for the kid. It kept him out of harm's way. It was also the best move for Jack. It meant he was free, completely, to focus on finding everyone else. Thea would have known that, he could see it in the excited way she told him the news about her plan to let Rankine take Ciaran away.

"Which means we've got a job to do from here on in. Have we got any further with locating where they were holding the rest of the kids? Did your guy check back in with you yet?"

"David, no," Jack replied, which he realised was strange. His former boss was unlikely to leave him out of the loop, whether he had found anything out or not. He reached into his pocket and pulled out his phone. "I should chase him up."

"Do what you've got to," Thea said, sitting down in the chair in his room. It had been a surprise for her to turn up at the B&B. Jack had told her where he was staying, but he hadn't done that as an invitation to pop round uninvited. It hadn't really crossed his mind. He looked at her as he waited for the call to connect. She wasn't looking back but scanning the room, taking in everything, just as he would have done in a new environment. That was something they shared, a need to be prepared wherever they were. A survival instinct that was an innate part of their ego, one that they couldn't stop. Even when he had begun to feel like he was out of the game, just before he took the call from Thea that had led him here, he still had those same base instincts. There was never a moment when some small section of his brain wasn't analysing and computing all the possible scenarios he might face in a room, trying to glean as much information as he could on what was happening around him. He was barely even aware of it, it was just who he was.

The call still hadn't connected. Which was very strange. Then there was a sound, a soft click, almost like a murmur, as the call was switched automatically to another line. Jack said nothing.

"Hello, Jack." The voice that answered wasn't David's, but he knew it all the same.

"Adam?"

"Hey, pal."

"What the hell's going on, man?"

"David was hit, we think, on the way back from you. He's alive, but he's not good."

"Damnit," Jack breathed. "How?"

"An HGV hit his car on the A1. The driver's dead. Heart attack."

"Of course he is," Jack sighed. "Son of a bitch. Is this linked to what I'm doing?"

"Looks that way. I think you've stumbled onto something big. We've uncovered evidence from a government computer that the place your kid came from was just one of many. There's a whole network of facilities up and down the country for these sick fucks to play out their fantasies."

"Jesus Christ. They've been farming them, haven't they?"

"Keeping the pigs in shit, so that they can control them afterwards, get them to vote how they want, turn a blind eye when they want, whatever. They must have decided David was a threat and that he needed taking out."

"I can tell you now, they're going to regret not going for me first. Do you have anything you can give me to get to these fucks?"

"We're sending up Mo. He's working for someone else now, but he discovered the files and sort of fell into our laps."

"He's out of the Regulators?"

"Couple of months after you. Seeing that kid go down, it broke him."

"How is he now?"

"Thriving I'd say. He's going to touch base with you in Leeds, feed you everything he can about the site and personnel you're going to come up against. You're also to pass it on to your CID friend."

"That's fine. Am I getting any backup?"

"Not from us, sorry. I think Lowri would rather keep that separate. I don't think she was too thrilled when I offered to brief you."

"No, she wouldn't be." Jack knew that would have been a massive leap of faith for Lowri to let Adam talk to him. "How is she holding up?"

"She's furious, obviously, but she's channelling it in the right places, as always. She wants these people taken down as much for David as anything else."

"It's on my mind as well," Jack acknowledged. "When is Mo getting up here?"

"Couple of hours. We're just putting everything in place, and then he's on his way."

"Great."

There was a pause.

"How's Laura and the little one?"

"They're good, man, bloody hell, really good."

"Enjoying parenthood?"

"You know what it's like, I could do with a bit more sleep. It's nice being out on missions. I get a bit of peace and quiet."

"I don't miss those days. Sleepless night for a stakeout is far more serene than being screamed at by a baby."

"How are your two? Kat still giving you nightmares?"

"She's trying to help me get over my toxic masculinity."

"So, that's a yes then?"

"In a whole new and alien way, yes. It's helping though. We're closer. Probably helps she's not got a boy on the scene, at least as far as I know."

"And Calum?"

"Same as ever, although he smiled the other day. I didn't ask at what, just nice to see him happy."

"It's the best isn't it?"

"You going to double up?"

"Probably. Laura's in no rush, but I'm sure we'll get there. I'd like to. Sooner, rather than later, you know, just in case it's too late."

Jack knew what Adam meant. There was always the risk in this job that today was the last day. What happened to David made that loom even more clearly right now.

"Do it, pal; you'll be fine."

"Thanks, Jack."

There was an awkward pause as each of them tried to work out how best to close the conversation.

"Stay safe," Jack ordered.

"You too."

There was a click, and the call ended.

"Was that?" Thea looked at him, her head cocked to one side.

"Yeah," Jack raised his eyebrows.

"What happened?"

"You're getting your info from Lowri."

"That's good but you know that's not what I meant."

"They took David out. He's in a coma." Jack still couldn't get his head around that.

"Who did?"

"They don't know yet, but it's got to be someone connected to this."

"I don't get it. How did they make David? Only Lowri and you knew he was coming here. Could she have sold him out?"

"No. Not Lowri, she wouldn't."

"You keep telling me how dangerous she is, that she's solely focused on doing what she believes is right."

"In terms of what's right and wrong, I don't think setting up a system of paedophile rings is ever coming down on the side of right in her eyes."

"Maybe not, but maybe there was something else she was covering up. It just doesn't make sense otherwise."

"The gamekeeper made him." Jack had no option but to confess.

"The gamekeeper?"

"John Braun, gamekeeper for Lord Brier. He was in the stack of photos you showed me. I recognised him from my first visit to the hospital. He was casing the place and got startled when he saw me. I thought he was just another person who double-took when they saw me coming around a corner, but I should have picked up on it at the time."

"You mean you didn't fucking tell me that you IDed someone?"

"No. Sorry."

"Jesus, Jack, everything you ever tell me ends up being a half-truth or just plain bullshit. How the hell am I supposed to trust you now then? It wasn't the job that made you a liar, it's you. You can't tell the truth because you don't trust anyone."

"And you do?"

"This has nothing to do with me." Thea stood and ranted, "Everything you've wanted to know about this case I've told you. So, I don't tell you about me? So what? That's my life and has nothing to do with you. You can't even do that. You close yourself off and wonder why you're here, alone. Everyone and everything walks away from you because you have to do it on your bloody own."

"That's not true!" Jack heard himself shouting now. Thea had hit a nerve there. He wasn't a lone wolf, far from it. "Look at Adam, look at my kids. I put people around me. I just don't want anyone to get hurt."

"Yeah, well, newsflash, you can't stop that, and if it happens, it isn't necessarily your fault. The fucking universe doesn't revolve around your fucking head." Thea's face flashed redder and redder with every word.

"I never said it did."

"You know what, you do your thing, we'll do ours. The right thing, the right way. I'm sorry I ever got you involved in this." Thea was walking out now, storming towards the door.

"Jesus Christ, what would you have done? Arrest him?"

Thea got to the door, stopped, and looked back. Her voice was quieter, stern, firm, but not shouting anymore. "You didn't even ask to find out at the time. Get in my way now, and I'll put you away."

She opened the door and walked out. She didn't bother to close it. Jack didn't follow.

33

Hearing from Jack again had been good, Adam thought, although he would have wished for it to have been under better circumstances. To be able to share just a little bit of what had happened in the last few months of his life had been a relief. He missed his old friend. He hoped genuinely to see him one day again, but for now, it was back to work.

The office was in a state of controlled frenzy as teams up and down the country were briefed for the upcoming operation. Adam would have given anything to be spearheading a task force to rescue some of the children, but he knew they had a far more pressing mission. Get the word to the press. That meant finding a journalist who would be willing to stick his neck out on material that wasn't one-hundred-percent verifiable. Someone who would take Adam's word as golden. Thankfully, Adam knew exactly the person he was looking for.

He sat back down at his workstation opposite Emmie who was busily typing something into her system. Critical, no doubt.

"How did it go?" she inquired without looking up.

"We're a go, as I'm sure you know."

"Can't help but notice," she looked up. "What's our role?"

"We need to deliver the data to a journalist who we can trust to publish it."

"Do you have one in mind?"

"I know a guy who doesn't mind publishing things that others might hold off on. He works at one of the slightly smaller tabloids, but they've still got a good reach."

"What's his name?"

"Nathan Nelmes. I'm going set up a meeting now."

Adam pulled a phone out of his drawer. He saw Emmie leaning over from her desk to look.

"How do you get in touch with him?" she asked keenly.

"Two burner phones. One for me, one for him. I send him a one-word text, which relates to a location; he replies with a code that relates to a time. Only me and him know what each one means."

"Smart," she lowered herself back into her seat. "Am I going to get to come along?"

"Absolutely, be good for you to meet him, although he can be a little bit jumpy. Being a journalist writing stories that tend to target pretty powerful people is a job that has about as limited a lifespan as ours. If he'd been born in plenty of other countries, he'd be dead already."

"I look forward to meeting him."

"Yeah," Adam smirked. "We'll see how you feel afterwards."

Adam's phone rang on the table in front of them. He picked it up and answered it, standing up and walking around the room as he talked.

"Morgan," Adam answered.

"Mr. Morgan. You won't be able to trace this call, and you will keep it one-sided. There is a mole in your office." A man's voice, calm and clear.

"Understood." Adam's mind raced. Who was this? Who were they talking about? More importantly, what did they want?

"We will be arranging transport. Be outside in five minutes." That was the last question answered. A face-to-face chat.

"It'd be helpful if you could just tell me," Adam sat down at his desk. "Busy day this end, babe."

Emmie looked up at him, and Adam raised his eyebrows.

"We won't keep you long," came the breezy reply.

"I bet."

"Outside." No negotiation, just an order. They knew Adam wouldn't be able to turn them down.

"Okay, hun, you're breaking up." The line went dead, but Adam carried on the charade. "Babe, I can't, listen I'm going to call you back." He put the phone down and shook his head. "It never rains, it pours."

"Trouble at home?"

"Don't get married and have kids. The two worlds don't work," Adam said standing. "I'll be right back, cover for me."

"Will do."

Adam checked himself out of the office, made his way down the narrow staircase before finding himself out on the street. He took his phone out, putting it to his ear, just in case anyone was watching, and they were bound to be watching.

The phone rang again. Adam answered. "I'm out," he said harshly, keeping his voice low.

"Head south, second left. An ambulance is waiting."

"Dramatic." Adam hung up and walked south, glancing back up at the office. He was putting himself on the line here. If he was missed, questions would be asked. If he never returned, they might not have an answer.

He reached the corner and turned it. There was the ambulance, twenty yards away. The back door swung open. He saw no one inside. He clambered up the step, sitting down on the stretcher and waiting. The windows of the ambulance were glazed to let light in but to obscure the view. Through it, he saw a shadow pass, then the door was closed. Seconds later, they were off.

34

Mo hadn't been to Leeds before. He had family who had been in Bradford for a while, aunts and uncles of some slight separation, but he had never visited them. So, this was, as far as he could recollect, his first trip north to Yorkshire. As the helicopter circled in over the city, heading towards the airport, he was able to watch it unfold beneath him as they headed northwest towards their landing site. The two Headingly Stadiums, which were used for cricket and rugby, were obvious, followed by the university as the clutter of the city began to give way to the suburbs. Finally, they were out of the city, touching down at a helipad just north of the town of Guiseley.

Within minutes he had been ushered to a waiting car, where silent men had driven him back the way the helicopter had come, returning him into the heart of the city, just as the sun began to set. He had been briefed already on what to expect, so there was no need to talk to anyone.

The car pulled up at the designated time in the carpark of Kirkstall Abbey. Night had fallen on their journey, and they were in darkness. The door was opened, and Mo got out. No one spoke to say goodbye or to check that there was anyone there to meet him. The door was shut, the car drove away, and Mo was left outside the abbey.

For a moment he wondered if there was anyone there at all. Then he heard a familiar voice.

"Mo."

Jack approached from the treeline opposite the abbey, emerging from the shadows, grinning. It was the happiest Mo had ever seen Jack look, so he smiled in return.

"Bloody hell never thought I'd see this day," Mo remarked on their reuniting.

Jack clasped his hand and shook it. "Me neither. Good to see you."

"You too."

"We need to get you to your people first, then we can make plans to go."

"Plans? To go where?"

"I want to check out a place."

"What place?"

"I think it's where they've got the kids," Jack said grimly.

"They have a plan you know, the Regulators. They're going to the papers."

"We're not Regulators, Mo. Besides I just want to keep an eye on it. I need to make sure no one does anything stupid."

"Bloody hell, Jack. Come on, man, let the professionals handle it. You're just one man on your own."

"True," Jack agreed. "You can come help me."

Jack had a car with him, and the two of them drove on into the centre, down Kirkstall Road, then turned off towards the area of Woodhouse. It was there that the Brotherhood had a safe house which Mo needed to visit and report back his findings. Again, the drive took place in near silence. Mo felt nervous around Jack. It brought back a lot of memories of the life he had left behind with the Regulators, as it had when he had seen Adam.

The difference, however, was that there was an easiness about Adam that wasn't always reflected in Jack. Jack had always been a man committed to the mission, right up until the last days of his time there, before things had started to change. It had been a subtle shift, but one Mo had noticed all the same. Now, though, he seemed different again. Focused, but free to do as he pleased.

"I know they know I'm coming, but all the same, it's probably best if you drop me off a street or two away," Mo said. "I think you going near the property with me might set off some alarm bells. We don't want to spook anyone anywhere."

Jack nodded. "Sounds sensible."

The car pulled up in a carpark not far from the safehouse, and Mo got out.

"I'll hang here," Jack said. "Hopefully shouldn't raise too much suspicion. If you're not back in an hour, I'll come knocking."

"Hopefully, I'll be much quicker than that. Drop this off, bring everyone up to speed and get the tactical lowdown.",

"Great, see you shortly."

Mo closed the door and walked out of the car park. It was dark now, but behind him lay a row of warehouses and a TV studio. That meant there were plenty of people around. Easier to blend in. He crossed a busy road which was lined with takeaways, sandwich shops, and other small businesses, then headed off onto a side street, up a steep hill flanked with traditional red brick terraced houses. He turned left once more, following an alleyway that ran between the rear gardens of two streets. It was deserted, and he counted the gates till he got to the one he wanted, all the while remembering his approach to the house in London and how that had ended. The sacrifices that had been made already for this were huge. They had to make sure that they pulled this off. Those people couldn't have died for nothing, those kids had to be freed.

There was a buzzer attached to a camera next to the gate. He pressed it and waited. A buzz and a click as the gate opened. No one asking who he was. This was clearly the right place. He pushed the gate open and walked in.

It wasn't too dissimilar to the scene that had greeted him when he had arrived in London. There was a small concrete courtyard that sat between the house and the back gate. A wall reaching to the ceiling of the ground floor rose all around it, whilst netting had been put over the top to ensure anyone looking in would have a hard time seeing anything. The house lay in front. A window would have once allowed him to see into the house, but that now had metal casing around it, the type used when a house was abandoned. The door to the house still worked, however. It was open, a man's face peering out at him.

"Come," the man ordered, and Mo followed.

It all felt so similar as he stepped into the house. Again, there was the same activity going on as he had seen in London. People working hard, glancing at the new face in their midst, briefly, with only what felt like mild suspicion, before returning to their tasks. This time he was taken up the stairs into what would have been the master bedroom, but now had three computers on three desks at which three men sat, one at each desk.

"Mo is here," said Mo's guide before turning and leaving.

One of the men stood up and walked towards Mo.

"Kasim Husseini." He thrust forward a hand and smiled.

"Moeen Younis," Mo replied shaking Kasim's hand.

"You've done very well, Mo, getting the files and getting to us."

"Oh, yes, of course." Mo grasped in his pocket and pulled out a small USB drive and passed it to Kasim.

"Wonderful," Kasim beamed. "I trust our new allies have their copies."

"They do, the police will shortly. It is all set, tonight they will be releasing the material to the press."

"Allahu Akbar, then the infidels who have committed these sins shall be punished in this life as in the next. A glorious day." Kasim smiled broadly. He sounded genuinely pleased like he had just been given news about a wedding or some other joyful occasion.

"Thank you. The man that I met here, he wants to go to the location, to keep an eye on things."

"We had a similar thought. We have our mujahideen assembling now and will be ready in an hour or so. In the meantime, I think you and your former friend should scout the location and report back to us any hostile activity."

"You want me to go in?"

"Moeen, you have led us bravely already. Now you will continue to do so on the front."

"You mean, you need someone to keep an eye on Jack."

"We have new allies, this is true. At some point perhaps, we will trust each other in the fullest possible sense, as we trust our own. It is a process."

"I understand." Mo nodded, and he really did. There was a real sense of paranoia for all of these groups, which served to keep them going.

"Check in with us if the situation changes. We will contact you nearer the time, to confirm the tactical layout for the operation. Here." Kasim passed Mo a mobile phone. "It's a burner which we will use now. There is a secure link app on there. You know the drill."

Mo did indeed. He took the phone, pocketing it.

"This morning," Mo began, feeling he needed to say something about why he had escaped the explosion. Kasim stopped him.

"Those that were martyred today will not have died in vain. We will continue their work in the name of their glory."

Mo said nothing, just nodded. Kasim put a hand on his shoulder and looked at him, smiling kindly. "They gave their lives so we could finish this. Without that, we would not be here now. That is what they lived for, that is what they died for."

Mo felt like telling Kasim that whilst he understood the concept, it didn't help make it any easier; but for now, he decided, that sort of philosophical debate could wait. "Thank you," was his reply.

Kasim seemed satisfied. "We will give you weapons, to protect yourself, and then you can go. Imran will supply you."

One of the other men stood and walked over.

"I will see you at the farmhouse. Allahu Akbar."

"Allahu Akbar."

Loaded with weapons and a host of information on his phone, Mo made his way back to the car, all the time nervous about the guns he carried in the backpack he had just been given. He feared that, at any time, some patrolling police officer might decide he wanted to see what he was carrying. He knew he looked suspicious. He certainly felt it, and what was it that all these cops on TV shows said? That they could spot someone acting suspiciously? He might as well have been brandishing a gun. But he saw no officer and made it back safe.

When he reached the car, he decided to place them in the boot, just to ease his own mind. They were travelling after all, what good would they be?

"Did it go okay?" Jack asked as Mo sat down in the passenger seat.

"They're happy for us to scout the location first. They're putting together their own team. They'll be about an hour behind."

"That works for me. Have we got a muster point?"

"Yeah." Kasim had programmed some coordinates into Mo's phone, prior to handing it over to him, and Mo brought them up on the map screen.

"No problem," Jack said. "It'll take us about an hour to get there."

"They should be just mobilising by then," Mo reported.

"Then we best get cracking. If you want to get some sleep, be my guest. I reckon you've had a long day."

"Thanks, Jack," Mo said. He didn't think he'd be able to get much rest, but the offer was welcome all the same.

He was wrong, however. He lay his head against the window of the car, felt the vibrations as it started up, then drifted off into slumber.

35

Never before in her professional career – hell, never before in her entire life – had Lowri ever felt so split by what she wanted to do and what she ought to do.

Being in the field office hadn't helped her. It seemed to be constant, a never-ending barrage of questions fired her way, or conversations she was half hearing. How had she never noticed the din before? How could anyone work in this?

In the end, she had sought solace in one of the meeting rooms, pulling the heavy glass door behind her and immediately enjoying the silence that followed. She had taken her laptop, her tablet, and she had been able to work, all the time maintaining a live feed to David's hospital room, his vitals displaying just below the video, just in case he woke up, or just in case he never could. Whatever happened, she had to know. This was her fault after all. That was the thing that was keeping her here and not sending her back to David's side. She had caused this. She had to fix it.

The starting point for her investigation had been the Armenian. It had been pretty clear early on that he had been a clean skin. Someone who had been picked for his vulnerability, the ease at which they could manipulate him. She would have seen him as an ideal mark as well. That was why she knew she was going to find them and beat them, because she thought like them. Only, she was better.

There were two things that Lowri wanted to find out more about. First was the camera blackout at the truck stop. That bothered her. That was clearly where the contact had been made with the driver. Again, it was a tactic she would have employed, catch someone in the moment, give them no time to back out.

There was something bugging Lowri about it all though. How could they have possibly known that the accident would have been bad enough to put David out of play. How could they have guaranteed that the Armenian would have even hit the right car? He wouldn't know who David was, and trying to spot what car was coming behind him, at night, was nigh on impossible. That meant there was a spotter. But where?

Witnesses on the scene hadn't spoken about anyone else at the crash scene, which meant that whoever was guiding the Armenian had been in a follow car, either behind the lorry or tailing David. David would have been aware of anyone tailing him for too long, but the A1 was a long, straight road that ran up the spine of the country, so someone being behind his car for a while would seem routine. David would have been employing some sort of tactic to root out a tail, speeding up and slowing down perhaps, but it would be more than possible for a follow car not to be spotted.

Traffic cameras had picked up a number of cars that could have been the one. At first, Lowri had looked for a car that had driven on past the scene of the crash, but no car had. That meant whoever was behind it had stopped. There were probably two reasons for that. One would be to ensure that no suspicion would have been directed towards the car. The other would be to ensure that there was no evidence of the plan. That meant both taking care of the driver, if he hadn't already been eliminated, and making sure that any signs of the communication device they had used was also cleaned up. Which meant that when the police arrived, they must have made a statement.

None of that explained how they had known David would be there, that was still the biggest mystery of all, but Lowri knew there were two threads that she wanted to pull at. She knew that would lead her to that answer at some point.

There was a knock at the door. Raf peered through tentatively.

"You said you wanted to be kept abreast of any updates?" he offered an explanation for the intrusion.

"Good ones?"

"Morgan has Nathan Nelmes onboard. Story should be live when we're ready."

"Good. Anything else?"

"Mo and Jack met with the Brotherhood and have now headed to a potential location. Looks like they've gone dark."

Lowri let that mull over. It wasn't completely unreasonable, for Jack had to do his own thing. But it did fit a pattern. What if he was the one who had betrayed David?

"Thank you," she replied coolly. Raf nodded and backed out the door, shutting it as he went.

That was a possibility of course. Jack Quinn would feel he had every right to be angry at the way he was treated. Lowri saw it differently. He had disobeyed an order and let a material witness go while she attempted to uncover who was behind an attempted detonation of a nuclear weapon in London. They had managed to stop the bomb, but the perpetrators of the plot remained at large, and at some point, they would be back. Jack might feel hard done to. Lowri felt he was lucky to still have his freedom, but she wasn't so dogmatic that she couldn't see where he would begin to put together a feeling of discontent that could lead him to turn on his former masters.

David and Jack though, that was a friendship. There were somethings that Jack Quinn was and somethings that he wasn't, and someone who would turn on friends? No, even Lowri didn't believe it. She would never discount it, but it had to remain near the bottom of her list of probabilities.

She looked at the computer screen again, a video now from the service station carpark, looking to see if she could make a match between the cars on the road and the cars that had stopped at the crash site. She didn't expect to. These people were professionals. Anything like that would have been too sloppy.

There was an answer though, somewhere in that service station, someone would have seen who the Armenian spoke to. She looked at the pictures once more. It was predominantly a truck stop, somewhere for long-distance lorry drivers to get a good night's rest. She picked up her phone.

"Raf," she said as it was answered. "Get me a chopper. I need to get to the crash site."

Most lorries these days had dash cams. There was a chance, a slim one, that someone would have captured something, and Lowri needed to go and check. While she was up there, she would also visit the officers who attended the crash. With a little bit of luck, she might be able to start putting this puzzle together.

36

"Shit!"

Jack saw Mo jolt out of his sleep, grabbing at the panels of the door and dashboard for security as the car pitched violently on the uneven track.

"What's happening?" a panicked Mo asked.

"We've been ambushed." Jack tried to keep the control in his voice. He didn't need Mo to freak out completely. That said, they had been ambushed, and that was bad.

The drive to the location for the stakeout had been completely routine until just after he turned down a dirt track that led to a copse where he hoped to conceal the car. The lights had been dimmed, and Jack edged the car along carefully, when the car had been bathed in the floodlights from two Land Rovers, one parked on either side of the road, obscured from view by the hedgerows, draped in camouflage netting and hidden further by the darkness.

The rear window crashed in behind them as a shot rang out from the lead chasing Land Rover.

"They're shooting at us!" Mo shouted.

Jack said nothing. He had to concentrate now on getting off this dirt track and onto something firmer. The saloon car they were in was a four-wheel drive, but alongside the Land Rovers, it was simply outmatched on the rough terrain.

The first Land Rover crunched into the back of their car, kicking the back end out to the left. Jack took his foot instantly off the accelerator, locking the wheel to correct the skid before quickly whipping it back and straightening it up. The driver of the

Land Rover knew he had the advantage and was looking to push it home.

"Can you fire back?" Jack asked Mo.

"I left all the guns in the boot."

"Shit." That wasn't good. They had to get off the track.

The road veered right. Jack's heart sank. The track widened but remained a bumpy dirt road, and worse, edged up a steep incline. Clearly a passing place, designed to allow farm vehicles both turning clearance and the chance to get past each other.

The Land Rover behind had known it was coming – Jack had seen them switch to the outside but didn't register why until it was too late. The Land Rover darted for the inside of the corner. Jack tried to counter, steering hard to the right, but the tyres bounced and struggled to find the necessary grip on the uneven road. The Land Rover was already on its way past as Jack's saloon clipped it. The Land Rover bounced, the rear left wheel coming up and then back down on the bonnet of the car, digging it further down in the ground, before coming to a rest immediately in front of the saloon. The second Land Rover pulled up behind.

Trapped.

"Damnit," Jack seethed.

"What do we do?" Mo asked.

It was a good question. Jack half expected a hail of bullets. The Land Rovers were high enough that if the shooters were smart, they could eliminate the risk of shooting each other, but nothing came. Instead, the passenger of the lead Land Rover leaned out of his window, a sawn-off shotgun trained on the front window of the car. From the other side, the driver approached, another sawn off, pointed always at Jack.

Jack glanced in the rear-view mirror. Both occupants of the second Land Rover were out now, guns trained on the car, one going each way around.

"Comply." Jack analysed and assessed the situation quickly. "It's our best shot at walking away. We're not dying here, so let's wait for a better opening."

Mo's mouth hung open a little bit. He said nothing, didn't nod, didn't shake his head, but Jack knew he understood. He raised his hands, and Mo did the same.

"Out of the car," the driver of the first Land Rover barked in a thick Yorkshire accent.

Jack slowly slipped his hand to the door and opened it, Mo following suit on the other side. They both stepped out of the car together, Jack now looking at each man trying to identify him. None of them were John Braun. They knew they were coming then, but they didn't know exactly where.

"Hands on heads." The leader continued to bark his orders. Jack and Mo continued to comply.

The two from the following Land Rover now approached them. One towards Mo and one towards Jack. Jack felt the man behind him pull his arms down in front of him, then place a sturdy and thick cable tie on his wrists before pulling it tight.

"In." The leader barked more orders as Jack was pushed forward by the man behind him, heading to the first Land Rover. He looked over and saw that Mo was being moved towards the rear one. Hopefully, they would both end up in the same place. It was unlikely that they had two facilities for holding people out here, but not something that could be ruled out entirely.

Jack placed his foot onto the step at the back of the Land Rover and pushed himself up, stooping as he got in. Inside there were two bench seats, one down either length of the rear cabin, facing each other. Up front, behind a wire mesh, was the cab. The door closed behind him with a decisive slam, and he heard the sound of bolts being pulled across.

He sat down, watched the driver enter and waited to see their next destination so that he could plan his escape.

The Land Rovers drove in convoy, leaving the saloon car behind, heading up the dirt track, bouncing Jack up and down. He tried to remember what he had seen from the map of the area. He knew there were a number of farm buildings, barns, and stores up ahead, one of which would likely be their final destination. Keeping track of the time in his head and monitoring the speed of the traffic, he hoped to have a rough idea of where they ended up, whenever they reached it.

The drive took less than five minutes, which meant that they were probably in Craggan's Farm, a dairy farm according to the records he had seen of the area. Lots of outbuildings, all of which could probably double up as a cell, well away from anyone else. Not a great start, but at least he had a rough idea where he was.

The door opened again, and he was helped unceremoniously out of the Land Rover. He saw the second one pulled up just a short way off, next to another building, but there was no activity there. The driver and passenger sat in the cab waiting. They didn't want him to see where they were going. A disappointing development.

The two men from his Land Rover grabbed him firmly, one on each arm, frog-marching him towards a large brick building with a thick wooden door. It was unlocked, the first man opening it with his shoulder as they approached, then they were inside, walking through the grey bricked corridors, hearing the sound of machinery in the distance, the smell of animals and manure unmistakable. The milking shed, most likely.

They came to a row of four metal-barred doors leading to concrete pens. They stopped outside the first one, as the first man took a key from his pocket and unlocked the door, before they all stepped inside.

On the roof was a hook, from which a metal chain dangled down. Jack was shoved unceremoniously under it.

"Up," the lead man ordered.

Jack looked up at the hook.

"Make me."

The second man, now stood behind him, kicked him in the back of the knee, hard, forcing him down on one leg.

"That's not helping," Jack said looking back over his shoulder.

The first man stepped forward, grabbing hold of the plastic cable tie that held Jack's wrists together, pulling him up hard by it. Jack obliged, but as he reached eye level, he unleashed a powerful headbutt on the first man, catching him square between the eyes.

The first man's eyes widened slightly, and his head rolled back, sharply at first, then hung in position as he blacked

222

out, his body crumpling like a sagging accordion to the floor. The second man barely had time to register what was happening before Jack was spinning. A double-handed clubbing blow landed centre of the man's chest, winding him, before a second blow, this time upwards into his jaw as the man started to double over, the meeting of the two intensified by their opposite motions. He went down like his partner, and Jack crouched alone over the two of them.

He waited for a moment. The sound of machinery drowned out almost everything else, aside from the odd moo of a cow somewhere in the yard. He searched the first man for the Land Rover keys, finding them in a pocket, as well as a knife, which he used to quickly cut the plastic cable tie.

He stood up, keeping the knife out, lamenting the fact that he didn't have the guns they had left in the Land Rover. Still, at least now he was armed. He walked cautiously to the door, checking the corridor. Clear.

Slowly he made his way back through the grey brick corridor, all the time scanning his surroundings, not only for anyone that might discover him but for some indication of where Mo was. He desperately didn't want to leave without him. Mo was or, at least, always had been, an analyst. He wasn't built for imprisonment and torture.

No one came down the corridor. The sound of machinery continued to hum around him as he made it back to the door that led to the yard. There were two more Land Rovers parked outside now. Which meant more bad guys. A doubling of the number perhaps. Still, not bad odds.

Jack knew he had to move fast. Whoever had arrived would be checking in on Mo, then checking in on Jack. They wanted them alive for something, which meant they were going to need to ask questions. They wouldn't be hanging around to do answer any.

Opposite him was a farmhouse. There were lights on in the building that Jack didn't recall seeing before. He bent down and crept towards the first Land Rover quickly, pressing himself up against the wheel arch and peering over the bonnet of the vehicle, through the gloom, checking that no one had spotted his progress.

All clear.

Jack was about to make his way to the next Land Rover when he saw something. Someone was walking through the farmhouse; he saw a shadow, nothing more. He lowered himself down, pressing himself closer to the Land Rover. He waited.

The door opened.

"Jack Quinn."

"Shit," he murmured to himself.

"Jack Quinn," the shout came again. "If you want your friend to live beyond the next ten seconds, I need you to make yourself known."

Had they seen him on some hidden camera? Had one of the men he'd incapacitated come to already? It didn't matter; the game was up. Even if he ignored the shout and left Mo to whatever fate awaited him, there was little chance now of making it out of the yard unnoticed. It could only be a matter of time before he was flanked, captured, or worse.

"I'm here!" he called, raising his hands above his head and stepping out from behind the Land Rover. He saw three figures standing just outside the door, illuminated from behind by the light from the house. One would be Mo. He was being held by another figure, this one with a gun pressed firmly against Mo's temple. The other was stood just slightly off, a little thinner than his colleague, a little taller, arms on hips, waiting. The person who had done the shouting. Jack couldn't make out his features, but he knew that the figure was looking directly at him. It had to be John Braun

"Walk out into the middle of the yard, then cross your legs, kneel down with your hands on your head, fingers interlocked," barked the figure.

"Don't do it, Jack!" Mo shouted, quickly taking a forearm to the back of the head from the man holding the gun. It wasn't a brutal blow, but a firm reminder.

Jack couldn't have backed out anyway. He was exposed completely now. He saw two more men coming through the door. Braun nodded towards Jack, and they both moved towards him, splitting off and circling him, taking no chances.

Jack waited for them to grab him and lift him up, but all that came was a powerful hit to his head, and he slumped forward into the mud, blackness enveloping him.

37

Thea watched the car carrying Ciaran, Rankine, and Rankine's wife as it pulled away, towing the modest looking caravan behind it, heading down the B-Road they had selected for its almost total isolation from the rest of the world.

It was the dead of night, and Ciaran had been bordering on sleep when they set off, fighting it as best as his ever-strengthening body could. He was excited for his first ever "holiday," the bond with Rankine strengthening with each and every moment they spent in each other's company. He was still cautious and reserved with everyone else. Maybe it was the food that Rankine always brought, Thea wondered. Whatever it was, it was working.

"I can go live with these people?" he had asked when Thea had told him the news.

"We'll see," she had replied, trying to cool his eagerness somewhat, but she had been buoyed by his enthusiastic reaction after her earlier argument with Jack.

That argument still bothered her. She had brought Jack in to help her, not to hide things from her. She knew she couldn't trust her own people. She thought that out of anyone, Jack would understand that feeling best of all, but he had done exactly the same. As Rankine drove off, she truly felt alone.

She got back into her car and started the short drive back to Malton. It was time to find out more about Mr. Braun, perhaps even pay him a visit. First, though, she needed to work out what was in store for her if she did. Rankine hadn't known much about Braun, other than he had a shotgun licence and worked for Lord

Brier. Nothing new. That meant going back to doing it the old-fashioned way.

There was no one around in the office when she returned, which was what she had been hoping for. Maybe they were out on a call, maybe they were out getting a late-night feed. It didn't matter, they were out.

Thea picked up a folder that had been left on her desk. She had asked one of the desk sergeants to dig up what he could on Braun. It wasn't much at all. A driver's licence, firearm licence, no convictions. A clean skin, which would be why he had been chosen. A further request to the military had been put in but was unlikely to find out anything interesting, but she did have one thing to go on. An address.

There was no point requesting a warrant at this time of night. It wouldn't happen anywhere quick enough for her to move, especially as she knew Jack was up to something. She had to get there first, not for personal pride, but to make sure this went down right. Right now, though, she had no smoking gun. Without that, she couldn't call on Wilkes to put the rest of the force behind it. She hoped the address would provide something.

As she walked back to her car, she wondered what her choices were? She could wait till dawn, but that ran the risk of turning up far too late. She could call someone. Briefly, she thought about calling Wilkes, but not knowing who she could trust meant that she could simply be putting herself in an even more compromised position.

No, Thea would go it alone.

Half-an-hour's drive later, she was at the address. It was a small house out in the middle of the Moors, standing on its own, surrounded by trees, part of the larger estate of Lord Brier. Thea assumed that it had probably been a gamekeeper's cottage since the day it had been built. It was the perfect spot for it after all. Deep in the heart of the estate, bordered by countryside. Secluded. Which made it all the more dangerous for Thea to be going in alone, but yet, here she was.

Approaching with lights off, she pulled over on the driveway a good hundred yards from the house. Already she could see there were no lights on. Either Braun was asleep, or he wasn't there. Given his role, either was possible, and both had their significant downsides when it came Thea being at the house.

The walk to the house seemed to take forever as Thea did her best to approach quietly. The ground was uneven and covered in debris from the plants in the area. Each step on a twig seemed to send an almighty crack echoing through the woodland, making Thea cringe and pause. Each time no one came. There were no movements from the house. The woods around her fell quiet again, and she carried on towards the house.

The house itself was made out of an assortment of different sized and coloured bricks, no doubt a factor of the time it had been built in. She could barely make out the colours in the gloom, but there were different shades of grey, some dark, some light. The pointing was wearing away, and it made the house look tired and uninviting. Not that Thea ever expected to be welcomed in.

Around the house was a low wooden fence, a couple of feet high, with a rickety gate that Thea was sure would make plenty of noise should she use it, so she opted to step over the fence and into what looked like a pretty poorly tended vegetable patch.

Still, no one came from the house.

Thea kept moving. It was twenty feet from the edge of the garden to the wall of the house, and she picked her way across the uneven earth as quickly as she dare. She jumped the last couple of yards, landing against the wall, freezing there for a moment, awaiting detection, feeling her heart beating.

No one came. All around her was silent and dark. She moved along the wall towards the door, creeping underneath the window to the kitchen. Once past it, she stopped, stood and peered tentatively inside. Darkness, no movement. She moved towards the door again.

She turned the handle slowly until she felt the expected resistance of the lock. Again, more waiting, just to make sure that every little move hadn't alerted someone. If it had, they were playing the long game and waiting for her to come to them.

She took the electric lockpick from her pocket and slipped it over the lock. There was the faintest hum as the machine did its work, but to Thea, it sounded deafening, echoing off every tree, wall, whatever.

The lock clicked, and still, no one came.

Thea pushed against the door, and it opened. Surely if someone was inside, they'd have dead-bolted the door, she reasoned. It seemed like good logic. No one was here, she reassured herself.

The door opened into a kitchen. In the darkness, she couldn't make much out. On her left side, she could see worktops, a sink and the shape of an Aga cooker. In the middle of the room was a small table, square, wooden, with just one chair placed at it. There was an old fridge on her right and a few cupboards. She moved left and into the house.

The other room downstairs was the living room. Again, it was empty. A small TV, the old type, small and unassuming with a bulbous back, sat in the corner, opposite a leather lounger. A small coffee table sat just to the side of the lounger. All set up perfectly for one person. One person on their own.

She made her way to the foot of the stairs, casting a glance upwards. Still no movement, but now there was definitely something. There was definitely light. She hadn't seen it from outside, which meant that either it had come on since she entered the house, or that it was behind a blackout blind. She hoped it was the latter.

There was no other way up but the stairs. It put her in a bad spot if someone was to appear, be it at the top or bottom of the staircase now, but what choice did she have? She needed to find something, anything, that could act as the smoking gun and allow her to get the backing of the rest of her force.

She made it to the top of the stairs. Still, no one came. The light was brighter now, shining from her right as she reached the landing. She eased her head forward, spying an open door. The light came from inside the room. She stepped out onto the landing, with every step praying not to find too squeaky a floorboard, to put too much pressure in the wrong place.

Making it to the door, she felt a sense of relief, as if she had crossed the line of some horrific obstacle course. She looked into the room. Still no one there. The light came from a bank of small TV monitors, CCTV screens, with black and white pictures showing a host of cameras each one showing a feed from a different room in some other building.

On one, she saw a room with a number of small mattresses lined on the floor, thin and sickly-looking children huddling together, lying on them, asleep, or trying to sleep. Their clothes were tattered, and there were bruises and cuts clearly visible on many of them.

Thea took her phone out, switching to camera mode and filming the scene in front of her. This was it. This was the proof she needed. If only she could work out where these cameras were feeding their footage from.

She scanned each screen individually, looking for something, anything that would lead her to the scene, to the place where these kids were being held, but there was nothing. All the shots were inside, there were no windows, nothing that stood out to her.

She kept scanning.

There it was. A yard at a farm. Finally, something outside. She counted three Land Rovers in the shot, noting down the registration plate of the one that she could make out, filming everything on her phone. Every single piece of information mattered.

She noted the positioning of the buildings, working out a bird's eye view in her head, something that she would be able to cross-reference on a map to work out where she needed to be. Then she kept scanning. More shots of the outside of a farm it seemed. A dairy farm it appeared, she saw cows in the background in a shed.

Then she stopped.

She saw Jack, stripped naked, hanging by his wrists from a metal hook.

38

Jack shook his head as he came too. It throbbed, and he could feel his heart pulsing across the back of his skull where the blow had landed. It hurt. It was going to hurt for a while. No use dwelling on it.

His arms hurt too. Already he could feel the pain in his wrists where the cuffs that held him upright had cut into his skin as his limp body dangled uselessly. His feet stumbled on the ground, struggling to find a purchase on the floor as his toes slipped, his heels unable to reach all the way down to the ground, putting more pressure on his wrists. There would be no respite for them.

The room was the one he had been taken to before. Cold stone walls surrounded him, and the stench of the dairy farm helped bring him to his senses even quicker. There was a wooden chair in the room, just off to the side, next to the metal-barred door that was now closed and no doubt locked. He looked up at the meal hook. It looked like it was sturdily attached to the roof, but he knew he would regret not finding out. Reaching his hands up, he grabbed the chains and pulled, driving all of his weight downwards, hoping that some lapse in concentration by a workman would come to his aid. It didn't. The hook and chains remained in place.

"Fuck it," he grunted. The physical approach wasn't going to work. No matter how much effort he exerted, he was staying put. He needed to save his energy for when an opening arrived.

His thoughts moved on to what had happened to Mo. Separation meant that they were likely to be questioning them about something, but what? If it was the location of the boy, Ciaran, then Jack felt desperately sorry for Mo. These weren't the sort of guys that were going to take no for an answer, but there was no answer Mo could give them to that question. They would keep asking until they could ask no more. On the other hand, if it was a question that Mo knew the answer to, he might be able to minimise his suffering, but only at the expense of jeopardising the mission. That would be a better outcome for Mo, a quicker death, perhaps even a stay of execution, a chance for them to fashion an escape. If Mo could find a way to smart talk himself into that situation, then perhaps there was a chance this could all pan out for the best.

For now, though, all Jack could do was wait.

He counted the minutes in his head, trying to keep his mind clear and focused. Just shy of twenty minutes, he heard the sound of footsteps in the corridor. They grew louder as whoever was coming got closer. Not one person, a host of them. Three, maybe four, and someone stumbling, the sound of scuffing footwear on the hard floor just about audible between the slaps of more steady feet that surrounded them.

They stopped just outside the barred door, and Jack saw them. Braun stood at the front. On each side were two of the men from the Land Rovers, the two passengers. They flanked Mo, who they were having to prop up, each one clasping an arm as Mo sagged between them, his head bobbing as he struggled to remain conscious. They'd given him one hell of a beating. Braun unlocked the gate, stepped in, and then to the side, letting the others in. Jack fixed his gaze on Braun's, doing all he could to blot out that last remnant of pain in the back of his head, fixating on his target, waiting for his opportunity.

The two men took Mo and half-placed, half-dropped him on the wooden chair, one of them stepping behind and pulling Mo's arms around the frame of the chair, taking a pair of handcuffs from his back trouser pocket, locking Mo in place. Braun watched all this, saying nothing.

Jack looked at Mo. His face was bloodied and battered, and a collection of cuts and bruises were forming over his exposed torso. They'd done a number on him, and they'd done it quickly. They were clearly after something fast. Had Mo given it to them? Unlikely. Mo was still alive, and so was he. If they had everything they needed, their captives would be expendable, and it was unlikely that Braun was going to run the risk of them escaping again if he could help it.

Braun stepped forward as the two men from the Land Rover skulked back, taking their places, one either side of the door. Braun looked at Mo, then at Jack. He sighed.

"I really, really thought that young Moeen here would be the weaker of the two," he lamented.

Jack smiled an invisible smile. Mo had said nothing. It didn't matter whether he knew it or not, he had made them believe like he might. He had made them decide to keep him alive, at least for now. Jack was impressed.

"Apparently, however, he stood up to the rigours of what we did to him. I admit, I would have liked a bit more time.

Extracting information is an art form and, done right, it always gets results."

"Not always," Jack countered.

Braun looked up from Mo, casting his eyes up and down Jack. He turned his body completely and walked towards where he hung in situ.

"No, perhaps not," he said coldly, reaching his hand out to touch a scar on Jack's arm. It was one he had received in a fight with a mercenary in Sierra Leone many moons ago, having been thrown against the branch of a rather unforgiving and sturdy tree. It had hurt like hell, but ultimately provided him with the weapon which he had used to beat his foe that day. It certainly wasn't a scar he had received due to torture, but there were plenty more he had. Braun started to circle him, and Jack knew he was taking in every little wound and marker, each one telling a tale of a moment, or sustained moments, of pain and injury and suffering that Jack had gone through. He had been tortured before, and he hadn't talked. He could deal with pain, and he wasn't afraid of dying.

"You've been asked questions before, I assume, Mr. Quinn?"

"Once or twice. People don't always like the answers I give though."

"I can see that," Braun reached out and touched another scar, this one a large gash along Jack's back. That was from someone asking "questions." A Moroccan people-smuggler who wanted to know where the crew of one his boats had gone. He had received his answer, finally, when Jack had buried him at sea at roughly the same spot where he had sunk the boat, crew and all. Braun went on, "The problem is, I need to like the answer, so I need to have you motivated."

Jack said nothing.

"Do you know what we did to your friend?"

Jack looked at Mo. He could make a pretty good guess.

"We beat him. At first with our hands, then with a cosh. Then we asked him some questions. You need to soften people up, let them know that you're in control, that there's no choice but to tell the truth, because trying to lie, trying to find a quick way out with bullshit doesn't land you anywhere. It just gets you hurt even more. So, we beat him and then we talked for a while. Then when he didn't cooperate, we beat him some more. We expected to do that for a while, but we did think he would crack. Our intelligence on him had him down as something of a soft target. You know there's nothing more frustrating than out-of-date intelligence."

Jack said nothing.

"We always believed that Mo's weakness lay in his need for self-preservation. We told him that we would stop if he talked. He didn't talk, so we didn't stop. We beat him and beat him and beat him till he blacked out. Then we woke him up, beat him some more, then asked some more questions. Still nothing." Braun's voice went up with a flourish at the end of the sentence as he spun around to face Jack.

Jack said nothing.

Braun paced forward as he spoke. "Everybody has a weakness, everybody has something that makes them want to talk. We thought we knew Mo's. We thought that he would tell us everything if we beat him to a pulp. We were wrong about Mo's weakness, but my god, I know, I am sure, I am absolutely positive that I am not wrong about yours."

Jack said nothing.

"You, Jack Quinn. You're here to save the world. You're here to protect people, keep them from danger, make sure that you right the wrongs of this world. I mean, why else would you be here, unless it's because, of course, you want to fuck that pretty little police officer? Personally, I wouldn't blame you, maybe it's a little bit of both, but we know that you don't think with your dick." Braun's hand reached out and flicked at Jack's penis, making him jerk backwards.

Jack said nothing.

"No, you think with your heart. Your big, soft, beating heart. It drives you to put your life on the line for others, to sacrifice yourself for all others. It's the noblest of causes and all that other bullshit, but it's also your greatest weakness. Which is what I'm going to guess everyone who has ever tortured you before has never ever cottoned on to."

Jack said nothing.

But he didn't like where this was going.

"You, Jack Quinn, are going to be asked a question soon and I am going to get my answer, and you better pray that it's the right answer because, if not, you will sit here and watch your friend die."

No sooner had the words come out of Braun's mouth, he was spinning around on the spot, unsheathing a knife as he did so, plunging it deep into Mo's stomach.

"NO!" Jack bellowed as Mo screamed in agony, his eyes opening, his body lurching backwards, hauled cruelly from the precipice of unconsciousness back into the world by the blade that protruded from his gut.

"That wound." Braun was pacing forward at Jack once more, the knife left in Mo. He put his face into Jack's, who strained at his chains trying to reach his tormentor, as he shouted in his face. "That wound is on you. He has hours to live, or he has minutes to live. You will watch him suffer, and then you will tell me what I need to know."

Then Braun turned, once more swiftly, abruptly, and was making his way back towards the door. He stopped and looked over his shoulder at Jack, a cruel smile played out over his lips.

"Almost forgot my knife."

He pulled at it, twisting it slightly as it came out of Mo's stomach. Jack knew he wanted him to see that he tried to make even more damage inside.

"You sick fucking son of a bitch. I swear, I fucking swear, I will kill you. I will fucking kill you."

"No, you will answer my question." Braun turned and walked out of the door, quickly followed by his two henchmen. The door slammed shut, Jack and Mo were alone.

39

The helicopter touched down on a playing field in the small market town of Retford, which lay just north of David's crash site, a short drive from the A1. Lowri hopped out to be met by two uniformed and one plain-clothes officer from the nearby station.

"Ms. Graves?" the plain-clothes officer asked, offering his hand as he battled the downdraft from the slowly decelerating helicopter blades.

"DCI Grigg." Lowri took his hand then showed him her badge. This time it was for the National Fraud Intelligence Bureau. Lowri had a host of fake badges at her disposal to ensure that, if she ever needed to, she could get access to whatever crime scene, whatever information she needed.

"I was a little surprised to get your call," Grigg said, ushering her away from the chopper. "I don't know how we can help you?"

"We've been tracking the movements of a group of sophisticated crash-for-cash scammers for a while," the lie flowed easily for Lowri. "We were hoping we could get to them before something sinister like this happened. Unfortunately, they beat us to the punch, so we want to move fast and ensure that this was them."

"Well, I can certainly provide you with the dash cam footage from our cars. You reckon they guided the driver?"

Lowri had told the team at Retford as much as she dared. She had told them the method by which the crash had been staged, that she felt a follow car had been in place behind the truck and that it had been destined to swerve and hit them, as opposed to the car it did hit.

"That was the plan, but for some reason, he must have hit the wrong car."

"And then gave himself a bloody heart attack when he realised." Grigg filled in the blanks, making his own narrative, as Lowri had hoped he would.

"That's the theory."

"I don't get why they would have stuck around though?" They reached the edge of the playing field. There was a road ahead of them that they needed to cross before they would be in the police station, an old Victorian building with sandstone bricks and tall windows. Far too grand to be a police station, Lowri thought.

"The A1 is littered with cameras." Lowri switched back to telling the truth. "I think they felt that if they drove off, they would bring more attention to themselves than if they simply stuck around like concerned citizens."

"Lucky for you." Grigg gave a little laugh as he thought about that. They crossed the road and walked up a small flight of stairs, entering into the lobby of the station. "I've got the videos all on the system already. We back everything up, as you know, it's all on the computer. I'll show you where you can get sorted. If you need anything burned off onto a DVD, that will be no problem."

"Thank you." Lowri smiled at him as he keyed in a code that took them through a door into the innards of the building.

The inside of the building was no less impressive, especially for a police station in the regions. The floor was black and white tiled, and the radiators that old metal type that were horribly inefficient if they were still attached to the original boiler, but it all served to give an old-world charm to the place. Like something out of the history books.

Grigg opened the door to a small side room, in which was a basic TV monitor attached to a computer on a grey desk. "Here we go," he announced.

"Thanks again. Is there any chance I can get a drink?" Lowri asked, wanting to try and get as much time on her own as possible.

"Tea, coffee, water?"

"Black coffee, please. No sugar."

"Coming up."

Grigg shut the door and Lowri was left alone. She knew how to use the system, she'd been sat at these machines many times before. Soon she was skimming through the dashcam footage from the patrol cars that had arrived at the scene. There were four cars in total, and Lowri didn't expect it to take her very long at all to find what she wanted. There were very few people at the crash scene, she could see that from the initial establisher. All she needed to do was get as clear a facial shot of each and every one, then she could begin to cross-reference them using the computer system the Vehm had at its disposal.

The first car on the system yielded nothing usable. They had been the first to arrive, and as such, their camera was facing down over the debris of the truck. Lowri span through the footage on a faster setting. The second parked up with the wreckage of David's car in front. Lowri slowed the playback to normal speed. Even though it was dark, the light from the patrol car headlights picked out the wreckage. She couldn't see into the car itself, not properly, but she could see a hand creeping limply from the wreckage. Not moving. Hanging. Lowri watched.

There was a knock at the door, breaking her from her trance. "Coffee, black." Grigg came in with her drink.

"Brilliant, thanks." Lowri's voice was a little choked up, so she took a big sip of the drink.

Grigg hovered for a moment, then clearly decided he would leave her to it. "I'm just down the corridor if you need me," he said excusing himself.

Lowri went back to the screen, this time spinning the footage forwards, watching as the fire crews and paramedics appeared on screen, busily going about their duties, tending to David, cutting him free, before loading him onto the stretcher. He was hidden behind the mass of bodies, but it was vivid enough for her to want to move onto the next camera.

The third car pulled up towards the back of the scene, behind both the patrol cars and a number of other cars that had stopped to help those injured in the crash. The angle it had parked at gave a nice wide field of vision. This could be the one.

At first, the action was confined to the distance, as everyone milled around the crash site, witnesses directing the officers and paramedics. Then the civilians started to amble away, having been told, no doubt, by the police officers to remain in their cars and wait for someone to come and take a statement, before turning them around and allowing them to continue on their journey. A horrible waiting game for most of them, but for one of them at least, the tension would be even higher as they hoped to avoid detection.

One by one, they would walk, often idly, past the camera. The picture quality wasn't the best. It was dark, and the camera wasn't a high-definition model, so the picture was grainy and it took a few attempts with each person for Lowri to be happy she had enough of their features captured to adequately run them through the facial recognition software.

There was one man, however, in a dark blue coat, collar up, shoulders down, who was doing all he could to avoid stepping in front of the cars. The untrained eye wouldn't have noticed his evasion techniques, but for Lowri they were obvious. Whenever he had to stand in front of the car, he turned his back towards it, looking at the crash, something which no doubt seemed a perfectly normal thing to do to those around him, but Lowri noticed it only seemed to happen when he was close to the camera. She skimmed through the footage, hoping to catch him with his guard down, hoping for a mistake, even for a split second, but it never came.

One more camera to go.

Lowri loaded it up, hoping, not believing she would get the result.

The footage opened with the car approaching without its blue lights on, driving at a relatively slow speed. A supervisor perhaps, on their way to the scene, keen not to end up coming into contact with anything or anyone in the dark, aware that the situation was under control from the reports from subordinates, so need to rush.

It pulled up alongside the third car. Slowly easing in, probably hardly audible with all the din of the crash site, the fire engines, the cutting machinery, the chatter of the emergency workers. It was certainly quiet enough to not be noticed by one officer and the witness he was interviewing until it pulled up right next to them. They both turned and looked straight at the car, straight at the camera.

It was the witness Lowri needed to see, but there was no need for a photograph. Lowri knew his face already. It was Nick Poole.

Lowri knew she should feel shock, betrayal, anger even, but there was nothing. If anything, it was a relief to finally have a suspect, someone to blame for what had happened to David. She pulled out her phone and called Poole.

"You took your time," he sounded smug. That wouldn't last, Lowri vowed.

"Why?" Lowri got to the point.

"Because the bigger picture is far more than one person. You know that."

"You've just signed your own death warrant. I'm looking at a picture of you at the crash site right now. In an hour, every Regulator in the world will have that, along with orders to proceed with maximum prejudice."

"No, no they won't. Because if they come for me, they're coming for you."

"Really?" Lowri couldn't believe the arrogance of the man. Was this really the dutiful Poole that she had been grooming for success?

"The problem you have is that I've had access to your systems for the last year and there is a paper trail that leads back solely to you. I've been planting it over time. Call logs, files, the sort of thing that goes unnoticed on a day-to-day basis, but over time, mounts up, looks incriminating. Plus of course, there is my confession."

"Confession?"

"Taped and ready to go, and let's be honest, I'm not trying to convince a court of law, or to overwhelm people with evidence, I'm trying to provoke a bunch of knee-jerk paranoid mercenaries into turning on one of their own. It won't be hard. So, you can come for me with your team, or you can come and meet me, one on one, and we can discuss what my employers want to happen next. It's your call."

"What happens next?" Lowri was getting angrier by the moment. Poole had no idea how close he was pushing her to the edge, and once he did, there was only one way this was going to go for him.

"Absolutely. You weren't so vain as to think this was all about you? You are a part of the plan, as am I. Removing you would fulfil a short-term goal, but I guess there is more you can do. First, though, you're going to delete that video."

"I'm not." Lowri was as blunt as she could be.

"You are, for two reasons. One, you want to know more about what's going on. If you don't do as I say, I disappear, and you'll lose your only chance of getting closer to the truth. At least, that's what you'll tell yourself you can get out of this."

Poole was baiting her, Lowri knew that. He knew she would want to know more, knew she would do the maths and see that deleting the file was a small price to pay if it meant getting closer to finding out who was behind this. For a split second, she berated herself for being so readable, but then she refocused.

"What's the second reason?" she asked.

"If you don't do as I say, right now, I pull the plug on David. I'm with him, not a hard job to get assigned." There was a ping on Lowri's phone as a message came through. She knew what it was without opening it. It would be a photo of David, from Poole, just to show he was serious.

"What happens after I delete it?"

"I have permission to meet with you, in a public place, to share with you further information. Eleven o'clock, St. Pancras Station."

Lowri moved the mouse with her free hand so that the cursor hovered over the file for the video. She clicked it once with the left button, once with the right and scrolled down to where a pop-up menu said, "Delete."

"I'll be there." She clicked the button. The file was gone.

40

The drive to wherever they had taken Adam hadn't taken more than half an hour, so they were somewhere still well within London. Other than that, he didn't really have much of a clue.

The ambulance began to reverse slowly, then stopped altogether. No one left the front of the vehicle, but the rear doors were opened by two men, both of them dressed in black T-shirts and tactical trousers. Adam stood and walked slowly towards them.

"Morning," he greeted them cheerily. There was no response.

The ambulance was parked in some sort of loading bay at the back of a red brick building. A warehouse and an old one at that. The brickwork was tatty, and the metal rail that edged the raised loading platform showed serious signs of rust through the flecks of drab green paint that still clung hopefully to it. Adam stepped across the small gap from the ambulance into the building, and the two men closed the ambulance door and then the loading bay door, before grabbing him by an arm each and escorting him into the building.

"Don't be rough," Adam warned playfully. "I don't like it rough. Not my scene." He may well have been worried, but he sure wasn't going to let them know.

The building was cold and damp, probably used rarely, for subjects such as himself. It wasn't designed for comfort, that was for sure. If it found another function other than its current clandestine use, Adam would have been greatly surprised. Much more likely, it would end up demolished and turned into something new, years of DNA evidence buried under some yuppie's flat. Adam hoped he wouldn't be a part of the foundations.

They reached a set of double doors with porthole-style windows and rubber runners on the bottom. His two escorts pushed them open, and Adam saw a table with three chairs in the middle of an empty room. One chair each positioned on three of the four sides of the table.

The two men walked Adam to the chair that was flanked on both sides and then sat him down. The chair was wooden, hard and cold, even through his clothes. The two men left and Adam hoped that whoever was coming through next would bring him a hot drink, not that he expected them to deliver.

It was another ten minutes before he heard so much as a sound. The building, whilst cold, had clearly been soundproofed. There was no traffic noise, nothing from any surrounding buildings, no birds in the air, not a single sound that one might expect to hear. Complete silence.

Then came the footsteps. Two pairs, almost in unison but not quite.

Two men walked calmly through the doors, saying nothing. They were both dressed in smart, Saville Row-looking suits, certainly not cheap. The first man had sandy coloured hair, smartly combed to the side. His face was thin but still showed signs of being muscular. The second man was roughly the same height, but younger. His hair was dark, buzz cut up the side to a slicked-back look on the top. Almost fashionable. He was broader in the face than his counterpart, stronger. Secret Service, Mi5.

Probably. One of them, the man with the lighter hair, came around to Adam's left, the other to his right. Both took their seats and looked at him.

"Mr. Morgan. Do you know who we are?" the lighter haired man spoke.

"Five, probably." Adam shrugged with indifference.

"Close enough. Let me fill you in on what we've been working on."

"Be my guest." Adam sat back and folded his arms, ready for the story."

The light-haired man leaned into the space Adam had vacated. "My job is to watch people like you. Vigilantes. People who think they know better. There's a small team of us dedicated to that role, and we do a pretty admirable job. Sometimes we stop you; sometimes we let you do the dirty work that an official agency couldn't do. You're a useful asset, but you need to remember that, if you cross a line, if you go too far, we are watching and we will pull your plug."

"Well, thank you for that. I appreciate the candour." Adam wasn't interested in getting into a power play game with them. It seemed like he was about to learn something, so he was happy to let them lead the conversation for now.

"Of course, you're not the only group. You might be the biggest, you might even have a case of being the best, that's not for me to decide, but you're one of many. Another one we've been monitoring is the Brotherhood. We knew they were planning something and we knew that we might want to know what they found because it touched on a problem within our government. If there was something afoot, we'd share that information and clean it up."

"Do you do any real work yourselves, or do you just try and take credit for our hard graft?" Adam raised an eyebrow. All this talk of knowing what was going on was relatively impressive, but at this point, there was a lot of talk and not a lot of action.

"Our job is to observe and react," the light-haired man continued. "We do it well. This time, however, we weren't the only ones observing. We became aware of an attempted hack on a Westminster server. We wanted to know what the information was, but it appears someone wanted to stop that information getting out."

"Which is why they went after the Brotherhood," Adam took on the narrative. "And that was a problem for you."

"It was."

"Because how did someone know what you knew?" Adam felt like he could read their minds. The light-haired man sat back, and the dark-haired man spoke.

"We stumbled on who was behind the hack by accident. The Brotherhood had been careful, they'd planned their exit and their routes to avoid every camera in the area. It was military precision. The only problem was, right opposite the door they exited was a bar that had placed a brand-new camera at their entrance that morning. The Brotherhood never knew, and so we had their faces leaving the flat later that day."

Light-haired man picked up the story. "We followed Mo and his friends. We wanted to see where they went, to follow them back to their safe house, then take them all in for questioning, which in hindsight was a mistake. Two of them were dead within the hour, and Mo disappeared. We, of course, assumed at that point that he was behind the hit."

"Mo? He's not a killer."

"We know that now." Light-haired shrugged.

"But that wasn't your problem. You had a mole."

"We don't deal in coincidences," light-haired man explained. "My experience is that there aren't any. I'm sure yours is the same?"

"For the most part."

"The trail was cold. We decided we needed to act fast, so we made the decision to raid a number of the Brotherhood's London safe houses. One of them, of course, was the one we were looking for. We didn't find Mo at the time, but on reviewing surveillance of the area, we were able to pick up a figure making their way to the river and escaping on a boat. We planned to intercept him, but someone beat us to it, which is where you came in."

"Those weren't your men then?" Adam asked.

"No."

"Well, that's a relief. I figure you might have been pretty annoyed with me if they were. So, who were they then?"

The brown-haired man cocked his head. "We were hoping you could tell us that."

"Me?"

"Your team, or someone from your group at least, cleared the bodies out," insisted the brown-haired man.

"I was under the impression the site was cleared before we ever got back," Adam countered.

The brown-haired man looked confused, whilst Adam saw the light-haired man pull his phone from his pocket. He swiped across the screen three times, then turned the phone over to Adam.

"This man works for you, right?"

Adam looked at the screen. There was a black van at the industrial site where Adam and Emmie had rescued Mo. The back doors were open, and two men in black loaded something into the back. It was hard to see exactly what it was, but from the way it hung and the way they were carrying it, Adam deduced it was a body bag holding one of the men they'd killed. The two men had their backs to the camera, but coming around the other side of the van was a third man, his face clearly on display. It was Nick Poole.

"Shit." Adam was already running the possibilities through his head. "He works for us, yeah."

"Who does he report to."

"Lowri Graves?" The light-haired man asked.

Adam said nothing.

"Is it possible that Ms. Graves could be working against our common good?" Dark-haired man went in for the kill.

Adam was asking the question himself. Lowri certainly would have no qualms with taking whatever action she deemed necessary to do what was right, but he was having a hard time believing that she could be involved, especially after the attack on David.

"I can't buy it. Lowri is a lot of things, but not this."

"Even if she felt it was for the greater good?"

"A fucking paedo farm?"

"Lowri Graves has a long and sordid past of doing questionable things for this country. She shed her conscience years ago." Light-haired man leaned in again.

Adam took a moment. He didn't want to believe it, but he also didn't want to believe that anyone from the Regulators had been involved. Nick Poole was proving otherwise. So where did that go? "Are you saying that this is something we've done?"

Light-haired man shook his head. "No, this is bigger than just you. We have a mole, we know that. Now you know you have one, at least. Maybe more."

"So, what do you want?"

"We want you to find Poole, then find out what he knows. We need to know who he's taking his orders from so that we can try and pull this apart. The least we can do is help each other find out who's really responsible and help us bring them to justice, whatever form that might take."

"You want me working for you?"

"We want you working for what's right," light-haired man continued the pitch. "Isn't that what you do anyway? Isn't your code that if it can be passed onto the authorities, it should be?"

"And Poole, Graves, anyone from our number?"

"They can be your problem. You can do what you want with them. We need to find the influencers in this situation and take them out. There's going to be massive upheaval in this country now. We need to make sure that no one is poised to exploit it."

Adam knew they were right.

"Fine. I'll get Poole, and if I have to, I'll get Graves as well. Just promise me this is a two-way street. You learn something, you tell me."

"I wouldn't have it any other way," the light-haired man smiled.

Adam was pretty certain he was lying.

41

Thea left the house as soon as she made the call for backup, requesting units to both the gamekeeper's lodge and the farm. It would take them a little while to get there, but she wanted to be in situ as soon as she could. While she rationalised in her head that it was because it would allow her to get a better tactical overview of the location, as she made her way quickly back to her car, she found herself contemplating how she was going to get those kids and Jack out of there.

She got into her car and started it up, hoping that no one heard the soft cough of the engine coming to life. She left the lights off and released the brake, turning the car around, doing her best to avoid using reverse. She didn't want her reversing lights alerting anyone that might be in the area. Eventually, she nursed the car around and made her way slowly, coasting as best as she could, to where she knew the farmhouse was located.

The call she had put out was for a possible hostage situation. That meant that at some point she would be getting tactical firearm support, but with this being rural Yorkshire, it wasn't going to be there as quickly as the local rank and file. She would feel better when it was. Rankine had been the only person she felt she could truly trust on this patch, yet she had sent him away. The more people she added to the mix, the harder it would be for anyone with ill intentions to be able to action them.

It took her a little over five minutes to be as close to the farm as she dared get in the car. Still, she saw nothing of her backup. She parked against a ramshackle stone wall, her low car sitting in the furrow created in the road over years of heavy machinery trundling up and down it. She opened the door slowly, slid out, and pushed herself against the wall. She must not be seen. The last thing she wanted was to end up in the same predicament as Jack, and out here, alone, she felt exposed and just a little bit scared.

Bobbing her head over the wall, she could see the coast was clear. No one was patrolling the house, and the windows that overlooked the road seemed to be unoccupied. She set off along the wall, keeping her head low, her feet crunching in the dirt and mud below. The road turned sharply right on its approach to the farmhouse, and as she reached the junction, she stopped to once again assess her route.

Still all clear. She could see the yard now, the Land Rovers still parked up, the sound of the cows and machinery now noticeable, mashed together in a cacophony of activity. She waited. There were no other sounds. No shouts of help, or of pain. No movement in the yard. Everyone must be inside. Was that a good or bad thing? She couldn't be sure.

Where was that backup?

She looked back towards the town of Malton, hoping to see lights on the horizon, bouncing and dipping as cars or vans made their way along the rough road towards her, or even the pulse of blue emergency lights cutting through the darkness, somewhere, just off in the distance, but she saw nothing.

She checked her watch. Nearly ten minutes since she had made the call. Should she make another one? Would that speed them up? If they were holding off until armed support arrived, then maybe it would, but if there was someone relaying her information or position to those in the house, she just ran the risk of further exposing herself. No, she would stay put. She was safe on this corner. She could see anyone coming in either direction. She had a view on the house, and if she heard something she didn't like, she could make the short run down into the yard and try and make a difference herself.

Her thoughts turned to Jack. Whoever it was who had captured him was clearly in no rush to dispose of him. That gave her time, but god, she hated herself for sitting there doing nothing. The thought of those children, spending just another minute in a cell, ate through her. She felt her anger rising. All she wanted to do was go in there, tear down that door, and get them all out and away from the sick sons-of-bitches.

She waited another thirty seconds, checking over her shoulder again in the direction she hoped backup would come from. Nothing.

Come on. I need you here! Silently she urged them to arrive. She looked back at the yard, fighting the urge to get up and move forward. She had to help the children, she had to help Jack, she had to punish those who were holding them all. She checked herself again. She wasn't the punisher, that wasn't her job. She needed to arrest them, nothing more. It wasn't her place to do anything more. She wasn't Jack. She was Thea Watts. Whoever was responsible would be brought to justice, but properly.

God, she needed to move. She needed to get in there, *now.*

She looked back. Nothing, she turned back towards the yard. Her heart raced. She glanced back across the field to her left. Something she had seen had caught her eye. She tried to focus in the darkness.

Nothing.

She looked back to the yard before quickly looking back to the field. She had seen something, she was sure. She scanned the field slowly. Was someone out there? Had they spotted her? Were they attempting to flank her, get around her and pin her down? She needed to know.

Still nothing.

She looked back over her shoulder once more. Where was that backup? She really needed it here, right now. Whatever she thought she had seen in the field had unsettled her now. It might have been nothing, it must have been nothing. Just a trick of her mind brought on by her hypersensitive state.

She looked back to the yard, but then her eyes cut back quickly to that field, to the hedgerow on the far side, about a hundred yards away.

It was so dark, it was impossible to pick out anything other than shapes. Even the hedgerow itself was a barely visible blur. She could only see it thanks to the slight reflection of the lights in the yard. It was unmoving, silent, devoid of interest.

Until she saw a figure, crouching, creeping towards the farm yard.

42

"Mo!" Jack's voice was full of urgency as he implored Mo to open his eyes. "Wake up!"

Mo's head rolled as if to signify he was still there.

"You've got to stay awake, Mo, you've got to stay with me here," Jack implored as he pulled at the chains hopelessly. "We're going to get out of this."

The analyst said nothing, just nodded his head softly, with barely any effort. Jack looked at the wound and saw the blood continue to pump out of his stomach, a new wave cascading down with each beat of Mo's heart. He didn't have long left, if it wasn't already too late. The colour was gone from his face and his fingers, his breathing was getting shallower and sharper. Jack looked around for something, anything, that might get them out of this. Seeing nothing, he pulled desperately once more at the chains, but they didn't budge. He was helpless. If only he could move, if only to hold Mo and let him know he was there.

Mo began to mumble something, Jack couldn't make out a word.

"Mo? Mo? What is it?" Maybe he had seen a way out of this.

Mo kept mumbling, and Jack listened.

"Wa bil Islami dinan."

Jack knew the words, he had heard men speak them before. They were a praise to Allah, an acceptance of fate. A prayer to be uttered before death.

"Mo, no, listen to me, you're going to be alright. Stay with me."

Mo kept reciting the prayer. "Wa bil Qur'ani kitaban."

What did they want from him? Braun had promised a question. Braun had said that if he didn't answer, then he would watch Mo die, but yet, there was no question, and Mo was dying.

"Damnit! Ask the question!" Jack shouted out, hoping that someone was listening.

Mo's eyes widened, he stopped his prayer.

"No," he spluttered, his speech a little slurred. "Don't answer."

"Mo, I have to. You're going to die if I don't."

Mo shook his head. "I die."

"Mo."

Mo raised his head and looked at Jack. Jack could see him fighting through the pain. He watched as Mo squeezed his eyes shut, summoning his last vestige of strength, then opened them, a newly found focus on display.

"You can't tell them anything. I watched people die for this today. They blew up a building so I could escape."

"Then that's why I have to help you, that can't be in vain."

"They didn't do it for me." Mo gave a little half laugh. "Thought they did. It was for the information. I get it now."

"You don't have to die for it. It's out there."

"We don't know that. If they find out, they could stop it. Not for me. No. These kids don't suffer another day to save my life."

Jack choked back a tear as he found himself agreeing with Mo. "Son of a bitch," he croaked.

"You save *them*. Not me."

"Mo, I can do both."

"How?" Mo smiled weakly. "I mean, you work it out, I'm all ears."

Jack didn't know how. He wished he did, more than anything in this world at this moment, he wished he knew how to save Mo without giving up the mission. A lie might be a stay of execution if they believed it. It could give them time.

Mo clearly saw what he was thinking. He shook his head slowly once more. "Don't bullshit them. This hurts, I don't want to hurt anymore."

"Mo." Jack didn't know what else to say.

"Just pray with me, or for me, or whatever."

"I don't know all the words."

"It doesn't matter."

Jack nodded. Mo went on.

"Wa bi' Aliyyan waliyyan wa imaman."

Jack was about to join in when he heard a noise. Mo continued praying.

Then it came again, and Mo stopped, his head lifting as his eyes rolled.

POP-POP-POP

"Shit, that's gunfire!" Jack felt his whole body tense up with anticipation. "Hold in there, Mo, just stay the fuck in there."

Mo didn't respond.

POP-POP.

POP.

It was getting closer all the time. Now came the sound of shouts, muffled, indecipherable, but shouts nonetheless. Someone was coming.

Jack looked at Mo. His head was sagging even more now.

"Mo! Mo! Don't give up, Mo, we're nearly there."

The shouts were louder now. Multiple voices, communicating with each other. Someone in control of a situation it sounded like. Clearing rooms probably, given the short, sharp bursts of speech.

The shooting had stopped. The shouts got louder. Definitely clearing rooms. Jack heard the shouts. "Clear." "Clear." Each one nearer, each one sharper.

"In here," he called. There wasn't a reply.

Finally, he heard the sound of footsteps approaching. Quickly, softly, coupled with the clanking and clinking of guns and equipment. An Asian man appeared at the doorway. "Got them!" he shouted.

"Help him! He's bleeding out from a stomach wound," Jack ordered as the man slid the key into the door and opened it.

"I got him," the man replied calmly.

More footsteps, this time running. Two more men came around the corner, both armed with compact Heckler and Koch MP7 machine guns, both perspiring.

"Are you Jack? What the hell happened?" he said, before turning to one of his men. "Get him down from there. Quickly." He turned to Jack. "I'm Kasim Husseini. I run this team."

A man stepped forward with another set of keys and began to release Jack.

"We got ambushed on the way in," Jack reported as he felt the shackles loosened and he dropped back down onto his feet. "They knew we were coming."

"How?"

"I don't know. They wanted to know who had the information."

"Someone talked." Kasim looked furious, but his voice was controlled.

"I know, but we can work that out later. Are any of them alive?"

"We killed three." One of the men answered matter-of-factly.

"There were a lot more."

"We will find them," Kasim promised. "I will have my men make a proper sweep. Now we go." He looked at his man who had picked up Mo. "Can you carry him?"

"Let me help." Jack answered, reaching under Mo's arm, softly telling him; "I got you, pal."

"We need to go," Kasim urged, turning and leading the way out. Jack and the other man followed, Mo propped between them, whilst the man who had arrived with Kasim brought up the rear.

They wasted no time in making their way back out towards the courtyard, emerging out into the light. Jack saw the three bodies lying on the floor near the Land Rovers.

"I need to see the bodies. Someone hold, Mo," he requested.

"Be quick," Kasim snapped.

Jack ran over to the bodies and looked at them. None of them were Braun. He ran back, taking his place back under Mo.

"Did you see who you wanted?"

"No," Jack said grimly. "Braun's still out there. The leader."

"We'll find him."

"Jack!"

Thea's voice echoed across the yard. Jack looked over his shoulder and saw her standing in the entrance to the yard. Blue lights began to cascade off the walls around her as more police began to arrive.

"Let's go!" Kasim ordered.

"Shit," Jack grimaced as they began to move off.

"Jack, freeze!" Thea shouted again. One of Kasim's men, just to Jack's right, raised a gun and fired a burst of machine gun fire in Thea's direction.

"No!" Jack bellowed, leaning across as best he could whilst still holding Mo, his hand reaching out towards the gun, pushing it away from Thea. He looked and saw her sprawling for cover, panicking for a moment, but feeling relieved to see her scrambling away, apparently unharmed.

"Go!" bawled Kasim. They needed no invitation

Jack and the other man half-carried half-dragged Mo with them as Kasim and the other man rounded the corner ahead, disappearing out of the yard.

Jack didn't look back. He couldn't look back. They reached the edge of the courtyard and saw Kasim again standing by a large 4x4.

"In," he barked. "Now."

Jack and the other man pushed Mo's limp body up and into the back seat of the 4x4, Jack scrambling in behind him, whilst the other man made his way around to the other side. Jack looked down at Mo. Was he even breathing?

"Is anyone following?" Kasim asked, quickly glancing over his shoulder.

"No one," the man in the passenger seat replied.

"Good work," Kasim said. He turned and tried to look to the three in the back seat. "How is he?"

Jack's head hovered above Mo's face, but with the noise of the car, the engine roaring, the sound of the suspension creaking as they bounced over the farm track, he couldn't tell and he couldn't keep his face level enough to be sure if he could feel that faint puff of air on his face.

His fingers sought out Mo's Neck. It was still warm. He pushed down. Was he in the right place?

Nothing. He moved his fingers, damn this car moving.

He felt something, a movement in his hand. And again.

A pulse.

Then it stopped.

He waited.

Nothing.

He moved his fingers.

Nothing.

Jack looked up at Kasim. It wasn't the first time he'd had to say it, not even the first time he'd had to say it about a friend, but something about this time left his voice cracked and straining.

"He's dead."

43

"Are you going to tell me what happened?"

It had been well over an hour that Adam had been out of the office. He knew that Emmie would have fielded questions about him in that time. She had covered for him and he owed her. Now, as they drove to see Nathan Nelmes, she was asking questions.

"Do you trust me?" Adam asked.

"Yes," Emmie replied coolly.

"Then trust that you don't want to know."

"Do you trust me?" This time there was a snap in Emmie's voice. Adam didn't necessarily disagree with her.

"Fine. When we get to Nelmes, I'll tell you, show you even. There's not the time now."

That seemed to placate Emmie. "Fine," she said.

Nathan Nelmes was sweating as they approached the booth in the corner of the bar in Hammersmith. It wasn't hot, but he was clearly nervous and not helped by his larger than life frame. His face was round with a reddish-brown fuzzy beard clinging around his two chins, whilst on top, his hair was straight, slicked to the sides and highlighted blonde. He was squeezed into a Ben Sherman shirt, buttoned up, with a Lacoste navy blue jumper over the top. Adam could see his Adidas shell toes tapping under the table as they approached. If he looked like a manchild stuck in the 90s, that's because he was.

"Hullo." He stood up, trying to greet them cheerfully, but in his nervous rush, banged his knee on the table, causing him to lurch forward and knock his beer, spilling a good third of a pint onto the table. "Oh shit!"

Adam smiled. "Mr. Nelmes. Covert as ever."

"Well, fucking hell, you know these things always make me nervous," Nathan said, futilely brushing beer from the edge of the table as it seeped towards his trousers.

"Shall I get a cloth?" Emmie asked.

"I'll get one, I'll get one," Nathan said quickly, hopping from behind the table and beelining to the bar.

Emmie and Adam sat down at the table and waited for him.

"Is he really cut out for this sort of thing?" Emmie kept her voice low.

"He might be a bit clumsy, but he's got integrity, *and* he's good at his job," Adam proffered the defence.

"How many times has he run stories for us?"

"Too many to mention."

"What sort of thing?"

"When the law turns a blind eye, sometimes it's better to let the public judge than throw someone in a cell. Certain folk we can't just disappear. Usually, their reputation is all they have to play off."

"MPs?"

"Yeah, for the most part. The odd minor royal, one of two celebs who've shagged their way to a degree of immunity, or whose parents know the right people from the right circles at the right schools. Nathan is my guy for putting them on the naughty step, so to speak."

"Will his paper really run this?"

269

"They have form. The editor isn't bought as far as we know, so fingers crossed."

Nathan was back now, a wad of the thick, blue tissue paper that seemed to be in every bar up and down Britain in one hand. He slumped back down at the booth unceremoniously and began dabbing at the pool of beer that had formed on the table. "Sorry about this," he mumbled again.

"You take your time, Nathan," Adam reassured him.

Finally, satisfied with the state of the furniture, Nathan looked up and smiled. It wasn't the most convincing smile in the world. He was still clearly nervous, as he was every time he met with Adam. Was this just his persona? Was he always nervous, or did the fact that Adam was here to meet him to share with him a story that would put him in the firing line make him act this way. He would have loved to have met Nathan outside of this setting, but Nelmes had already been brought into the fold by Jack, by the time Adam had been introduced to him.

"Right, a story I guess?" Nathan stammered out the obvious before turning his attention to Emmie. "Sorry, Nathan Nelmes." He offered his hand.

"Emmie Weston."

"The new Jack? Not quite the same model." Nathan laughed at his own joke.

"No, well, we need to move with the times." Adam placed his hand in his pocket, took out a USB drive, passing it over the table to Nathan. "This is your big lead for the next month."

"Month? That good?"

"It's the story that will define you. Just be careful where you watch it."

"Not safe for work? I mean, other than at our jobs?"

"You could say that. Word of warning, you aren't going to want to sit through it."

"Right, fine. Do we have any headlines?"

"We've collated the key bits into an easily digestible document in the top directory, but there's a lot in there. You're going to need a team on this, but only once you've backed it up a lot and run the opening story. Trust me, they're going to try and shut it down."

Nathan looked at Adam. "How badly?"

"We've got your back. You just make sure the people get to hear about it," Emmie promised.

"I'm not going to lie," Adam decided to be honest and expand. "This came from a government server. It's got all the hallmarks of the intelligence agencies all over it, but if we expose them, then we can clean this all up. We just need to get it out there and on the streets so that they can't sweep it all under the carpet."

"When?"

"There's kids' lives at stake."

"Kids? Shit, that sort of not safe for work. Great." Nathan pulled a face somewhere between disgust and disappointment. "Fine, I'll make sure we put it out there as soon as we can. What's your timescale?"

"The next couple of hours. If you get to work now, it's just a case of letting you know when to press the button. You probably don't want to tell anyone until it's ready though."

"I get you. No problem. Right, well, this is a jolly way to spend an evening, talking about paedophilia with the implied threat of being murdered. Anyone for a beer?"

Adam stood up, taking a ten-pound note from his pocket and placing it on the table. "Can't drink on duty, but you get yourself another one, then crack on. My treat."

"Thanks, mate." Nathan nodded at them as they edged their way out of the booth. "Nice seeing you again and pleasure to meet you too, Ms. Weston. If that is your real name."

"You'll probably never know," she smiled.

44

The first patrol car was in the yard just seconds after Jack and the other men left. Thea was cursing the fine margins as she stood, trying to brush the mud and muck from where she had sprawled for cover. She heard the car doors open and the squelch of footsteps in the wet yard.

"You alright, ma'am?" One of the officers jogged over to her, placing his arm on her shoulder in a show of reassurance. Without thinking, she brushed it off, feeling guilty straight away.

"Yes, fine," she said, trying her best to not sound annoyed but knowing she failed.

"What happened?" the officer asked.

"Four suspects, all armed, made off that way. I need them chased down. Where's the aerial unit?"

"I don't want to have my men chasing them down, not if they're armed like that."

"No." Thea didn't necessarily agree with the officer's fears. She needed everyone bringing in and fast. A little danger was the price you paid for being on the frontline.

"I'll find out about air support though." The officer unclipped his radio and barked the request into it. A distorted reply came through, and although Thea heard it, the officer repeated it back to her. "Five minutes out."

"They're going to be long gone by then," Thea admitted.

The more she thought about it, the more she realised they had been delayed and spared, rather than just got lucky. Anyway, there were kids somewhere in the facility, and they had to be the priority. "There are kids here, somewhere in one of these buildings."

"Kids?" the officer's eyebrows raised. "What do you mean like?"

"I saw a video feed of a room full of children."

"Jesus Christ."

"We'll get whoever did this, but we'll get them later."

"Of course." The officer turned and called to his colleagues. "I want this place turned over. There's some kids in here, we need to get them out."

"Thanks," Thea said.

"Did you see what room they were in?"

Thea looked around her. It would need to be a decent-sized room to hold as many children as she had seen. Somewhere where they wouldn't be able to escape or raise the suspicions of anyone who might end up in the vicinity. "Is there a basement to the farmhouse?"

"I would reckon so. We'll check it out first."

The officer turned and jogged towards the farmhouse. Thea hoped that he was someone she could trust. She didn't know his name. Looking around, she realised she didn't know any of the officers here. She stood alone for a minute, watching as another car arrived and more officers jumped out, quickly joining in the search of the premises.

She looked to the end of the farmyard where Jack had made his escape. He had been helping someone who looked badly wounded. Whatever they had been doing here had gone badly wrong. Had it gone so badly wrong that the children had been compromised? God, she hoped not.

The sky was starting to grow lighter now, though it was heavy with cloud cover which looked likely to release its load of rain at any give moment. The orange glow of the farmyard floodlighting tinted everything in the yard, giving it a strange, washed out light that glowed like firelight in the morning murk.

"I hope you're alright, Jack," she sighed. If only he had come to her, had let her know what was happening, but she had pushed him away. She should have known that, to be able to keep tabs on someone like Jack, she'd need to keep him close. At the time, she had hoped that pushing him away would lead to him thinking twice, especially given his isolation from anyone else in the area. Judging by the team he had around him, he'd managed to address that problem.

That left another question. Were they Regulators she had seen with Jack? Given Jack's continued reluctance to involve them, she thought it unlikely. The men she had seen all looked Asian in descent, Indian, Pakistani, or something similar. Was this something else?

Thea looked back at the house. Jesus, this thing wasn't getting any simpler.

The officer she had been speaking to appeared at the door of the farmhouse.

"We found them!" he called.

"Fuck," Thea gulped to herself. Had they been in time? She ran towards the house, the officer stepping aside as she barged in. To her left, she saw movement, another police officer coming out of a white wooden doorway that fed into a set of stairs.

"I've got ambulances coming," he said coldly.

275

Thea said nothing, she squeezed past him, through the door, down the stone steps that had been worn away so much that they dipped in the middle. They were so smooth she almost slipped as she approached the bottom.

A dim light hung from the ceiling, barely giving off enough illumination for the space, but there were additional spots of brightness from the torches of the officers working down there. It was enough for Thea to see the group of children she had seen on the CCTV back at the gamekeeper's house. They were all there. Thin, gaunt, scared, but most importantly, they were all still alive.

45

"I need a weapon," seethed Jack.

Kasim went around to the back of the four-by-four. They had parked up in a ramshackle barn missing one wall, but still offered shelter from the dirt track thanks to the other three and from the air by the corrugated metal roof that somehow, despite the rust that covered it, held on grimly to its perch on top of the walls. The rear of the four-by-four was already open, and Kasim pulled a black plastic box forward, opening it.

"Sig Sauer MPX. Red dot scope. Thirty round magazine. Silencer." He pulled the body of the gun from the box, assembling the relevant parts as he went, before shoving the gun into Jack's hands. "Moeen was a good man. He died for this cause. Remember that when you catch up to this man."

"I will," Jack said gruffly. Mo's body was being wrapped in a white sheet by the other two men as they spoke. They had already bathed him, cleansing him quickly, a part of the Islamic funeral ritual. There was no way Jack could forget. He went to walk away. Kasim put his hand out to stop him.

"Will you?"

"What the hell is that supposed to mean?"

"Braun needs to die, one day. He needs to answer for his crimes, but not everything needs to happen in the here and now, and not everything needs to happen at our own hand. Allah, God, the universe, whatever you want to call it, it all moves in mysterious ways and to the beat of its own drum."

"And if I feel it move through me?"

"We are not the architects, but, Inshallah, we are, sometimes, the messengers." Kasim's tone softened, and he took his hand off Jack's chest.

Jack looked at Kasim, not knowing what to say. Was there even anything left to say? The man was right, Jack knew it. He knew that when he caught up with Braun, he would have to stop himself from ripping the man limb from limb, at least as long as it took to get the information out of him that he needed. The problem was, even right here, right now, he couldn't promise that. He felt something stirring in him that had been locked away for a long time. A need to get revenge, not just deliver justice. A need to get even against a man who had mocked him, taunted him, and then made him watch his friend die. Braun had rendered Jack helpless. Braun had shown him how powerless he was, and in that instance, Jack had sworn never to be powerless ever again.

"Thank you," Jack said. "For everything." He looked toward where Mo's body was being wrapped.

"We will make sure he is buried properly."

"And his family?" Jack knew they would never know the full truth, just as his wouldn't. A part of the job that he tried his hardest not to think about.

"We will release to the media that he travelled to Syria to join an aid convoy and that he was killed saving the lives of countless others. He will be remembered as the hero that he truly is. You are sure you don't need any help tracking Braun?"

"No. I know where he is."

"I would ask how, but I am sure you will not tell me."

Jack put his hand out to Kasim's. The man took it and shook it. "Until we meet again," Jack said.

"Until we meet again."

The how of Jack finding Braun seemed obvious to Jack. To others, it would seem like a complete shot in the dark, but Jack knew different. Braun would have a set of tasks he would need to complete should the operation be compromised, a clean-up. Anything he would have wanted to have done at the farm itself would have gone out of the window the moment Kasim and his men took control of the site. Braun would have retreated the moment he saw that the tactical situation was against him. That was just good soldiering, regroup and await another opportunity, rather than go down in a blaze of glory.

Losing the farmhouse would have been problematic for them, but if it had been used solely as a prison, the exposure wouldn't be so great. There would have been nothing there tying anyone to anything. It wasn't a part of Lord Brier's lands, and the deeds would no doubt lead to a dead end. There would be a base of operations that had to be dismantled, quickly. Jack knew where that would be, and he knew that would have to be where he started his search. There was only one place that Braun would want that to be. His house, the gamekeeper's lodge, on Lord Briar's estate.

Their escape from the farm had taken them nearer to the cottage. Jack didn't expect to be ahead of Braun, but he knew that he wouldn't be far behind. If he got there in time, then he could catch Braun in the act. If not, the trail would still be warm, and the chase would be on.

Dawn hadn't broken yet, but it was getting lighter and lighter every second. Birds were echoing their morning calls to each other from across the treetops as Jack left the dilapidated barn, heading north. He was now dressed all in black, hoping to stay close to hedgerows and blend into the shadows, should anyone be watching for him. He had no doubt they would be, on both Braun's side and Thea's.

Thea was another problem. She would be pissed off now, and rightly so. She had cut him out of the investigation when he knew that he should have brought her into the loop. It had played on his mind throughout, especially when he was at his most helpless, dangling from those cuffs watching Mo die.

Don't be stupid. If you brought her in, you could have been watching her die. He knew that was true. Thea would never have taken a watching brief. She would have insisted on being involved, she would have been there in that car with them as they were ambushed, and she would have been the third prisoner in that cell. Who knew what twisted plan Braun would have hatched for her? It was better she was angry at Jack than in Braun's custody.

That didn't make his tactical situation easier, however. They would be looking for him and Braun. Not just the police either. Soon enough, as the story broke, the media would begin to turn up. That was always a part of the plan, to make the areas as hot as possible, to discourage anyone from trying to intervene in their efforts to free the children, to make sure that anyone trying to escape would find it harder to remain anonymous. A pretty flawless plan if they weren't still trying to operate covertly in the area.

It was getting lighter and lighter now. Jack figured they'd be in full daylight by the time he reached the gamekeeper's lodge. Nothing about this was going to be ideal.

Mercifully, the journey to the gamekeeper's lodge passed without incident. The fields that led to it were flanked by woodland, with Jack able to use the treeline as cover, merging with the growing shadows, hiding his approach from both the air and the land. He picked up the dirt road that led directly to the house about a half mile away, skipping across it, moving further into the woods that circled the house, keeping his profile low to the ground and narrow to the house. You never know who might be watching.

Slowly he crept forward, listening now to every sound. There was nothing out of the ordinary. Just the usual woodland noises as the natural world carried on regardless, not noticing or caring about the problems of the world of man. The woods slowed him down somewhat, stepping carefully through the undergrowth so as not to trip nor alert anyone to his approach, always scanning ahead and around for anyone watching and waiting.

Finally, he saw the house. There was a Land Rover outside, similar, but not the same colour as the ones that had chased him and Mo the night previous. It was parked right next to the house. Just down from that was a police officer four-by-four, lights flashing. Jack stopped.

The doors of the police vehicle were open. Had Braun been apprehended? He listened.

Nothing.

The engine was off on the four-by-four. Whoever had gone in, had gone in a relative hurry if they had left the doors open, but not so much of a hurry that they left the engine on. Jack edged closer, hoping to get a better look inside the house.

He stopped. Something on the floor was reflecting the sunlight that was now starting to find its way through the branches of the trees above. What was it? Jack pressed himself up against a tree, using it to disguise his body as he pulled himself upwards, looking to the ground by the four-by-four. He finally saw the culprit. A fluorescent strip on a bright yellow jacket, dead police officer still shrouded inside. His left leg was bent backwards where he had fallen as his bodily functions instantly ceased, most probably due to the large wound that had been gouged into the top of the man's chest. A gunshot.

"Shit," Jack lowered himself back down. The officer must have been shot pretty much as soon as he stepped out. Risking another look, Jack tried to see the other side of the four-by-four, but he couldn't. The door was open, however, and the relative silence of the scene suggested that a similar fate had befallen the partner of the first officer.

There was barely time for Jack to decide what to do next when he heard the sound of tyres slowly making their way up the track. He ducked quickly down, glancing over his left shoulder, looking behind to see another police vehicle, an estate car this time, single-crewed, making its way along the path.

"Oh no." Jack felt himself rise subconsciously for a moment, his natural reaction was to warn the officer of the danger, but he stopped himself. Revealing himself to the police officer would only serve to make them both targets. The officer would want to cuff him, put him in the back of the car, and make him a sitting duck. Jack would just have to hope this guy had better luck than his colleagues.

He watched as the car got closer to the four-by-four, slowing as the officer started to assess the situation. The lights quickly flashed on and stayed on. The officer had seen the body. Jack could see him leaning over in the driving seat, talking into his radio, looking at the other side of the car. Definitely a second body, Jack thought.

The house remained silent. Jack wondered if whoever had shot the first officers were still there? They must be, Jack thought. There was no way that they could have got back and cleaned out the house from anything incriminating already. He tried to peer around the tree so he could see the windows and door better. The door looked a little ajar, he couldn't quite tell from here, but he was fairly certain it wasn't properly shut. Was someone standing just inside with a gun drawn, waiting for the cop to step into their sights?

Jack wasn't going to have to wait long to find out. The door opened to the police car, and slowly, tentatively, the officer began to get out, edging his right foot forward, creeping and keeping low behind the door of the car, just in case someone was in the house waiting to take a shot. *Smart,* thought Jack.

The officer's head was locked on the house. Jack could see he wasn't moving much, deciding, probably, about whether to approach or not, no doubt assessing the condition of his colleagues as best he could. Jack knew, as the officer must surely have done too, that they were dead. The body of the one he could see was crumpled up in such a way that only came when all life is

283

snubbed out. He couldn't see the other side of the car, however. Maybe the second officer was still hanging in there?

Slowly, the officer moved out from behind his cover. Eyes on the house. Waiting for something, anything to happen. Jack looked at the house. The door hadn't moved. There was nothing happening in any of the windows.

CRACK!

The officer dropped on the spot, his body tottering and falling in on itself, left shoulder rotating backwards just a little bit as he went down. Sniper.

Jack made himself smaller. He figured that the sniper hadn't seen him yet – he was still alive after all – but if he wanted to stay that way, he had to find the shooter.

Jack shuffled slowly and carefully around to the left-hand side of the tree. The way the officer had fallen suggested the bullet had come from his right. From the force of the shot, the shooter was probably using a big calibre hunting rifle. It needed some force to make the officer's body spin as it went down. Once he was sure he was as covered as he could be, Jack risked a look.

Nothing.

No one in the treeline. No one moving to check the body. A sentry then. Someone who had the job of making sure no one went in the house whilst whoever was in there could carry out their job quickly and without worry. Smart set up, but where the hell were they?

Jack couldn't see any elevated areas, any structures in the distance. Whoever it was couldn't be too far away. There was too much foliage around, too many tree branches getting in the way of a clear shot. That meant they were near and probably elevated.

A hunter's perch. It had to be. Hunter's perches were structures that you could find dotted all over parts of the countryside where shooting took place. They ranged from sturdy wooden hides raised into the air on tall wooden legs to more simplistic, crude designs. One Jack had seen in a wood near Stansted Airport was nothing more than a plastic chair bolted to the trunk of a tree, with a rest for the rifle. Jack didn't know what sort of perch the shooter was using, but he was certain he must be using one.

Easing himself up slightly, Jack found a gap between the trunk of the tree and a large branch that sprouted out to the right. It was sturdy enough for him to be able to slide his right arm along and grab hold of it for support, pulling his head slowly out of cover to look at the scene. As long as the shooter was preoccupied looking for people who were still to come into the target zone, Jack figured he'd be okay.

Once in place, he waited a moment, looking for movement. Nothing. Where was the shooter then? A perch would have to be accessed by something like a ladder, be it rope or wood, or even something attached to the tree itself. Jack slowly scanned each tree, looking for something out of the ordinary.

There it was. Just past the house, giving the best angle straight down the road, which explained why his approach hadn't been noticed. Black rubber grips screwed to a tree trunk, the sort of thing that you might find on a ladder to stop your feet from slipping. They made six small steps, jutting out of the bark, up to a small wooden platform, on which a man was sat, black combat boots, green camo fatigues, rifle resting on a wooden beam in front of him, crouching forward, waiting for his next victim.

It wasn't going to be Jack. He eased the snub rifle that Kasim had given him forward, resting it on the curve of the branch and the trunk. There wasn't an extended stock to steady it as much as he would have liked, but he settled into the shot and waited for his heart to slow and his breathing to regulate. The man in the tree was going nowhere, so neither was Jack. Not until he'd removed the threat.

He looked through the sight, lining up the red dot on the man's chest. Almost there. He slipped his finger around the trigger, slowly adding a little more pressure, building up to the moment. Breathing under control. Heart rate steady. A little squeeze more.

The man moved.

Just a small move of the head, a glance across the yard. Maybe even a smile.

Another shooter.

Shit. That was the last thing Jack needed. It wasn't just back to square one, it was a whole new ballgame now.

He eased the gun back in behind the tree, slowly, being careful not to catch anything on a branch or some other obstacle that might give him away. The other guy must be over to his left, on the other side of the track in. That would explain why he couldn't see the body on the other side and why there hadn't been a concerted response that surely would have followed had the original pair of officers managed to get a radio call off, detailing the drama unfolding.

Looking out across the road wasn't as easy. The cover there was made up of a couple of bracken brushes, nothing more, as the treeline faded away. It made Jack hard to spot, but if he were spotted, then there was little in the way of density to slow a bullet. It also made it hard for him to get a clear shot lined up, but he was going to have to.

It didn't take him half as long to find the second shooter. Knowing where the first one was meant that it was simple trigonometry to work out the best position for a second shooter. Create a field of fire where nothing was left to chance. The second shooter had be off to the side of the road, similar height, aiming downwards, about fifty, sixty yards from the road, about seventy or eighty yards from him. The harder shot.

Which meant take it first. He found the man, just a little further out than he expected. A similar, if slightly more robust looking perch, this one with a wooden roof on it, but the same camouflage, same pose, rifle trained down the road, watching for incoming. Not watching for Jack.

Jack shuffled down onto his belly and moved backwards. The shot was on his left-hand side; he was right-handed. He needed to give himself a little more clearance from the tree to make the shot. It meant exposing himself. The moment the first shot went off, the second shooter would be looking for him. He would be open, he would have to move, he would draw attention to himself. At that point, it would be a straight race to the trigger. Jack was fast. How fast was the other guy?

Jack lined up the shot slowly. He placed his left arm out in front of him, resting the gun on it, cocking the barrel upwards, bringing the sight to his eye. No wind, nothing to really account for. A simple shot, if it was just one shot. Breathe. Relax. Visualise.

He ran it through in his head. A fluid process. Squeeze the trigger, drop the guy, bring the gun up and right, rest on the tree, find the second guy, fire. There was a lot going on in the middle of the process, but he was out of better ideas.

He ran it through one more time. Was there anything he could do better? It all rested on the motion. Be fluid, be loose, let it flow.

It was time.

His heart was beating steadily. His breathing was controlled. In. Out. In. Out. In Out.

PHUT.

The bullet zipped out from the muzzle of the gun, the suppressor doing its best to mask the sound. Jack knew it was true, aimed dead centre of the man's chest. He was already moving up and to his right as he heard the yelp. He found the first shooter, looking across to where the shout had come from, spying his friend. Costliest mistake he would ever make.

Jack was steadying the gun on the tree, doing all he could to compose himself. Focus on the process. Own your actions.

"Contact!" A shout from the first shooter. Jack could have done without that.

PHUT. PHUT.

Two shots now, central mass. There was no further shout from the first shooter. He whipped backwards, then slumped forward. Dead.

Jack had to go back to his left. He had to know the other shooter was dead. He looked. The man was sprawled backwards. He looked dead.

PHUT.

But you can always be more certain.

46

Nelmes hadn't been exactly comfortable with the idea of the two Regulators waiting in his office as he drafted the story, Adam and Emmie had been made well aware of that, but he hadn't really had much of a choice. Adam knew that getting the message out into the public domain was integral to the plan. If they learned of Nelmes' story, it made him a target, and with that in mind, Nelmes acquiesced.

The newspaper was situated on the twelfth floor of a modern office block at the north end of Canary Wharf. Nelmes' open-plan office looked out over Billingsgate Market, and had Nelmes been lucky enough to have had a window seat, he would have been able to see the merchants and traders beginning to come and go as the market prepared for its early morning opening. There was no time for window gazing now. Nelmes was focused on the narrative that was shaping in front of him, a stern and resolute look on his face, just a slight trace of a sweat on his brow.

Adam watched Nelmes' from where he and Emmie were stood in a canteen area, silently drinking a glass of water. The journalist was silhouetted by the iridescent blue glow of the computer screen, one of the few lights that was actually on in the office. Outside was dark, but not pitch black. It never was in the city, especially not this part, where the lights of the high rises that surrounded them shimmered and sparkled like beacons.

"You going to tell me what happened?" Emmie encouraged Adam.

Adam put the glass down and looked at her. Could he trust her? Now was as good a time as ever to find out. "I got into a conversation with some friends in the intelligence game."

"New friends or old?"

"New," Adam admitted.

"Did they bring anything interesting to the party?"

No going back, Adam thought. "They've got proof that we have a mole. Nick Poole, Lowri Graves' assistant."

"Shit," Emmie mulled it over. "Why aren't you telling anyone?"

"Because if he's involved, Lowri could be too. Or anyone. I don't know who I can trust." Adam was being totally honest. The situation worried him. He felt like they were all now massively exposed.

"You expecting something to happen?" Emmie asked, without even the slightest hint of worry.

"Always," Adam answered, again, honestly. "Truth is, as high profile as this place might be, it's still almost completely deserted, so we're exposed. The right people, the right team, with the right plan, could easily come in here and neutralise us all, without anyone ever being any wiser. Poole knows we're here, so you've got to think it would be a high probability."

"Should we call for backup?"

"That might tip him and anyone else off that we're on to him."

"So, we're bait." Emmie wasn't asking. She didn't sound like she was disapproving either.

"Best plan I can come up with on this short notice." Adam tried to raise a smile.

"How would you do it?" quizzed Emmie.

"In on the ground floor, remove security, then cut the power right as I got to the door to the office. You've got a split second of confusion as the light goes out to move and make that first chance count."

"Us two standing here in a confined space like this kitchen, probably makes us sitting ducks. Nowhere to run, nothing to give any real cover." Emmie ran her free hand over the MDF unit that would no doubt house communal bowls and plates.

"Yeah, you're right," Adam agreed, looking around the room, taking it all in. "I'll go check on our friend, see how his piece is coming together, you can patrol the perimeter. Might get a little advance warning if anything is amiss."

"Okay, but try not to get killed while I'm gone."

"I'll try." Adam screwed up his face as he nodded back sarcastically.

Emmie put her glass down and headed out of the office, watching Nelmes as she went. Adam couldn't help but be impressed with her. There was a confidence to her that he hadn't expected when he first saw her. She was in control of the job, in control of herself. Now she was in his circle of trust.

Adam walked over to Nelmes slowly. The journalist was typing quickly, his fingers rattling the keyboard against the desk with every stroke.

"We're getting there," Nelmes said without looking up from the screen.

"Great stuff. Pulitzer prize-winning?"

"That's an American thing," Nelmes rebuked him, "We get the British Journalism Awards. Not quite as cool a name, but it does exactly what it says on the tin."

Adam circled in behind Nelmes, placing his hand on his chair behind him. "Well, whatever the award, I'd be dusting down the mantlepiece. This is going to be a big one."

"Once I've worked out my backstory of how I came to get this information you mean. They don't tend to give it you for just copy and pasting,"

"We can help you with that. We specialise in backstories."

"I dread to think." Nelmes' hand flicked up his head to wipe away some sweat. He barely broke the rhythm of his typing.

"What's the angle you're going for?"

"A pretty brief overview of the story, some of the bigger names, conspiracy, yadda, yadda. We'll run more in-depth stuff throughout the week, I'm sure, but for now, I want to get the key points out and get people hooked in. Speaking of which..."

Now Nelmes stopped typing and swivelled his chair to face Adam.

"You are going to be going to the police with this, right?"

"They're already involved."

"Can I put that in the story?"

"Absolutely."

"Good, because the last thing I want is for people to think I've sat on this. That's enabling." He swivelled back to the screen and began typing again. "These fucking loons on social media, they need just one little slip-up, and they're on you like a pack of rabid thundercunts."

"Thunder whats?"

"It's a word, and it fits. Seriously though, if you have any sort of political leaning, and I don't mean just left or right, anything. Anarchist, socialist, fascist, even centrist, if you are politically minded, someone, somewhere from one of the other sides will try and batter you down in one hundred and forty characters or less. Not going to the police would be the thing they hung me on here."

"So, put it in."

"It's in, trust me."

"Good." Adam placed his hand on Nelmes' shoulder and gave it a reassuring squeeze. "You keep cracking on. Give me a shout when it's about to go live."

"Fifteen minutes, tops."

"Great."

Adam stepped away. It was best to let the man do his work. He turned and walked slowly towards the window, looking out over London. There were still a few more hours of darkness, but by the time the sun had come up, as people up and down the country began to go about their daily lives, Adam knew that the story they were writing here would be in the process of drastically changing the political landscape of the country. They were so close to it now.

His phone vibrated in his pocket. It was the office.

"Morgan," he answered.

"How far off are we on the story?" It was Grant. He sounded annoyed. Not angry, annoyed.

"Minutes."

"Can we go any faster?"

"I'll ask, why?"

"It's all gone off in Yorkshire. They've found the house and the kids, but I don't think Watts has the data we sent. There's no chatter about other operations." Grant almost hissed the name Watts.

"Can we not get through to Jack?" Adam asked.

"He's gone dark. Last we heard he was heading towards the same address with Mo and the Brotherhood."

"Fuck."

"I know."

Adam looked back into the room at Nelmes. "As soon as we're good to go, I'll let you know."

"I need to get that data to the police now. Lowri should never have done it so small scale. Too easy for it to go wrong."

Adam had to agree. If Lowri was working with Poole, compartmentalising the data release whilst secretly doing all she could to stop it getting out there would be a way of deflecting attention. "Keep me posted," Adam said, his mind racing.

Grant hung up. Adam watched Nelmes for a moment, then looked out the window. It was getting lighter. If someone was coming, it would be soon.

47

It quickly fell completely silent again around the house. Jack waited, hoping to hear the sound of someone trying to make a break for it from behind the house, but he heard nothing.

He dared a quick look towards the house. The door hadn't moved, the windows seemed empty, although he couldn't be sure. The house was dark inside, no movement, no sign of life, but he needed to make his move soon. Sooner or later, this place was going to be crawling with police.

He burst from his position, racing for the door. If someone was waiting to take a shot, they were going to have to be quick off the mark. Stumbling through the undergrowth, head down, making himself small, counting down the distance, twenty feet, fifteen, ten, five, zero. He slammed into the door. It was ajar and swung open. Jack ducked down, rolling into the room, a small, moving target. Hard to hit, should anyone be waiting. No shot came, but there was another sound.

The back door, just a creak, but definitely a noise. Jack was up again and darting through the narrow corridor, grazing past a table that threatened to jut out and knock him off track, before reaching the small kitchen that overlooked a ramshackle back garden, lined with broken concrete slabs and weeds that protruded through every crack and clump of earth in sight. There, in the middle of the garden, running away from the house, was Braun.

Jack fired. A quick burst, shattering the window of the kitchen. Something hit Braun. He wobbled and toppled then regained his composure and struggled on, darting behind a terminally neglected shed. Jack let off another round, into the shed, hoping a bullet would pass through the rotten wood, finding his target. In the next breath, he was chasing Braun down again, following his footsteps, out into the garden, hopping over the wobbly paving slabs, making for the shed.

Jack raised the barrel of the gun again, arcing away from the shed just enough to give himself the chance to take evasive action if Braun was standing waiting, but he wasn't. The area behind the shed was empty. Braun was gone, leaving just a small smear of blood on the wood. Not enough for Jack to tell the severity of the wound.

"Braun!" Jack bellowed. He wanted that son-of-a-bitch to know he was coming, that he would not stop, that he would catch up to him. He wanted him to know fear like never before.

Past the shed was a small bush that seemed to mark the boundary to the garden. Around it was more woodland, just like to the front of the property. Jack didn't think, he just followed. He had to keep on the trail, Braun knew the area after all. Losing him for just a brief second could be all it took for the trail to go cold.

He wasn't out of sight for long, but already Braun was moving into the distance by the time Jack reacquired him. He continued to head north, as Jack had expected, away from the road, putting as much distance between him and the police as possible. Jack raised the gun and tried to find an angle for the shot, but the trees made it impossible to get anything clear. He fired anyway, and Braun ducked. Enough to slow his stride and keep him nervous. Reeling his quarry in.

Whatever injury Braun had suffered didn't seem to be slowing him, much to Jack's chagrin. He was fast, surefooted, decisive. Jack had never been the best sprinter; his frame wasn't built for that. Too much extra muscle. What he was good at, however, was holding a good pace longer than most. Fatigue didn't bother him. He could switch that part of his brain off, especially when he was as focused as he was now. Be it running down someone who wanted to escape him, or fighting to the bitter end; Jack could always turn off the pain receptors that would inhibit others. He could run through walls and not notice. Right now, there were no walls, but the branches and brambles of the woodland snatched out at him. Jack didn't feel as they stung him. He ran on. Straight line, as fast as he could, straight at Braun.

Braun wasn't looking back, which was a mistake. It meant he was darting, diving one way and then another, just in case Jack was waiting to line up a shot. A longer route. Jack was closing. Not quickly, not enough yet, but he was definitely getting nearer.

Braun glanced over his shoulder. He must have seen the gap narrowing. Jack waited for him to take a shot back. He didn't. Jack couldn't see a gun in either hand. He pushed himself harder, forcing every muscle to strain that little bit more to propel him as fast they could towards his target.

Braun stumbled, not to the ground, not quite, just enough to need to put a hand down to steady himself. He would have made it back to his feet had Jack not barrelled into him, driving a shoulder into Braun's left side, almost directly on his kidney, pushing up and into his ribcage, trying to take all of the air out of him, to put him on the ground, unable to get up.

Jack tried to hold onto Braun as they fell, but his hands didn't find a grip quickly enough, and he found himself rolling over Braun, landing in front of him, his back momentarily to his opponent.

He twisted around, planting his feet firmly into the ground, bringing himself back up. Braun was still on the ground, spluttering, winded, his right arm reaching across his midriff, grabbing at his side where Jack had hit him.

Jack lunged.

The right hand came away from the ribs, a gun in it. A bluff. Braun had suckered him in. They were now in a split-second race for who was going to land their blow first, and it was heading for a photo finish.

There was the unmistakable pop as the pistol in Braun's hand went off just as Jack fell onto him. Jack felt a sharp pain on his left-hand side. A momentary pain. A graze. Not enough to put him down, not even close.

Jack crashed into Braun, an even heavier blow this time, his left hand instantly coming up, his hand wrapping around the wrist that held the gun. He drove his right forearm down and into Braun's throat, then slammed his left hand down, once, twice, three times, till the gun came loose.

Braun squirmed under the pressure, and Jack sneered down at him.

"This is going to hurt."

He lifted his right forearm up, then brought it down sharply into Braun's temple, knocking him clean out.

Jack ran for a good half an hour with Braun on his shoulders, until he was sure they were a decent distance away from where the police would now be congregated. The weight was heavy, and his shoulders ached, but he had to put more distance between himself and the gamekeeper's lodge.

Braun hadn't shown any sign of coming around, which made it easier than it could have been. Even when Jack dumped him down on the ground. There wasn't even the slightest resistance. Jack dragged his limp body to a tree, sitting Braun up against it, wrapping his arms backwards around the trunk and then cuffing them. He searched his pockets and found a set of keys with an electric fob that he pocketed. He checked where the bullet Braun had fired had hit him. He found an inch-long gash halfway up his side, just under his ribcage. It was still bleeding lazily and would need a clean and patching up, but nothing more. He sat down, watching Braun, and waited.

Braun came to about ten minutes later, his eyes rolling in his head, which rose then drooped up and down three times before he shook it, clearing the fog.

"Fuck. You shot me."

"Likewise." Jack fixed his eyes on Braun, his voice calm and measured. "For you though, it was just a prelude."

"Yeah. I figured as much." Braun looked at Jack, his face resigned. "How bad was it?"

"Flesh wound, just above your hip."

"Shame it wasn't something more serious."

"You're definitely going to think so." Jack stood up.

"What happens now?" Braun sounded defeated. *He should do*, Jack thought.

Jack looked away from the tree, letting the moment linger. He was in no mood to give Braun a quick and easy passage. There was work to be done, but it would be done at his pace. The woods thinned in front of them, a small ridge looking down towards a field with a drop of about twenty feet. It gave Jack a little bit of reassurance to know no one could creep up in that direction. He turned back to Braun.

"Let's talk about Mo."

"A brave man," Braun almost sounded respectful, but it was too late for any kind of redemption.

"Very brave."

"You didn't give him the credit he deserved."

Jack felt his temper rise, as Braun no doubt would have wanted. He didn't react though. He just smiled at Braun, a small, slight, smile. No warmth.

"He died a hero, which is more than most of us will ever get to say."

Braun said nothing.

Jack knelt down in front of him.

"You made me watch him die."

"It's your weakness. If we'd have had another half an hour in there, if you'd have seen him on death's door, you would have talked."

Jack ignored the provocation. "You stabbed him in the stomach, and you made me watch him die. Now I want to do both to you."

A look somewhere between confusion and panic shot across Braun's face. Jack pressed home the advantage and slipped out the knife Kasim had given him. He held it in front of Braun.

"I'm going to take this knife, slice across your gut, then I'm going to reach on in there, pull your intestine out, so you can see it. Then I'm going to slice it in two, walk away and let you watch your insides spill out on the floor as you die in agony."

Braun was going white.

"There is nothing, absolutely nothing you can do to save yourself," Jack explained. "You pushed me. You thought you could break me, maybe you nearly did. But you didn't finish me. That will cost you your life."

Braun swallowed, his tongue flicking out quickly over his drying lips.

Jack pulled up Braun's shirt, pressing the knife against Braun's abdomen.

"Any last words?"

Braun's eyes were wide, but he stayed silent.

Jack pressed the knife in, red blood trickling down Braun's chest. He began to slowly draw it across.

"Wait!" Braun's voice was shrill.

"I said no redemption." Jack pulled it slowly, another half an inch.

"Please. Please. Let me help you!" Braun begged.

"Help me?"

"The people you're up against, you have no idea what you're dealing with."

"We have the files. We know."

"You think the people behind this are linked to the files?" Braun looked at him incredulously. "You really are amateur."

Jack ignored the barb, but pulled the knife away, sitting down. "Go on," he insisted.

"There is a group of people, government officials, but not MPs, Secret Service guys, this country and others, all of them. They have these arrangements, honey traps for people who they can manipulate afterwards to do what they want, be it voting for legislation, the shit they write in their newspapers, the interest rates they vote for, whatever. Every part of our lives, they influence in whatever way they can."

"We worked that much out for ourselves."

"Yes, but you don't know who they are."

"I'm finding it hard to believe you do."

"Lord Brier hired me to do more than just caretake the children. You've seen my record; you know what I can do."

"What did you do?" Jack asked.

"I got names, that's what I do. He wanted an insurance policy, something he could use against them if he wanted to get out of jail free, which I'm guessing he'll want to, right about now, if this thing is about to be blown open."

"Tell me some of the names."

Braun shook his head. "I don't know any names. They're on a drive, back at Brier's. Hidden away somewhere that they would never be found, but I can show you."

Jack stood up, putting the knife away, sighing. "You know what, most of that I believe. There is a drive, there are names on it, and Brier is going to be using it. Thing is, I don't believe you don't know any of the names."

"I don't, but I can take you to it."

Jack pulled out his pistol, pointing it at Braun. "You already did."

He pulled the trigger, shooting Braun at point blank range in the head. He dropped the pistol next to Braun, then scrambled down the embankment and ran.

48

"How long?" Adam asked Nelmes, who was still typing at his computer. They were closing in on the fifteen minutes he had specified.

Nelmes didn't answer. He remained fixed on the screen, typing still. Concentrating, Adam realised. He was back at the kitchen, watching from a good twenty feet away, so Nelmes must have tuned him out. He called again.

"We nearly there?"

Nothing. Adam stepped from behind the counter and idly began to walk over. The fingers will still brushing the keys on the keyboard, the eyes fixed. He was really sweating now, a collection of beads of perspiration collecting on his forehead, glistening from the light of the computer screen.

"Nelmes?"

"What?" The journalist turned and looked at Adam.

"How long?"

"Uh, I'm not... minutes?" Nelmes mumbled.

Adam saw it then. It wasn't just a few beads of sweat on his head. He was dripping, sweat pouring from his head, his armpits, down his chest. His skin looked grey, it had been hard to tell before, illuminated only by the ghostly light of the computer screen, but at this distance, it was much clearer.

"You feeling okay?"

Nelmes went to say something, his mouth opened, but no sound came out, it just hung there limply, closed slightly, then dropped open again, a thread of dribble pooling, then falling from a corner of his mouth.

305

"Shit!" Adam exclaimed as Nelmes pitched forward from his seat, his body tensing, hitting the ground with a heavy thump as he started to convulse violently on the floor. "Emmie!"

Adam dashed to Nelmes, dropping to his knee, scooping an arm under him and rolling him over, trying to grapple with his thrashing body. His eyes were completely rolled back into his head, and where the saliva had been falling from his mouth, now white foam bubbled and gushed out, coating his chin and neck in a slimy foam.

Emmie came into the room. "Where are you?" she called.

"Nelmes desk, here. He's having a seizure."

"What the hell?" Adam heard her response, then the sound of her running on the soft carpeted floor. She was with them seconds later. "How?"

"I don't know," Adam answered, "he was fine, at his desk, then he just keeled over."

Emmie took off her coat and balled it up, pushing it under his head. The convulsions had already started to subside from their first furious moments into more rigid twitches as Nelmes arms and legs began to draw up.

"We're losing him," Adam triaged him in his head, noting the symptoms, knowing they were so far away from the immediate help they were going to need. "Hold him for me."

He placed a hand on Nelmes' chest as Emmie shuffled over and took up his spot. Adam stood and looked around. Someone had poisoned Nelmes, but what with? There was no glass or mug on Nelmes' desk; Adam hadn't seen him take a drink. Maybe something had been slipped to him before they got there? Maybe it was nothing but coincidence?

"Did he get the story done?" Emmie looked up at Adam.

Adam looked down at the screen, reading the last paragraph. It looked complete. "I don't know. I think he wrote it but didn't publish it."

Adam went to press the keyboard when he heard Emmie shout, "Don't!"

He felt her grab his jacket and pull him back, hard, unbalancing him so that he fell to his behind.

He turned to look at her and saw her holding one of Nelmes' wrists with her other hand, pointing the hand towards Adam. He saw the fingers. He saw the skin blistered, broken, cracked, already red raw, bubbling in places, in others turning black with infection.

"The keyboard," Emmie explained. "It's on the keyboard."

"Jesus Christ." All the time they had been waiting for an attack, but it had already taken place. Adam got up. "Wait here."

Getting his phone out at the same time, he headed for the kitchen. The call was already connecting to the emergency services by the time he was opening the drawers looking for what he needed. Normal protocol would have been to call this in to the Regulators emergency medical team, but he wanted Nelmes to have the best chance of survival, and he knew that London's emergency services could be on the scene far quicker and ready for this.

"999, which service would you like?"

"Ambulance." It didn't matter if he said any of the services. What he was going to say next would mean there would be a multiagency response that went above and beyond. As he waited and listened to the operator connecting his call, he found a pair of metal salad tongs and a fork in a cutlery drawer and made his way quickly back out of the kitchen to Emmie and Nelmes.

"How is he?" he asked as he got there, taking the tongs and placing them around the mouse.

"Not good," Emmie replied, looking on hopelessly as Nelmes foamed and spasmed on the floor.

"London Ambulance service, can I take your name please?"

Adam ignored the request. "I'm on the twelfth floor of the Golden Dock building at Canary Wharf. I have a male who has been exposed to a nerve agent. He is unconscious and needs atropine quickly. This is a hot zone, two other people, unknown substance, probably absorbed through the skin."

Adam heard the sound of the call centre in the background as the operator took a split second to take it all in before her voice came back calmly and authoritatively.

"Is the patient breathing?"

"Yes, but he's not got long. Whatever he was exposed to, he's had a big dose. There's nothing we can do for him, other than try and keep him comfortable."

"We're on our way, sir. What was your name again?"

Adam hung up. He'd been on long enough.

"They're on their way," he told Emmie before turning his attention to the computer. He guided the mouse using the tongs, moving the cursor until it hovered over the publish button, then he took the fork and used the handle to press the mouse button. A small wheel icon appeared over the word publish. Then the screen changed, a new message displayed itself on the screen.

"Your article has been published."

"Job done," Adam sighed. He let go of the fork and tongs, leaving them on the desk, kneeling back down next to Nelmes and Emmie.

"What's going to happen now?"

"We're out of the game for a little bit. We need to be decontaminated, just in case, then the Met and the spooks are going to start asking questions. How long that lasts depends on how long someone can get us out of there."

"What are we talking?"

"Hours, days, I genuinely don't know." He looked at Emmie. "Thanks, you saved me back there. If I'd have touched that keyboard, I could have been lying next to him."

"No problem. Let's hope we saved him too."

Adam looked at Nelmes and wondered if it was already too late.

49

"Listen, I don't know if you've thought this through or not, but we really ain't got anywhere to be sticking all these kids."

The custody sergeant in front of Thea looked harrassed, beaten already by the problem that had been bestowed upon him.

"They're kids and they're scared. Just get them somewhere comfortable to sit, and something nice to eat and drink." Thea hadn't wanted to sound aggressive, but she knew from the reaction of the sergeant, as his head pulled backwards, that she had been.

"Fine, fine" came the flustered reply, and he turned and walked away. Thea sympathised with him. At no point in his career would he have expected to have had a situation like this on his hands. Neither had she, even though over the last few days she had become more and more aware of what was happening.

Thea turned back and looked at the children as they were being brought in. Already a few had found their way onto the plastic chairs that lined the waiting area of the station. They all looked scared and confused. Some sat with knees drawn up, others stood just staring at the new world they had just been dumped into. Ideally, they would have gone to the hospital where they could be checked out and given a bed, but Malton hospital was still closed and wasn't set up for this sort of event, so this was the next best step. She needed to get them out of this room, however. It was too exposed to the outside world, and Thea wasn't prepared to take any risks. The sooner the sergeant found them a more secure spot, the better.

She slowly moved over to one child, a young girl, not more than six or seven, dirty face, scruffy, filthy blonde hair, but with the most piercing blue eyes that searched the room, watching everything. She looked confused, scared. Thea knelt next to her.

"Hi," she said softly. The girl's head turned slowly to look at her. She swallowed but said nothing, so Thea asked the first question that came into her mind. "What's your name?"

There was a pause where the girl looked like she was working out the answer to the question, in the same way Thea might have expected any other six-year-old when faced with a maths question, but not simply what her name was.

"Jade," the girl replied softly. Thea smiled.

"Hi, Jade, I'm Thea. I'm a police officer."

Jade nodded.

"How old are you, Jade?"

Thea waited and watched again as Jade tried to make sense of the question. This time, however, there was no connection. Thea felt her heart sink. How could a child not know how old they were?

"Can you remember your mummy and daddy?"

Jade nodded. "They died."

"I'm sorry," Thea said, then she wondered if that was true, or if it was just something that Jade had been told. "Who told you that?"

Jade shrugged. "Everyone. All our mummies and daddies died, so we had to go to the house."

"Is that what the people there told you?"

Jade nodded again.

"Okay, well, we'll find somewhere for you that's safe."

Jade lurched forward and grabbed Thea's arm. "I don't want to go back," she pleaded, tears suddenly cascading down her face as she cried out with ear-shattering terror.

Thea wrapped her arm around Jade, pulling her close, hoping to do something that would abate the cries. "You're not going back, I promise. Never. You're safe now."

Thea found the tears forming in the corners of her eyes. She buried her head into the back of Jade's neck and let herself sob.

She let herself cry with the girl for a couple of minutes before handing her over to one of the specialist officers who had begun to arrive. They, along with a team of doctors and social workers, were going to be carrying out the first part of what would be a long process of tests, physical and mental, to determine what was the best next step for each child. Thea had asserted that no less than four people should have eyes on each child at any one time. She didn't know who she could trust still, so she was taking no chances. The doors to the area where the children were being kept were to be guarded as were the exits and entrances to the station. No one was taking these children back. They were going to be safe while she was around.

Her next job was to bring Wilkes up to speed. The Sergeant had arrived ten minutes ago and had told Thea he needed an update as soon as she was free. Wilkes was one of the people Thea desperately hoped she could trust. Her boss had been one of the few good things in her work life since she had arrived in the north. Now wasn't the time for him to reveal a different side.

"Quite a mess," he said as she entered his office. Wilkes was perched on his desk, one leg stretched to the floor, the other dangling around the corner where he was straddled. In one hand was a tablet computer, his other hand flicking across the screen as he looked at what Thea assumed were images from the farm. "No suspects in custody?"

"It was a warzone up there, sir. I don't know what else to tell you."

"Three officers dead, Watts, you need to tell me something."

Thea had heard on the radio about the bodies at the farmhouse. Instantly, she had felt guilt. She ordered it secured; her call sent those officers to their deaths. Wilkes would know that.

"I'm sorry, sir."

"So am I. You know we're going to need to go through the whole thing with a fine-tooth comb." He stood up from the desk and put the tablet down. "Jesus, Thea, come on, tell me what the hell is happening here because you and I know straight up that you didn't just stumble on that house by accident. The kid you've been looking after has disappeared, I'm going to guess he's off with one of the officers here who just booked in a holiday after working with you on that. Then let's get to the fellow who was supposed to be his uncle. I've got lads down there who swear blind he was running from the scene of the shooting at the farmhouse."

"Sir…" Thea paused. How far could she trust Wilkes? Should she be honest, or should she shut him out, leave him with a few half-truths? She thought back to her last conversation with

Jack, the anger she had felt, the betrayal, when she realised he hadn't been honest with her. Now was the time to trust someone. "Sir, I'm going to need you to call Professional Standards."

"Why?"

"I've reason to believe that there's a far-reaching conspiracy to kidnap and abuse children, and I fear that we're going to uncover a number of names from the police force have been involved when we start digging. More than the police force too. This thing, it goes everywhere."

"So I've been hearing."

Thea panicked. How could he know? Wilkes answered the question for her. "It's all just broken in the last hour online. All over the internet, the news channels. Someone leaked some information to one of the papers. That's great, backs you up. What it doesn't do is exonerate a single thing you've done here. People are dead because you did things the wrong way." His voice grew louder as he reached the end of his rant, his face getting redder.

Thea looked down. She didn't want to anger him. She didn't want to anger anyone. She'd tried to do the right thing, but she knew she'd failed on so many levels. The children might be safe now, but at what cost? She bowed her head to the ground. "I'm sorry, sir."

"Fuck your sorry," he snapped. "Do the right thing, for once."

Thea's head rose. "For once? All I ever do is the right thing. Sir." She felt her anger rising as she met the challenge headon.

"Did you? Three bodies out there say otherwise."

"Three bodies that I didn't pull the trigger on, so don't you even begin to lay that on me. I called in a hostage situation, I called it in as armed, so each and every one of those officers knew what they were going in there expecting to see, and believe me, when I say that, I'm not shifting blame on them, I'm putting the blame firmly on the shits who pulled the triggers."

"And who were they? Who were the shits who pulled the triggers? Because without them, and without a bloody good reason for you being there, this all just becomes your mess."

"I was there because I had reason to believe the occupant of the house was involved in the abduction of the lad we had in."

"That's funny because I've got no log of that. No call in from yourself to let anyone know where you're going to be. I've just got you calling officers into two locations, both of which turn out to be ambushes."

"Are you saying you think I'm involved?"

"No, for fuck's sake, Thea, I'm saying you're irresponsible. You're bloody dangerous. You don't think things through, and you get people hurt."

"How could I? I didn't know who to trust!"

"We do things by the book, we do it the right way, that's why we're the bloody good guys."

"Only we're not. We've been infiltrated. The people behind this are inside our system, they work in our offices, they answer our phones. Those kids could have been at risk if I put the call out too soon."

"You don't get to make those choices." Wilkes sounded exasperated. "We're the police. If we start doing things outside of the rulebook, we're pointless. You know that, but let's be honest,

315

you've never done it the right way. We both know your record. This is you, Thea, you're a bloody loose cannon."

Thea knew where this was heading, so why wait, she figured. "Come on then, let's get to the crux, shall we? Let's get to the bit where you fire me, or suspend me, or put me on gardening leave. Whatever, sir, let's get to it."

"I'm not giving you an out." Wilkes looked at her with something nearing disgust. "You think you can make this mess and walk away? You're totally barking up the wrong tree. You're going to see this case through, then after that, the Office for Police Conduct can have you and do as they will with you. I don't know what you've done Thea, I don't know how many laws you've broken, and frankly, it's bottom of my list of priorities right now. You need to go downstairs, sort this shit out, get these kids safe, and then, fuck it, you're not my problem."

Thea shook her head and ran her hand through her hair. She allowed herself a little laugh and then looked at Wilkes. "Fuck me, Wilkes, all that you've just said to me and then you come out with that. Fucking hell."

"What do you mean?" Wilkes screwed his face up.

"You don't even know what a hypocritical little shit you are."

Thea turned, walked out of the room, slamming the door. She didn't want to wait to hear what Wilkes said next; it was all just noise to her now. How could he chew her out for what she had done, when he was just as prepared to ignore protocol to get these kids safe?

Her feet thudded heavily on each stair as she raced to get back downstairs. She'd wasted enough time. She needed to put a proper plan into place to make sure these kids were safe.

Back in the waiting room, it was quieter now. The children had been moved on, and all that was left behind the desk was a lone officer.

"Where are the children?" Thea asked.

"The sarge cleared everyone out of the canteen." The officer sounded a little disgruntled about that. Perhaps he'd missed his morning coffee.

"Great, a little bit quieter in here for you," Thea tried to cheer him up. She'd pissed off enough people for one day, she thought. Why not try a new tack?

"For now," the officer shrugged, his tone resigned. "Don't know how long it's going to stay that way."

"What do you mean?"

"Take a look." The officer nodded to the door. "I reckon these are just the first. Be more soon enough, once they're all up and out their beds."

Thea stepped around the counter and walked towards the door. Outside she could see a rabble of people outside, huddled together in the cold morning air, talking to one and other. Normal looking people, a multitude of ages, men and women. Everyday people. Thea opened the door and stepped outside. They must have heard the door, stopping their chatter and turning towards her as she headed their way. One of them, a woman in a pink puffer jacket and grey knitted hat, probably in her early fifties, stepped out of the group and approached her.

"What's happening in there? Are they safe?" her tone was sharp, almost accusatory, Thea thought.

"Who?"

"The kids. We know that the police were involved in what happened to them, so we're not going anywhere till we know they're safe."

"They're safe," Thea said in the most non-confrontational tone she could muster.

"And you are?"

"DC Watts, CID."

"Well, DC Watts, I've lived around here all my life and I've never seen you before, so I'm sorry, I don't know why for one second I should trust you."

Thea stood for a moment, nodding thoughtfully at the woman's provocation, all the time trying to look like she was mulling over giving a reason as to why she should be trusted, while in truth, she was convincing herself that it would be more trouble than it was worth to hit the woman in pink in front of her.

In the end, Thea Watts said nothing. She turned around and walked back into the station.

"Lock that damn door. Anyone comes near, call for backup," Thea said to the officer at the desk.

50

The emergency services arrived a little under ten minutes after the call had been made. It probably would have been much quicker had they not been on the twelfth floor.

First, firefighters decked in protective clothing, most probably from the nearby Millwall fire station, had arrived, then two paramedics in similar bright yellow plastic suits had come in. They had immediately begun to tend to Nathan Nelmes, whilst the firefighters had taken Emmie and Adam down one at a time in the lifts.

Decontamination had been an annoyance. Clothes and phones confiscated, which left them naked in two senses. The standard issue phones of Regulators were encrypted, but protocol dictated that they'd had to purge them anyway prior to the emergency services arriving. Adam had briefly checked in with the office, apprising them of the situation, and had been told curtly to sit put while they tried to work out a way to get them out.

Now they sat in the back of an ambulance, both in blue NHS gowns that they had been given to cover their modesty, watching out of the open rear door as they waited for someone to decide what would happen next. In front of them was a scene that looked chaotic to the untrained eye but was anything but. Blue lights flashed from a host of emergency vehicles; fire engines, ambulances, police cars. The police were erecting a cordon around the building, evacuating the remaining members of staff. Adam tried to watch as many as he could, committing faces to memory, looking for someone who looked like they didn't belong, but seeing no one obvious. Two fire officers in hazmat suits came down carrying plastic bags, in which Adam could see the keyboard, mouse, and screen of the computer, whilst another followed, carrying a sealed plastic box, in which no doubt was the tower of the computer and the monitor itself.

"How much trouble are we in?" Emmie asked from behind him.

"With the authorities, quite a lot. With our bosses, probably even more," Adam said grimly. The computer would contain traces of whatever had been used to attack Nelmes. As he watched the largest concentration of it being taken away, he knew their chance of using it to help track down the attackers was probably disappearing with it. However far the Vehm's reach was, it would be a while before they would know anything about the substance.

"I'll back you up," Emmie murmured. "Whatever the story you want to go with, let me know."

Adam turned and looked at her. "The truth works for me."

"Even for the police?"

"Well, perhaps not for the police or anyone else official looking. Sometimes it's best just to say nothing in those cases. They might hold us for a couple of days at most. Might be that the Vehm decide that's a fitting punishment, to let us stew, but if we say nothing, we can't incriminate ourselves."

"We didn't do anything though."

"Not to Nathan, no, but we do break the law every day by being Regulators. That, we need to keep quiet about. Eventually, someone will come."

"You seem certain about that."

"They have to. They've got just as much to lose as we have if we end up talking," Adam shrugged as he explained, a shrug of indifference, trying to present a calmness to Emmie. She didn't seem worried, far from it in fact. Her questions were cold and procedural, no hint of fear or emotion in her voice. She trusted him.

"Of course, that doesn't clear up the other problem," he added.

"Who did it?"

"I think we know who did it."

"Poole?"

"Yeah, I'm far more interested in who gave him the order."

"It can only be one of a few people." Emmie had done the math, and she'd probably come up with the same figures Adam had. None of which he liked very much.

"Someone who knew the op, knew where we were, knew what we were doing."

"That's a limited number."

"I know. Me, you, Lowri, and Grant."

"And Quinn."

Adam shook his head. "Not Jack, no way."

"He knew," Emmie pointed out.

"But he wouldn't have done it."

"I'm still on your list."

Adam felt the twang of guilt. She was still on his list. She had to be.

"I've known Jack for a long time," he began the defence of his partner.

"But you haven't known him for a long time. I mean, when was the last time you saw him? Who knows what might have happened in that time. This isn't about you trusting him over me. It's about coming at this right, coming at this from all angles."

"Yeah, well, that's just not an angle that makes sense. I mean, I get it, he has every right to be pissed off with the Regulators, with the Vehm, but to take that and turn it on innocent people? On kids?"

Emmie cut him off. "Maybe he doesn't see them as innocent?"

"On friends then," Adam objected. "On David, on me. That's not who Jack is, grudge or no grudge."

He had hoped that would be the end of it, but he could see Emmie readying her next salvo. She opened her mouth but then stopped, looking over his shoulder. Adam turned. The paramedics were back, two of them, still in their protective suits. No one was taking any chances.

"How are you feeling?" the first paramedic asked, a woman with what looked, from behind her visor and hood, to be short, blonde, spiky hair.

"So far, so good," Adam said truthfully and with more than a little relief. Being that close to whatever had been used on Nelmes had huge risks. The possibility that they had been infected too was very real. He'd pushed it to the back of his mind as best as he could, but the truth was that he'd feel a lot better with an all-clear from a doctor.

"That's good to hear. We're going to take you to Newham University Hospital. You'll be assessed by the team there, and hopefully, they'll be able to give you some positive news."

"Hope so," Emmie said.

"Take a seat," the paramedic nodded. "We'll get going soon."

"Thanks, will do," Adam replied.

The door closed and Emmie sighed. "Let's hope she's right," she said as she sat down on one of the seats that lined the side of the ambulance.

Moments later, the engine started up, the ambulance began to move. All Adam could do was wait.

51

All morning long, the crowd grew. Each time Thea looked out of the window, there was another handful of people joining the group. There were easily thirty to forty people standing outside, waiting for something to happen. Thea wondered if they knew what that something was, or if they just felt compelled to be there, but all the same, for a town the size of Malton, it was quite a large gathering. They spilled from the pavement onto the street, every now and again irritating a passing motorist, but so far, no tempers had been frayed too far. There was still a sense of calm.

A couple of rooms along from where she had looked out of the window was the canteen area where the children had been returned and were currently eating what Thea guessed was their first decent meal in a very long time. One or two had eyed it suspiciously at first, but most had tucked straight in with ravenous vigour. Within minutes, the plates were all but clear.

Thea watched them from a distance. She had been told that she should observe the children only. It was hard. Jade's story had hurt, and as she sat there, she saw the young girl, a little cleaner now, a little more energized, guzzling squash from a plastic cup.

"Watts?" The custody sergeant was back. Thea nodded back at him, realising she still didn't even know his name. "I need you to come and look at something," he said.

"Something good?" Thea tried to raise a smile.

"We weren't born that lucky."

The custody sergeant took her back to the custody desk, a tall, raised structure that looked over the booking area. The place was deserted at the moment. Mornings weren't a big time for crime in Malton, clearly.

Behind the desk was a laptop used mainly for checking in suspects, but at the moment, as perhaps would be the case on any work computer, anywhere, a social media page was open.

"What's this?" Thea asked.

"Local group, you know, online community forum. Place where folk come and air their woes, take pops at the council, that sort of thing. Sometimes we get some good stuff from it, sometimes it's just trash."

"I know what you mean. This is the Malton one I'm guessing?"

"Aye, certainly is, and it's full of stuff about our guests, look."

The custody sergeant turned the laptop towards Thea, and she began to read the top post in the thread. It was an angry diatribe about how the police had been found culpable already in the scandal and were now holding some of the victims "hostage" in stations up and down the land until they could be rehoused in other centres where they would continue to be abused.

"Same shit that they said outside. And people are buying it?"

"Some, which is more than a worry."

Thea looked at the original post again. There was something about it that unsettled her. The whole thing was constructed perfectly; there was a real attempt to build emotion in the reader. There were a few spelling and grammar mistakes here and there, but the more that Thea looked at it, the more she felt they were deliberate.

"Do you know this person?" Thea clicked on the name of the author, bringing up their profile page.

"Let me have a look," the custody sergeant said, peering closely. "Nope, not a name I know, but then, there's a fair few folk around here I don't know."

"Can you check the records?"

"I can do that, sure. You reckoning on paying them a visit?"

"More that I want to know if they're real or not," Thea admitted.

"Fake news?"

"Fanning the fires at least. Can you keep an eye on this page, let me know if anything else happens?"

"That's just it, I want you to check this one as well."

The custody sergeant took the browser back, and the conversation thread came back again. He scrolled down the page, stopping at another comment. Thea read it.

"What do you think?" the custody sergeant asked.

We need to be prepared to go in and get them. Bring whatever you need.

"I think I hope no one reading that is that stupid."

"There's a few folks what are saying they are. They could be, what's the word, trolls, I suppose?" the custody sergeant offered helpfully.

"They could be, but even if they are, it's all positive reinforcement. Mob mentality is a shit."

"You reckon they're coming in?"

Thea pulled a face as she thought about it. It made no sense. "They might, but I don't know why. I mean, this feels orchestrated, but what are they after?"

"The kids?"

"How are they going to get them though? The people who they'll be using as their mob will be doing all they can to protect the kids. If that's their end game, the moment they show their true colours, they'll be overwhelmed."

"Okay, so it's not the kids. Must be you then?"

Thea looked at him. She went to say something, but before she could, an alarm cut through the building.

"What's happening?" Thea asked as the custody sergeant quickly moved to a bank of CCTV screens to his right.

"Bloody hell. The idiots are trying to come in through the doors."

Thea looked. They were. A number of the protestors were at the front door, kicking at the already broken glass, barging into it with their shoulders, and as they watched, two came up with a long-pointed piece of metal and wedged it into the doors, trying to force it open.

"Where's the riot gear?"

"Kit room is down the corridor there." The custody sergeant waved his arm down the corridor that they had entered through.

"Get yourself kitted up, get some help, and hold that front door," Thea ordered.

"Where are you going?"

"I'm going to make sure those kids are alright."

By the time she got upstairs, panic had set in with the children. Some were crying, all of them looked scared. They were huddled into the middle of the room, officers at every door. Wilkes was sat with them, talking to a couple of them, trying his best to keep them calm. He looked up briefly at Thea as she entered before turning back to the children.

Thea looked around the room. It looked secure, there wasn't much she could add, other than another body, but something about the way Wilkes looked at her made her feel she should be elsewhere. On the outside of the room, however, maybe there she could be a stop gap.

She stepped back through the door, closing it behind her, waiting.

Her radio cackled. "They're in, they're in, falling back."

Not good. Once the outer perimeter was breached, it would only be a matter of time before someone made it up the stairs.

Then there was a noise. Not from downstairs, not from the canteen, but one of the side rooms. A dull thud, as though something or someone had fallen over. Thea pulled her baton out and flicked her wrist, extending the pole. She reached toward the door, opening it slowly, not knowing what she might find. Friend, foe, or nothing.

The door eased open, Thea could see nothing. She stepped slowly inside. Still nothing. No one in sight. What had made the noise? She looked around, then up.

The skylight was open.

She spun around quickly, but it was too late, she felt a strong arm grab her, pinning her arms, while another brought a gun up to her head as she was thrown sideways down onto a table.

"Where's the boy?" a voice hissed.

Thea struggled and looked up at her assailant. A tall, strong man in a balaclava.

"Where's the boy?" the question came again, a little more vehemently this time.

"I don't know who you mean," Thea replied through gritted teeth.

"Ciaran, where is he?"

"Gone."

"Where?"

"I don't know."

The man peered at her through his balaclava. He must have believed her because she felt the grip loosen. She began to relax. Then he brought the butt of the pistol crashing down on her head, and she felt nothing.

52

Everything was muffled and confused. There were noises, but no sights. Someone's voice perhaps. Thea tried to concentrate. Her head felt like it was in a fog and she needed to find her way out. What had happened to her?

The noises became clearer. Someone was saying something. A man. She could hear a man's voice somewhere in the distance. It almost sounded like it was calling to her.

She felt her eyes open, and she saw light and shapes, but she couldn't make anything out. Something was moving toward her, hovering over her. Jesus, her head hurt.

"Thea!"

She felt one hand on her arm and another on her neck, lightly pressing on the side like someone was checking for a pulse. Why were they checking for her pulse? Nothing made sense.

She wanted to get up, but she couldn't. It felt like her body was heavier than it should be. She tried to talk, but she couldn't.

"Thea, are you okay? Can you hear me?"

She knew the voice. Wilkes. That was who it was. What was he doing here with her? She tried to ask him, but all she could muster was a croak. What was going on?

"Take your time, mate. Take your time."

Wilkes' voice was soothing. She focused on it, her vision slowly becoming clearer. She could see his face now. He looked somewhere between concerned and caring. She felt the pain in her head, and it started to come back. The man in the room, being hit, him wanting Ciaran.

"Ciaran," she said groggily, trying to sit up. Her whole world spun as she did, but she knew she had to fight through it.

"What happened?" Wilkes asked.

"There was a man." Thea tried to get her brain to kick into gear. "He wanted to know where Ciaran was."

"What man?"

Thea looked at the skylight, which was now closed.

"He came in through the roof. Wanted Ciaran, knocked me out when I said I didn't know."

"The roof? How?"

Thea took a moment, trying to put the pieces together, hating the delay in everything she was trying to do.

"I don't know," she sighed. It felt like a confession.

"What sort of guy?"

"Professional. He had a gun."

Wilkes pulled his radio out. "What did he look like?"

Thea shook her head. "Balaclava. Black clothes. He was white, I think. I couldn't see anything else."

"This is Wilkes to all units. Be on the lookout for an IC9 male all in black, last seen in the vicinity of Malton station." Wilkes fired off the information into the radio and then returned his focus to Thea. "Don't worry, we'll get him."

"You won't," Thea said as she pulled herself groggily off the table. "What happened outside?"

"Some protestors got in, we arrested a couple, and the rest turned back."

"It was a diversion."

"A diversion?"

"Yeah, they wanted to get in unnoticed and secure Ciaran."

"Why?"

Thea was wondering that herself. Her head throbbed still, but she knew that even if her head had been clear, she would struggle to put the pieces together.

"I don't know," she admitted. "Are the other kids okay?"

"They're fine."

"So why him and not them?" Thea was asking herself as much as she was asking Wilkes?

"Did he say anything? The guy who was in here?"

"He just asked where he was and, when I said he was gone, he hit me."

"Where is he?"

Thea shook her head. "I really, really don't know. I didn't want to, I figured he was safer that way."

"He probably is, especially with Rankine in tow."

Thea groaned, placing her head in her hands, the world still spinning slightly. "I wish we had a way to contact him, just to let them know that people are looking for them. Might help them keep their heads down a little more."

"You didn't leave a burner phone or anything like that?"

"No. He was to go away for two weeks, then check in with the station and see if the coast was clear. They needed to go dark."

"Shame he hasn't got social media or anything like that. We could leave a message or something," Wilkes lamented.

"Social media. Shit." The lightbulb went on in Thea's head. "Sarge, if you were looking for a suspect who you knew was in hiding, what would you do to flush him out?"

"I'd make an appeal."

"Which would end up on social media."

"Absolutely. Jesus, do you think they're going to use social media here?"

"I would."

"How?" Wilkes wasn't so sure, Thea could see. "I mean, it's not going to come from an official police website, and they won't even know where to target it."

"They won't need an official source. Look at what just happened. They'll use community groups, set them up somehow, call them a part of the conspiracy. They'll have half the bloody population looking for them by the end of the day if it goes viral, which on something like this, it's bound to."

"People will react?"

"There's posts still doing the rounds about missing kids who have been found years ago. People like to help, and when it comes to kids, it kicks in a whole different side of them. They'll do whatever they think they can to help."

"So how do we find them?"

"You need to put a team together to monitor these groups. Find where the posts are made, read the answers and hope we can react fastest when someone says they've found something."

"Will that be enough?"

"It has to be. It's all we've got."

"Fine," Wilkes pursed his lips, probably trying to work out where he was going to get the manpower to assemble a team. "It still doesn't explain why they're after Ciaran. Was there anything he said, anything at all that might explain that?"

"No. Genuinely, I'm stumped. He's clearly special to them. I just don't know why."

53

Hammerby House was a grand-looking building, yellow-grey bricked, rising up over only two storeys, but standing the same height of a regular three or four storey building might. The front of the house was lined with tall windows that reached up and arched to the ceiling of the first floor, whilst smaller windows on the second floor mimicked the style of those below, just on a lesser scale.

A perfectly manicured, green lawn, lined with evenly spaced fir trees, spread out in front of the house, cut through by a yellow stone driveway that stopped just in front of the house, a water feature acting as a roundabout in the centre. The double doors to the building were tall and impressive, made of dark wood, and flanked by pillars that held up a stone roof to create a porch for waiting doormen to stay sheltered from the weather whilst receiving guests.

Today, there was no one around, at least not that Jack could see. He crouched low next to a tree, watching the scene through a small field telescope. All of the windows had seemed empty, and whilst there were cameras dotted around the approach to the building, he was certain he'd managed to pick a route that would allow him to get in unnoticed.

He ducked back into the treeline of the woods that ran along the east side of the estate and made his way about a quarter-mile further along until he was towards the rear of the property. There was always the risk he would be detected, but he had a feeling that Brier's regular guards would have either been incapacitated or picking up a host of other tasks due to their diminishing numbers. If Jack had been in charge, there would be a perimeter, a hard one, but it would be a lot smaller and a lot tighter. Given the size of the estate, they'd have to fall back. The question was, how many remained?

Jack took up position behind another tree, a tall and sturdy-looking Scots pine. He was near to the back of the house now. It was nowhere near as deep as it was wide, but there were still tall windows on the ground floor. Jack scanned them with his telescope again. He could see a grand dining room that looked out over the side and rear gardens, but it was deserted. Next to that was a small, innocuous-looking door. That was what Jack was aiming for. There was a camera above it, looking down at the space just in front of the door, where anyone wanting to get in would have to stand. Jack didn't have much of a choice. That was his way in.

One last check to ensure that there was no one looking out on his route before Jack made the short sprint across the lawn to the door, pressing himself against the wall just to the side of the door, directly under the camera, doing all he could to minimise the time he might be visible.

He took the keys that he had taken from Braun and placed the electronic fob over a small, black, oval scanning pad on the wall. A green light flashed on the top of the scanner, and he heard the sound of an electronic lock being released. A good guess. Jack quickly moved to the door, grabbing the handle and opening it in one smooth motion, darting inside, hoping he had been on the camera for as little time as possible. Every advantage would count here.

The door opened up into a small hallway which had two other doors running off it. One to the left, the opposite side to where the dining room ran. It was a big, white, industrial-style door that jutted out from the wall, with a large white handle. A walk-in freezer. Not what Jack wanted.

In front lay another door, already open, with metal beads dangling down in the doorway to stop flies or other unwanted pests getting in so readily. It would also make more noise than Jack wanted when he had to pass through it, but there wasn't another way in.

Softly, he paced forward, taking the beads in one hand, pistol drawn and pointing in front of him in the other. He moved the beads slowly out of the way, minimising the noise as best he could, creeping into the next room. It was a large commercial kitchen, the place where Lord Brier's team of chefs would prepare all his meals, as well as the bigger, more extravagant banquets that he would host in the dining room. No one was in there now, the lights were off, the room only being lit by emergency lighting and the blue neon glow of two fly zappers that hung on the walls behind and directly in front of Jack.

Easing the beads back into place, he took a moment to assess the room. There were three rows of shiny metal workspaces in the middle of the room, where the chefs would normally be working. To his left was a bank of tall, dark-doored fridges; to his right was a grill space and some industrial-size fryers. The darkness and clutter made it hard to be certain there was no one lurking. He moved away from the door, both hands now on his gun, letting it slide from side to side in front of him, gliding through the air, looking to seek out and lock onto any targets that might crop up.

Still none came.

Jack slowly made his way across the kitchen to another door. Reaching it, he opened it with the same caution he had the beads. It brought him out into a small corridor that ran along the length of the kitchen. Jack turned right, following the corridor as it took a left turn, past a marked pair of toilets, stopping at a security door. There was another oval pad, which the fob once got him through.

Now he was in the actual hall itself, not behind the scenes. He was standing underneath a mezzanine area that clung to the wall above, reaching around the edges of the whole room, accessed by the grand staircase that stood behind the double front doors he'd seen earlier.

He wasn't alone any more.

Lord Brier was standing in the middle of the room, hands behind him, dressed in a smart tweed suit, looking directly at Jack. Jack trained his pistol on him, centring his shot on Lord Brier's chest.

"There's no need for that, Mr. Quinn." Lord Brier brought his hands out, showing he wasn't holding anything. "I only want to talk."

"Then talk to the authorities." Jack stepped forward, never letting the gun move off target, but doing his best to scan the room, especially the landing area above him.

"They won't do what I want them to, unfortunately. I am hoping you will."

"I've got a feeling I won't."

"Come." Lord Brier turned and walked slowly towards another door.

"Stay where you are!" Jack snarled.

Lord Brier glanced back over his shoulder. "You're not going to kill me yet. You have questions, and I have answers. Let's talk and make an arrangement."

Jack gave another quick glance around the room. Brier saw him.

"The place is completely deserted. All my men are out on the task in hand. You have nothing to fear from me." He looked away and walked to the door. Jack hesitated and then followed.

Brier led him through to a room that was accessed from a door just behind the staircase. It was a library, what looked like a large one to Jack, but he had to concede that in the context of the house, it was probably one of the smaller, more snug rooms. Tall bookshelves lined with all different colours of books flanked both sides of the room, leading down to a perfectly placed window that gave a sumptuous view out to the gardens of Hammerby House. Jack could imagine it was a place that Brier came to a lot, somewhere where he found solace, which added to the intrigue as to why he had chosen that spot now. It was clear that Brier had been waiting for him, that he would have had time to plan what he was going to say and how he was going to say it. He would have picked that room for a reason. No one did things like that by coincidence.

Brier gestured to one of two brown leather chairs, the sort that one might expect to see in a stately home library, English antiques, exquisitely upholstered. Jack went to the chair he had been offered and sat down, watching Brier's every move as he did the same.

"So, I suppose you have questions?" Brier said calmly as they sat.

"Not many. What was the plan here, and when are you going to turn yourself in?"

"Ah, straight to the point I see. I like that. Braun was the same."

"That's a line you don't want to go down," Jack warned.

"I take it you got to him?"

"I only wish I'd had more time with him."

"Shame, he was loyal. A quality I seem to see less and less of these days."

"I don't care." Jack quickly tired of Brier's civility, mock or otherwise. "Tell me about the kids. Why did you do it?"

"Oh, I had to, dear boy, I bloody had to. They gave me no choice in the matter. They knew some of the damn silly things I'd done as a young man, and they blackmailed me. A simple enough transaction, I do as they say, I keep my freedom."

"And that was a price worth paying, was it? The innocence and freedom of all those children and god knows how many more, for your own?"

Brier looked at the ground, and for the first time, Jack sensed something bordering on regret or shame. "I will never profess to being a good man. I made a choice based on many things. The name of my family, the hurt I would cause to loved ones, but mostly, yes, to save my own hide. I put myself first, something I have regretted at times, but I will not lie, I have benefitted from at others. It gave me the chance at a life, at a family."

"Aren't you lucky?" Jack wasn't warming to Brier. Not even slightly. The old man was clearly a confident orator. He could turn it on when he needed to, Jack could tell that, and on another day, someone else might have felt pangs of sympathy for him. Right now, Jack just wanted to break him into pieces.

"I preserved the legacy, something I will come back to soon, but I did it under duress. I need you to remember that. They came to me, asked for use of a farmstead we owned, nothing more. It was only once it was in place that they revealed what they were using it for."

"Who are they?"

"Ah, now, isn't that the big question? They, dear boy, are everything and they are nothing."

Jack shifted in his seat and sighed. He had no time for this. Brier saw the expression change, and his own face dropped, just a little, knowing he needed to hurry up.

"There is a group of people, a little bit like yourselves I suppose, who take it upon themselves to operate outside of the law and bring the world to heel according to their own worldview."

"Then they're nothing like us," Jack snapped, before correcting himself. "Or what I was, what the Regulators and the Vehm are. They're still bound by the law of the land. They don't cross that line."

"Don't they?" Brier looked at Jack, raising an eyebrow slightly. "I could have sworn you were on the outside because of that very reason."

Jack said nothing.

"Anyway," Brier carried on. "They don't have a name. They're a collection of individuals, all over the world. Some politicians, some businessmen, some nobility. All with huge sway and influence, but perhaps not the direct power they feel their positions deserve, or as is more often the case, they simply know that their vision needs implementing by others and that they would rather simply stay out of the limelight."

"So, they create a trap for people like you. They set up facilities like this, then once the deed is done, the person is in their pocket."

"Exactly that, then from that point on they can exert their influence. Don't fancy a certain piece of legislation going through? Use those in your thrall to lobby, canvass, and ultimately disrupt any motion. Want to change the discourse of a nation? Get enough journalists, TV and film producers, even bloody internet nobodies, get them all singing from your song sheet, delivering diatribes, making programmes around a common theme, soapboxing on your phone screen in a hundred and forty bloody characters. It really is that simple."

"Names."

Brier placed his hands on a cigar tin that sat on the table next to him. He looked at Jack, silently asking for his permission. Jack nodded, and Brier opened it and pulled out a USB drive.

"Names," he said, placing it on the table and pushing it to Jack. He withdrew his hand, and Jack took it, pocketing it.

"I would be careful though, Mr. Quinn," Brier warned. "They have a plan for you."

"For me?"

"Of course, they have a plan for everyone. Believe me, my boy, I would not want to be crossing them, and you've already stepped on some toes, I believe."

"Me?" Jack let a smile come across his face, not a genuine one, but an attempt to elicit more from Brier.

"Yes, you rumbled some big plot they had. Cost them a couple of years. Cost you more, it seems."

Jack guessed what Brier was referring to. The attempt to detonate a small nuclear device in central London. He and his team had believed it to be a plot to frame and discredit the far right, something that, in principle, Jack had no issue with if it didn't involve the mass murder of thousands of innocent civilians. It had been the case that killed his career as a Regulator. The question was, how did Brier know that? Only the Regulators and the Vehm knew what had happened after.

It wasn't time to ask that question yet.

"You said you wanted me to do something for you?" Jack asked.

Brier said nothing for a moment. Reflecting on something, Jack thought. *He doesn't want to tell me everything.*

"I need your help, not something I am sure you want to readily give, and it's going to seem a strange, perhaps even unpalatable request, so I shall start by saying that this matters more to me than anything else has ever mattered in this world."

Brier looked gaunt all of a sudden. The red flush from his cheeks had evaporated, his hand had clenched around the arm of the sofa, sending his knuckles white. Jack said nothing. He wanted Brier to volunteer everything here, he was more likely to say more that way. When people wanted something as badly as he

343

seemed to, they always overshared if there was no question to fixate on.

Brier waited for Jack to speak, but when it became clear he wasn't going to, he went on.

"I need the boy back. The one that got away. I need him returned."

There was almost a hint of emotion in the voice now. Something was really unsettling Brier, something about Ciaran. Jack was beginning to have suspicions, but he wasn't about to ask. Not just yet.

"If you know where he is, I need you to return him to me. I need him with me, where I can keep him safe."

"Safe?" That was the blue touch paper being lit up for Jack. His eyes widened, and he said it again. "Safe?"

"Yes, safe," protested Brier, his voice almost a wail.

"Because he was so safe with you before?"

"He was." Brier changed in an instant from sad to angry, his voice now sharp and aggressive. "He was safer here than you can ever know. I did more for that boy than anyone could ever know. I saved his damn life. He would be dead without me, and I will do all I can to keep him safe till the day I die."

"How did you save his life?"

"Because they would have killed him. They would have taken him from me and killed him."

"Oh god. No." Jack knew, but he couldn't bring himself to say it.

"Yes."

"He's your son?"

"Yes!" He shouted defiantly. Now there were tears on Brier's face. Real ones.

"How?"

"Oh, come on. It's obvious, isn't it? I messed about with them to. That's how they got me; I had a thing for little girls. The problem is, they don't stay little forever, and sometimes accidents happen. Usually, they would take care of it, one way or another, but this time it was my accident, my child. I hid his mother and then when he was born, I hid him."

"But he was in there with all the others. He was abused. How could you?"

"I hid him for as long as I could. I sent him to live with another family, away from all this. Friends of mine who I could trust, but they found out. Their tentacles reach everywhere and, as I said, loyalty is so bloody hard to find. Someone sold me out, I never found out who, and they came for him. Killed the people who looked after him, put him in the system, and then snared him up, brought him here, right into that goddamn hallway out there and showed him to me. They gave me a choice. Put him to work, let him serve his time, then they would set him free, or they would kill him, right there and then. What the hell was I supposed to do?"

"You're meant to find a way. He's your flesh and blood." Jack heard the anger in his voice. He couldn't begin to imagine what he would have done had it been his son, Calum. He knew he would have done everything in his power to stop them from harming him, even if it cost him his own life.

"There was no way. If I could have broken him out, I bloody would have done."

345

"He found a way."

"He's a very smart and resourceful little boy, and he deserves the chance to have a life. I can give him that." Brier pointed his finger at his chest vigorously. "I can give him a life he could never imagine, a life he could never dream of."

"Living with the man who raped his mother?"

"Living with his father."

"You're no father. Being a father isn't just about siring the latest heir to your legacy. It's about giving your everything to your kids. Giving them all they need, every hour of every day."

"Like you're in a position to lecture me on that."

"We're not talking about me. We're talking about you."

"No, we're talking about Ciaran. My son. Right now, they're out there looking for him, just like I need to be."

"They? You mean the people behind this?"

"Yes, they need Ciaran because they need me onside. When your friend Miss Watts kept it off the records, it gave us the chance to keep it from them. We were working out a plan of how to rescue him from the hospital."

"Rescue him?" Jack spat the words back at Brier, not trying to hide his contempt.

"Why is that so hard for you to believe?"

"Because you let that child be raped. His life was a hell."

"At least he was alive."

Jack shook his head and stood up. "I can't believe this. You know I'm not going to help you, right?"

"But you must. I gave you names!" Brier sounded genuinely shocked as if Jack was cheating him on a deal.

"No." Jack turned and levelled the gun on Brier. "No."

"Please. He's my son."

"A technicality."

"You love your children, you know you'd do anything for them, you wouldn't stop, neither will I. I will do right by him."

"Prove it."

"How?"

"Show me some sort of sign of what he means to you. Prove your love. If you really want my help."

"I… I…" Brier was struggling. Jack knew there wasn't a lot he could do. Not a lot he could say. There might be one thing, however. that's what Jack was banking on. Brier's eyes lit up. He thought he had it. "My will." He cried, hand thrusting in front of him as if in a victory salute.

"Will?"

"Everything is in his name. The whole estate. There is no one else, after all. Braun was designated to look after him. I suppose that won't happen now, but other than that, yes. That's how I prove I love him. I will give him my all."

Brier looked so pleased with himself.

"Fine. I believe you. I just need you to do one thing for me in return." Jack made his final bargain.

"What?" Brier's mouth dropped. "I swear, I will do all I can to look after that boy."

"You'll do more in death, and believe me, I'm only telling you this because I think you do, in your own, messed up way, love him. Consider this me giving you purpose in death. He'll inherit all of this, and I'll make sure they never get him. I promise you that. I will do all I can to give him the best life possible. Not for you, but for him."

Brier went to say something, probably in his own defence, but he stopped himself. He said nothing. He bowed his head and closed his eyes, accepting his fate.

54

Thea took the ringing phone from her pocket and answered it.

"Watts?"

"It's me. Quinn." Thea knew the voice straight away, she didn't need the further explanation. "I know why they're after Ciaran."

"Why?" She didn't mean to sound short, but she did. The anger at Jack added with the stress of everything else that was happening leaving her unable to stop the aggression in her tone.

"He's Brier's son."

"What? How?"

"He got one of the young girls there pregnant. Ciaran is the offshoot."

"I thought he'd had a foster family."

"He did, he tried to hide him," Jack recounted Brier's story. "The people who organised it all found out and used him as leverage against Brier. I sort of think he really didn't know what to do for the best."

"Are you with him now? What's he going to do?"

"I'm not with him, he's gone. He's going to give Ciaran the best chance he can." There was something enigmatic about Jack's answer that left Thea unsettled.

"Is he dead?"

"It was the only way to stop them chasing him."

"Killing Brier?"

"There's no leverage there anymore. He's pointless."

"Jesus, Jack, it never ends does it?" Thea thought about yet another body added to the pile. She had no sympathy for anyone involved in this, but indiscriminately handing out such harsh justice was just wrong. "They came here looking for him," she added.

"To the station? Shit. Where is he?"

"I don't know. Rankine took him and disappeared into the countryside. We're monitoring social media now looking for any leads."

"Get a team out to Hammerby House. Brier's body is there, make it official, then they'll call off the hunt."

"Are you sure?"

"As sure as I can be."

"That's not enough. I need to find him, make sure he's safe."

"If there's anything I can do."

"I'll let you know."

"Thea," Jack sounded like he wanted to say something profound. Thea wasn't really in the mood for it, she had work to do, but all the same, she decided to hear him out. If he was brief.

"What?"

"I'm sorry and good luck."

"You too."

Thea hung up. Of course, he was sorry, he had to be.

She looked back at her computer screen. She had volunteered to be one of the four people Wilkes had put together who would spend however long it took monitoring the different social media channels where someone might post something about Ciaran and his trip with the Rankines. So far, they had drawn a blank, but Thea knew they were looking for a needle in a haystack.

Wilkes, to his credit, had been as accommodating as he could be. He had given her the team, had given her free reign to call the shots as she saw fit. He'd also arranged for a police helicopter to be flown to Malton, on permanent standby to take Thea to whatever location Ciaran was found in. The chopper had landed around ten minutes ago in a school playing field just a couple of minutes sprint from the station. If she needed to be somewhere, she could be.

The three people that Thea worked with all knew Rankine well. They were officers from Malton station, friends of his. Thea hoped that would have two benefits. Firstly, that they would know the spots he liked to travel to, where he might be likely to hide out, and secondly, that it might give them that extra added motivation to help their friend if they knew he was in jeopardy.

On one of the walls of the room was a map of North Yorkshire, with notes attached in the approximate locations of places where Rankine had been known to have visited before when holidaying. Alongside those were the name of any social media forum active in that area that might have information that would point them in the right direction.

At first, they had simply watched the groups, waiting for any sort of post regarding Ciaran or the Rankine's. There had been nothing at first. Then they had begun. Innocuous posts at first. People claiming they had heard that someone had "kidnapped" one of the children from a police station. Then other, more conspiratorial posts about the police orchestrating a cover

351

up. People started posting pictures, mocked up police bulletins, the registration number of Rankine's car. It was all there online, and people were buying it.

The anger that accompanied some of the posts was shocking. Thea knew people were capable of saying the most incredible things when hidden behind a keyboard, but to see it directed at someone she knew, someone who she believed to be a good, honest, decent man, was unnerving. Most of it was bluster of course. Levels of violence that your average person couldn't bring themselves to inflict on anyone. It was the case of the little dog on the lead with the big bark. But there would be some reading it who would want to act. More often than not, they would say nothing. Thea hoped one of them didn't spot Rankine and Ciaran first, because if they did, a post on social media might signify that they had been too late.

So far, however, no one was biting. There were no sightings. Rankine was doing his job.

The search wasn't just confined to North Yorkshire. Thea had them looking in the whole of the north of England, right up into the border regions of Scotland. Rankine had a good head start and, if he had any sense, would have wanted to have put as much distance between himself and Malton as possible. That was a large amount of land, a vast number of towns and a host of different forums. None of whom had seen them.

Thea was just contemplating how long she would have to wait before calling in reinforcements when one of the other officers, a young female PCSO, shouted out excitedly.

"I think we've got something."

Thea spun her chair around and looked at the screen of the PCSO. It showed a video, a live video, being taken from inside someone's car, following a caravan that had Rankine's number plate on it.

"Where is that?" Thea asked.

"It's on the Dumfries forum, but, I mean, that could be anywhere. They haven't said yet."

"Keep watching, you get a location, tell me."

Thea was out the room in seconds, calling into her radio for the helicopter to prepare. She was just about to leave the station through the rear doors when Wilkes came toward her with two armed response officers.

"Sir?" Thea asked, worried he'd come to put a stop to it all.

"I figured you could use a little help." Wilkes offered.

"Always," Thea said, relieved and pleased in equal measures.

"Good, let's go."

The four of them exited the station and jogged through the carpark. They came out into the street, past the now dissipating crowd outside the station, some of whom watched on in awe as armed officers ran past, then to the field where the helicopter was now ready for take-off, engine roaring, rotors at full speed. A voice came through on Thea's radio.

"They're heading towards Loch Ken," the PCSO reported. "The video has finished, but looking at it, I think they're a few miles away, to the east. We'll keep updating you."

Thea got into the front passenger seat of the helicopter and told the pilot their destination. He nodded, eased the throttle forward, and they were airborne. Thea took out her phone and looked at the built-in map application, doing the maths. It would take them a little over an hour to get to the Loch. Thea just hoped it would be long enough.

55

Adam sat alone on a trolley in the infectious diseases wing of Newham University Hospital, his bed surrounded by plastic sheets that distorted the view outside. He could see shapes passing by but couldn't make out any faces. He had been seen already by a doctor and a nurse, both dressed in protective clothing. They had taken his blood, checked his temperature, his pulse, and blood pressure and promised to return with results as soon as they could. Adam had asked what had happened to Nathan Nelmes, or if they knew what had been used against him, but they both remained tight lipped.

Now he was waiting for answers.

He felt fine. He was no doctor, but he had seen the way that whatever had been used had taken hold of Nelmes and he felt certain that if the same thing were to be happening to him, even on a smaller, slower scale, he would be feeling some sort of effect by now. He hoped Emmie wasn't symptomatic either. He hadn't seen her since the two of them had been ushered off in different directions on their arrival at the hospital. Understandably so, Adam thought. Infectious disease wards weren't set up for people to be sharing.

He saw a shape working through the plastic sheeting towards him. As they approached the final layer, Adam saw the doctor who had visited him before. This time, he wasn't wearing a protective suit, just smart trousers with a salmon shirt tucked in and a navy blue tie. He stepped through the final layer and smiled.

"All clear, Mr. Morgan. You got lucky," the doctor announced.

"Thanks, Doc." Adam jumped up off the bed, offering his hand. The doctor took it and shook it. Definitely all clear then, Adam thought. "When can I get out?"

"Not my decision. I'm sure there are a few people who want to talk to you. In the meantime, I'll have someone bring you some clothes."

"What happened to my old ones?"

"Burned, just to be safe."

"Ah, I liked those jeans." Adam protested. "What about my phone?"

"Gone the same way, I'm afraid, but," the doctor looked over his shoulder. "I was told to give you this." He passed Adam a phone.

"Thanks, Doc." Adam took it off him, wondering where the phone had come from.

"They said they'd get in touch," the doctor added. "I'm sure someone will be along soon."

With that he was back out and through the plastic, leaving Adam wondering just who it would be who called him.

He didn't have to wait long. Within a minute, the phone was ringing.

"Hello," he answered cautiously.

"Morgan? It's Raf."

"Thank fuck for that." Adam breathed a huge sigh of relief. "I really didn't know who was going to be at the end of the line. Could have been the mother-in-law for all I know."

"Happy not to be, trust me," Raf replied. "You okay?"

"All clear," Adam replied "What's the latest on Nelmes?"

"He's critical. Outlook's not good, whether he lives or not."

"Do they know what it was?"

"Not yet. Something from the eastern-bloc most probably. There's plenty of stuff that went missing off the back of lorries during the fall of the Union."

"Yeah, great. I guess I should count myself lucky." Adam was more than a little unnerved by the use of a nerve agent. "One other thing – is this line secure?"

"It is now," Raf replied, clearly altering something in the system to take his call off the grid. "What's up?"

"We've got a mole."

There was a silence. Adam visualised Raf looking around to make sure no one was listening, cautious as ever. "Who?" he said in a hushed tone.

"Nick Poole. At least him."

"Lowri's guy? Is she?"

"I don't know yet. Someone must be pulling his strings, but whether that comes from inside or out, I don't know yet."

"Shit, she knew where David was. No one else did."

"I know, but I can't believe she'd hurt him. They were too close-knit."

"We need proof one way or the other. Have you got any idea how you're going to get it?"

"I can get you footage of Poole, but I can only put stuff on him for now. Where is Lowri?"

"She was up north, checking out the footage from the traffic cars and the truck stop. Her chopper left about fifteen minutes ago."

"Have you spoken to her?"

"Briefly, I got the feeling it was a bust," Raf replied.

"Do me a favour. Get in touch with the traffic unit and ask them to transfer the footage to you," Adam requested.

"What do you hope to see?"

"In truth? Exactly as she says, dead ends." Adam really did. He wasn't convinced that Lowri was the mole, and admitting that she was would be to admit that everything he knew about the Regulators, about the Vehm, was a lie.

"I'll get it and get back to you."

"Thanks, Raf." Adam felt a sense of relief from sharing the burden. Raf would do what was necessary and without prejudice. If there was someone at the Regulators who Adam could trust not to go above him to Lowri, it was Raf. He was always keen to prove himself, to show he could do the job, so this would be another notch on that particular bedpost for him.

Raf was calling him back two minutes later.

"What do you know?"

"I just spoke to the traffic unit Lowri just visited, they were only too happy to send over the footage. Only problem was, one of the files was missing."

"Missing?"

"The person I spoke to swore blind they were all there earlier. Says someone must have deleted it."

"We know who," Adam replied grimly.

"What does she want you to do?" Raf asked.

"She wants me to bring in Poole. She's set up a meeting with him at St. Pancras. I'm to go in place."

"Sounds a bit like a trap," Raf observed.

"Doesn't it just."

"Want back up?"

"I'm going to take Emmie. She's proven herself already today."

"Okay, well you know where I am."

"I sure do." Adam hung up.

One more call to make. A call that made him nervous and excited in equal measure.

"Hello?" came the cautious response.

"Jack, it's Adam."

"Hey, mate, how you doing down there?" Jack's voice brightened up instantly.

"Hoping we're on the final stretch. You?"

"Adam, sorry man, Mo didn't make it."

Adam heard the words like a sledgehammer. Mo was dead?

"How?"

"He went down like a hero. They wanted him to talk and he wouldn't. He wouldn't let me talk either. He was far braver than I ever knew." Jack's voice trailed off at the end. Adam wasn't used to hearing his friend moved.

"Holy shit." Adam was lost for words.

"It's been evened," Jack said by way of consolation.

"Thanks. Fuck, man. How are you?"

"Got some files for you lot. After that, I'm done. Everyone else is tidying up, everything else unless, of course, you've come to ruin my day?"

"Would I?"

"More often than not."

Adam had to laugh. In an instant, Jack had found a way to pick him up when he needed it. "What files have you got?"

"Brier said they were the names behind the plot. I've not had the chance to look yet, but I think it's a fair bet they're encrypted. I'm sure you've got someone who'll have the key your end. I'll upload them to a server for you as soon as I can."

"I'm sure I will, and thanks again. You didn't have to do any of this."

"I did," Jack replied.

"Listen, in return, I want to pick your brains," Adam went on.

"Not my strong point, but I'll give it my best shot."

"Did you speak to Lowri before David arrived?"

"No. I've not spoken to her personally since I left."

"Did David have anything to say about her?" Adam was trying to find a motivation for Lowri to take out David. He was struggling to find one.

"He said she was rattled, which didn't sit well with me. Lowri doesn't do rattled. She's cool and in control."

"Did he say what about?"

"An old operation, operation Malice. Said that if it worried her, it worried him."

"Okay, now I'm really going to push you," warned Adam jokingly. "What's your best guess?"

Adam heard Jack sighing as he mulled it over for a second. "Lowri doesn't get rattled. She's in control because she knows that she will get the answers. She trusts the machine she's part of."

"She lost trust?"

"Or her trust was betrayed. These cases have been going on for a long time. We've investigated them for a long time ourselves and turned nothing up."

"Which means we were either inept," Adam began.

"Which would anger Lowri but not rattle her," added Jack.

"Or someone was working to hide the proof from our inside."

"And that would unsettle her."

"It would. Final question, would it unsettle her more if it was her doing the covering up?"

There wasn't an immediate answer. Jack was putting it altogether. "I wouldn't believe it," he finally replied. "I'd need to see proof."

"What about this for proof?" Adam offered. "Her deputy, Nick Poole, carried out the hit on David, and she covered up the evidence."

"That would be pretty damning if it were true. Does it sit right for you?"

"I don't know anymore," Adam confessed. "I didn't think anyone would cover this sort of shit up, honestly. I couldn't imagine it. It's fucked."

"It's the sickest shit I've ever worked on, no doubt, but never underestimate the lengths people will go to."

"Could be that the politicians that were being manipulated ended up doing things that worked best for us?"

"Not according to Brier. He's dead by the way."

"Good."

"He said that this was another group, like us, but with ulterior motives. It's clear we've been infiltrated. Want my advice?"

"I didn't call to hear your dulcet tones."

"Take her in. Do the investigation thoroughly. One way or the other you'll make this right."

"Thanks, pal, appreciate the input. You stay safe, yeah?" It was a question, as much as a piece of advice.

"Always, mate. Love to the family. See you on the other side.

56

Jack hung up the phone and paused for a moment. Adam's call was worrying, but what could he do? He wasn't a Regulator anymore; this wasn't his fight. It was right to pass on what he knew and his advice, but he couldn't fix this for them. Was Lowri a traitor? She was ruthless, and anyone could pull the wool over your eyes. If you'd have asked him a couple of years ago, he would have said no. But now, who knew?

He was nearing the bed and breakfast. It was time to leave this town. The job was done here. Thea was looking out for Ciaran, she'd get to him, get him safe, then they'd tell him the incredible news. He was rich. Nothing could make up for what that kid had been through, him and all the other poor children who had suffered, but hopefully, this would give him a chance to one day be happy. Jack had already promised himself he would look in on Ciaran at some point, but right now he needed a sleep before his journey back. Then he *had* to see his kids.

There was no one around on the ground floor of the B&B, which came as a relief. Jack was a muddy mess, he could see that much, and he was sure that his face showed that he'd been in a couple of scrapes over the last few days. It certainly felt that way.

He climbed the stairs wearily, hearing each one creak as he stood on it. There was no point being stealthy now. This wasn't a hostile environment; this was his safe zone. He opened the door planning to do nothing more than slump onto his bed, kick off his shoes, and sleep. Instantly he realised that wasn't going to happen. There, sat on the chair next to the window, was Eamon Grant.

"You look tired," Grant observed.

"Shattered," Jack responded, walking past Grant and sitting on the edge of the bed. "I was hoping to get some kip."

"Sorry to disappoint you."

"What is this then?"

"We need to debrief you. Orders of Ms. Graves."

"After I sleep, fine."

"I'm afraid not. There's a train out of here to York in half an hour. We're going to be on it, then we're going to catch another one to London. You've got time to pack your bags."

"Can I sleep on the train?"

"You can do whatever you want. We won't be talking till we return."

"Return where? I'm not returning anywhere."

"Back to the field office."

Jack lay back on the bed. "I'm really not feeling this, you know. I'm a civilian now, I'm not beholden to you or Ms. Graves."

"Are you beholden to David?"

Jack closed his eyes. When Adam had asked his thoughts about Lowri's potential involvement in the wider conspiracy, he had told his former partner all he could think of off the top of his head, but there was always the chance he'd missed something. A thorough debrief after some sleep could reveal more. It wouldn't be the first time. Re-examining events, what people said, how it sounded, often allowed for subtle tells to come to the fore. He couldn't rule out the possibility that they might be taking him with them just to put him in a cell for the rest of his days, but Jack thought it was far more likely they would have just put a bullet in his brain the moment he opened the door. It would have been cheaper.

"Fine. I'll get my stuff together." Going with the flow seemed to be the best decision. "Here." He took the USB drive from his pocket, passing it to Grant.

"What's this?" Grant asked gruffly.

"Names of those behind the plot. Brier had it as his insurance."

"Jesus, Jack, that's brilliant." Grant looked like he'd won the lottery. Jack wondered if this was the first time he had ever seen Grant smile.

"You're still not going to let me kip, are you?" Jack asked, more in hope than expectation.

"I'll give you an hour to get things sorted," Grant said. "But then we really do have to go."

An hour and a half later, they were sat on a four-carriage train, a smaller regional service that operated from east to west Yorkshire and back again, heading for York. The first train took under half an hour to get into York. They sat in silence, the train being crowded, but the second train they boarded was much larger, an inter-city service that would take them all the way to London's King Cross station. Grant led Jack through to the front carriage of the train, first class. It was deserted, and they had the pick of the seats.

Jack settled into his chair, tipped his head back and closed his eyes.

"Comfortable?" Grant asked.

"I'll make it work." Jack shrugged.

"Before you do, do you mind me just asking a couple of questions?"

"I do, but do you care?"

"I don't."

"Carry on then. Sooner we're done, the sooner I sleep."

"What happened with Brier?"

"I put a bullet in his head."

"Because of the boy?"

Jack opened his eyes and looked at Grant. "Because of the boy."

Grant nodded. "And David, before he left, did he speak to anyone? Have contact with anyone?"

"Not that I was aware of, other than when he was scouting the area around Brier's house. He said he made Braun. I'm guessing Braun made him."

Grant nodded. "I guess that makes sense."

"Although how he knew to be on the lookout for him is another question."

"I assume we'll never be able to ask?"

Jack shook his head and said nothing. He didn't feel like telling Grant anything more right now. Grant must have sensed it.

"Get some sleep, I'll wake you when we get to London."

Jack closed his eyes. The train juddered out of the station, rattling him around, and he wondered how much sleep he'd manage to get. Within seconds, he was snoring.

57

The Eurocopter EC135 had cruised northwest for nearly an hour, running at near its top speed of 140 kilometres an hour. It was cramped in the back. There was room for six, but the two armed response officers took up more space than usual with their MP5s at their sides. Wilkes had insisted that Thea and he wore body armour as well. Each and every decision made it a little cosier in the back of the helicopter.

They had been receiving updates throughout the journey as different sightings of Rankine and his caravan came in on social media. They seemed to be pointing in one direction, heading north along the Loch Ken. There weren't many places to turn off, but they hadn't stopped yet. That was probably a good thing. Who knew what sort of vigilante nut was out there waiting for a chance?

Sat next to the pilot was the observation officer. He turned back to address everyone in the rear cabin, even though they could only hear him through the internal radio.

"Air traffic control just got in touch. There's a chopper coming in towards the Loch from the southwest. They've tried to hail them, but they're hearing nothing back."

"Someone else has worked it out," Thea shouted into the microphone.

"Who's going to get there first?" Wilkes asked.

"Neck and neck, they reckon," the observer passed on the information he'd been told.

"Give it all you can," Wilkes ordered, receiving a nod of confirmation from the observer. He turned to Thea. "I'm glad I brought these guys now."

"We'll keep everyone safe," reassured one of the response officers.

Thea hoped he was right.

The Loch appeared below the helicopter, and they banked right, heading further north. The road to the east was where they expected to see Rankine and Ciaran. Wilkes was on the left-hand side, and he began scanning the horizon for the other aircraft.

"I think I see them," Wilkes said, arm pointing out toward the window of the chopper. Thea looked. It took a moment, but she saw the rapidly enlarging shape of another helicopter heading towards them, nose down, moving at speed.

"They're on an intercept. Shit, what's he playing at?" the observer said.

The pilot reacted, dipping the nose and banking right, then left, trying to create some separation. The second helicopter came in above them, banking hard left just after, spiralling down back on their level, and then cutting across the nose of their chopper.

"He's trying to put me down," the pilot shouted as the chopper lurched further right and off course.

"Or take us away from where we need to be!" Thea replied.

"He's not going to do that," promised the pilot, flicking a switch above his head before pushing the throttle forward. The nose dipped, and he banked left, back down now towards the road, no more than fifty feet over the ground. They levelled out abruptly, and Thea tried to look for the other helicopter. She couldn't see it.

"Where is he?" she asked.

"Dead ahead!" came the shout from the pilot. Thea looked between the two pilots and saw the second helicopter, swinging in from above the Loch, over the road. It turned, side on to them, as if blocking the road.

"Gun! Gun! Gun!" the observer cried out.

Thea saw it. The side door of the other helicopter had been pulled back, and two men peered out from the exposed cabin. It was hard to see at that distance, but from their position, their stance, it was obvious they were holding guns, aiming them at the police helicopter.

Thea ducked. She felt the chopper pull up and right in a steep, hard bank, trying to turn the underside of the helicopter to the gunfire to minimise what precious machinery could be hit. They weren't fast enough, and Thea heard the pinging of metal, the whine of bullets, then the screeching of alarms.

"We're hit!" someone shouted. Thea had no idea who.

Everything stopped making sense. Thea tried to look out of the window and see the horizon, but she couldn't. There was only grass. She was pushed back in her seat as the helicopter entered a spin. The alarms screamed, and the engines coughed and spluttered, something was wrong. They were spinning faster and faster now; the ground was getting closer. She heard the shouts and cries of the pilot as he tried to bring the chopper under control. It was all in vain, she knew that. They were going down. She leant to her left, away from the ground. It was getting closer.

The helicopter pitched up. For a moment, Thea was sure they'd saved it, that they would be okay. The G-force eased, she could move in her seat more easily. Then it all stopped. She felt her stomach flip as they seemed to hang in the air, weightless. The helicopter rolled over on itself in a stall. More alarms. Where there was ground, now there was sky.

They fell to the ground with a sickening thud, then Thea heard the sound of machinery as the helicopter ripped itself apart. The cabin spun as the rotor blades dug into the ground. Shrapnel was flying through the cabin. Something hit her leg, something heavy bounced into her side, winding her.

Then it was still and silent.

Everything hurt. Every single bone felt like it had been hit by a hammer, her muscles felt tortured and pulled, her ears rang and her head buzzed even more than it did when she woke up from the blow dealt to her by the intruder in the police station.

Thea was still strapped into her seat, staring out of the front of the shattered window of the helicopter which now lay on its left side. She grabbed at the buckle with one hand, holding onto her seat with the other as she loosened the buckle and felt gravity try and snatch her down. She swivelled out of the chair as best as she could, letting her legs drop down to the crumpled metal that was once the side of the chopper.

"Wilkes?" she croaked.

He was still strapped into his chair, his head hanging down to the side, blood seeping from a cut on his head. He muttered something, his head rolling. At least he was alive. More than she could say for the officer at her feet. She looked down at the body, seeing eyes staring up into nothingness. She couldn't see the injury that had done it. Everything looked how it should have been, but the expression of the officer's face said all she needed to know. She bent down, running her hand over his face, bringing down his eyelids for the last time.

"Is he dead?"

The voice of the other officer came from above her. That answered that question, she thought, looking up to him.

"Sorry," was all she could think to say.

"We all might be in a minute. He's coming back around." The second officer dropped down inside the cabin, shouting. "Get down!"

More bullets ripped into the chassis of the chopper. It sounded louder without the backdrop of the noise from their own engines. Each clang of the bullet Thea heard, she felt herself bracing, expecting to feel metal ripping into her, but she didn't. None of the bullets found her, and when she dared to look up, she saw the three of them in the back had somehow all survived.

"The pilots?" she asked the officer.

"Couldn't tell," he answered bluntly.

"Fuck this." Thea grabbed the gun that was currently lying on top of the dead officer. "I'm not sitting here waiting to be killed."

She scrambled up on the chair, pulling herself towards the open door.

"Thea?" gurgled Wilkes as she made it halfway up.

"Stay put, sir. It's a bit mad out there."

Clambering out onto the side of the helicopter, she had her first chance to take stock of where they were. The helicopter had come down about sixty or seventy feet into a field that bordered the main road running along Loch Ken. She could see people next to cars looking at the scene, not daring to cross the field with the second helicopter buzzing around. Where was the helicopter?

She spun her head around looking for it. She could hear it. The thud of the blades echoing across the field. It was near, circling. The pitch altered, it was coming back towards her.

"Your six." The armed officer was up with her.

He'd spotted it, and Thea swivelled, turning her body all the way around, looking away from the loch. There it was, bearing down on them. Thea raised the gun, took aim, and waited. She needed it to be closer.

Out of the side of the helicopter, she could see a man hanging out, weapon trained on them. They were planning to strafe them again, coming in along the length of the downed aircraft to give the two shooters the best view of their prey. Already the helicopter was offsetting its angle of attack, trailing to the left. Thea aimed just in front, tracking with it, hoping she was judging the distance right.

"Wait for it," she urged the armed officer, although she was sure he didn't need her input.

The helicopter was closer now. Still not close enough. Thea tracked it, trying to keep her movement as fluid as possible. She started to put a little more pressure on the trigger.

Any moment now.

Both shooters became visible as the chopper got nearer, heading left. From the edge of her vision, Thea could see that they were lining up their shots, no doubt trying to focus on her and the officer. They had actual targets now, not just fish in a barrel.

"Here they come!" came the warning. Thea didn't need a further invitation. That was as long as she was prepared to wait. She fired off her first burst.

The sound was louder than the bullets that had hit them moments before, a staccato rattling as they both opened fire on their attackers. The attacking helicopter kept on heading toward them, no change in its flight path. Thea tried to work out if she was hitting anything, if her shots were actually finding a mark. She saw the two shooters ducking for cover. Something had rattled them but not hit them. They seemed intact. Was it her shots or the other officer's? She kept firing.

The attacking chopper came nearer. Now the two shooters had regained their composure and were firing back, albeit from more concealed positions, making their bodies as small as they could.

"Take cover!"

Thea heard the shout and dropped down inside the hull of the crippled helicopter, just as the first salvo bit into the metal. There was a shout of pain from the officer as he fell in next to her, missing his foothold and slipping down. The burst of shots ended as the helicopter thundered past.

"Are you hit?" she called.

"My shoulder, shit!" he exclaimed. He sounded more like he was angry at himself than in pain. "Shouldn't have let that last round off."

"Can you get back up?"

"Yeah, I'll do my best." He clutched at his right shoulder already, his arm hanging uselessly down by his side.

"We need to end this," Thea determined. "You're going to struggle with that."

"Don't you worry about me."

Thea nodded. "Come on, let me help you up."

She clambered up to the hatch, then leant back down, holding her hand out for the officer to clasp on and pull himself up.

"What's your name?" she asked.

"Peterson, ma'am."

"Peterson, you hold the position here. I'm going to try and get a different angle."

"They'll pick you off," Peterson warned.

"They'll try." Thea smiled.

Peterson got himself up into a position he was comfortable with.

"You haven't got long." He motioned to where the attack was coming from.

"We best make it count then. Good luck." Thea pulled herself fully out of the hatch.

"You too."

Thea jumped down into the field behind the helicopter, shielded from the sight of their assailants. She pulled her weapon into position, readying it for where she expected them to be, then she tracked to her right, hoping to come in as shallow as possible on the flight path of their attackers. She wanted her to be as small a target for as short an amount of time as possible. Her plan was simple. Get inside the arc of fire and put as many bullets as she could into the cockpit of the chopper.

She got to the end of her cover, the nose of her helicopter. She peeked out. They were seconds away from being in range.

She dashed out, firing instantly, moving further and further right, using the angle as her cover, looking to hit the cockpit.

God, she hoped she didn't bring that thing down on top of herself.

Squeeze, release, squeeze, release, squeeze, release. Her finger moved smoothly on the trigger. No jerking, no pulling, everything controlled. She tried not to think about the other shooters or their bullets. If this didn't work, she was probably dead anyway.

A patch of turf near hear started to kick up. Someone had seen her and was making their best effort to get at her, but already she was almost level with the nose of the incoming helicopter.

Squeeze, release, squeeze, release.

The nose of the helicopter pitched awkwardly, nodding down, then bouncing upwards as it sailed over her. *At least it's not going to hit me.*

The nose dipped again, this time fatally, and the helicopter ploughed into the earth with a sickening thud, metal and sod flying into the air.

"You okay Peterson?" Thea called back.

"No more holes, ma'am," he replied.

A cloud of dust hung over the crash site as Thea turned and marched towards it. She kept her gun trained ahead of her.

"Armed police," she barked. "Get on the ground."

There might not be time for any more warnings, she told herself. It could be a case of her or them.

The dust was settling. She could see the chopper now. The front of the wreckage was embedded into the ground with the tail sticking up into the air, broken, cracked in half like a twig, strung up only by the control cables, swaying to the right. On the floor next to the crash site, lying motionless, was one of the shooters. Thea had seen enough dead bodies ejected from crashes to be able to tell from the contorted state of his body that he was long gone.

Where was the second shooter?

Someone fell from the fuselage of the aircraft, landing on their chest, staggering upright and away.

"On the ground!"

The figure spun toward her, as if drunk. Thea saw the gun in his hand. That was all she needed. She already had her sights trained on him.

Squeeze, release.

A short, sharp burst from thirty yards and the man slumped down on the spot to the ground, bending his legs backwards at the knees.

Thea paced forward, carefully, gun trained on the lifeless body. She was pretty certain he was dead, but never take anything for granted. She glanced back and forth between the body and the smouldering wreckage. She might have only ever seen two shooters, but that didn't mean there wasn't anyone else lurking, waiting for a chance.

She reached the man's body. He was wearing a balaclava like the one the man who had attacked her was wearing. There was no way to tell if it was the same man. He was definitely dead, however. Three rounds had hit the centre of his torso but had found the Kevlar vest. The fourth, however, had done the trick, landing just a little higher as the gun had kicked up, tearing a hole into the base of the man's neck. Thea felt for a pulse all the same. There was none.

She edged over to the wreckage of the chopper. The cockpit had been completely crushed by the impact. There was no way anyone had survived that, but Thea needed to be certain there was no one else on board. She wanted this to be over. This was the last step in the process.

Nervously, hopefully, she approached the body of the craft. The door was still slung open where the two shooters had been firing out. First glance, it looked empty, but she had to be certain. She pulled herself up into the cabin, scanning under the seats, in every nook and cranny.

The helicopter was empty.

Thea hopped down back into the field and looked around. The crowd was still watching nervously from behind the stone wall at the edge of the field. Thea put up her arm and gave an "okay" symbol with her hand, to offer comfort, if anything. When she did, she was surprised to see someone hop the fence and start to run towards her. He looked like a civilian, but all the same, Thea felt herself tense. He was coming straight for her. Dressed in a burgundy rain jacket and light brown chinos. Then she saw the red hair, thinning on top, and the red complexion. Relief hit her more than she would ever dare to admit. It was Rankine.

She ran to him, the two of them meeting in the middle of the field in a tight and genuine embrace.

"Bloody hell, lass, what the hell are you doing here?"

"Ending this," she said, trying to keep herself together.

"Ending what?"

"All of it. I think. They were onto you, but I think we've stopped them. Think we've stopped them for good."

"Well, that's a shame. I don't fancy cutting my holiday short," Rankine smiled. Thea laughed. For the first time in a long time, she felt happy.

58

St. Pancras was without a doubt one of London's finer looking stations, both inside and out. The red brick façade towered over the immediate area and led into elegant shopping and eating areas which channelled passengers through to the platforms which would take them across the UK or onto mainland Europe. Lowri wasn't there to look at the architecture, however. She was there to deal with a traitor.

There were a number of cafés and restaurants that Poole could have chosen, but he had taken one that sat at the far end of the upper concourse, finding a seat near the balcony, looking down at everyone who passed through. Lowri saw him way before she reached him and knew that Poole had probably spotted her way before that. It was a smart spot for Poole to pick because it not only gave him a grandstand view of everybody else, but it meant that Lowri would be forced to sit opposite him, with his back to the world and just the platforms in his field of vision.

Lowri made her way up the escalator to the upper concourse, turning around halfway up as if scanning the area. Everything seemed so normal, so calm. Lowri didn't like it. The nearer she got, the more she found herself questioning what was going on. Poole had seen her, he was looking directly at her. He was smiling. Had she fallen into some sort of trap?

She reached the top of the elevator and went to step forward, only to be stopped by a gaggle of tourists who were ambling past, dragging suitcases and taking photographs as they admired the architecture. Lowri stepped backwards and then to the side. It was then she felt the hand on her arm.

"Keep walking," came a harsh whisper in her ear as the hand pushed her to the right and they started circling the top of the station. Lowri saw Poole stand up and begin to follow, then she looked at the man who had grabbed her.

There were two of them. One on either side. Both well dressed in smart suits, one with dark hair, one with blonde. He was the older of the two, with a slightly thinner face. Definitely spies, thought Lowri. Mi6 or Mi5. Not good.

"Would you not prefer a chat over a coffee and croissant?" Lowri offered, hoping to engage them in some sort of chat.

"Not a pastry man," the light-haired man replied without looking at her.

They carried on through the hustle and bustle of the station, walking along the mezzanine floor that overlooked the concourse, then away from the main area to where two doors, both marked "PRIVATE", stood. The dark-haired man approached one and entered a code into the key lock. By now, Poole had caught up with them, and the four of them walked through the door, letting it swing shut behind.

They edged through a narrow corridor, down some steps, then into a small area with two double fire doors leading out, with two doors on either side, presumably leading elsewhere in the station. A sign on the doors warned that they were alarmed, but when they were opened by the dark-haired man, no alarm sounded. They were out on the pavement. Directly in front was a large Range Rover, black with blacked-out windows. They walked to it, dark-haired man continuing his role as doorman, opening it so that Lowri could step in before he circled around to the other side. She climbed in, sitting in the middle between the two men. There was already a man in the driver's seat. Poole came around the front and sat on the passenger side.

The doors were shut, and the driver pressed a button locking them all in before starting the car and driving them away.

"I didn't know you had friends, Nick?" Lowri said calmly.

"Clearly, there's a lot you don't know about me," Poole goaded.

"I'm guessing you were never really fired from Six?"

"I was never at Six," he corrected her.

"Oh, so you're all Five. Well, that's good to know. So where are we at? Are you the boys behind this honeypot operation?"

"I wish it was as simple as that, Ms. Graves." Poole looked at her earnestly. "No, you see, the honeypot is someone else's toy. I was simply sent in undercover by my team to get as much evidence as possible to put you away for multiple crimes. Murders, theft, you name it. You're done. Game over."

"I think you forget where I keep my friends." Lowri let her tone slip a little from pleasant to peeved.

"And I think you overestimate how far they're going to be willing to put their necks out after you just put the spotlight firmly on wrongdoings at Westminster."

Lowri swallowed. Poole had a point.

He went on. "We came here to take you down. Now we have you and your deletion of that file and sudden disappearance, alongside the man who betrayed them all, will cause enough panic around your organisation to render you completely redundant, at least in the short term. Today's a big win for us."

"You certainly have me there, but if I may just ask one question. Why David? Why go after him? Why jeopardise that operation."

Poole looked at the light-haired man who nodded. Poole looked back at Lowri. "There are some people who, when they pass you an order, you simply have to follow it through."

Poole leaned back, waiting for a response, but Lowri didn't give him one. After a moment he turned and looked out of the driver's window. Lowri did the same from her position, wondering who he meant, fearing the implications. She watched London winding away in front of her and wondered when, if ever, she would see it again.

59

The vibrating of his phone in his inside pocket woke Jack up. He didn't know how long he had been out, but looking out of the window, he could see just from the scenery that they had made it a lot further south.

He pulled his phone out of his pocket.

"Do you mind?" he asked Grant who still sat opposite.

"Go ahead." Grant shrugged.

Jack looked. It was Thea. He answered. "Hello?"

"It's over, Jack. Ciaran's safe. I just wanted you to know."

Jack could have cried, right there and then. Whether it was the tiredness or not, he didn't know, but for a moment, it very near all came bubbling out of him. He wouldn't have cared either. It was the best news he had heard in a long time. "Oh, god," he gasped. "That's amazing."

"He wants to see you, to say thank you."

Jack cursed silently under his breath. "Sorry," he said. "They've got me heading down south for a debrief."

"They?"

"It's the way it is."

"Oh." She was disappointed, Jack knew that sound. He'd heard it a lot from his ex-wife in the later throes of their marriage.

"Sorry, I really am. Look, if I get out soon, whenever, I'll come see him, come say goodbye properly."

"I know."

Jack hated himself. Thea's disappointment was one thing, that couldn't be avoided. He wasn't upset with himself about that. What he was upset about was that he was planning to leave without saying goodbye to Ciaran, and that was just selfish.

"Are you okay?" he asked eventually.

"Bit beat up. We got shot down in a chopper. I'm okay though. We lost two officers, another critical, another serious."

"What?" Jack couldn't contain his surprise. "How?"

"I guess the word about Brier never got to them in time, and they were still chasing."

"Shit, I'm sorry. Should have killed him sooner."

Jack saw Grant's eyebrows raise and his eyes dart around, reminding him that he was a civilian on a civilian train.

"That's not on you."

"Thanks." Jack appreciated the sentiment, but all the same, he wished he had killed him sooner.

"Listen, I'll let you know where Ciaran is going to be when he's settled, so you can come find him."

"That would be great," Jack replied, knowing full well what was coming next.

"But I wanted to say goodbye as well."

"Goodbye?"

"Goodbye."

Jack couldn't blame her. He had brought nothing but disaster into her life. People she knew and cared about had been hurt, some had been killed. That she had turned to him in the first place had been a surprise.

"You're a good person, Thea, keep away from this world."

"I will."

"Good luck and goodbye."

"You too."

The line went dead.

Grant looked at him. "You okay?"

"Just got word that the kid is safe."

"That's good news."

"Absolutely."

"I'm sorry we're dragging you away from it all. I know you've bonded with a lot of people up there. I'm sure you wanted to say goodbye properly before you got back to your family," Grant went on.

"I probably should have done," Jack agreed.

"If it helps with the debrief, I can bring in Adam? I assume it's been a while since you spoke?"

"That would be great. We spoke a couple of days back, but you know, always like to see his ugly mug." Jack figured it was best to leave out that last conversation. He had no idea where Grant's loyalties lay.

"I'm sure he'd say the same," Grant smiled.

Jack shifted his weight. Grant was being nice here. There was something more going on. "Lowri okayed that," he said, looking out of the window as if pondering a point. "She must be mellowing in her old age."

Grant said nothing. Jack turned and looked at him. Grant had a solemn look on his face. "What?" Jack asked. "What's happened to Lowri. They haven't got her as well?"

"She's fine," Grant said. "She uh…"

"What?"

"Can I trust you, Quinn?"

"I hope so."

"She may well have been in on all of this."

"Really?" Jack feigned surprise. He hoped he feigned it well.

"We don't know yet. They'll be questioning her to find out more."

"Jesus." Jack sat back. This wasn't normal. This was volunteering. Why though? Did Grant think he was in on it? It was possible, given that the last person who saw David was Jack. "How did they get inside?"

"We may never know, I suppose, depends if she talks."

"Everyone talks," Quinn echoed Braun's words.

"I heard you never did."

Being tortured was a chapter of his life Jack wasn't keen on getting too entangled in. "They didn't find my button. I thought someone might have done recently, but a friend saved me."

"A good friend to have," Grant concurred.

"I don't have many, and those I have are getting fewer in number by the day, it seems."

"I'll keep you off the Christmas card list."

The train began to slow. An announcement came over the intercom, letting them know they were approaching Stevenage. Probably about half an hour to go.

"Nearly there," Jack noted out loud. Grant just nodded.

The train eased into the station. Jack watched out of the window at the people on the platform. It was grey and raining outside, and there weren't many people about to board. It was way past the morning rush, but there were still a smattering of people, some tourists heading to the city, others in for work.

The train pulled to a stop. Just one man looked like he was going to get into their carriage, a tall, severe-looking man in his late fifties, early sixties, dressed in a fine suit. Jack heard the sound of the alarms on the doors going off as they were unlocked. He looked away. Then there was another noise. A banging. Jack looked back. The man was banging angrily on the door before turning, muttering to himself, and walking down to another door.

Jack looked away. No one had been inside the carriage when he had dozed off, but they had been joined by a small handful of people since. There were four of them. Three men and a woman. All sat on their own. All fixed on laptops or tablets in front of them. No movement. Jack looked further up the carriage. The door was closed at the other end. He saw someone stepping onto the train, pushing the door release. Nothing happened. He turned away and walked into the other carriage.

Jack looked again at the four people he and Grant shared the carriage with. One at a time. The nearest to him was a woman with her back to him. Red hair, a little taller than average with broad shoulders, in a smart white blouse with blue pinstripes. It was hard to be sure of her age. The next along was a young man in his early twenties, again dressed in a suit that was perfectly tailored to him. He had cropped hair and looked like he worked out a bit. Jack could see his face, illuminated by the glow of a tablet computer. It showed a mean-looking scar above his eye.

Further back were the other two men. Jack couldn't see much of them as they were hidden behind seats, but they were taller than average, given that he could see more than normal of the top of their heads.

"You okay?" Grant asked.

"Just trying to work out where the toilets are," Jack offered his explanation.

"I think they're down the back there," Grant replied helpfully.

"Thanks," Jack said, standing. "I'll be back in a minute."

"Jack." Grant put his arm out to stop Jack as he passed. Jack stopped and looked down. "Remember, you're not supposed to flush in a station."

"That still a thing?" Jack laughed, trying to be nonchalant.

"As far as I know."

Jack smiled and walked on, past the other two men. He managed a quick glance, enough to tell him what he needed to know: they were younger than him, early thirties at most, all well-built.

There was no point trying the door to the next carriage. The lights that usually encircled the button that would activate the doors were off. The toilet door worked, though, and he was able to lock it behind him.

He figured he wouldn't have long before they got suspicious, so he set to work immediately. First, he opened up the drop-down table that would be used for changing babies. On it was a strap designed to help keep the baby in place. Jack ripped it from the plastic and coiled it around his left hand. Then he turned his attention to the handrail that went up alongside the sink, nearest to the toilet. It was a short, metal pole, about a foot in length, screwed into the plastic that edged the mirror. Jack didn't have a screwdriver, but he did have brute force.

Grabbing the pole in both hands, he placed his right foot on the mirror, pushing hard down on it while planting his left foot hard on the ground. On a normal train service, that might have been a little trickier, had the floor been covered in water and urine, but as no one other than the six of them had been using the carriage, it was mercifully clean. Jack bent the pole left and right, left, and right, feeling the plastic begin to bend and give away before coming away with a satisfying but obvious crack.

That would be the final warning for those in the carriage that something was up. From the moment he left, they would have been on edge, waiting for his return. Now they would be springing into action. Their problem was that so was Jack.

Slipping the bar up his arm, Jack turned and stood by the door. He waited until he was certain that someone would be there. He reached his hand out to the unlock button. Breathed and pressed it.

The door swung open; the redhead woman was there. She looked up at him as if wanting to step around him. A ploy, perhaps, to disarm him. Send in the girl, make him think twice.

Jack didn't think twice. He stood his ground. Clearly, the redhead woman wasn't expecting that and found herself caught between the lie she was supposed to perpetrate and her instinct to strike first. She tried to step around him but only stepped into him. He said nothing. She looked up, then decided to go for the second option.

Her hand went behind her back, looking to grab something. Jack didn't give her the chance, pulling her by the head and her left arm and slamming her into the frame of the toilet door. She bounced off it, backwards, tumbling down to the floor, out cold.

One down.

Jack turned and strode quickly into the train carriage. The other three were still playing dumb, but the moment that they saw him enter alone, they were up and running. Jack passed the luggage rack and stopped. He was in a gap between the seats and entrance, a dead space for wheelchair users. It gave him an area to work in. The three approaching him were stuck in a small funnel, forced to come down one at a time. They didn't stand a chance.

The first one raced at Jack. He needed to be cleared quickly before anyone else could get into the space with him. Jack let the bar drop down from inside his jacket sleeve and swung it down and across the man's face, scattering his blood across the seat to Jack's left. A second later, the man slumped down across the seat and the aisle. Another obstacle for the others to contend with.

The second man hurdled his unconscious comrade but walked straight into a backhand from the bar. This time he was caught under the chin, his head whipping back, the pole bending with the force. Jack wasn't sure, but from the way the guy fell, he knew there was a pretty real chance he'd broken his neck.

The third guy checked his approach for a second, trying to play it smart, working out how he might get a shot in to overpower Jack. Jack discarded the bent pole and took the strap in both hands. It seemed to be the signal that the last guy was looking for, like he thought the pole was all that Jack needed. It wasn't.

The final guy attempted a sort of rugby tackle, ducking his head down, trying to wrap his arms around Jack's waist and take him to the ground. Jack dropped his arms, letting the strap go below the man, spinning as he went, catching the man in the strap, under his left arm, over his right, pulling him up. The man kicked out backwards, but Jack was in control, and he spun the man around into the luggage rack. It wasn't enough to put him down, nowhere near. The man swung his right hand backwards, missing his target completely, as Jack lifted him up using the strap then slammed him forward into the wall of the carriage.

Still not enough. Jack slung him right, then left, then right again, trying to disorientate the man before releasing his left hand and barging the man forward against the door. The man spun around, blood pouring from his nose. He stepped forward, swung a lazy right at Jack who ducked under it, firing a sharp shot into the man's gut. It winded him, doubling him over, letting Jack get the strap around his neck and pull, choking the life from him.

"Jack!" Grant shouted.

Jack spun the man around in front of him so he could see Grant. He was holding a tablet up in front of him. Jack pulled the strap tighter.

"Think of your family Jack," Grant warned, walking towards him.

Jack looked at the screen and focused. A video, filmed it looked like, from inside a car. The camera was static, watching a house. Jack knew the house. He used to live there.

Jack pulled the strap tighter. He felt the fight going out of the man.

"Let him go, Jack."

He pulled it a little tighter.

"Jack, I have to make a call when we get to London. If they don't hear from me, they go in and kill your family."

Jack pulled the strap tighter. The man slumped in front of him. Jack released the strap, letting the body hit the floor. He stepped over it and smiled at Grant.

"That gives me about twenty minutes. Plenty of time to hurt you enough so you're begging to make that call."

60

Waiting was never fun. Not for Adam. He was the sort of person who wanted to be always active. Moving from one thing to the next, not necessarily physically, sometimes just in terms of progressing a case, but he needed that motion in parts of his life. Waiting in the ward, his bed isolated still by the reams of plastic sheeting that hung from the ceiling, was limbo for him. Knowing the promise of impending release, as well, made it even worse. Each and every step he heard could be the footsteps of the person coming to release him back into the world. But half an hour after the doctor had told him that he hadn't been infected by whatever was eating away at Nelmes, he was still in that same room, still waiting to go.

He sighed and stretched out on the bed, leaning back on the pillow and looking at the ceiling for the umpteenth time. What choice did he have? As much as he hated it, he was going to have to wait.

His phone started to ring. Raf.

"What's up, Raf?"

"Are you alone?" Adam heard the worry in his voice. What the hell was happening now?

"Chronically," Adam said, sitting up.

"Listen, I've been trying to get hold of Grant, but I can't. I don't know who else to come to with this, but it needs to be out there." There was something really worrying Raf. He didn't sound right at all, his words rattling off at a fast pace. "I think Lowri has screwed us over."

"What?" Was this Adam's worst fears being realised? "Why do you think that?"

"She returned from her trip up north, her driver picked her up and took her to St. Pancras. Apparently, she told him to wait for half an hour. When she didn't return, he called it in."

"Did she run? That doesn't make sense, why come back?"

"No, she didn't run. We've got the footage. She meets Poole and two other men. They disappear into a side door, then they're never seen again. The cameras outside the station were turned off. She went dark, and we lost her. We've got teams sweeping the building now, but so far, nothing."

"Can you send me the footage?" Adam was still clinging on to the hope that something was being missed.

"I'll get it over to you. Has anyone been in to see you at the hospital?"

"The doc has given me the all clear, just waiting for permission to go from the police and associated acts."

"I'd get out now," Raf warned. "Lowri was our most direct link to all the sort of agencies that are going to be poking around this. If someone starts asking the wrong questions, I don't know who is going to be there to bail you out."

"Fair point, understood. I'll get Emmie and get the hell out of here." Adam hadn't thought of that, but he knew Raf was right. Lowri pulled so many of those strings, he didn't realise how reliant on her they had been. Now though, those jobs she did were beginning to come under the spotlight.

"Video is on its way to you. Good luck." The line went dead, and Adam was alone again. There would be no waiting now.

He was up and on his feet, brushing quickly through the plastic sheets, out into the main area of the infectious disease ward. "Where's my partner?" he asked a nurse who turned around sharply from the station she was working at.

"Your partner?" The nurse didn't seem to understand the request.

Adam replied in calm but commanding tone. "Emmie Weston. Where is she?"

"Room four," she blurted, looking over Adam's shoulder in that direction.

Adam was in the door and through the plastic sheets in seconds. Emmie was sat, just as he had been, on her bed in the middle of the room. Waiting.

"You alright?" he asked.

"All clear," she replied.

"Come on, we're going. Now." Adam hoped his tone would convey urgency. It seemed to because Emmie was up and following before she asked any further questions.

"What's going on?" The question came when they were in the corridor.

"Lowri might have been turned."

"You found proof?"

"She met Poole. The two of them and two men disappeared at St. Pancras."

"That's not proof," Emmie cautioned as the two of them reached the door to the main hospital building.

"It's not, but I don't want to be sat here exposed either way," Adam said, pressing a button that had "door release" written above it. Nothing happened.

Adam pressed again. Still nothing.

"Shit," he said, turning and heading back to the nurse. "Open the damn doors," he called when he saw her.

"I can't," she protested. "No one gets in or out."

"We're clean," Adam snapped.

"That's not how it works."

Emmie stepped quickly to the nurse, grabbing her by the scruff of her uniform and pulling her towards the wards. "Open the door, or I'll find a room with someone really sick and stick you in it."

"Okay, okay." The nurse pulled at Emmie's hands, wriggling free. "I'm just doing my job," she said by way of mitigation as she hurried towards the door and swiped a key pass against a reader then pressed the door release button.

The doors swung open, and Emmie and Adam were out into the hustle and bustle of the main hospital, jogging.

"Would you have really thrown her in a room with patient zero?" Adam asked as they rounded a corner and followed a sign that said "EXIT."

"I must have been convincing if you're not sure." Emmie smiled back.

They clattered down a set of stairs, round another corner, and then found themselves faced with a busy reception area. Darting between people, they were through the doors and out at the front of the hospital.

"Where now?" Emmie asked.

Adam stopped, taking a moment to formulate a plan.

"Oh shit." There they were. Two men, smart dark suits, not too dissimilar to the two men he had met off the ambulance, stepping out of a black saloon car. Another group of intelligence-agency workers, clearly keen to pull apart their story and get to the bottom of what was going on. He didn't think they had seen them yet, but he didn't want to wait and find out. "Run."

Emmie quickly looked, Adam saw her register, then the two of them ran in the opposite direction, heading around the front of the hospital, away from the road, towards a grass verge. Take the car out of play, no way for them to use that to chase them down.

They both hurtled down the grass verge, barging through a bush at the bottom that bordered a dual carriageway. Cars charged in each direction. They had to get across it. A lot of people would take their time, hesitating, waiting for gaps, taking one lane at a time. Adam and Emmie didn't. They ran down the side of the road, then, when spying a gap that would just about do it, the two of them darted and sprinted for the central reservation.

The central reservation was a knee-high metal barrier, designed to keep crashing cars from careering over to the other side of the road and causing more chaos. Adam and Emmie vaulted it. Adam risked a look back. No sign of anyone following, but that might only mean they were chasing them down in the car. Keep moving. They ran along the centre of the dual carriageway, cars flashing their lights and sounding their horns to warn them about the danger they were in, as if they didn't already know.

Another gap, another quick sprint across the two lanes. The other side of the road. It was lined with trees, the other side of which Adam could see a small pond. No roads. No chance for the car to catch them, if it was following at all.

"Through the trees," he panted at Emmie, and the two of them ploughed their way through the undergrowth, dodging branches and bushes, coming out on the other side and circling the pond like a pair of Sunday morning fun runners.

The pond led onto a small playing field, still lined with trees. They were thicker now, more cover. Perfect spot to check if anyone was following, Adam decided.

"Let's regroup," he offered, bending his run into the treeline.

Ducking down and short of breath, the two of them waited. No one came. For five minutes they waited, not daring to move. This time Adam didn't feel restless. He didn't feel the need to move on. He felt exhilarated. Thrill of the chase.

"I think we're safe." Emmie moved her feet, repositioning herself before her legs seized.

"Yeah, for now, I hope so." Adam was still scanning, still waiting.

"What's going on?" Emmie asked.

"We're fucked," Adam said, turning and smiling. "That's the short of it. Long of it, Lowri may or may not have been turned, but whatever happened, she's gone."

"Gone?"

"Gone."

"Where?"

"They don't know, she met Poole at St. Pancras and two other men. I've got footage."

Adam fished around in his pocket for the phone, pulling it out. Raf had sent the file as promised. He still hadn't seen it himself. Was this really the proof that Lowri had been playing them? That this whole thing had been part of her plan from the off?

The video began. A CCTV video, wide angle, looking over the top mezzanine level at St. Pancras, focusing on the area where the escalator offloaded people on the first floor. Adam couldn't see anyone he recognised. They watched.

Then Lowri appeared, the top of her head gliding along as she was ferried up the escalator. Adam watched intently. He couldn't see Poole. Lowri reached the top of the escalator and got off. She was looking at something or someone. Her eyes were fixed on one point. A rabble of tourists got in her way. She stopped. Then Adam saw it.

"Oh no," he croaked. The two spooks who had met him off the ambulance came up behind her, one, the sandy-haired one, grabbed her arm.

"What?" Emmie asked.

"That's not a betrayal. That's a rendition."

"How do you know?"

"Those two men were the ones who came to me with the footage of Poole. They sowed the seeds." Adam watched as Poole came into shot, following Lowri and the two spooks offscreen. "Then they took her off the streets. Left us to cast aspersions at her, undermine everything she did to make us tick."

"You can see her being grabbed though; people will notice that. They won't believe she turned on us, not on David."

Adam put the phone in his pocket. "They'll just say it's all an act. That it's part of her ploy to cover up what she did. I don't believe for one moment that these two were working alone. There are people in our group and the Vehm who helped them. There's a bigger picture that we're missing here."

"Then what do we do? Tell people about the two men you met?"

"For now? No. We say nothing."

"Nothing?" Emmie looked confused.

"Lowri needs someone to work this smart. Work the long game. If we come out all guns blazing now, we're going to get picked off. Look at the hospital. They were coming for us."

"Surely they'll keep coming?"

"They'll try, but the only thing that's going to keep us safe now is if they think they have our silence. If they think that I'm so scared I'll be implemented, I'd rather cover up knowing who these two are."

"Which you will be doing," Emmie pointed out.

"I will," Adam smirked. "But at the same time, covertly, me and you are going to find out who they are, what they did with Lowri, and why they're going after us."

"That sounds like a huge ask. It could take years."

"I don't think we have years. Something like this is a planned strike on the Vehm, the Regulators, to limit our capabilities. To make us less effective. You take out your enemies' capabilities just before you're ready to strike."

"Strike where?"

"That I don't know," Adam admitted. "That's what we need to find out. Come on. Let's get out of here. We need to get back to the office and check in."

He was trying so hard in his voice to keep his tone calm, to make out that this was no big deal, but inside he knew it was anything but. The two of them were the only people that knew for certain that Lowri had been taken against her will. They were going to hide that in part to protect themselves and in part to bring out those who had allowed this to happen. For however long it took, this would be the confidential mission. It was without the biggest job he had ever undertaken. It was the job that ultimately could save the Regulators.

61

Grant had agreed to call off the surveillance of Jack's family quicker than Jack had expected. The mere threat took him to the edge, and a couple of well-thought-out pressure points sealed the deal. Grant had called his operative, and Jack had watched as the car drove away, the feed still playing so he knew that they were safe.

"You made a smart move, Grant," he said soothingly. "If you hadn't have done that, I'd have had to kill you. Now we can move onto the why? Why do you want me? What more trouble could I possibly have posed?"

"You know how it works, Jack. You don't do as you're told, you're a liability to the Vehm. They want you gone, so sooner or later, you're going to die."

"I'd kept off the radar for a long time. I kept up my side of the bargain."

"But then you came back." Grant shook his head. "You just couldn't keep away. I guess that what's scared them."

"Who gave the order?"

"I don't know, Jack. It came from the Vehm. Could be any of them."

"Lowri?"

"It could have been, but she didn't do it in person."

Jack believed him. Grant was a man who followed orders, did as he was told. Jack leaned forward, reaching into Grant's inside pocket and pulling out the USB drive.

"Did you tell them I brought them this?"

"Jack…" Grant began.

"Did you?"

"No, I didn't. Don't tell me you think it would have made the slightest bit of difference?"

"Would have been nice to find out."

"Call it in then. If that info is what you think it is, call it in now, use my tablet to upload it."

"You're being very helpful, Grant." Jack raised an eyebrow.

"Believe it or not, I just want the right thing to come out of this. I want the bastards behind it to be caught and punished. That doesn't change because I was sent to bring you in. Different game."

"Fine, let's do it. Give the office a call."

Grant took his phone out, bringing up the details, dialling, then waiting for the call to connect.

"Raf?" he said as someone answered. "I've got Jack Quinn with me. We've got some information we need to upload to the system and look into," he explained before answering an unheard question. "Evidence about who set the honey trap apparently."

Grant gestured for Jack to place the drive into the tablet.

"Put Raf on speakerphone," Jack said as he slipped the drive in. Grant pulled a face, but he did as he was told. "Raf, it's Jack."

"Hi, Quinn, long time no speak."

"Yeah, figure it might be the same again after this. There's some data coming in now. I got it from Lord Brier, said it was his safety net against whoever was behind this. Hopefully, it's usable for the right people, whatever way."

"Do you know what we might find?"

"Not yet."

"Fine. Grant, can I talk to you in private?" Raf sounded a little concerned by something, as if he was eager to impart some information. Jack nodded, watching Grant as he took the phone to his ear, waiting for him to say something. He said nothing, just listened intently. Whatever news it was, Grant was clearly caught a little off guard by it. His eyes raised for a moment. He said nothing, however, placing the phone back in the middle of the table and putting it back on speaker.

"Program is working now. You should be getting the results on your screen."

"Thanks, Raf," Grant replied. "Want to guess where this is going?"

"Brier said politics and money. There's a lot of both of those around, I wouldn't want to cast aspersions as to who might find pimping kids as a palatable plan."

"No, nor me," Grant said grimly.

The screen in front of them flashed. A folder opened up, documents began to appear, cascading onto the screen. A whole heap of information dumped in an instant onto the tablet. Video files, photographs, emails, audio transcripts. The works. A dossier of evidence that proved without doubt who had been pulling the strings. Braun had done an incredible job.

"Let's see who we've got." Grant tapped the screen of the tablet. An audio file began playing. Two men, talking in the Queen's English. Well-to-do. High society.

"And they'll vote the way we want?" said one.

"Home secretary is so scared that we'll put that video of him and the kids out to tender that you could ask him to do the Bolero in a tutu and he'd be quite obliging," came a second.

Grant's face went white. "I know that bloody voice," he squeaked.

"So do I," Jack concurred. Pretty much everyone in Britain would.

Grant's hand moved across the tablet surface, picking through a couple of files until he found what he was after. A photograph of Edmund Jarvis, the Prime Minister of the United Kingdom.

"The bloody PM?" Grant said in complete disbelief.

"Appears so."

"What do we do?"

"We do nothing," Jack said, reaching forward and snatching the tablet computer. "I'm giving this to the authorities."

Grant opened his mouth to say something, then stopped. He settled back down in his seat. "Fine," he shrugged.

That unsettled Jack. He'd already wondered why Grant had been so obliging. Why he'd quickly decided to back down with the surveillance of Jack's family, why he was happy for Jack to view the material on the tablet. It was all a ploy. He was stalling.

"How many?" Jack asked.

"How many what?"

"People on the platform."

"Not just the platform, Jack. Whole station is locked down. You've nowhere to go."

"Son of a bitch," Jack hissed, standing up.

The train was slowing now as they eased their way through the capital. At most, there were ten minutes to go. He took one last quick look around. None of Grant's men were moving.

"You're out of time," rasped Grant. "End of the line."

"Not yet." Jack reached down and pulled Grant up from the chair.

He frog-marched him toward the front of the train. As they reached the door that led between the carriages, Jack stopped Grant before reaching to take the hammer that was normally used to smash out the windows in an emergency. Then they marched out of the carriage, into the connecting area between carriages. Grant staggered along in front, Jack holding firmly onto his coat as he guided him forward.

"Stand right there," Jack ordered, pushing Grant up to the door.

"There are people waiting on the platform. If you want to live, let me take you in," Grant kept bargaining, but Jack had made his mind up.

"I've got a better idea."

Jack slammed his fist against the emergency call button, alerting the driver to a potential problem in the train. He knew he was banking on the driver not being involved in Grant's plan, but what other choice did he have?

"What's the problem?" the driver sounded worried.

"If you don't stop this train, I'm going to smash the windows and put this man's head through the window." Jack looked up at the security camera that he knew the driver would now be watching him through. He reached his arm out around Grant's neck and pulled him in front of him.

"What the hell are you doing?" Grant squealed.

Jack said nothing. He slammed Grant into the wall, stunning him and dropping him to the floor, then turned, swinging the hammer into the window of the door. Over and over, cracking and chipping the toughened glass. It was designed to stand up to a lot, but not this. Four, five, six, seven hits… the glass was almost all gone. Enough for Jack to get Grant's head out. He picked Grant up, arms wrapped around him in a full-nelson lock. He wrestled him to the door, head positioned over the window. He looked at the camera. The train didn't slow.

Jack pushed Grant's head forcefully through the remaining glass, making him scream in terror and pain as the broken shards sliced through his head.

For an exceedingly long couple of seconds, there was no braking, no deceleration. Jack wondered if the driver had decided he was the victim of a prank. Then the train shuddered, and Jack and Grant were slammed against the wall of the vestibule as the train lurched to a halt, the brakes slamming on, causing the train to wobble, the carriages to concertina into one and other, bouncing off each other in a controlled but powerful, sudden stop. Grant went to tumble, but Jack caught him, pulling him back upwards as the train finally ground to a complete halt. It wouldn't move again now till the brake system was released.

Jack pushed Grant to one side, then wrenched at the emergency release for the door. It sprang open.

"They'll get you. They *will* get you," Grant spat from where he lay on the floor.

"They'll try," Jack retorted before jumping down onto the track.

An hour later, Jack finally felt safe. He had escaped the track via a siding yard, before disappearing up each and every side street he could find. He'd taken a taxi from a back street minicab firm and now found himself walking down a deserted B-Road somewhere looking for a phone box. Ten years ago, that wouldn't have taken half as long, he lamented.

He found it eventually, in a little village called Widford. Not the classic red British phone box, but one of the later models, a see-through plastic box essentially, with a silver metal phone. He slipped a few coins into the slot then dialled the number.

"DCI Watts please," he asked. The operator explained Watts wasn't available. "Can you connect me to her mobile?" Jack insisted. "This is critical to her case."

The operator relented, and Jack waited.

"Hello?" Thea sounded tired. Not surprising. She'd probably been trying to catch up on some sleep.

"It's Jack. Sorry to bother you, but I need someone I can trust, someone who'll do it right."

"Jack, I said I didn't want to hear from you. I don't want this vigilante shit."

"This isn't vigilante. The opposite. I'm taking this off them, giving it to you."

"What is it?"

"When I went to Brier's, he gave me evidence about who was behind the plot."

"You have it?" Thea suddenly sounded perkier.

"I do," Jack said coldly. "I need to warn you though. If you see this, you're going to be in deeper than ever before."

"I don't care. You know that." Jack did know that, that's why he had called.

"It's the PM."

"What?"

"He pulled the shots. I've got audio, video and more. I'll get it to you as soon as I can. Just be ready to move when you do. Make sure you copy this as well. They're going to come hard."

"Thanks. I will," Thea sounded breathless. No doubt excited. This was huge after all.

"Take care," Jack said.

"I will. What about you?"

"I'm out. They came for me today, so the moment I give you this, I need to disappear. Otherwise, they're going to come for me and kill me."

"Why?"

"I crossed too many lines. This will be another one."

"Jack…" Thea began, but she must have realised there was nothing more to say.

"Good luck, Thea, and goodbye."

Jack hung up the phone and looked around. He pressed send on the tablet, the data transferring over the 4G connection to Thea. They would know he was here right now. Inside ten minutes, a drone would be above him, maybe sooner. Half an hour, boots would be on the ground searching for him. Jack would evade them, that was what he did. He would disappear, he would go dark, and he would never come back.

THE REGULATORS WILL RETURN IN
DEADLINE

READ CHAPTER ONE OF THE NEXT BOOK ON
THE FOLLOWING PAGES

VISIT WWW.BENBRUCE.CO.UK TO SIGN UP TO BE THE
FIRST TO HEAR ABOUT THE NEXT THRILLING
ADVENTURE, AND IF YOU ENJOYED THE BOOK,
PLEASE DO LEAVE A REVIEW.

DEADLINE

1

Nathan Nelmes always wanted to be a journalist. From an early age, writing stories for the school newspaper, Nelmes had enjoyed the buzz of telling his peers what was happening in the school. Sometimes that had gotten him in trouble. He had a nose for a story, as the old cliché went. He didn't care who he upset either, and if there was a tale of a teacher being unfair or crossing a supposed line, Nathan was always more than happy to put it down in black and white. More often than not, those stories never made it to print in the school paper. Teachers would intercept them, Nathan would end up in the headteacher's office, and the world would be none the wiser. For some people, that would be a lesson learned. Not for Nathan. That became his fuel.

Nelmes' passion for breaking stories upset as many editors as it had teachers. At first, especially when he worked for local papers, far more used to telling stories about school fetes than scurrilous exposés of corrupt local councillors, especially without always being able to back up the accusations he made in the surest sense. There were other publishers, however, that loved him. The rise of the internet meant that his specific brand of investigative journalism found a home online. His reputation grew. Stories were broken. Scandals were exposed. Nathan Nelmes became the scourge of those who had something to hide. The *Daily Inquirer* offered him a role as their chief investigative journalist, and his reputation was cemented.

That had brought him to the attention of David Warner. David was the head of an underground vigilante group, the Regulators, an organisation that targeted those who skirted the law and avoided punishment for the crimes they committed. More often than not, the same sort of people Nelmes targeted. Corrupt politicians, people in power who abused their position. Both sides could offer the other information. Nelmes often filled in blanks in David Warner's investigations and, in turn, when it was decided the best punishment was publicly exposing these people, Nelmes would get a huge scoop. It was a profitable relationship for both. Warner had moved upstairs in the Regulators, so contact with Nathan Nelmes had been passed to Jack Quinn, then Adam Morgan. It was Morgan who, two years ago, had brought Nelmes his biggest story.

The Regulators had stumbled upon a honeypot operation, where young children were used to entice and entrap politicians and other people of influence with the purpose of compromising and controlling them. Morgan had brought a dossier to Nelmes, and Nelmes had written the story breaking it. It had nearly cost him his life.

Unbeknownst to Nelmes or Morgan, their plan to reveal the story had been uncovered, and Nelmes' computer had been doused in a nerve agent that left him in a coma for seven weeks. He had survived, but at cost.

Both his forearms had been amputated, and he had been confined to a wheelchair for the most part, barely able to move more than a few painful steps at a time. It had barely been a life.

Now Nathan Nelmes was dead.

His name had cropped up in a police bulletin. The Regulators monitored all the usual methods of communication for the emergency services. One of the key factors in their job was to move fast so as to ensure their actions are kept covert. Nelmes' name had been listed as soon as he became an informant. The sad reality was, it had to be. Sooner or later someone was going to catch him out.

The alarm had been raised by a neighbour who hadn't seen Nelmes for a week. Police had entered and found the scene. Forensics had been called, and the alarm had been tripped. Adam Morgan and his partner Emmie Weston had made it to the scene just before the circus had arrived.

"ID." The officer at the front of the house put his arm out to halt Morgan and Weston as they approached. Both reached confidently for their badges, handing them to the officer. He scanned them, never noticing for one second that the Security Service IDs he was looking at were fake. He handed them back. "Didn't realise it was this big, sir." He looked a little taken aback. Clearly, he'd never met a real spy before.

"It might not be, but we need to be sure," Emmie reassured him.

"Uh, yes, of course, ma'am." The officer turned his attention to her, his face flushing as he realised he'd forgotten to address her. "In you go."

The overwhelming smell of decay hit Adam the moment they stepped through the door.

"Fucking hell," he groaned, looking at Emmie who was also pulling a face. There was no doubt there was a dead body in there. The smell lingered heavy in the air, and Adam half expected to actually see signs of it floating past. They walked through towards the sound of officers talking, along a narrow corridor and into a bedroom. Now there was no doubt.

Two officers stood just inside a dirty and untidy bedroom. The window was closed to preserve the scene, but Morgan was sure that the officers must have debated opening it. The smell in here was even more intense. The bedsheets were twisted and stained, falling half off on the bed to the floor like a linen waterfall. They were stained with sweat, bodily fluids, and blood. More blood was on the wall. Smeared on the bed, the cupboards, beside table, and hand prints on the wall, and then finally, the centrepiece, the word "Judas" scrawled in what Morgan presumed was Nelmes' blood. Under the morbid motif was Nelmes, tied by his ankles and the stumps of his amputated arms at each end, stripped naked as if party to some extreme sex game, electrical tape over his mouth. Dried blood stains marked the cream bed sheet on which he lay. There was a hell of a lot of blood. He was a mess. Hundreds of little cuts littered his body where his assailant had taken their time picking him apart. His toe nails were gone. One testicle missing. Both eyelids removed. A massive slice carved up the middle of his abdomen, like a surgeon had been preparing to go in for open heart surgery. Adam stepped forward, pulling on some blue protective gloves.

"Anyone checked?" Adam asked the two officers, who shrugged back.

Adam pulled the tape back, confirming something he already knew.

"You think he talked?" asked Emmie, who was still staring at the room, looking at the blood and guts mural that had been created

"He couldn't," Adam grimaced. "No tongue. They didn't come here for information. They already knew who he was talking to and what he'd said and he'd have given up anything a long time before they got this far with him. They just wanted to leave a message."

"To us?" Emmie looked at Adam.

"Probably," Adam sighed. "But it could be to anyone else who was thinking of doing the same. Jesus, we need to get a copy of the forensics report quickly."

"I'll get Raf to forward it on." Emmie peered down at Nelmes who was staring at the ceiling. His face still looked scared. Petrified, Adam thought. "You think we might get lucky?"

"No. This was a professional job," Adam lamented. "But sometimes you get lucky, and sometimes they get sloppy. Whoever did this revelled in it, they might have taken their eye off the ball for just one moment. All we need is a print or a hair."

"There's a number of CCTV cameras in the area as well. We can get the footage and see if we've got anyone coming in or entering the property in the last week." Emmie walked through the process.

"It's a shared property so we might not have much success." Adam knew that it would be impossible for him and Emmie to canvass the neighbours without raising suspicion. If they over stayed their welcome, someone with more authority and clout would begin asking questions.

"I'm going to guess that there's no computers left," Emmie surmised. It was a fair assumption. Adam knew that whoever had done this had all the time in the world to carry out a full and thorough search. If they were looking for something, they would have found it and taken it with them. A power lead sat forlornly on a desk in the far corner of the room as if to highlight the fact. "It looks like they cleaned up."

"Well, looks like we're starting from scratch."

"You think this is to do with the dossier?"

"I don't know." Adam paused looking at the room. "The Judas thing makes me think that it wasn't. It doesn't fit. This suggests more like he was betraying some sort of trust."

"Or it could be a red herring?"

"Like I said." Adam looked at her. "We're starting from scratch." He looked down at Nelmes once more. He couldn't help but feel guilt. He hadn't brought Nelmes into this world, he doubted anyone could stop him, but he'd certainly put him in harm's way more than once. All the same, no one deserved to be subject to this level of brutality in their final moments. He took one last look at the tortured look on Nelmes' face. "I promise you, though, we're going to find out who did this, if it's the last thing I do."

Printed in Great Britain
by Amazon